MW01439918

Shiver

Chandler McGrew

This one is for my kids.

A chair leaned against the motel room door that was locked, deadbolted, and chain latched. The windows were bolted as well, the curtains drawn tightly.

Although it seemed impossible that the men who had murdered Katie had any idea of his whereabouts– certainly not *Mark Townsend's* whereabouts–the man now *known* as Mark Townsend simply could not sleep anywhere, anytime, without making sure first that his *lair* was as secure as possible. He'd been an intruder himself often enough to know that even the best of security could be breached. He felt for the pistol underneath before plumping the pillow and rolling over onto his back.

In his mind, the first movement of Gustav Mahler's *Symphony No. 1 in D Major,* with its eight full octaves of harmonics echoed the deep night outside the motel. He knew that before the work reached its fanfare, he would be asleep.

Mark's life had always been orchestrated to music.

His father had been a symphony conductor known the world over for his unique interpretations of older, half-forgotten works. His mother was a concert Cellist who enjoyed newer, more eclectic music. But the two of them found a synthesis together, a symbiosis that went far beyond their chosen *genres.* With his father wielding the baton, and his mother playing as star cellist, they had performed with the finest symphonies in the world.

Mark had been born with an *ear.* By the age of ten, he played the piano well enough to give a solo performance in the local high school and had already written a libretto.

But all that was from what he thought of as the first chapter of his life. He hadn't touched the keys in over ten years–since his parents' deaths. All that remained was the inner music that would never go away.

By the time he finally drifted off–thinking as always of Katie in those moments before sleep took him–the clock on the bed stand was just shining a digital, green 2 AM.

When a light tapping awakened him the gun was already in his hand. He sat on the edge of the bed trying to place the sound. When the tapping returned, he slipped over to the window and peeked through the curtains. The brightly lit motel sign flashed above the office fifty yards away draping bright streamers of bloody neon ribbons across fresh rain puddles in the parking lot, but the rain had stopped.

The clock read 4:04.

When the tapping did not return, he aimed the pistol at the door and peered through the tiny peephole, careful to keep his eye a few inches away. He got pretty much the same view he had from the window, only distorted by the fish-eye lens.

Silently he removed the chair from the door into the adjoining room, unlocked the door, and checked out the view through that room's peephole. No one there.

He slid the chain lock aside. Just as carefully, he turned the deadbolt. Finally, he opened the door just a crack.

Cool night air rushed in bringing with it the smell of ozone and fresh bread from a bakery down the street. He eased the door fully open, counting cars. There were a couple of new ones in the lot, but one was a two-year-old station wagon, and the other a beat-up mini-van.

He relaxed, clicking the safety on the pistol.

A well-aimed foot–wearing a patent leather shoe–swung around the door frame like a baseball bat, catching Mark in the solar plexus, driving the wind from his lungs and bending him double. His fingers tightened instinctively on the gun, but his thumb could not seem to tweak the safety again.

Not that it mattered. Before he could raise the weapon a fist the size of a dinner plate struck him in the jaw and knocked him on his ass, his pistol skittering away across the carpet.

He could just make out the fuzzy outlines of dark suits as three men pinned him to the floor, gagging him with a strip of duct tape, binding his hands behind his back with something that felt like a clothesline. He was jerked to his feet, and a gun jammed in his back convinced him to follow two of the men submissively around the side of the small motel and across the shadowy back lawn. Before they'd gone twenty steps Mark had the knots out of the rope, but he was still groggy from the blows, and he didn't see an opening yet.

As they rounded a small storage building, he spotted a heavy round concrete cover–shaped like a manhole and eight inches thick–laying on the grass like a discarded beer cap and understood immediately that this was to be his final resting place.

He lashed out with his elbow, driving it into the ribs of the man to his right, but before he could turn, the giant behind him was already shoving him stumbling into the hole. Mark caught himself painfully on his elbows, but two glancing kicks to the head took the fight out of him, and he dropped into the icy water. As soon as he bobbed shivering to the surface, he ripped off the rope and jerked the tape from his mouth.

"You must have the wrong man!" he screamed as the stars disappeared, and he heard the unmistakable scrunching creak of the manhole being dragged across the top of the concrete tank. "What do you want?"

He really didn't expect the mistaken identity ploy to work, but it was the best he could come up with on short notice. He had to convince them to let him out of the tank, to give him one last chance to defend himself. If they closed the lid or simply shot him now, he had no chance whatsoever.

"Scream all you want," said the biggest gunman, smiling over the top of the thick concrete cover. "You'll sound like a mosquito if you put your lungs into it."

The lid dropped into place with a final thunk that reverberated through the water, and Mark knew that he would never be able to lift it. The icy liquid would quickly leach the heat out of his body, and hypothermia would kill him.

Immersed in mind-numbing total darkness and with the terrible sense of being buried alive, he ran his fingers around the circular cover, scratching at the fingernail-wide opening between it and the top of the tank, wondering if it admitted any air. Would he suffocate before he froze to death? He clung to what felt like a concrete crossbeam, struggling to get his brain to function.

Regardless of his attacker's warning, he did try screaming again. But the tank was buried in insulating soil, and the eight-inch-thick cover merely reflected his cries back inside.

He swam in small circles, blindly discovering the dimensions of his prison. When he reached another crossbeam, he realized the tank was divided into at least three chambers. There was just enough room to pass between the support and another just like it, submerged about a foot-and-a-half below the surface. He dove, slipping between the beams like a harbor seal, surfacing to search the next chamber by feel. There was another manhole there, but once again he didn't have anything to stand on.

He slapped the concrete—a sharp pain shooting up his arm and into his shoulder—and he recalled that he hadn't noticed any other covers on the lawn when his assailants had dragged him out. Any other tank openings than the one he'd been tossed into were probably auxiliaries, buried beneath the sod.

Trembling, he swam back through the center of the tank and into the far chamber.

Same thing. Another lid. No place to stand.

But for the first time, he noticed the sound of running water. He followed the gurgling noise to the corner of the tank where a powerful stream of icy liquid poured from a pipe in the ceiling. The tank was filling up.

This had to be a storage cistern for drinking water. The motel must be serviced by a well, and they needed enough backup so that in high-usage periods they wouldn't suck the source dry. But it was the middle of the night, no one would be bathing or flushing toilets. So, the tank was refilling for the next day. He reached up to the lid again and realized it was already easier to reach than when he'd first been tossed down into the hole only minutes before.

So, he wasn't going to suffocate, he was either going to die of hypothermia or drown.

He wracked his brain for a way out, struggling futilely one last time to raise the tank lid. He couldn't explode through the concrete walls, and he wasn't going to shrink himself and get sucked into someone's toilet tank.

Although it was the last thing in the world he wanted to hear, he couldn't keep Martha Argerich's rendition of Rachmaninov's *Third Piano Concerto* from popping into his head.

For Mark, the raucous sound of the music juxtaposed against the maestro's clarity and confidence had always accompanied the threat of his imminent demise. Because it had happened often enough in the past, he had known for years it was the music he was destined to die to, and it looked as though tonight was the night he really would see Katie again.

But the image of flushing toilets stuck in his head.

He swam quickly around the perimeter of the third chamber until he discovered a larger pipe that disappeared into the water beneath his feet. Shaking from the cold he ripped off his pajamas and balled the soggy cotton into a mass he could clutch in one hand. Taking three deep breaths he dove.

The bottom of the tank was closer than he'd thought. His feet had only been floating a foot or two off the bottom. The tank was much larger than a coffin, but not too big for a sarcophagus, and an image of his bloated white body floating up and down with the rising and falling liquid level was extremely unappealing.

He found the end of the intake pipe a few inches above the concrete floor and wound the cotton tightly around the filter, wrapping it again and again, tying it with the clothesline before shooting to the surface, gasping for air, trying to remember how many cars had been in the parking lot.

The motel had to have a hundred rooms, and the lot had been three-quarters full when he'd checked it before going to bed. If there were seventy-five rooms occupied, and each car averaged two people he could probably count on eight or ten of them getting up in the night, flushing a few toilets. There was a night manager on duty at the front desk. With any luck, he might be a beer drinker.

But how long would it take to drain the pressure tanks in the building? There had to be some since this cistern wasn't pressurized. Mark was forced to accept just how slim his chances were of shutting down the motel's water before he froze or drowned, but at the very least they'd find his body the next day, not a month or days from now. Little consolation, but something. Wearily he struggled back through the beams so that he could hang on beneath the one lid he was certain was not buried.

The fire and ice feeling of Argerich's rendition of the music began to ratchet up in his head.

The *Third* was probably Rachmaninov's most demonic work, and Argerich had a way of revealing the Satanic influences in the outer movements like no other pianist. Mark supposed that if he did have to die, being trapped inside a water-filled crypt with Martha wasn't such a bad way to go. Better than being blown to bits like his parents. He just wished Martha would choose some other less devious symphony to lull him into the afterlife, but he probably deserved that as well.

It had to be his imagination, but he felt colder without the cotton pajamas, and the sound of the water splashing seemed not so loud. Then it dawned on him that that was because the level was still rising, and the flow had less distance to fall. He could touch the ceiling of the tank now without stretching, and the water completely submerged the upper cross-member. He tried to estimate how long he'd been in the tank. Not nearly so long as it seemed, or he was sure he'd be dead already. Maybe twenty minutes max.

People could live in icy water for up to forty-five minutes if they were in really good shape and managed to stay awake and afloat. After that, he'd either die of hypothermia or drown. If help got to him fast enough after that they might be able to revive him even after a couple of hours. Maybe. But the doctors in Houston didn't have nearly as much practice as even firemen did in Boston in reviving cold water drowning victims. And did he want to be resuscitated after his brain had been deprived of oxygen for who knew how long?

Why his attackers hadn't simply put a bullet in his head was confusing, but then probably someone at the top had decreed that Mark deserved a more interesting death than that. The worst thing was that now Katie's killers would never see the justice they deserved. That thought sent a heat raging through him, and he prayed that if he was doomed to die here there *was* a hell so he could finally get his hands on the men responsible. He had lived for months on hate, rage, and grief. To die so ignobly, so stupidly, and without revenge was more than he could bear.

He thought he heard a humming noise from the other chamber, and he floated over to investigate. There was definitely a high-pitched vibration, and he hoped it was the pump trying to suck water through the plugged intake pipe.

Flush those fucking toilets!

The pipe began to make thumping noises as though it had built up an intolerable vacuum and was struggling desperately to fill it. With any luck, the damned motor would burn out. However, the owner or plumber might spend hours installing a new pump somewhere inside the main building without figuring out that the equipment had died because of a plugged intake.

Mark slapped at the cover again, shouting for help. There was nothing else he could think of to do now, and saving his energy so he could languish here for another few minutes seemed silly. The lid was almost close enough to bump his head on, his body was growing numb, and he was getting so sleepy he could barely grip the concrete beam. Now and then his head bobbed below the surface, and he splashed back up spluttering.

Katie's face flashed in his mind. She was the most beautiful woman he'd ever known, the sweetest, most caring individual he'd ever met, and the fact that she loved him as deeply as he loved her was proof of miracles, but the image that came to him now wasn't a peaceful one. He could feel her limp body in his arms, see her face–so restful in death–taste the salt of his tears. His heart pounded against his ribs in frustration, and the thought of her dead still had the power to drive the wind from his lungs.

From a great distance, he thought he heard a voice, and he knew his mind was playing tricks on him because it sounded like Rory, murdered the same day as Katie. Mark forced his mind to picture the two of them on another, happier day, tossing a Frisbee on the front lawn of the house he and Katie shared in Maryland. He could see the sun over the tops of the tall oaks that bordered the road, warm and inviting. He could feel it on his skin like a caress. He smiled at Rory, and Rory smiled back, winking conspiratorially in Katie's direction.

Everyone that Mark knew lied to Katie. Rory lied to Katie, too.

We had to. I never wanted to lie to you, my darling. But we had to.

That it was a fact gave him even less solace now than it had then. And though it seemed incongruous on that warm sunny afternoon, there was the sound of thunder or the echoing rumble of something heavy grating on stone.

"There you are," Rory's voice seemed impossibly close, and the sudden flash of light that wasn't *quite* the sun burned Mark's eyes. His arm slipped off the beam for the last time, and he felt himself sinking back under the water as huge hands grabbed him by the shoulders, lifting him like a small child, out of the tank, onto the grass.

"Boss says you get a reprieve, asshole," said the voice, and Mark felt himself lifted higher, into great, powerful, warm arms.

And then he slept.

A STARTLINGLY BRIGHT RAY of late afternoon sun slashed across the windshield of Tracy Roger's Camry, temporarily blinding her and causing her to pounce on her brakes. When her vision cleared, she glanced nervously in her rearview mirror, but no one had come close to hitting her bumper, and none of the cars following seemed suspicious.

She feathered her short brown hair back into place with jittery fingers, at the same time rubbing a bead of cold sweat off her brow.

Her hands shook on the wheel, and her mouth was dry as charred cotton. It had been less than thirty minutes since she had seen her best friend, Stephanie, murdered and the dregs of adrenalin still jarred her nerves. She had to force herself to drive slowly through the tree-lined suburbs of DC, past red brick townhouses and condos.

She was stopped at a light behind a long line of automobiles when she spotted the grill of Ash's powder blue Lexus in her mirror. Cars in the lane beside her hemmed her in, but she managed to ease onto the shoulder around the Cadillac in front of her and whip into an apartment parking lot. She leaped out of her car and ran.

When she spotted two ominous black sedans on the side street ahead, she turned toward the entryway to the building to her left. Miraculously she made it inside the small lobby without hearing anyone shout her name or shoe soles slapping behind her, but she knew that very soon the place would be surrounded by the same men in dark suits who had murdered Steph.

She raced down the long, bleak hallway–decorated with plastic potted palms and beige carpet–testing each door, glancing over her shoulder at the glaring sunlight through the glass entryway. When she rounded the corner at the end of the hall there were four more doors, an elevator, and then the entrance to a stairwell. She hit the panic hardware on the door to the stairway with both hands, bursting inside.

The basement would be a trap. But what would she do upstairs if all the doors were locked? Hell, what would she do if they weren't? She couldn't hide for long in someone's apartment, and there was no use calling the police.

Ash owned the police.

The squealing tires of more cars pulling up out front echoed around her.

She'd failed.

Instead of discovering the truth, she'd somehow betrayed herself, and now *she* was the hunted. She was going to end up disappearing just like her parents.

She raced up the stairs to the next floor, hurriedly checking every door in the L-shaped corridor. When she burst through into the stairwell again, she heard footsteps below, and she leaped up the next flight of stairs three risers at a time, the sound of pursuit speeding up behind her. She exploded out onto the roof, sucking in great gulps of air as she raced to the ledge. Across the street, she saw more black-suited men running toward the building.

She spun back toward the door, steeling herself for the inevitable.

Without warning a man slipped around the rear of the little stair enclosure, appraising her with cunning, dark eyes. He was slightly less than six feet and maybe a hundred-and-eighty pounds, wearing a long-sleeved white shirt and dark slacks over shiny dress shoes. He looked like your average office worker on lunch break, and he clearly wasn't one of Ash's cold-blooded killers. Tracy let out a slow breath, feeling sorry for the guy. Whatever twist of fate had brought him to this place, this time, it was bad karma, and there wasn't even any time to warn him. She didn't think the men racing up the stairs behind him were about to leave any witnesses.

Suddenly the door burst open, and one of the goons stepped through it aiming his big black automatic pistol first toward her, then swinging it toward the man.

The man's hand swept out in a blinding arc. At the same time, he performed a pirouette that any ballet master would have been proud of, and suddenly a bright fountain of blood sprang upward from the gunman's throat as he dropped like a sack of cement onto the roof. In the same movement, the dancer kicked the door hard on the wrist of a second gunman.

The man's pistol clattered to the floor, and the hand jerked back inside. The dancer reached down beside the door and shoved a wooden wedge under it, kicking it solidly into place just as someone began pounding on the door from the inside. The man, with his back still to Tracy, took a deep breath, leaned to wipe his bloody fingers on the dead man's shirt, and then turned and strode over to her, studying her face.

She scrutinized him as well, wondering who the hell he was, how he'd done what he just had with his bare hands, why he was on the roof, and how he knew about the wedge. The thought also entered her mind that he had now definitely signed his own death warrant, and the idea of being responsible for yet another murder shocked her into near immobility. She had been raised to be a pacifist, and yet she had intentionally wormed her way into a world that seemed to exist for nothing but killing. Hiding from such a world she knew how to do. Surviving within it was something she was *not* trained for.

The man's eyes, now that she got a closer look at them, were not just dark. They were black. But within that blackness, strange sparkles shone, like quartz chips in a coal shard. He had raven hair with an errant lock that hung almost into his eyes, and he appeared to be in his early thirties, with a hairline scar that followed his left cheekbone from his chin to his temple. When he smiled the scar tugged that side of his lips downward in an accompanying frown, giving him an ambivalent look. Still, he was handsome in a self-assured, if disconcerting way.

"Those men are here to kill me," she said, glancing past him toward the door that was bowing outward from the pounding it was taking. "They'll kill you, too, if you don't get out of here."

Of course, he had no more chance of escaping now than she did. After defending her against Ash's men Ash wasn't likely to leave the man alive in any case.

"How many are there?" he asked.

She'd expected him to sound shaken. Instead, his voice was a calm alto with a slight southern lilt, as though the fact that he had just killed a man, or that many more were coming to kill him meant little to him.

She shook her head. "I have no idea. It doesn't matter, now."

"We should talk somewhere else."

She just couldn't dredge up a laugh. "Where would you suggest?"

"Come on," he said, reaching for her.

She jerked away instinctively, and he stopped in mid-stride, still holding out the hand that had somehow sliced through a man's throat.

She noticed small patches of blood still clinging to the knuckles.

There was nowhere to go, unless he was planning on doing a *Matrix-style* jump to the building across the street. But he stood there calmly, with those sparkling eyes burning into her, waiting as patiently as though they really did have all the time in the world, even when the men in the stairwell started firing wildly through the door.

Finally, he spoke again. "You coming or not?"

She sighed, placing her hand in his. The feel of another human's touch for the first time in... was it really a year... struck a deep and dangerous chord, but she stopped herself from jerking her hand away yet again. This man had put his own life on the line to save hers. If both of them were doomed the least she could do was treat him with a little dignity.

When he dragged her around to the rear of the stairwell, she was certain he was crazy, but what had it cost her? She'd humored him in their last few minutes alive. Maybe she'd get a couple of karma points for that.

The back of the little structure was clad in vinyl siding, warped and cracked by too many summer suns, and when the man let go of her hand she leaned against the creaking hot plastic, still struggling without hope to figure some way out of their predicament. They couldn't jump three floors, and even if they did and survived, Ash's men would be waiting for them in droves down there. Neither one of them would even be able to crawl as far as the street before being gunned down.

"Come on," said the man.

She turned to face him again and blinked.

The roof was covered with tar inset with pebbles, the material forming one solid brown surface the width and breadth of the building. But directly in front of her, the man was disappearing into a hidden hatchway that she had not noticed before. In fact, she knew that it could not have been there, and yet it was.

He waved her inside, and she knelt to crawl past him into a narrow, metal-lined space that twanged noisily each time she shifted her weight.

"Farther down!" he said. "I have to close this."

She scooted forward on her belly, her shoulders pressing the sides of the enclosure, her head banging on the ceiling each time she inched her way farther along. There was a creaking sound then a buzzing blue light that blinded her like a welder's flash. Then suddenly it was pitch-black, and she squeaked as a heavy vibration ran through the tunnel.

"Quiet!" he whispered.

She felt his legs squeezing alongside her, his shoes resting against her hips.

"What is this place?" she whispered.

Footsteps pounded directly overhead, and she could hear muffled shouts, but couldn't make out the words. There was no way her pursuers would not find the hatch if this man had. They were about to be trapped like rats and die just as ignobly.

"The main air-conditioning duct, I think," he whispered back. "Now shut up!"

He *thought?* How could he know about this place and not know what it was?

As she lay there the air grew hot and stuffy, and she wondered if this was an air-conditioning duct why no one was using the AC. Couldn't *someone* turn the thermostat down and give them a little air?

A voice sounded directly over her head, muffled by the floor above.

"Where the fuck did she go?"

Then pounding footsteps all around.

Eventually, she heard more footsteps hammering down the stairs again, and more voices, closer this time. She realized that some of the men were in the room directly beneath them, and now she *could* make out what they were saying much clearer, as though they were only separated by the thin metal of the ductwork.

"Bitch has got to be here somewhere!"

"Fan out and find her!"

TRACY SAT LOW IN the car, her eyes level with the passenger window, as the steel and concrete businesses south of New York City shot past. The night outside was dull and dreary, rain just beginning to fall, mirroring her somber mood.

Her savior drove calmly, the combination of cheap chinos and the scar lending him a disarmingly casual yet swashbuckling appearance, like a modern-day pirate, or perhaps a movie stuntman. He certainly didn't look to her like someone who would be cruising around in a brand-new Beemer, and after watching him in action she had to doubt seriously if it was his.

She wondered just how long it was going to take to get pulled over, the info to go out over cop radios, and then for Ash to show up. She had no illusions about custody or being protected by the cops. As soon as the two of them were captured Ash would know, and the strings he could pull would far outweigh any story she chose to tell.

"Who are you?" she asked for the one-hundredth time.

"My name would mean nothing to you."

"Where are we going?" she asked, not really expecting an answer to that question, either, since she'd asked it before.

He shook his head. "I'd rather not say just yet."

"You should drop me off somewhere. You're already way too mixed up in this. There's no reason for you to die for your crimes."

She was sick of people dying. Now Steph was just one more person that she might have somehow saved.

He laughed mirthlessly, and once again she was surprised by his melodious voice.

"My crimes," he mused, almost sadly. "What do you think I've done that's a crime?"

The question and the way he said it–as though he were both amused and genuinely curious–took her by surprise. She recalled the ease with which he'd broken them out of the building still filled with Ash's men–although she still could not credit *how* he had done it. He was a man trained in arts that no law-abiding man had ever practiced, that much was certain.

"Murder. Breaking and entering. Car theft? I suppose interfering with some kind of government operation, but I don't think that one would ever come up in court."

He nodded slowly.

"No. None of what happens to you, or me is ever likely to be heard in a court of law... But do you think self-defense or defense of another is a crime? The car, by the way, is not stolen. As to the government operation, I do not recognize this government." He seemed to consider that for a moment. "At least I do not recognize these men's authority in it."

"That sounds like something my father might have said. But you'll recognize it pretty quick when they catch up to us."

He frowned, turning his attention back to the road.

"Your father sounds like a wise man."

"I thought he was."

"But not anymore?"

"It isn't relevant. What were you doing up there on the roof?"

"Looking for a hiding place."

"From whom?"

"Obviously from the men who were trying to kill you."

She shook her head. "You're saying you knew I'd be there, that they'd be coming?"

"Yes."

"But you had no way of knowing that. I didn't even know I was going there. Who are you?"

"I'm a friend. You seem to need one." He sighed. "I couldn't leave you to those men. I've seen too much killing."

"Me, too. But why pick me to help? What do you know about Ash? About what's going on?"

"There is a balance that needs to be maintained. Those men were about to unbalance things. I couldn't allow that to happen. Not again."

"You don't make any sense."

"I suppose I wouldn't."

"Can't you please at least tell me your name?"

He sighed.

"You can call me Shiver."

"Shiver?"

He smiled again, and she discovered that she liked that expression a lot better than his frown. In spite of his odd demeanor, she felt safer in the car with this mysterious man than she had in a long long time.

"Where are you from?" she asked.

"You might say I'm from New Mexico," he said, frowning again.

"You don't sound like you liked it much."

"I didn't at the time I was there."

"Did you get into trouble there?"

"It's mostly *here* I seem to get into trouble," he said, smiling even more enigmatically this time. "But, yes, you could say I got into trouble there as well."

"You don't volunteer much, do you?"

"I've learned not to. Tell me about your childhood. Anything about before you moved to Washington."

"Why?"

He shrugged.

"Because there are two people in this car, two human beings, and that is what we do. We talk, as much to assuage our own instinctive fear of silence as to communicate with one another. Silence is too much like a mimicry of death, and we don't like death. I don't, anyway. Besides, those men wanted to kill you for a reason. To find out what that reason is, I have to know who you are."

"I grew up in California."

"Nice state. Not a great deal of storyline, though."

"Let's chat about something else. How about *your* past"

"You had an unhappy childhood? A falling out with your parents?"

"They're gone," she said.

She didn't speak about them even to people who might one day become *acquaintances*, and certainly not to weird strangers.

"Gone. Not dead." he said, smiling more to himself than at her. Even for a good Samaritan, he had an uncanny knack for rubbing her the wrong way. "So, you moved to DC to make your fortune."

"I took a job with AventCorp for the benefits."

He nodded.

"Doing what?"

"Office manager."

"AventCorp," he said, nodding to himself. When she frowned, he smiled again. "Do they kill many office managers there?"

"Not that I know of."

"So why are they after you?"

"I'd rather not say."

Heavy drops of rain suddenly began to slap harder on the windshield, and he turned the wipers up.

"Now you're learning. But I did save your life."

"For which I'm eternally in your debt."

"But you won't tell me what you found out there that made them want to kill you?"

"I didn't find out anything."

"But you were looking."

"Yes."

"Why?"

"It's personal."

"It is for me, too."

"What do you have to do with AventCorp?"

"That is a very long story and one I'm afraid you wouldn't believe if I told you."

"Which you're not gonna."

"Correct."

"Why?"

He sighed again, and the sadness seemed to return, darkening the glints in his eyes.

"Because it is a very personal pain, and I am dealing with it in a personal way."

"Me, too," she said, turning away.

But she saw his reflection in her rain-drenched window as he glanced at his watch.

"Right about now," he said, enigmatically, "evil men are doing evil things."

Some errant thought or memory tightened his jaw.

Then he shook his head, took a deep breath, and returned his attention to the road ahead.

"THIS IS WHERE I leave you," said Shiver, nodding through Tracy's rain-streaked window toward the doors of the Boston bus station.

Horns blared, tires screeched, and sirens shrieked, echoing off the tall marble and granite buildings as did the sound of jackhammers and the cries of pedestrians and construction workers.

In between the heavy showers, occasional shafts of cold gray sunlight struggled down through the forest of stone, steel, and glass to bounce dully off the new asphalt and ancient cobbles. A young man in a glistening poncho struggled up the temporary plywood ramp, shouldering his way into the revolving doors of the station, dragging his duffle bag behind him.

Tracy shook her head in disbelief, staring at the green vinyl bank bag on her lap. "You're just going to dump me here?"

Shiver tapped the bag with the back of his hand.

"You have everything you need to survive now. Just follow instructions."

"Why are you doing this? How did you know where to find me?"

"The driver's license is real," he said. "So are the credit cards, and the birth certificate, and the cash. You are now Mildred Jones."

Tracy laughed hollowly. "Who thought that up, F. Scott Fitzgerald?"

"A friend. Anyway, I like the name."

"*Mildred Jones?* It sounds like a Broadway musical from the thirties. Why don't you just put a sign around my neck that says *Hiding! False Identity!"*

Shiver frowned, reaching to adjust the mirror sunglasses on her face.

"They look nice."

"Thank you for buying them. I could have done it."

He shrugged.

"I didn't want to chance you being seen in the store."

"They add to my persona as Mildred Jones, I'm sure."

He sighed.

"What more can I do for you?"

"Tell me what's going on. What is AventCorp really up to? How did you know where to find me? How did you do those things you did? And how could you possibly have created a new identity for me so fast?"

He shook his head.

"If I tried to explain it would take far too long. Even then you wouldn't believe me."

He glared out into the steady afternoon rain, his eyes seemed to harden like slate, and suddenly Tracy was afraid of him.

"What did they do to you?" she asked, more fearful than ever as he turned to face her again.

The scar on his cheek was livid. His eyes took a long moment to register on her, but when they did, they slowly softened, and he relaxed in his seat.

"A great many things, I'm afraid. But one in particular for which I cannot forgive them. Ever."

The way he said *ever* chilled her to the bone. She sensed a terrible sadness and at the same time a rage that reminded her of her own, but there was a violence in this man that seemed far beyond anything she had ever felt. A forced calm kept his hands resting idly on the wheel, and yet at the same time she was certain that at any moment he might explode again like a human stick of dynamite.

"What do you know about Ash?" she asked.

His eyes flashed, but once again he remained calm, merely shaking his head.

"You need to be going. You'll miss your bus."

"I'll take the next one."

"It isn't safe for you to be seen even here. I told you, stay in the restroom until the bus is ready to board. Don't talk to the other passengers. Just pretend to be asleep."

"Why are you putting me out here, then? Why not take me farther away? If they've followed us to Boston, you're just leaving me in their hands."

"We weren't followed. Or at least we have bought a little time."

"How do you know?"

"I know."

She believed him.

Over the past twenty-four hours, he'd exhibited strange skills, like his disconcerting ability to change lanes in traffic without using the rearview mirror, and the uncanny knack of seeming to know what she was thinking, like the sunglasses. They'd barely reached the outskirts of Baltimore with the sun sinking behind them, and Tracy had been wishing that the people in the passing cars couldn't see her so clearly. Shiver pulled into a small gas station and told her to remain in the car, returning with the mirror shades.

He knew what she was thinking maybe, but not necessarily her tastes.

"What if I just sit here? What if I won't get out of the car?"

He sighed again, staring at the parking meter that was ticking out the last of their ten minutes.

"Then I will leave you the car. Perhaps that would be better. Do you want me to do that?"

"I'd follow you."

"You wouldn't be able to."

She knew that was true.

"I have to find out what's going on. I have to," she whispered.

This time his eyes were even sadder than before.

"You can't do that. You have no idea how dangerous the men are who are after you."

"Yes, I do," she said, glaring through the windshield. "They murdered my only friend, and I think it was because of them that several other men died, and my parents ended up the way they did, and now they're gone, too. I won't allow them to get away with that."

"They aren't going to get away with it. I promise you. But *you* need to stay away from them. All you're going to do by not listening to me is get yourself killed."

"Take me with you. I can help."

He shook his head.

"I can't. There are things I have to do that you couldn't understand. Places I have to go that you couldn't follow. This is where you belong now, and I belong somewhere else."

"Where?"

He shook his head, placing his hand on the handle of his door.

"No," she said. "You take the car. I'll do as you say."

He nodded, reaching out to grasp her arm as she opened her door. She turned back to him, rain trickling down the shoulder of her blouse, gluing her hair to her head, flowing down her cheeks like tears.

"Live long and prosper, Mildred Jones," he said, stretching the scar in another grin.

"You, too," she said, slamming the door, and racing through the deluge.

ASH STOOD IN FRONT of the massive multi-paned window, watching the line of traffic out front. The storm that had blasted through the city had finally blown away northward, and the late afternoon sun glinted off the Capital dome, causing him to squint, but he would not look away.

It was a dangerous game he had played since boyhood, a battle between himself and the sun's reflection–rarely the sun itself, he wasn't often *that* stupid–and although more than one ophthalmologist had told him he was ruining his vision, he couldn't stop. He made up for the progressive loss by wearing dark prescription glasses most of the time. But occasionally–as now–he could not resist doing battle barehanded, so to speak.

Across the wide expanse of his office sat a short, chubby man in his late forties, wearing thick spectacles of his own and a business suit that seemed new, but rumpled. He looked like an accountant, his pen poised in his stubby fingers, hovering over a yellow legal tablet.

Ash turned to the man and shook his head in disgust.

"You don't often come to my office," he mused.

"I'm a busy man."

"You're an idiot, Walsh."

"You've often told me so, Ash."

Ash smiled, cutting his blocky face in half with a slash of teeth.

"But you're loyal, aren't you?"

"As the day is long."

Ash chuckled. The sound was like old bones being dragged through dry dirt.

"I'm going to enjoy torturing every last secret out of that girl and whoever helped her if they happen to get brought in alive."

"I thought your orders now were to kill her."

Ash shrugged.

"I rescinded that when she wasn't taken care of immediately. It's obvious she has outside help. I want to know who it is. I will enjoy finding out what they know."

"I'm sure that will be fun for you," said Walsh, writing rapidly on the pad.

Ash frowned.

"What are you taking notes about now?"

Walsh read from the pad, tipping his glasses with one hand.

"That will be fun for you, I said."

Ash turned back to the windows.

"Just make sure you keep that shithead on the hill off my ass for a few more days."

"You're certain that's all the time you need?"

Ash nodded.

It wasn't a matter of how much time he *needed*, and even an idiot like Walsh was aware of that. They were about to hit a wall. If their mission was not completed by then, if they failed... the consequences were unthinkable. If the damned senators in the Energy Committee had any idea of the real situation, they would be running around like chickens with their heads cut off, or more likely screaming that the sky was falling, which it was.

"Just keep him occupied."

"I'm trying, but even Aventcorp doesn't have unlimited pull with a Senate committee much less the President of the United States. You haven't given him much to go on."

"I need the original device. I'm within inches of getting it."

Walsh nodded. "If there was an original device... I'm not arguing just postulating... Something went wrong with it. Terribly wrong. Why are you so sure you can control it?"

Ash made a swiping motion. "What other options are there? We have to have energy. The Pentagon Brass remind me of kids who have just learned all their toys are about to be burned. An army or navy without gas is as useless as tits on a boar hog. But if we inform OPEC that they *will* sell all or even most of their oil only to us the rest of the world is about as likely to stand for that as the President is of letting me perform brain surgery on him. Which might not be a bad idea. We're about to go to war, and he's too stupid to understand the outcome."

Walsh swallowed a lump, nodding. "I'll try to finesse him."

"You're good at finesse, aren't you, Walsh?"

Walsh nodded. "I have my talents."

"Yes, you definitely do."

Walsh nodded. "To your success."

Ash flicked the fingers of his right hand, signifying that the meeting was over. He watched Walsh waddle out of the office, and when the door whooshed shut behind the man, he pressed the button on his intercom. "What have you got for me?"

"A security guard in the Boston bus station saw a girl that looked like our pigeon."

"And her *helper?"*

"No sign of him."

"Did the guard find out where the girl was headed?"

"No. But our man did."

"Who?"

"I sent Trevor. I thought it was time to quit fucking around."

Ash frowned.

"Good. I want her in our hands by nightfall. And our mysterious Mr. Townsend?"

"He's being taken to Terra Diablo, as you ordered. Are you going there?"

"Soon."

Ash turned back to the window. Cars and buses scuttled through the streets, planes flew overhead, and vendors on the Mall hawked ice cream and hotdogs. It was all so ordinary. So American.

And it was about to come crashing down so fast the Joes and Janes walking along the sidewalks out there wouldn't have time to crap their pants or panties. The last report by the United States Geological Survey on oil reserves had been the first ever to be classified. Ash had been instrumental in convincing the Director of the agency that it would be in his and the country's best interest if he *revised* that one before publication.

People weren't stupid, though. With gas prices where they were everything else went up. Wal-Mart was taking a hit because it was cheaper to buy local produce from the farm stand and to get your nuts and bolts from the local hardware than to drive to get them. Electric vehicles were taking over, but solar and wind production of electricity would never meet the demand for all those rechargeable batteries.

It was a mess.

Ash felt like the little Dutch boy with his finger in the dam, and new holes were popping up everywhere. There was only one hope for the country he truly loved, and hardly anyone believed in it but himself and a handful of crackpot scientists. But if they could pull it off, they could not only save the good old US of A from ruination but put her back into the forefront of world powers. More than that, it would give the US not only unlimited energy but a source of power beyond belief, a weapon no other government on earth would question or want to face.

Ash was ready to go to any extreme to succeed, although he didn't want anything for the accomplishment. He sought neither fame nor fortune. Just doing it would be enough.

And maybe sticking the knowledge up his father's ass.

TRACY'S SAVIOR HAD MADE one mistake.

While he went inside the convenience store to buy sunglasses for her she had rummaged through the glovebox and discovered a small spiral notebook. Glancing through it she found names, phone numbers, and addresses, along with what looked like bank account numbers and a little biographical data on each person. She'd been so intrigued that when she noticed Shiver heading back around the front of the car she slammed the box shut and slipped the book into her pocket. Once on the bus, realizing she still had it, the little book had seemed to point her naturally in the next direction of her quest for information.

Instead of following directions and heading for Canada she switched buses in Lewiston, Maine, and headed for Cleveland where she caught a cab. She could have called an Uber, but Shiver had warned her that Ash would be able to follow even a burner phone. She'd believed him. Her phone was now on another bus. Tracy had simply tossed it into the baggage compartment when the driver wasn't looking and then vanished.

Now in either direction, the Ohio landscape drifted away idyllically beneath the full moon. Open fields rolled in low waves around groves of low-slung oaks. One farm seemed to cover the entire dell, but because the barn off to one side was hardly bigger than a two-car garage, Tracy knew that the owners of the house were gentlemen farmers, the land more than likely leased to someone else. The cab driver sat in the car at the end of the walk, staring at her through the passenger window, but she still hadn't made up her mind to knock.

The house reminded her of the idyllic part of her childhood, its long, covered deck constructed with wide, square posts and a waist-high, cedar-shingled railing. The porch was a place toddlers could romp in safety while the adults chatted on the worn wooden swing and sipped drinks in the late afternoon sun, or perhaps a place for an older couple to relax in the evening. This was not a spot where federal agents would roar into the drive and drag your parents down the steps like men corraling mad dogs. Not a home masking a terrible secret, even from its most timid and impressionable occupant.

Or was it?

She knocked lightly on the door. The porch light came on, drapery on the other side of the oval glass was pulled aside, and a woman's face appeared, with hesitant but friendly brown eyes, and a quick smile. The door opened, and the woman head taller than Tracy and built broadly but not fat–stood waiting. She wore a jersey, calf-length skirt, and black pumps that Tracy felt would be more fitting on someone a lot older than the woman who seemed to be in her late fifties.

"I'm Mildred Jones," said Tracy, feeling silly using the name. "Are you Beatrice Smith?"

"Yes," said the woman.

"I was wondering if I might speak to you?"

Beatrice's eyes narrowed, but her smile remained.

"About what?"

Tracy shrugged.

"I don't know where to start. Might I just come in for a moment?"

Beatrice studied her, but apparently found nothing in Tracy's demeanor to fear. She stepped aside and waved toward a set of double doors through which Tracy saw a sofa and end table. Tracy nodded her head at the cabbie, and he drove away. She tucked the small backpack she'd purchased at Wal-Mart tightly under her arm, following Beatrice into the house.

The home was suggestive of an older widowed woman, and it wasn't just the smell of scented candles. Everything was done in floral prints and lace, and the worn, hardwood floors were covered with handmade throw rugs. The pictures on the walls were mostly black-and-white prints in faded frames. There was no smell of a man, nor any men's magazines or memorabilia. Just the photos.

"Family?" said Tracy, stopping in front of a picture of two women on a deserted beach.

The bathing suits were all one-piece, the women not stout but full-figured. Something about the picture was off, the out-of-focus buildings along the far shore seemed foreign. When Tracy looked closer, she noticed that none of the pictures had any of the same people in them, anywhere. If they were family shots it was one large, scattered family.

"Yes," said Beatrice, herding Tracy to the sofa where the two women sat nervously regarding each other.

The small parlor had a high picture rail lined with more old photos. The walls themselves were ancient pine panels, and a small brick fireplace was centered between two brass stands filled with umbrellas and canes that *did* look masculine. Maybe her initial reading had been wrong.

"Now please tell me what I can do for you," said Beatrice. "Oh, my. I'm forgetting my manners. Would you like coffee, or something cold to drink? Perhaps some strudel?"

"Thank you, no," said Tracy, noticing that Beatrice seemed thankful for that.

The woman was naturally polite, but anxious. That might just be normal apprehension at having a stranger in the house, but Tracy didn't think so.

"I was wondering if you'd ever met a man who called himself Shiver."

Beatrice tried hard to disguise her shock, but there was no missing the sudden intake of breath, or the nibbling of her bottom lip that she quickly hid with a touch of her fingertips.

"Shiver?" she said, tittering nervously. "What a strange name."

"So you've never heard of him?"

"No. Why should I have?"

Suddenly the woman's face–still trying to hold onto the smile–exhibited a cunning behind the dark eyes.

"I found your name in a notebook that he'd been writing in," said Tracy, watching the eyes tighten. "I assumed you knew him."

"Might I see the notebook?"

Tracy tried not to frown. Beatrice sounded more like a spider inviting a fly in for a cup of tea than the nice middle-aged woman she'd met on the front porch.

"I'm afraid I don't have it with me," she lied, trying not to clutch at the pack. "I left it back at my motel, but your name and this address are in it, I assure you."

"I believe you," said Beatrice, nodding. "Why would you lie?"

Why indeed? Maybe as a pretense to get into the house and murder her. Why was she so easily convinced?

"And how do you know this...Shiver?" said Beatrice.

"We met in Washington, DC."

Beatrice nodded.

"Under what circumstances?"

She knew something. Only what? Tracy had just assumed that the names on the pages were people who worked with Shiver somehow, perhaps people he had helped like herself. But what if there were people on the *other* side? What if Beatrice was somehow connected to Ash? That didn't seem likely. What could this woman living alone outside a small Ohio town have to do with secret research or a man like Ash?

But nothing had added up in a long time.

"What do you mean?" she said, stalling.

"In my experience, men named Shiver don't just appear out of nowhere for no reason. How did you meet him?"

"You've had experience with men named Shiver?" said Tracy, playing the game.

Beatrice frowned, her voice suddenly businesslike.

"I think you know what I meant. Now why are you here, and what do you want?"

"I want to know what's going on. I want to know who you are, who Shiver is, and why he helped me."

The eyebrows looped upward.

"So he helped you."

"Yes."

"He saved your life."

"I didn't say that."

"You didn't have to."

"So you do know him."

"I didn't say that."

"You didn't have to."

"I think I will brew some coffee," said Beatrice, rising. "Make yourself comfortable."

"If you don't mind, I'll join you in the kitchen," said Tracy rising.

A wry smile replaced the frown.

"You're a quick learner."

"You're not the first person to tell me that."

The old house was a maze of dark hallways and tiny bedrooms, but the kitchen was light and airy.

"How long have you lived here?" asked Tracy, watching Beatrice scoop coffee into an old-style stainless-steel percolator on the white tile counter.

"Seems like all my life," said Beatrice wistfully, her back to Tracy.

"Are all those photos really of your family?"

Beatrice's shoulders stiffened and then released.

"They remind me of them."

"Shiver sent you to live here, didn't he? He gave you this new identity."

Beatrice plugged in the pot and sat down next to Tracy at the old chrome-legged table.

"Beatrice is my real name."

"Tell me how you met him and what he did for you."

"I'm afraid I can't do that."

"Why not?"

"Because I promised."

"But you have met him. You know who he is."

"I can't say."

"He saved my life. I have a hunch he saved your life and the lives of all those other people in the book. But I don't know who they are or what's going on, and I don't know what to do."

"What did he tell you to do?"

"He told me to go to an address in Quebec and start a new life under the identity he created for me."

"Then I suggest you do that."

"Why? What are you hiding from? I have people after me that want to kill me, but what about you? Who did you work for? Did people want to kill you, too?"

"You have no idea what trouble you're in," blurted Beatrice.

Her eyes flashed, and then watered, and Tracy knew she'd opened a vein.

"People are trying to kill me," repeated Tracy. "I think I *do* know."

"There are things worse than dying."

"Who are the people on the list?

"I'm not supposed to say."

"Please."

"Friends," said Beatrice, sighing. "I can't tell you any more than that. You shouldn't ask."

"Do you live here alone?" asked Tracy.

Beatrice nodded.

"My husband died ten years ago."

"Is that him in those pictures?" asked Tracy, pointing to several photos of a tall dark-haired man over the antique side table.

"Yes."

"He was a handsome man."

Beatrice smiled.

"He was very gentle and kind, and very brave."

Tracy smiled back.

"You don't have any children?"

"No."

"Do you work in town?" said Tracy, trying to break the rhythm, searching for any road into Beatrice's tightly closed world.

Beatrice shook her head.

"I wouldn't know how."

Tracy nodded.

"Shiver left you well enough off that you don't need to work."

"I'm not wealthy," said Beatrice defensively.

"I was just wondering where he gets all the money," said Tracy thinking of the notebook filled with names and bank account numbers.

If every one of them had received the same type of largess as her, then Shiver had to be an incredibly wealthy man, and he certainly hadn't looked it, except for the BMW.

"Is that important?" asked Beatrice, frowning again. "He helped me. He helped you, and all those other people, as you say."

"I don't know for a fact that they're all in the same situation as us."

"But you suspect."

Tracy shook her head.

"I have no idea what to suspect. I was working for a research company in DC, but I believe that was just a cover for something that a man named Ash had going on the side. Now he obviously thinks I know too much, although I don't understand why. What I really don't understand is who Shiver is, who all the people are in the notebook, or why a man I've never met risked his life to save my own."

Beatrice seemed to relax. She carried the coffee cups over to the sink, staring out the window into the lowering sun.

"It isn't always good to know things," she said, turning on the water.

"It seems like I've spent half my life not knowing things," said Tracy.

"Why not just let it go?"

"Because I can't," said Tracy. "Because I have to find my parents or what's happened to them. I have to know if they did things they were said to have done, that I thought they did, or whether it was all some kind of setup by Ash and the company."

"Who are your parents?"

Tracy shook her head.

"It doesn't matter. What does is that I think now maybe I was wrong about them all along. I think I made a terrible mistake and they paid for it. I have to redeem myself, if only for myself."

"Is it worth your life?"

"Yes," said Tracy, without hesitation.

Beatrice turned to face her with a sad expression.

"Sometimes the best thing you can do is accept things as they are."

"I guess I should be going, then," said Tracy, starting to rise. "I should have kept the cab."

"It's late now," said Beatrice, turning toward the window again. "Where will you go?"

"I'll get a motel for the night," said Tracy, realizing she'd just trapped herself in a lie. "Or I might just hop a bus again. Maybe it's better if I keep moving for a while."

Beatrice nodded.

"Throw the hounds off the scent. Then go where Shiver told you to go."

When she turned back toward Tracy, some of the anxiety had left the older woman's eyes, but Tracy read little more in them than concern for another human being, and perhaps loneliness.

"Why don't you stay the night? I don't often get visitors." Beatrice laughed at herself. "I *never* get visitors. Please stay."

A warning sounded in the back of Tracy's head. *Keep your distance. You let Steph in and now she's dead.* But she wasn't making friends with the woman, not really. She'd given up nothing of herself, and the offer of a room in a real house, with another real breathing human being right down the hall seemed almost too good–too safe–to pass up.

"Do you have luggage?" asked Beatrice.

Tracy fanned her hands, nodding toward her pack.

"I have no clean clothes. Nothing really. We left Washington in kind of a rush, I suppose you can imagine. And

I only stopped long enough in a store to grab this pack and some fresh underwear."

Beatrice nodded.

"I know the feeling. I have a nightie that should fit you, and you look like a shower might cheer you up. There's a bath down the hall. In the morning you can wash your clothes if you like."

"Are you sure?"

"I can't help you. Not really. The least I can do is feed you and see you get a good night's sleep before you're on your way again."

"Thank you."

The bathroom, like the rest of the house, seemed like something out of time, and Tracy wondered if the home waiting for her in Canada was any more modern. But the old cast iron tub was deep and comforting, and she found packages of toothbrushes still in their cellophane wrappers in the stainless-steel medicine cabinet.

Beatrice tapped on the door, handing Tracy a bathrobe without entering. The steamy air in the room, and the comforting sense of the woman at watch on the other side of the door relaxed her more than she'd allowed herself to relax in months. She slapped on the robe and followed a mouth-watering aroma into the kitchen.

"How do hot ham and cheese sandwiches suit you?" asked Beatrice, *scritching* the fork in the pan.

"Fine," said Tracy realizing she hadn't eaten anything but fast food since DC. She dropped into the same chair she'd used before. "Can I ask you one more question?"

Beatrice didn't exactly stiffen, but her head cocked back a little.

"I wish you wouldn't."

"Tomorrow I'll be gone," said Tracy. "You'll never see me again. I don't know what's going to happen with my life, and I just wondered if you could tell me why you live the way you do. Am I expected to lock myself in my new house, and never come out?"

Beatrice sighed.

"I don't know what you're supposed to do. Most likely you'll find instructions in the house when you get there."

"So Shiver told you to live like a hermit? I mean you do, don't you?"

"Yes," said Beatrice slowly. "I mean, no. We weren't told to live this way. Please turn the sandwiches."

She dropped the fork onto the counter, and raced out of the kitchen, leaving Tracy wondering if she shouldn't learn to keep her mouth shut.

Tracy had plates filled when Beatrice returned to hand Tracy a yellowed sheet of paper. Tracy held it beneath the light over the sink, recognizing the jagged script immediately as the same hand that had written the names and addresses in the notebook she'd stolen from Shiver.

The instructions detailed a life Beatrice and her husband could have led. They instructed them where to find their college degrees, and other background information in the house so that they could obtain employment. The paper was so detailed it even explained why they had left their previous employers–who would give each of them glowing references–and where to find the local church.

Tracy lay the faded old legal sheet carefully on the counter away from the splattering pan. One thing bothered her. The paper looked pretty old and frayed to have been written by the same man she knew. Unless he'd written it when he was five. Then it dawned on her that Beatrice had said her husband had died ten years before.

"How long had you been living here before your husband died?"

"A while," said Beatrice, not meeting her eyes.

"How old was Shiver when you met him?"

"Young."

Like maybe an infant?

"I can't imagine the organization it took to set something like this up," said Tracy.

Beatrice nodded.

"But did you ever get a job? Did you join the church?"

Beatrice removed the eggs, and placed them on two plates, adding toast and pieces of bacon, carrying them to the table while Tracy found silverware, and poured each of them another coffee.

"We did for a while. My husband was more religious than me, but neither of us ever worked except to keep a few farm animals."

Tracy frowned.

"You think you would be bored to death," said Beatrice, shaking her head. "But my husband could spend hours in the study with nothing more than a pencil and paper, and I have always been happy being a housewife. There's more than enough to keep a woman busy with a man around. Then, when my husband died of a heart attack, I tried going to church, and some of the congregation came by for a while. They were very nice, always trying to draw me out. But it was just too hard keeping my stories straight, and I finally managed to shoo them away."

"I'm sorry about your husband," said Tracy, meaning it.

Beatrice shrugged, staring away into the distance.

"It was strange that we should make it here... to safe ty...only for him to die in so senseless a manner. Even though they did not actually kill him, I still blame them for my husband's death. I suppose some things are just meant to be."

"You must have been incredibly lonely."

"They took my whole life. My husband, my friends. They stole the time that should have been ours. They took everything. They would have taken my life, too, if not for Shiver. A lot of times I wish they had."

"I'm not going to live like that."

Beatrice stared at her.

"Don't. You go out and make a new life for yourself. Make new friends. You're young and strong."

Tracy shook her head.

"I'm not going to let them take my life from me. I'm going to find out what's going on, and then I'm going to do something about it."

"How?"

"I don't know yet."

Beatrice shook her head.

"They'll kill you. You have no idea how powerful they are. But before they kill you, they'll force you to lead them to each of us."

Tracy frowned. She hadn't thought of that.

"The notebook you mean."

Beatrice nodded.

"You should destroy it."

"I guess I will."

But she knew she wouldn't. She needed the book in order to find someone who would tell her what was going on. Surely not all of the people listed had complied so perfectly with Shiver's wishes as Beatrice. Beyond that Tracy had the uncanny feeling that she and Shiver would meet again if for no other reason than him returning to claim his notebook.

She ate greedily, watching Beatrice pick at her sandwich. When they were both done Tracy insisted on helping with the dishes. The two women worked in silence as the sun disappeared over the high backyard fence. When Tracy placed the last dish in the strainer Beatrice stared at her.

"When you get wherever it is you're going, I want you to call me."

Tracy was touched and embarrassed. She'd come here to question this woman, not to make a friend, but it seemed as though she had.

"Are you sure?"

Beatrice nodded slowly.

"I feel responsible for you in a way, now. I just want to know you're all right. Just call and say you're all right, and then hang up. Use a pay phone. I'll give you some money if you need it."

Tracy shook her head.

"Of course," said Beatrice, smiling. "You wouldn't need money, would you? We're kind of a club."

Tracy smiled back.

"It's an odd organization."

"Yes. We're the survivors of our own little Holocaust. Perhaps that's fitting."

The idea seemed to strike a deep and hidden chord for Beatrice. Once again, she stared blankly out across the backyard–her hands still immersed in the soapy water–and Tracy was reluctant to disturb her, slipping quietly away into the living room.

THEY SPENT THE REST of that uncomfortable evening together in the parlor in front of an ancient color TV, neither paying attention to what was on, both dancing nimbly around the strange events that had brought them together.

It was clear that Beatrice was not about to tell Tracy who she had been in her former life, or what she might have known or seen that had driven men to want to murder her and her husband. Nor did she ask to hear any more about Tracy's background. So, the two women ended up discussing current events, and Tracy was surprised to find how well-informed Beatrice was. Apparently, she watched the cable news channels all day.

As Tracy rose at last to head for bed Beatrice unexpectedly hugged her.

"Please, do not do what you are thinking," whispered Beatrice. "Just go where you were told."

Tracy sighed. It would be so easy to lie to the old woman, to allay her fears, but she could not. She'd told far too many lies over the past year.

"I can't," she said, quietly. "I have to find out what's going on. I owe that to my mom and dad, that much at least."

"Life is so very short and precious. There is a balance-"

Beatrice's words hung in the air, echoing what Shiver had said, and Tracy stared at her, waiting for her to finish. But the old woman's lips closed, and she smiled.

"What were you going to say?" asked Tracy. "Why did Shiver help you? Why are you special?"

Beatrice shrugged, refusing to speak again, and Tracy felt a sudden anger at the woman that she tried hard to hold at bay. They were both in this–whatever this was–together. Why couldn't Beatrice see that? Finally, Tracy sighed and shook her head.

"When you see him again," she said, turning toward her bedroom. "Tell him that I'm not going to quit."

Beatrice's whisper seemed to reverberate in the air long after Tracy lay alone in bed.

"If I ever see him again, I will have many things to tell him."

THE NIGHT WAS DEEP and dark, the fields shielded from the preying moon by a thin layer of clouds. As Tracy lay wide awake in the back bedroom, sniffing at the odor of lilac and mothballs, she heard what sounded like a key in a lock and bolted upright in bed. There was another tiny clicking noise from down the hall, and she stared at the dark shadows through the open door, swallowing a thick lump in her throat. Who else besides Beatrice would have a key to the house?

She was sure Beatrice was sound asleep two doors down. She'd heard the older woman snoring only a few moments before and then a rustling when Beatrice must have awakened herself and rolled over.

Tracy carefully slid aside the bed linens and tiptoed to the door, glancing nervously down the long hall. A man's figure was silhouetted through the oval curtain of the front door, and a cold surge of panic raced through her. She backed into the bedroom, snatching at her clothes that lay scattered across an antique settee in front of the window. The front door creaked, and then the chain lock clinked, and Tracy froze. She could see a sliver of moonlight slicing along the hallway carpet.

When no further sounds disturbed the house, she silently picked up her tennis shoes and socks. She threw the pack over her shoulder, tiptoeing around the settee.

She hoped that the intruder didn't know the layout of the house. He would come to Beatrice's room first, and Tracy realized at that instant that he might very well kill the older woman. As her fingers reached the window latch a pang of guilt stabbed at her heart and her hands fell away. She turned back to the door, shaking with fear, but knowing that she could not run out on the old woman. She gasped when a silhouette filled her bedroom doorway, and her heart drummed in her chest.

But it was Beatrice.

The old woman tiptoed to meet her at the foot of the bed.

"A man-" whispered Tracy.

"I know," whispered Beatrice, taking her by the shoulder and aiming her at the window again. "I heard his car and went to get this," she showed Tracy a heavy wooden rolling pin. "Go!"

"I'm not leaving you."

Beatrice turned as a heavier metallic clicking sound told Tracy the man had just snipped the chain lock.

"I can tell him nothing about the others," whispered Beatrice, still shoving her toward the window. "*You* have the book. You must go. He's more interested in you than me. I'll distract him. Now go!"

She shoved Tracy toward the window one last time, and then headed back toward the hall. In the doorway, she turned back to wave quickly, both fear and determination in her eyes. She peeked down the hall, turned quickly in the direction of the kitchen, and then she was gone.

Tracy knew that there was no way she was getting the old woman out of the house now. Beatrice had made her decision. Now if *she* didn't go, Beatrice's courage would be for naught.

Tracy twisted the tarnished brass latch, praying the window didn't make a sound when the pressure was released. She felt a draft as the front door opened, and she thought she heard a footstep in the hallway. Then there was ominous silence again.

She stared blindly into the gloom outside. The night was overcast, and the porch light out front didn't seem to make it around that corner of the house. The old window continued to resist, and Tracy wondered if it might have been painted into place. A sudden scuffling sound came from down the hall, and another knife of guilt stabbed at Tracy. But she used the sound to cover the light scraping noise of the window as it finally gave in to her constant pressure. She reached for the screen latch only to discover that there was no screen.

All she had to do was slip through the window silently, and get away. But her hands were full of clothes and shoes, and the pack swung loosely against her back, one more thing to snag in the window or make a noise. She held her breath as she stuck one leg out into the darkness, her bare feet digging into some kind of bushy shrub. Fighting a cramp in her other leg, she slid her butt onto the sill and slipped outside, snagging her nightdress. She jerked nervously at it, finally freeing the flannel, but she was wedged between the shrub and a tall fence that blocked her from the front of the house.

She considered trying to reach the window again and pull it closed. That might give her a few more moments before she was discovered–since the intruder was bound to see the bed had been slept in–perhaps he'd search the house first. But when something crashed inside, Tracy shuffled toward the rear of the house, leaving the window open.

It seemed unusual to her for a farmhouse to have a backyard with a privacy fence. She couldn't picture Beatrice sunbathing in the nude, but it might just be that the only way the woman felt safe out of doors at all was when she was surrounded by the tall, reassuring border.

As she inched her way along the high, vertical boards, a little moonlight eked through the branches of the giant oak trees but didn't manage to really reveal the backyard. The grass was damp and cool beneath her feet, and even though the night was warm she shivered. She was searching for a gate, but it dawned on her that there might not be one. Beatrice might like the sense of being totally surrounded by the tall barricade so much she'd brook no entrance other than the one from the house. In that case, Tracy was going to have to climb. She reached high overhead but could not touch the top of the wood slats.

It seemed only seconds ago she had slipped out into the scratchy shrub, and yet in her mind hours had passed inside the house, and the intruder must already know that she had escaped into the trap of the yard. She bumped into the back fence, and started along it. But as she hurried, still clutching her clothes in a tight bundle under one arm, the pack bumping her butt, a light flicked on in the kitchen, sending a sharp yellow beam slicing across the grass, illuminating a single chaise lounge and a small umbrella table.

A man's head and shoulders passed by the window, but the man seemed intent on what he was doing, and quickly disappeared again, extinguishing the light.

But where was Beatrice? What had he done with or to her? And now what? For all Tracy knew the bastard was still standing right in that black window, waiting for his eyes to adjust, for her to move. But that made no sense. If he was looking for her outside he'd never have turned on the light in the first place.

She continued along the fence until she reached the next corner, turning toward the house again. There was just a little more light there, enough to finally reveal the gate.

She sucked in a quick breath and raced to it, pressing her back against the house, listening to her heart pounding. Through the crack between the gate and the fence, she spotted a big black sedan out front with no one in it. She craned her head in both directions, but there didn't appear to be any other cars on the road. If she could get out of the trap and across the front yard, she might be able to hide long enough to put her clothes on and slip away through the fields and into the nearest trees.

As she lightly fingered the rusted old gate latch, she heard the distinctive sound of brush rustling behind her. The sonofabitch was climbing out the window! She forced herself to open the gate slowly, hating every infinitesimal creak, finally easing through when the opening was barely wide enough for her to pass, taking the time to draw the gate closed to keep the light from the porch from seeping through. When she heard rushing footsteps behind her she ran.

But there was no way she was going to outrun the killer barefoot, in her nightclothes, packing her ungainly bundle. As she raced across the lawn, imagining bullets burning into her back, she was shocked to hear the low rumble of the car's engine. She dodged around the hood and ripped the door open, tossing her pack inside and dropping into the seat, jerking the shifter into gear. Behind her, a dark-clad figure barreled across the lawn, and as she floored the accelerator, she wondered how many such escapes one woman could be expected to make.

MARK TOWNSEND AWAKENED SLOWLY from a heavily drugged sleep, listening to tires humming loudly across the asphalt. As he fought his way back to consciousness, he became aware of booted feet directly in front of his eyes and the painful cramp of handcuffs on his wrists behind his back. He followed the boots up to a pair of jean-clad knees, and when the van rolled to a stop a scowling face appeared between them.

The man's high-pitched voice didn't match his wide, chiseled cheeks or razor lips.

"So, you're up, Sleeping Beauty. Thought for a while we might have killed you."

The vehicle lurched and Mark had the sickening feeling of falling, as though the road had disappeared from beneath the tires. Suddenly his body pressed painfully into the floorboard, but there was no accompanying crash.

"Get up," said the booted man, nudging Mark with his toe.

Mark tried to edge onto his elbows, but he was still groggy, and he barely managed to roll over onto his side.

Some guy behind him grabbed his arms, jerking him roughly out the back doors of the van.

They were parked in what seemed to be a large indoor garage, and two more men appeared suddenly to grab Mark's arms and lead him staggering toward a set of double doors ahead. Lights hung from the dark ceiling in long fluorescent fixtures, illuminating the huge empty floor, and Mark wondered where all the other cars were. Maybe it was late at night and everyone else had gone home, but he had no idea how long he'd been under. As his vision cleared, he noticed that the space was, in fact, a giant cavern, but it must have been geologically unstable because steel shoring beams ran between the stalactites high overhead like a fishnet stocking over a hairy leg, and in his drugged state the image struck Mark as funny.

At the far end of the cavern, a concrete wall reached away to the high ceiling like the facade of an immense funeral crypt.

He was dragged through a door in the wall–that looked for all the world like the bulkhead on a submarine–into a narrow and brightly lit corridor.

"Where am I?" he gasped.

"Tell him?" the guy asked the bigger man behind Mark.

"Ash didn't say. Better keep your mouth shut."

"Ahh," said the first guy, mimicking a sympathetic expression. "He's not going to tell anyone. Are you, pretty boy? I mean, who's he going to tell, ever?"

Mark didn't care for the sound of that, but then he'd pretty much decided that he wasn't getting out of this alive unless he did something drastic. Only he couldn't for the life of him think what that might be, with his hands cuffed behind his back, his muscles turned to

Jell-O and these two mammoth guards just waiting for him to make a move.

When they reached another set of double doors, Girly Voice pressed his hand to a security screen, the locks clicked open, and Mark found himself in what appeared to be a large conference room with thick beige carpet, a long, dark cherry table surrounded by comfortable looking leather armchairs, and a huge flat screen on the far wall. He was surprised when he felt a small key being placed in his hands, but when he turned his captors were already closing the door behind them.

Mark fiddled with the key, fitting it to the hole in the left cuff. When he had freed himself, he dropped the manacles on the floor, pocketing the key, and inspected the room.

The double doors were solid as stone with heavy steel bolts at the top and bottom securing them into the thick metal jamb. He thought that he might be able to disassemble one of the chairs and use part of the base as a bar to break out, but he had no reason to believe that he would be able to without setting off numerous alarms. And even if he did get out, where was he going to go? The men who'd brought him here were certainly somewhere outside in those endless corridors, and even had he been able to make it back as far as the cavernous parking lot, there was only the one van, the driver was certainly armed, and he had no idea how to get out.

He was surprised when Ash's face appeared on the screen, his eyes burrowing into Mark. Mark noticed the small glint of a round lens high in the corner. He also noticed that the little he could see of the *room* behind Ash looked like the interior of a private jet.

"Yes," said the husky voice that was so familiar. "We can see each other, Mr. Townsend. Please sit down."

So, he didn't know who Mark was, or else he was playing the game out. Ash had always been good at games.

Mark shook his head.

"I'd rather be sitting in a plane seat," he said, disguising his voice.

"I'm sure you would. Unfortunately, that isn't going to happen. So make yourself comfortable."

"Why am I here?"

"Are you being philosophical?"

"Are you being funny?"

Ash shrugged.

"Call me Ash."

"I've heard of you."

Ash's eyes glinted.

"Why does that not surprise me?" he said, and Mark thought that he was doing his best not to shake his head in disgust.

"Nice place you have here," said Mark.

"I like it. It *is* very special."

"I'll bet it's not in this year's Guinness Book."

"No. That isn't possible, I'm sorry to say. But it could be for more reasons than you can count."

"I noticed there's no late shift."

"What do you mean?"

"The parking lot was empty."

"The parking lot?... Oh...I see." Ash disappeared off camera for a moment. When he returned, he was wearing dark glasses. "I'm sorry, Mr. Townsend. I have to protect my eyes for... for other things."

"What are you working on here?"

"I'm not here to give you specifics about the facility. In fact, *you* are here to give *me* information."

"Such as?"

"Such as what you know about Project Feedback."

"Feedback on what project?" said Mark, frowning.

"Don't play games. I have no time for them at the moment."

"I'm not playing games. I don't know what you're talking about."

"Mr. Townsend, I will arrive there in person in a short time, and I can assure you, you will give me all the answers I require. You will find it much easier if you give them to me now."

"So you can what, have Girly Voice shove me down a drainpipe?"

"Girly Voice?"

"One of the goons who brought me here."

Ash smiled.

"I don't know those men personally. But rest assured I'll inform your captors of your opinion of them when I arrive."

"Like they can kill me twice."

"You are so naive. Dying is easy. I will ask you one last time to tell me all you know about Project Feedback."

"Go screw yourself."

The wall went ominously blank again, staring back at Mark like the eye of some giant unblinking predator.

THE NIGHT HAD TRANSFIGURED itself into late morning without fanfare by the time Tracy pulled into a gas station outside the little mountain village of Tarrelton, New York.

She was too exhausted to keep her eyes open, and the adrenalin that had sustained her for the past seven hours was being replaced by bile and lactic acid, so that her stomach burned, and every muscle in her body exhibited low-level aches. She desperately needed to stop somewhere and rest, but she was afraid that if the men pursuing her could track her to Beatrice's house, they could find her anywhere. She kept trying to tie the address on the second page of the notebook to the map on the seat that wove in and out of focus. She had plenty of reason to believe there had to be a tracking device on the car, and even if there wasn't she feared using its built-in GPS.

Since racing wildly away from Beatrice's farm she had stopped only long enough to call the police and inform them of the break-in, then later to gas us up just before dawn. Oddly enough the late-night attendant had been able to find a real live map in a dusty box in the storeroom, although he seemed to think she was crazy. But she was almost out of gas again and dying for something to drink. She rummaged around in the pack for the money Shiver had given her, searching for something smaller than a hundred.

Inside the station's convenience store, she grabbed a couple of sodas, a large bag of potato chips, a couple of candy bars, and a quart of chocolate milk. It wasn't haute cuisine, but there wasn't a hell of a selection. She figured if she could put *anything* into her stomach and find some place to snatch at least a few hours' sleep she might be able to get her brain working again. When she dumped the junk food on the counter along with a twenty, the redheaded, teenage boy on duty gave her a funny look.

"What's the matter?" she asked.

"You look like you've had a hard night, that's all," said the youngster, tweaking one of his earrings.

"I have. It's been a long drive."

As he rang up the food items he glanced at her license plate.

"You sure you're okay?"

"I'm fine."

"I don't mean nothing," he said, shaking his head. "It's just you don't look like someone who'd be driving a rig like that."

"It belongs to my father," said Tracy, a little too quickly.

"Yeah, okay," said the kid. "He a secret agent or something?"

Tracy sighed. If this kid could spot the car so easily, how the hell was she going to get away with driving it around in broad daylight?

"I'm looking for a man named Dietrich Reich. He lives at 101 Ressler Road."

The kid frowned, cocking his head.

"Is there a problem?" asked Tracy.

"Why do you want to find Mr. Reich?"

She shrugged.

"It's a private matter. So, you know him?"

"Maybe."

"Are there a lot of Reichs living around here?"

"Maybe."

She sighed.

"I just want to talk to him, that's all."

The kid nodded. "

And you're driving a government car."

Tracy was too exhausted to argue. Against her better judgment, she decided to take a chance. If the conversation went screwy, she could claim to be joking.

"I stole it."

The kid's face lit up.

"You serious?"

"Yes."

"Want to get rid of it?"

"What?"

He leaned across the counter, giving her the leering look of a drug lord in a B movie.

"I know some people that might be looking for a car just like that."

"Are you kidding?"

"Only if you are."

Tracy thought fast. Whatever this kid was into it wasn't something Ash was likely to know anything about.

"I need a place to crash," she said. "And the car really is hot. In fact, I'm afraid there might even be some kind of locator somewhere in it."

"Really?"

"I'm not sure. The people I stole it from haven't caught me yet, but I've only been gone a few hours. I'm just warning your friends, or whoever they are. So here's the deal. A place to crash, and they get rid of the car, and I mean *rid* of it."

"Give me a sec," said the kid, shoving the bag of food toward her and disappearing through a door behind the counter. When he returned the drug lord's face was replaced by the greasy look of a well-oiled politician. "My friends'll be here in two shakes."

"You'd better not double-cross me," said Tracy, trying to make the meanest face she could.

The kid looked hurt. "We don't do that shit," he said, nodding his head. "You'll get a good night's sleep. I promise you that. Before you leave town the car will be history. What did you get yourself into?"

"The less you know the better."

"I'm no friend of Big Brother."

"I need to get my stuff out of the car."

When she returned to the store the kid was just hanging up the phone again, a little too quickly. Tracy eyed him nervously.

"I just called to set everything up," he said, holding up both hands.

Tracy nodded, not quite assured.

"Shit," she said, as a town cop pulled up to the pumps behind her car.

"Through there," said the kid, waving Tracy toward the door behind him, snatching up the junk food at the same time, tossing it under the counter.

The kid turned off the light in the tiny office and closed the door. But Tracy reopened it an inch so she could see out into the store. In a couple of minutes, she got a glimpse of the cop–a tall, blond fellow with hands big enough to play professional basketball. He had placed a coffee and two stale donuts on the counter.

"On the tab, Milt?" said the kid.

"Yeah, Rank. Where's the owner of that government sedan out there?"

"Went to the can," said the kid.

There was a little too much silence.

"What's the matter?" said the kid.

"Nothing. Just wondering who he was and what he was doing up in this neck of the woods. What's he look like?"

"I didn't pay any attention. How can you tell it's a government car?"

"Right make and model, black. But anyway, it has US government plates, and there's a sticker on the bumper, says NSA."

"What's that?"

The cop laughed.

"The National Security Agency."

"Big Brother."

"Yeah, to you. Personally, I never met an NSA guy, and I'd kind of like to."

"Think he'd tell you why he's here?"

"Probably not. But a lot of times you can learn things by what people don't say."

"Is that right?"

"Yeah, it is. How long's he been in the can?"

"Not long. Just before you pulled in."

Tracy saw a shadow pass the crack in the door as the cop moved away from the counter. In a few minutes, he was back.

"Taking a long time in there," said the cop.

"Maybe he's cleaning up. People do if they've been on the road for a while."

Tracy wondered what would happen if Rank's friends showed up while the cop was parked out front. Surely, they were smart enough to drive on by.

"You got another key for the door?" asked the cop.

"No," said Rank. "Where are you going?"

"To check it out. Maybe the guy is sick."

"Damn," said Rank, as the front door closed, and the little bell rang.

He slipped inside the darkened room with Tracy and speed-dialed a number on his cell phone.

"Yeah," he said. "I know. This is going to have to happen fast. We need Coot to get his ass into the woods out back right now and make some noise like he's sick or something. Lead the sucker into the forest...Okay, then screw you unless you got a better idea."

Tracy heard a burbling conversation on the other end of the line.

"Hurry the fuck up, then," said Rank, slipping the phone back into his pocket and turning to Tracy. "When you hear me say go, I want you to walk straight out of here, and climb into the back floorboard of whatever car's at the curb. Don't stop for anything. Got it?"

"Got it."

"Cool."

Tracy crouched in the small office wondering why fate had sent her to this gas station. Was she supposed to get caught and killed? Or was this the only place in creation where she had a chance to get away from Ash and his men? She tried to imagine what the cop was doing outside. Surely, he'd realized by now that there was no one in the restroom. Or did he think the driver of the sedan had passed out in there? Was he preparing to kick in the door, and if so, what would he do when he discovered the restroom was empty?

Tracy heard the low rumble of a car motor outside, and at the same instant Rank called to her.

"Go!"

She straightened, grabbed her pack, and hurried around the counter and out the front doors, climbing into the back seat of the Jaguar sedan and dropping onto the floor catching only a fleeting impression of the young woman in the driver's seat. Tracy expected the car to peel out, but instead, they eased out onto the highway and drove slowly away. They were miles down the road before the driver spoke in a soft voice with a hard edge.

"You can get up now."

Tracy slipped up onto the seat, staring at the girl in the mirror. She was petite with brown eyes that contrasted with her short blond hair. A nasty-looking black automatic pistol nestled in a fabric holster attached to the upholstery above her head.

"Where are you taking me?"

"A safe place."

Tracy could tell by the set of the girl's shoulders that she was done talking, so she leaned back in the seat, watching the night slide by as the car wound first down one mountain road, then another. She was drowsing when the Jaguar rolled to a stop in front of a house trailer surrounded by tall spruce trees.

"Get out," said the driver.

Once they were both inside the girl gave Tracy a good once over.

"I'm not a bellboy," she said, glancing at Tracy's pack.

"I didn't expect one. I just need a place to sleep and hopefully a ride in the morning. I paid for it."

The girl nodded, pointing down the hall. She followed a little too closely as Tracy slipped into the first bedroom.

"Why did you want to know about Dietrich Reich?" asked the girl.

Tracy shook her head.

"I need to talk to him, that's all. Do you know him?"

"Maybe."

"That's what Rank said."

"Good for him."

The girl pointed at the very inviting four-poster bed. Tracy dumped her gear beside it, and when she turned back the girl was regarding her evenly.

"I'm Marilyn."

"Millie," said Tracy.

"You're safe here, Millie," said Marilyn. "At least for the moment."

"I'd like to believe that," said Tracy, removing her top, and tossing it onto the dresser.

She dropped wearily onto the bed, wishing only that the girl would leave so she could sleep.

But Marilyn's eyes continued boring into her.

"We'll talk when you wake up."

Tracy sighed.

"I have to get moving at first light."

"Get some sleep," said Marilyn. She stopped and turned in the door. "And rest easy. I'm a crack shot."

"YOU ARE A THOROUGHLY amazing man, Mr. Townsend," said Ash. "And I must say that I am not often admiring of other men."

The room spun around Mark like a wobbling fan blade, and although most of the nerves in his body seemed to be firing out pain signals, he could no longer feel his hands, tightly bound behind him, nor his feet, equally tightly trussed to the base of the heavy chair. He could barely make out the wires attached to his bare chest, or the others leading away from his crotch. Unaccountably, his interior music box kept playing *Tiny Dancer* by Elton John, over and over.

He liked Elton. The man had class and talent for a rock star. But after seven or eight renditions, the singer sounded frazzled, and the piano playing rather mechanical.

"You are either the bravest man I have ever met," murmured Ash, adjusting one of the leads taped under Mark's arm, "the most resistant to pain and suffering, or you are the stupidest imbecile on the face of the planet. In any case, you are a remarkable specimen."

"Don't know anything else," Mark managed to mutter.

"Yes," said Ash. "So, you keep saying."

Mark shook his head, trying to stave off another round of torture. He had no idea how long he'd been out from the last session, but consciousness seemed like a feeble thread holding him in the room, and he was certain that if he passed out again, Ash would kill him. The thing was that Ash had simply never asked the right questions. He wanted to know what Mark knew about Derek Maynor, which was practically nothing. He asked what Mark was researching, and Mark told him old Nazi research. But he seemed to accept that Mark was who he claimed to be, a lowly assistant. He never asked about Mark's past, so Mark never told him they had been raised by the same father.

"D...Derek," stammered Mark. "Derek Maynor."

"Yes," said Ash, adjusting another lead. "I know all about Professor Maynor, and when I catch up with him, I'll be asking him some questions also. Of course, you know that no one at MIT has ever heard of him."

That information just wouldn't register. He'd been to the man's office on campus. Of course, they had never met in person, and–still trying to get his brain to function–he realized that none of the other researchers he'd spoken to knew much about Maynor, either.

Maynor had contacted Mark in Florida and asked him to do research. Mark hadn't intended that the background information he'd created for his new identity actually get him work. But then Maynor had surprised him by insinuating that the research would include Avent-Corp.

"You really didn't know," said Ash, frowning. "Is that all this is about? Are you really that stupid, just a patsy? No. You couldn't be."

But Mark had decided that he was, indeed. Whoever Maynor was, whatever he intended to do with the little information Mark had managed to dig up, it hadn't helped Mark.

Ash reached for the large black rheostat knob again, and Mark screamed.

When Tracy awakened with a jolt she rolled quickly to the edge of the bed, leaning over to unzip the bag inside her pack and count the money and credit cards. Everything was exactly where she'd left it including the notebook.

She found Marilyn—wearing a pair of cutoff jeans and a halter top—curled up on the sofa reading a weathered old paperback Tracy recognized called *Steal This Book*. Glancing around the trailer, Tracy realized that she had passed through it before in a daze. It was almost like waking up in a new location.

The room smelled of rosewood incense and lavender body oil and some underlying odor that Tracy knew she should recognize. The furniture was all old and well-used but clean, the fake leather upholstery scarred but not torn. And the carpet was lightly stained and worn enough to be the original. The place had the appearance and feel of a well lived in home, and yet there were no photos, no knickknacks on the side tables, no lived-in-recently *feel*. Tracy got the sense that the girl was as much a visitor here as herself.

Marilyn smiled at her. "I've never seen anybody conk out like that."

Tracy frowned. "What time is it?"

"Seven in the morning. You slept a whole day away."

"Are you joking?"

Marilyn shook her head, rising. "You must be famished. Come on, I'll make you something to eat."

The girl turned out to be an excellent cook, and Tracy praised her work by downing four pancakes, three slices of ham, and four pieces of toast along with lavish amounts of strong black coffee. By the time she pushed her chair away from the table she felt bloated and content.

"Thank you," she said, as Marilyn lit up a joint, and offered it to her. So t*hat* was the other smell. "And no thanks."

But she discovered that there was little of the coldness in her voice that had been her constant companion for the past year. She didn't smoke pot, didn't drink, not because she looked down on either practice–her parents had had friends that used both drugs–but because chemicals broke down barriers, and she had spent far too much time and energy constructing her interior walls. Still, she found herself instinctively trusting this girl more than she had allowed herself to trust any other person in recent memory.

Except Shiver, she reminded herself, and Beatrice. The thought of Beatrice sent a chill through her, but she had to put that aside for now.

Marilyn shrugged, sucking the sweet-smelling smoke deep into her lungs and covering her mouth politely as she coughed.

"Helps me relax," she hissed between clenched teeth.

"I'm afraid to relax," admitted Tracy, realizing that that very admission was another step out of her shell, and she felt a tingle of fear listening to the wall crack.

Marilyn nodded, turning her head to blow out a long train of smoke. "I keep telling you, you're safe here."

"I know you think that, but I'm afraid it's not true. The longer I stay here, the more I endanger you and your friends."

The girl's face took on a harder expression.

"Tell me why you wanted to talk to Dietrich Reich."

"You wouldn't understand."

"I might understand more than you think."

"What's that supposed to mean?"

Marilyn shrugged.

"You don't look like one of the bad guys. You don't act like one. But you were driving a car registered to the NSA."

"I told Rank I stole it. I should probably ask who you and your friends are."

"You're not getting anything else out of me until you tell me why you need to see Dietrich Reich."

Tracy sighed.

"Because he's a name on a list. Because people are trying to kill me, and I think it has something to do with the people on that list, but I don't know what or why."

Marilyn frowned.

"You don't know who the other people on the list are?"

Tracy shook her head.

"But you came looking for Dietrich Reich first?"

"No. The first place I went I found a woman... Beatrice. I'm afraid she might have been kidnapped or murdered."

The frown spread across the girl's face, and Tracy could have sworn she was about to cry.

"You don't know for sure?"

Tracy shook her head.

"I got away. I ran...I left her."

When Marilyn stared at her silently Tracy found she had to explain.

"She insisted I go. She claimed that the man breaking in wouldn't want her, that he was after me. I wanted to believe it, so I ran. But all that time, driving, I kept going over and over the scene again in my head, and I'm just not sure. I'm afraid I just deserted her out of fear. God help me if that's true."

Marilyn nodded, staring at the floor. When she finally spoke, her voice was low and choked.

"You're lucky you got away from them at all."

"How do you know that? What do you know about *them?*" whispered Tracy. How could this girl possibly know anything?

"I know they're evil," said Marilyn. "But maybe you're right. Maybe they didn't kill her. Maybe they just took her somewhere."

She sounded as though she wanted to believe that with her heart, but her head wasn't listening.

"What do you know about any of this?" said Tracy, insistently.

Marilyn chewed her lip.

"Let me see the list, again."

"Again?"

Marilyn shook her head, realizing she'd slipped up. But she held out her hand.

Tracy dug the notebook out of her pack and opened it to the page bearing Dietrich Reich's name.

"What are the numbers?" asked Marilyn.

"Bank accounts, I think."

"You have my dad's bank account numbers?" said Marilyn, instantly realizing she'd screwed up again.

"Dietrich Reich is your father?" said Tracy.

"Maybe."

Tracy sighed loudly.

"Can we please get past this? I need to speak to him very badly."

Marilyn's frown was even sadder.

"Unfortunately, that's not possible."

"Why?"

"Because men broke into our house and took him the day before yesterday."

"Oh," said Tracy, wondering that the girl could speak of such a thing so calmly. "Are you all right?"

"No, I'm not all right. I want to know who has my father, and what they want with him. I wanted to get him back, but until you showed up, I didn't have a clue. I came here because he told me that this was where I was to go if anything ever happened to him. He never explained what was going to happen, just that there were men who might come for him one day. For a long time I told myself that was crazy, that maybe Dad was a little...off, you know? That's what I wanted to believe. Then I came home and saw the cars out front. Just like the one you were driving. I parked down the street and waited. They loaded my dad into one of the cars and drove off. I followed for a little ways, but when one of the cars slowed down... I knew they were checking me out. I dropped back and came here. I shouldn't have left him."

"There was nothing you could have done," said Tracy, knowing her assurance meant as little to Marilyn as the girl's had to her. The fact that Marilyn had thought her father might be crazy stung Tracy, opening her own old wound.

"Tell me everything you know," said the girl, her features suddenly tight.

There was obviously a lot more to her than her tiny frame and pixyish face revealed. Tracy told her everything that had happened since she'd begun to run. About Steph. About the attack on the roof, and Shiver, and Ash.

"That *is* crazy," said Marilyn, when Tracy was done. "But it sounds like you're telling the truth. My father always told me that if anyone ever came looking for him, asked for his address or phone number, or just mentioned his name in town I was to come here and hide. This place is owned by a friend who has known my family for years."

"Somehow your father was tied to the other names on the list," said Tracy. "He never told you anything at all about why those men might be looking for him?"

Marilyn shook her head.

"He just said there were men who might one day show up, government men, and that if that happened, we had to go and go quickly."

"What about your mother?"

Marilyn's face took on a sadder expression.

"She died when I was twelve."

"I'm sorry. But didn't you wonder if maybe your father had broken the law?"

Marilyn laughed.

"My father wasn't the kind to jaywalk, much less break any *real* laws. He told me that a long time ago he did something for the government, and one day they might want him to do it again, and he didn't want to do it."

"What does your father do for a living?"

"He runs an appliance repair shop in town. My dad can fix anything."

Tracy shook her head. What in the world would Ash want with a widowed tinker?

"My friends found all kinds of electronic stuff in your car, by the way," said Marilyn.

"Like what?"

Marilyn shrugged.

"There was a GPS tracking system, but luckily for you, someone had turned it off. There was also quite a bit of very expensive radio gear, and a lot of guns, and some specialized grenades."

The thought of driving around for hours in a stolen car with a tracking system sent a chill up Tracy's spine. But the deadly weapons were almost as bothersome to her. She hated guns, and had abhorred them her entire life.

"I'm sorry about your father," she said.

Marilyn nodded.

Although the girl's eyes had taken on the characteristic redness of a chronic pot smoker, she didn't appear fazed by the stuff. Her steady gaze made Tracy nervous. She couldn't help sensing some great mill wheel rolling inside the girl's pretty head, crushing everything in its inexorable path toward her.

"I need to be going," Tracy said.

"I'm coming with you," said Marilyn, dropping the joint into an ashtray on the table.

Tracy shook her head.

"You're going to look up those other names, right?" said Marilyn.

"I am. But I'm afraid this is going to keep getting more dangerous. The best thing for you would be to do as your father said and stay hidden here."

"I don't know who the people are that took my dad or what kind of power they have, but they aren't going to keep him. And you never told me why they're after you."

"It's because of something I read," said Tracy, not ready yet to tell the girl about her life *before* the company. "But it didn't make any sense. It was just a date."

"What date?"

"June 8th, 1959."

Marilyn frowned.

"Why would anyone care about that?"

"Good question."

"Your family must be worried about you."

"Both my parents disappeared a year ago," whispered Tracy.

"I'm sorry. Were they in the notebook?"

"No."

Marilyn studied her face.

"You weren't just working for this company, were you? You were investigating them."

Tracy nodded.

"So then what else do you know about this *Ash?*

Tracy couldn't escape the idea that Marilyn was older than her eighteen years. Evidently, her father had taught her to use her head under pressure.

"He holds a doctorate in nuclear physics, and another in mathematics. Rhodes Scholar. Summa Cum Laude from Yale. He has the diplomas on his walls, but each of them has been wiped out so that only the one name is there and no dates. I heard some people whispering about him in the cafeteria one day and slipped over to join in the conversation. Everyone shut up when they realized I was there, but I guess they finally decided that I wasn't a stoolie, and they began to talk again. One of them had been doing some snooping and couldn't find any record of a man named Ash having been Summa Cum Laude from Yale after all."

"So, he forged the diplomas."

"Why forge diplomas then erase the first name? Why not just put in Ash to begin with?"

"You think he removed his college records? From Yale?"

"Yes."

"That would take some doing."

"I don't think it would be hard for Ash."

"What were your duties?"

"I answered the phone, directed traffic, arranged appointments."

"With whom?"

"I had a database of names and numbers. Mostly scientists, on very rare occasions senators or congressmen, sometimes spooks."

"Government agents."

"Yes. You could always spot them. It's something in their eyes. They look dead. Doesn't that sound stupid?"

Marilyn shivered.

"I don't think it sounds stupid at all. What did Ash do with the spooks? What did they talk about?"

"I have no idea. I was never privy to any of the meetings. I just knew they were extremely important, and very secret. Everything that crossed my desk was mostly in some kind of code although it took me a while to realize it. At first, I thought it was all just trivial paperwork, shopping lists, memoranda on something called *Feedback*, canceled plane tickets, weird stuff."

She frowned, remembering.

"It was almost as though the stuff was purposely left on my desk sometimes, like they wanted me to read it."

"Why would they do that?"

Tracy shook her head.

"I wondered sometimes if they didn't *know* who I was and what I was really doing there."

She realized she'd slipped up with *who I was*. But Marilyn passed over it.

"Did you ever find out what *Feedback* meant?"

"No."

Marilyn sighed loudly.

"So, all you saw was a date?"

Tracy nodded.

"What did this guy, Shiver, have to do with all the people in the book?"

"He definitely helped Beatrice and her husband, although I don't know how he could have. According to Bea she and her husband had been living in their farmhouse for years. Shiver didn't look any older than me. She wouldn't explain how that was possible, but I know she believed it. I'm just guessing the story's the same as the others, but I could be wrong. Either way, they all must know something."

"What were you supposed to do after he dropped you off?"

"He gave me a new identity," she said. "I was supposed to go there and start a new life."

"So, you aren't really Millie?" said Marilyn, smiling. "No kidding."

Tracy smiled back.

"He said a friend came up with that name."

"Then he has partners."

"Apparently."

"Maybe it was one of them that helped Bea originally."

"Maybe," said Tracy, trying to recall her conversations with Bea. She was certain no partner had been mentioned.

"This is all so weird," said Marilyn, shaking her head. "I thought my dad was crazy, talking about working for the government, people after him, hiding out here. I just humored him."

Once again Tracy was surprised at how close to her own guilt the girl was living. Only Marilyn hadn't done anything to feel guilty about other than disbelieving her father, and that wasn't a crime. Tracy had been to blame for her parents being locked up like animals. She had testified against them, and then, mysteriously, they had disappeared.

"It's as if there's this whole other reality," mused Marilyn.

Tracy frowned.

"What do you mean?"

The girl shrugged.

"Ash and his people after my dad and you. This guy Shiver helping you, claiming to have a friend who creates new identities. That sound like everyday life to you?"

In fact, it sounded too much like a life her parents had once described to her, but that was a long time ago... She could hear her father's soft, firm voice.

You can't always believe what you see, Tracy, and you can believe a lot of things you can't.

"How are we going to travel?" she asked, wondering how easy it was to accept Marilyn as a partner. The girl acted much older than her years, but even so, a part of Tracy still felt reluctant to drag her into what could very well turn out to be a deadly trip.

Marilyn placed her cup in the sink.

"By now your car is a couple of hundred miles from here. Not that we'd want to use it, anyway. We take mine."

"They may be looking for you, too."

Marilyn nodded.

"It's okay. The Jaguar is registered in a friend's name."

Tracy squinted at the girl, trying to read between the lines.

"A friend?"

"Actually, a friend of Rank's."

"He won't mind you driving off in a very expensive car?"

"He won't be using it for a while. He's doing five to ten for car theft."

"And the car?"

"Let's just say the registration will hold up under a cursory inspection."

For just a moment Tracy wondered if she might be in more danger traveling with the girl than without her, but what choice did she have?

"You're absolutely sure you want to do this?" she asked.

Marilyn frowned.

"Whether you like it or not, you're stuck with me. I don't know why those men took my father, but I know I'm going to get him back."

"Just so you understand. I'm not very good at this. In fact, for the past couple of days, I've been doing more running than investigating, and I've mostly been lucky at that. I don't like guns, and I've never fired one. So, if we run into any of Ash's men again, I really don't have a clue what I'm going to do."

Marilyn shook her head, her gaze hard and firm.

"My father taught me how to use a gun, and I won't have any trouble killing any of the men who took him. I can promise you that. Maybe you need me as much as I need you."

"All right," said Tracy, quietly, "I still think you're making a mistake, but I have to admit I'll be glad for the company. I just hope you don't regret your decision."

"If I do that's my problem, not yours," said Marilyn. "Let me see that notebook again. We might as well start with the closest person on the list."

"YOU'LL DEFINITELY HAVE TO forget the girl, now," said Walsh, cleaning his glasses on the tail of his sports coat. His squat body lolled precariously along the sidewalk beneath the flags of the Avenue of the Americas and sweat trickled through the furrows of his brow. "You're running out of time."

Ash glared at him like a man looking at a particularly loathsome piece of garbage that had mysteriously appeared on his dinner plate.

"I have plans for that girl."

Walsh frowned.

"If your errand boy, Trevor, hadn't turned off the tracking system in his car—as usual—we'd have her by now. Forget her."

"You keep forgetting why we hired her."

"I know why we hired her as well as you do, but nothing came of it. Forget her and get rid of the Townsend gentleman. You didn't get anything more useful out of him than you did the girl, and you don't have time to waste on sideshows any longer. You never told me how you knew where Townsend would be staying, by the way."

Ash shrugged. Better that Walsh did not know about his informant. Maynor had only recently begun to prove his worth. Ash still had no idea what the man wanted for the tidbits of information he was leaking, or why he had sent Townsend first to investigate and then given him up so easily, but he wasn't about to share that with Walsh. Why should he?

He maintained his composure by staring up into the sun through the maze of buildings.

"Is the equipment ready?" asked Walsh.

"It's almost ready," Ash fudged. "Yes. It will be ready on time."

"Will it work or not?"

"It'll work. I'd stake my reputation on it."

Walsh's laugh was sharp as glass.

"Your reputation is rather... enigmatic, shall we say? And you're staking a lot more than that."

Ash nodded, coming to a decision he'd been putting off for a very long time. Walsh needed to have a nasty little accident.

"Now," said Walsh, completely oblivious to the fact that he was a dead man. "What are you going to do with Townsend, and are you going to forget the girl, or not?"

"Townsend is going to be our next guinea pig," said Ash, smiling now as he replaced his sunglasses and turned back to face Walsh. "And the girl is my business. If you're stupid enough to let her run around out there with critical information in her head, fine. I'm not nearly so inefficient."

"I never said you were inefficient," said Walsh, ignoring the slur. "I merely mentioned that the information means nothing to her, and there's no way she can hurt us. She learned nothing that could help her *or* her parents."

"We've found some of the missing scientists."

"What? Where?"

Ash shrugged.

"All over the place."

"How did you find them."

"I got an anonymous tip."

Walsh frowned.

"Forget them. They're hopelessly out of date. Surely the girl has no more idea of what happened to them than we do, and I don't think using Townsend is a good idea, either. Why not a monkey, or one of your lab techs?"

"We've already tested a monkey and one of the techs," said Ash, enjoying the look of consternation on Walsh's face, but refusing once more to give out more information than was necessary. He had no idea why Maynor suggested using Townsend in the machine, but the idea had instantly tickled Ash's fancy, just as the man's knowledge of the device's existence had sent him into near paroxysms.

"Why wasn't I informed?"

"You were busy with one of your fundraisers, or kissing some congressman's ass," said Ash, enjoying every last minute of Walsh's brief life.

This time Walsh frowned at the insult.

"You'll push me too far one day, Ash. I assume you videoed the test?"

"Of course. You'll have a copy when you return to your office."

"And I further assume it was a success."

"The monkey's doing fine. Or he was until we vivisected him."

"No organ damage?"

"None whatsoever."

"You didn't mention the tech."

Ash frowned.

"There was some glitch with the settings."

"He didn't make it?"

"Parts of him did. Apparently, we needed to allow for not only the larger mass but for the increased cranial electrical activity as well. But we've made adjustments."

"You're saying the procedure is perfectly safe for humans now."

Ash didn't allow his frown to spread. There was no sense in telling Walsh about the primate's strange behavior *before* the euthanization. As he'd said, all the organs were fine. It wasn't the test subjects that were the problem now, it was calibrating the equipment correctly. Apparently, the way they were sorting for the destination was a problem, but they were getting closer. It would all work itself out shortly.

"We want to conduct a couple more tests. Townsend will do. I assure you he's being very helpful right now, and under the influence of drugs he will be completely pliable."

"And what will it prove, using him?"

"That a human being can survive the process, of course. If we could just find some more suitable technicians-"

"The techs that I've managed to keep on the staff are all good men, regardless of what you think of them, and they know how important this is. They're well trained at what they do but volunteering for this-."

"Cretins," muttered Ash.

"Do *you* want to do it?"

Ash laughed.

"You've already made it clear that my testing the apparatus is not an option. I'd be happy to... When the time comes."

Walsh nodded.

"The Senator doesn't think that's a good idea for any number of reasons."

"I can imagine."

"You have four days."

"I'll be ready," said Ash, spinning on his heel and striding away down the walk.

ELROY KLIEBNER WAS DEAD. Claude Weise had disappeared, leaving no forwarding address. Tracy was afraid that meant the same thing. Now they were on their second day of the search.

She turned toward Marilyn, who leaned way back in the driver's seat, her head pressed against the rest, her eyes half closed. She'd told Tracy more than once that she was fine, that she enjoyed driving, so Tracy hadn't asked to take over again, even after they'd passed through Vermont and into Maine.

"How far to the coast?" Tracy asked, staring at the blanket of stars over the mountains.

Marilyn studied a folded map, then slipped it back between the seats.

"A couple of hours maybe to where we're going. Have you given any thought to the possibility that all the rest of the people on that list have been kidnapped... or they're dead?"

Tracy could tell the girl didn't want to admit to herself that Kliebner and Weise's fate might have been no different than her father's. There was no telling what had been done with him once they'd spirited her father away from his home.

"I don't believe that. It would be too much of a coincidence that the first name I chose was Beatrice, and she was alive. And your father was taken alive. If they wanted him dead, they could have murdered him right there."

"And left too much evidence, maybe," said Marilyn, glancing away out the window.

"Maybe. But wouldn't you say coincidences like me finding you, and also finding Beatrice and her being alive, too, was stretching chance just a little bit?"

"There's another possibility," said Marilyn, frowning. "Maybe this is some kind of con, and this guy Shiver is in on it."

"Why give me a whole new identity," she was about to say, *and* a small fortune. "Just so someone else could kill me? Why save me on the roof? Besides, he had no way of knowing I'd end up with the list, or that I'd use it to find Beatrice. And I think she had been in that house for a long time."

"How long?"

Tracy shook her head.

"She said her husband died ten years ago. The place looked like it had been lived in a lot longer than that."

"One man couldn't have set all that up," said Marilyn. "Whoever Shiver is, he must be connected to something bigger. Besides my family's been in that same house for over twenty years."

The thrum of the engine and the tires on the road ticked off the minutes as the car sliced through the night. With each passing second Tracy could feel the strands of an invisible rope forming a noose around them.

"How were you associated with Rank?" asked Tracy, wanting to change the subject.

Marilyn shrugged, glancing away.

"We got to know each other in school. His family's a little weird."

"And he's a car thief."

"He calls himself an *Automobile Relocation Specialist.* Rank doesn't like the establishment."

"And you trust a thief?"

"*You* stole that car."

"I hope you understand there were extenuating circumstances. Is he your boyfriend?"

Marilyn shook her head.

"He wishes."

When the girl spoke of Rank it was clear there was friendship between them, but something else as well. Perhaps she'd been trying to reform the boy and failed, but Rank was history now, and Tracy needed to clarify the relationship between herself and the girl. The last thing she wanted was Marilyn blaming her for anything.

"What if we can't get him back... your father, I mean?"

The girl's face flushed, and her fingers whitened on the wheel.

"Then I'm still going to find out what happened to him."

"And then?"

Marilyn's eyes flashed in the reflected glow of the headlights.

"Then I'm gonna kill the sonsofbitches that took him."

That seemed to clarify things.

IT WAS ALMOST FOUR AM before they found Earl Carter's place along a section of rocky coast that jutted out into the ocean like a gnarled finger, beckoning the North Atlantic inland.

The chill air was dense with the smell of pine and salt. The steep-gabled, run-down, shingle-sided house was surrounded by tall firs on three sides, perched high over the granite sea cliff. Though the stars hung in stately immobility overhead, and the ocean lay calm and dark as glass below, Tracy felt anxious as she and Marilyn quietly closed their car doors.

"Should we wait until morning, you think?" asked Marilyn.

Tracy shook her head. With every ticking minute she sensed time running out for the two of them.

Earl was alive.

At least the fellow at the all-night convenience store down the road had said as far as he knew that was the case. But he had given them a strange look when they asked for directions. Now she understood why. The entire yard was littered with old televisions, stereo sets, and miscellaneous refuse that all seemed to be trailing snarled strands of multi-colored wires like the tentacles of a swarm of plastic-and-glass jellyfish washed up on some rogue wave.

Earl was a dump picker.

"Bet my dad could fix a lot of this stuff," mused Marilyn.

They carefully wound their way through ancient tube radios and console TVs stacked three high on the front porch. Tracy rested her pack on the porch floor, unwilling to leave it in the car even long enough to find out if Earl was home. She frowned as the sound of classical music seeped through the walls. Either Earl was a real night owl or an incredibly early riser.

"An educated man," said Tracy, glancing around at the conglomeration again as she knocked, then knocked again.

"Yeah. Coming!" said a raspy voice.

The door swung open just enough for a man to fill it, and Tracy found herself staring at a throwback.

The guy was well over six feet tall with a long, bushy brown beard and a thick, braided ponytail draped over his shoulder. He wore a tie-dyed t-shirt, ratty bell-bottom jeans, and sockless sandals. The house smelled of patchouli and pot.

Marilyn smiled appreciatively.

"Earl Carter," said the man, smiling and extending his hand as though strangers often showed up on his doorstep in the middle of the night.

"Millie Jones," said Tracy. "And this is-"

"Drew Barrymore," said Marilyn, taking Earl's hand. "Can we come in?"

"Sure," said Earl. "Just a sec."

Tracy gave Marilyn a look as Earl disappeared, and the grating sound of something metallic being dragged recklessly across a wood floor assaulted the air.

"Drew Barrymore?" Tracy whispered.

"Just popped into my head," said Marilyn. "Nobody gave me a new identity."

The door swung wide, and Tracy was shocked to see that the hodgepodge of old electronic equipment outside was nothing compared to the accumulation inside the house.

Every square inch of the floor seemed to be buried beneath something involving a plastic case, vacuum tubes, or dials and switches, much of it stacked to the high ceiling. Even the stairs were entombed beneath radios, reel-to-reel recorders, adding machines, and picture tubes, leaving only the narrowest of spaces alongside the wall for anyone to access the upper floor. Angular shadows shrouded most of the narrow, dust-smothered spaces between the equipment, and Tracy wondered what might be living there.

She stared nervously down at her feet.

"Follow me," said Earl, leading the way through the electronic maze into a well-lighted area near the back of the house from which the music seemed to emanate. That room turned out to be furnished in late Thomas Alva Edison just like the rest of the house.

"I'm afraid it's a little bit of a mess in here," said Earl, tossing stacks of Popular Science and Mechanics Illustrated magazines off a lone sofa in front of a television that was a blur of snow.

In the corner, atop yet another pile of console stereos, sat an antique phonograph, now playing something that Tracy thought might be Bach.

Earl caught Tracy's eye.

"You like the music? A friend gave me a collection of old vinyl, all classical stuff. I don't know what all of it is, but I got to liking it better than rock and roll."

Tracy smiled.

Earl slapped the couch, and a cloud of dust arose, causing him to cough.

"It's the only place I have to sit," he apologized, covering his mouth and waving for them to take a seat.

Tracy sat in the center, facing Earl.

"I don't know quite how to start," she said.

Earl nodded as though he'd expected that.

She sighed.

"Do you know a man named Shiver?"

Earl laughed.

"You bet I do! It was him give me the records."

Tracy was nonplused. If Shiver had saved him from the same unknown fate as the others on the list and told him to keep quiet about it, Earl would have forgotten the warning before *Shiver's* dust had settled on the sofa.

"How do you know him?"

"He saved my life."

That at least tied in with her theory about the notebook. Now she wondered about the two men who had died or disappeared. According to the locals, Leroy Kliebner had simply passed away of old age, but Claude Weise had disappeared leaving no forwarding address. Tracy was now the custodian of a lot of people's lives, and she vowed once again that at least her copy of the book would never fall into the wrong hands.

"Why?" she asked. "And how?"

Earl frowned for the first time, and Tracy could tell that it wasn't a well-oiled expression.

"Who are you people?"

She sighed again.

"Shiver saved my life, too."

The frown turned back into a smile, and Earl nodded vigorously.

"So, you know, then."

"Know what?"

"What I do."

"I'm afraid I have no idea."

"But you know Shiver."

"I met him only briefly. Just long enough for him to give me a new identity, and then disappear."

"He does that," said Earl, seriously.

"What did you mean, what you do?" asked Marilyn, leaning around Tracy.

Earl's smile broadened until it threatened to rip his beard.

"Wait!" he said, racing through the maze to vanish down the dark hallway.

Marilyn grinned and shrugged.

When Earl returned, he was lugging a heavy-looking aluminum box covered with dials, gauges, and toggle switches. Atop that he had coiled extension cords, and a smaller black box with its own cord on one end and what looked like an electric guitar jack on the other. He plopped the whole array onto the old console tv, and dropped to his knees, burrowing through the mess, apparently in search of an outlet.

When he reappeared, he was beaming, and lights had begun to glow on the aluminum box.

"It's kind of dangerous doing this in here with all this stuff," he said, frowning again, then brightening suddenly. "But we should be okay. Just don't move. Sometimes it's attracted to movement."

"It?" said Tracy.

"You'll see."

He fiddled with the dials on the machine, flipping a toggle switch, humming to himself, flipping the switch back off, and all the time Marilyn and Tracy exchanged curious looks, like two people accidentally seeing more than they were supposed to of someone's private madness.

Earl looked like a kid revving up a new go-cart.

"Keep your heads down," he said, excitedly. "Sometimes things happen."

"Sometimes?" said Marilyn.

"Most times," he corrected himself.

Tracy had the odd sense that the room had gotten smaller. The wild mélange of equipment and parts seemed to creep closer around her and Marilyn, and the distant, painted-metal ceiling appeared almost low enough to touch. But Marilyn was focused on Earl and the machine.

"There!" said Earl, peering around the room, pointing behind Tracy, then quickly turning back to the dials of the device.

It took a moment for Tracy to understand what Earl was pointing to amid the clutter. One antenna of a pair of rabbit ears behind her seemed to be melting. Molten metal dripped along its length, and for the first time, Tracy became frightened.

What the hell was the machine doing, emitting some kind of radiation? She noticed that the melting metal wasn't bright red as she would have expected. Nor was it any longer chrome colored. She rose to her feet and waded through the morass of equipment. To her surprise, she discovered that she could touch the metal. Whatever it was doing, it wasn't exactly melting.

"Don't," said Marilyn, reaching across the back of the sofa toward her.

Earl shouted.

"Oh, shit! I told you not to move!"

Something heavy struck Tracy a glancing blow across the temple, and for just a second everything went black. She stumbled. A high-pitched buzzing filled her ears, and then she felt a body pressing down on top of her. When the sound finally stopped, she realized that she wasn't blind as she had feared. The lights had gone out, and Marilyn was slowly climbing off her. Tracy could hear Earl, cursing, striking a match.

"Just take me a minute," he said, to the accompaniment of slapping shoe soles and flickering match-light. "Got to find a fuse! This old place doesn't have breakers."

"I'm okay," said Tracy, as Marilyn helped her back to her feet and led her through the darkened maze out into the hallway where a bit of moonlight worked its way in from the windows beside the front door.

"You sure? You got a nasty clip on the head."

"From what?"

"Looked like a box of chocolates."

"Where did it come from?"

"Off the top of one of the televisions I think."

"Who threw it, Earl?"

"Nobody. It just took off."

"Because of that machine?"

"As my father would say, I hesitate to make that assumption," said Marilyn.

"Meaning yes."

"Meaning I hesitate to make that assumption."

"What the hell is that thing?"

"I guess we'll have to wait for Earl to tell us that. I don't have a clue."

The lights came back on, and Earl appeared in the parlor behind them again, assuring them several times that it was safe to reenter before he convinced them to do so. When they were all seated on the sofa, Earl beamed at them.

"See?"

"What exactly was it we just saw?" asked Marilyn.

"Zero Point," said Earl, nodding vigorously.

"What's that?" asked Tracy.

Earl frowned. This time his eyes seemed to follow suit.

"I thought you were friends of Shiver's."

"I am," said Tracy. "I told you. He saved my life."

"Okay," said Earl. "So how come you don't know what Zero Point is?"

"Because she doesn't," said Marilyn. "Neither do I. What is it, and why is it so important?"

"It's just the most powerful thing in the galaxy. Hell, in the universe! Where have you been?"

"We've been busy," said Marilyn. "Tell us more."

"Zero Point is an energy that exists everywhere, all around you, all the time. Theoretically, if you could remove every last atom from the universe so that there was nothing here but vacuum, and the temperature was absolute zero there'd still be the same amount of Zero Point energy."

"That's impossible," said Tracy, shaking her head.

Energy and mass were the same thing, one converted to the other. The Law of Conservation of Energy said that nothing was destroyed, but conversely, nothing was really created. Without mass, there was no energy. To Tracy Earl's blabbering, all sounded a little too much like one of her parents' half-baked theories. Next, he'd start talking about crystal power and the astrological alignment of the pyramids.

Earl laughed.

"That's Zero Point. It is impossible. But it exists. It has to. Or else all the best theories about how the universe works, how natural laws fit together, quantum physics, relativity, none of that stuff can ever be finally proven. It's the last factor in any unified field theory that has any chance of working."

"And you've found a way to harness it," said Marilyn, nodding as though it all made perfect sense.

"Not exactly," said Earl, nibbling his lip.

"What did you just do in here with that machine?"

"I'm not sure."

Tracy rubbed her temples hard.

"Then what were you trying to show us?"

"Just what might happen. There was a pretty good probability that something was going to."

"And what did?" asked Tracy. "I saw the antenna melt."

"It didn't melt. It transmuted."

Marilyn shook her head. She rose from the couch and ripped what was left of the antenna off its plastic base, returning with it. Tracy peeled away a couple of drops of the soft yellow metal, kneading them with her fingernails.

"Is this what I think it is?"

Earl shrugged.

"I'd have to do a chemical analysis, but probably it's gold. Sometimes I get lead or platinum. Mostly gold."

"You have to be shitting me," said Marilyn, scratching one of the globules with her thumbnail.

"The machine transmutes metals. Sometimes it flies things. Well, you saw that," said Earl, glancing apologetically at Tracy.

"*Flies* things?" said Marilyn. "That's what you call it?"

"Yeah. I almost killed a couple of government scientists once."

That information seemed to amuse Earl no end. His smile was absolutely contagious.

"Now we're getting somewhere," said Marilyn, also apparently liking the sound of that. "Where did you do this to the scientists?"

"New Mexico," said Earl. "I used to live in Santa Fe, before Shiver came and got me. But they were working at a place called Terra Diablo."

"You were at Terra Diablo?" said Tracy.

Earl nodded.

"What's Terra Diablo?" asked Marilyn.

Tracy stared at Earl, but when he remained silent, she spoke.

"Supposedly it's a top-secret government research facility in New Mexico. I heard my dad talking to my mother about it a couple of times when I was little. Whenever I'd ask about it, he'd shake his head and get this look in his eye... He told me never to ever mention the name. When I was little I thought it was like some kind of hell."

"Kind of like hell," said Earl, the fear behind his eyes reminding Tracy incongruously of the sadness she'd seen in Shiver's.

"Tell us why you were there and what happened," said Tracy.

Earl shrugged.

"A guy named Ash heard about my experiments and wanted to see them."

Tracy stared at Marilyn who raised an eyebrow as if to say *what did you expect?*

"Doctor Ash," said Earl. "He sent a couple of his flunkies to my house because he thought everything he'd been hearing was bunk. I sent his guys back with a shoebox full of gold, and they came right back asking me to please bring my machine to show him. But I got the idea they weren't really asking."

"And?"

"We had some technical difficulties when I tried to get my machine to work in their lab," said Earl, frowning.

"Like what?"

"The first day I couldn't get the machine to do much of anything except twiddle their instruments a little. I worked all day and half the night without much success. It was the second day that things got hairy."

Earl frowned, glancing at the machine again.

"Go on," said Tracy.

"I turned a couple of steel bars into gold, and Ash liked that, but he wasn't as excited as I'd thought he'd be. He kept pressing me to *push* the machine. That's what he said, push it. I asked him what he expected me to do, and he just looked at me like I was a cretin or something. I'm not stupid. People shouldn't treat me like I was stupid."

"No," said Tracy, staring at the tiny bead of gold in her palm. "They shouldn't."

Earl smiled. "So, I pushed. I gave it all I had. All kinds of things started floating around that big old cave. For a while there I thought the place was gonna explode, but the more I pushed the more pissed off Ash looked, and I knew I wasn't coming close to what he was looking for. When one of the metal tables started to transmute, I got a little nervous and started to back off, and that's when it all kind of went to shit." He glanced apologetically from Tracy to Marilyn. "Sorry. Excuse my French."

"What do you mean went to shit?" said Tracy, smiling reassuringly.

"I think Ash was really frustrated. He never said what he thought my machine could do, but while I was all wrapped up in trying to tune it back down, he reached past me and started twisting the dials and flipping switches, and all hell broke loose. There were people screaming and diving for cover, things crashing into the walls, floor, and ceiling, and the machine had set up this sympathetic vibration with the whole freaking cave. Everything was humming this low-pitched sound that kept getting louder and louder. Ash and I were kind of locked into the machine."

"Locked in?" said Tracy, frowning at the box.

"Yeah. I never had that happen before. No one ever touched the box while it was running but me. See it isn't just a machine. It's more like some kind of musical instrument. I think it's kind of in tune with me as much as I'm in tune with it. When Ash locked onto it everything got all screwy. It was like the two of us trying to play a piano duet, but only one knew how to read music. I couldn't control the machine at all. Hell, half the time I don't think I'm controlling it, anyway, but that day it was like it went crazy."

"You must have gotten it under control," said Tracy, watching Marilyn rise and meander away down the hall.

"Yeah," said Earl, as the girl disappeared. "But Ash said he was fed up with me. Called me a dunce. But when those fellas took me home again, they kept my machine. That one there is another one I built after Shiver came and got me and brought me here."

"Why did he come and get you if they took you home?"

"I think they changed their minds pretty quick," said Earl. "Shiver showed up on my doorstep, and we got out of there."

"He told you Ash's men would be coming back, and you just believed him?"

"Not at first. Mainly I just went because I wanted to check things out."

"Check what out?"

Earl seemed to think that there were a great many things that should be self-evident to Tracy that most definitely were not.

"If you see him again, you tell him everything's working fine now," blurted Earl.

"You mean the box?"

Earl nodded.

"And me. I was kinda sick for a while afterward."

"After the demonstration you gave at Terra Diablo?"

"Well, yeah," said Earl, frowning. "But I mean after-"

"We have a little problem," said Marilyn, sticking her head back in the door, and waving for their attention.

"I'll just be a minute," said Tracy, leaving Earl sputtering to himself.

"What's the matter?" whispered Tracy out in the hall.

"A black car just pulled in at the end of the driveway," said Marilyn, pointing toward the front door.

"Earl," called Tracy, as Marilyn slipped back down the hall to the door, "what did Shiver tell you to do if any of Ash's men came back?"

A frown shot across Earl's face, and fear registered in his eyes.

"He said to go. Don't wait for nothin' just go."

"And how do we do that?" asked Tracy, as she saw Marilyn hold up two fingers in a v.

"Now our friends have friends," said the girl, hurrying back to Tracy's side.

"Come on," said Earl, waving them back into the parlor.

He led them through the clutter, stopping only long enough to unplug the box and lock it under one arm. Then they raced through another room that was only distinguishable as the kitchen because the refrigerator and one side of the sink peered out from under more piles of dusty appliances. They stepped out onto a creaky back porch beneath the light of the moon that sent a long silver wake toward them across the impossibly flat Atlantic.

"There," said Earl, pointing in the direction of a wall of bracken bordering the property and running as far as the cliff's edge.

"Where are we going?" asked Tracy.

"I keep a van parked in the woods," he said, heading toward the trees.

Earl ambled along like a bear, the device snatched up under his arm like a flopping salmon. As he led them through what appeared to be an impenetrable wall of brush onto a narrow trail, Tracy heard the unmistakable sound of car doors slamming behind them.

Mark dragged himself up off the cot in the room in which he'd just awakened and stumbled to the tiny bathroom, staring into the mirror in disbelief.

Through however many days he'd been tortured—strapped to the chair with Ash nearly always there when he came to—he had been certain that he was disfigured for life, that skin had been ripped or burnt from his flesh, that his face was a mass of whelps and lacerations. But In fact, he could not find a scar anywhere on his body, and even the bruises were small black-and-blue spots on his arms, thighs, and chest.

The image in the mirror was the face of a man who had just awakened from a long bender, not one who had lived through hell and was searching for a means to commit suicide.

But of course, there was nothing in the cell with which he could hurt himself. He pounded on the mirror with both fists, hoping to shatter it into shards that he might use to slit his wrists. But it appeared to be stronger than glass, and it occurred to him that it might only be opaque on his side. He peered into the reflective surface, but all he saw was sallow skin and a three-day growth of beard. That at least gave him some intimation of time.

He rubbed his chin thoughtfully as he staggered back to his cot.

The walls of the tiny room were concrete blocks, thickly coated with off-white paint. The floor was one solid sheet of heavy beige vinyl, and the ceiling–which at the moment seemed impossibly far away–was an ugly shade of green. A lone fixture loomed in its center, the light seeming to droop toward Mark as he lay back groggily, resting his head on his hands because there was neither bedding nor pillow.

He felt a nagging sting from the crook of his elbow, echoing the prick of numerous needles. He had no idea what Ash had given him. Narcotics, hallucinogens, and drugs tailored to break down his inhibitions and force him to tell the truth. But the truth was he had very little idea what Ash was doing, and *Project Feedback* was a complete enigma. Luckily Ash seemed to assume that Mark had never been anything other than what his records showed, a lackluster graduate student working on his Ph.D. by doing research for a crazy professor.

But the fact that *Mark* knew that it was Ash who did the torturing, had made the hell of the past days all the more unbearable. In the back of Mark's brain there had remained enough thirst for revenge–and enough rationality to realize that death would deny him that release–that he had managed not to blurt out his overweening desire to rip Ash's throat out. Graduate students didn't do that.

A light breeze fluttered across his body, and he sensed it the way an anemone senses the tide. He noticed a difference in the light that he hadn't appreciated before, and then he realized that it was because there was a shadow on the far wall that looked vaguely manlike. His eyes and ears still didn't seem to be working in concert, because as he watched the shadow taking three steps into the room, the sound of shoes striking the concrete floor came later, as though resounding from a great distance.

Suddenly Ash was leaning over him. The man's face seemed huge, far too large for his body, like a Halloween mask. All the horror of the past hours or days flooded through Mark's mind, but instead of giving into the terror and clawing backward on the thin cot, he reached out with both hands for the hateful face. Impossibly his hands just kept on reaching. His arms seemed to snake away like fire hoses, and yet they never reached their target.

Ash shook his head, and when he spoke his words weren't any more in synch with his lips than his footfalls were with his feet. And he seemed to be doing a jig.

"I'm afraid we need you again, Mr. Townsend."

Mark shook his head.

"N... no," he managed to mutter. "I'm gonna kill you, you fuck."

He finally realized that the reason Ash seemed to be dancing was that *he* was shaking uncontrollably. The aftereffects of the drugs and rage and adrenalin were causing convulsions. Ash's laughter echoed like exploding artillery shells.

"I think not. It is you who are eventually going to die. But first, we are going to put you to good use. Bring him along."

For the first time, Mark realized there was another man in the room, one of the burly goons who had first brought him here. Ash waved a hand that looked like a snake at the man and then disappeared out the door.

"What's Ash experimenting on here?"

"That stuff's way over my head," said the goon. "I just do what I'm told."

"Nice job."

"Pays the rent."

Mark figured that a part of this guy's housing was about to be funded by *his* death. So, he ended the conversation.

In any case, they'd reached another heavy bulkhead door, and the goon had to rest Mark against the wall to open it. When the huge shining door swung open the goon lifted Mark again and carried him into what turned out to be an elevator. Mark leaned against the wall, supported by the man's giant hand on his chest until the doors opened again and a new tunnel appeared, the goon depositing him rudely in the plastic seat of a golf cart. At least he wasn't going to have to walk to whatever was about to happen to him.

He couldn't figure out whether the ride was really as long as it seemed or whether it was the drugs, pain, and exhaustion again, but the tunnel seemed to go on forever. When the cart pulled up to another thick steel door, the goon jerked Mark just as roughly out of the cart as he had thrown him into it and again half carried him through the door.

The giant space was so brightly lit Mark could barely keep his eyes open, and he noticed that the goon had put on a pair of dark glasses. If there was anyone else in the room Mark couldn't make them out, and no one offered him a pair of shades. As his eyes slowly adjusted, he noticed that the ceiling was far overhead, clearly the shored-up roof of another natural cavern like the one he had been in—when was it days? —before.

He was led staggering across the wide expanse of floor toward what appeared to be the source of the light, and the closer he got the more he noticed a dull buzzing noise that seemed to radiate from the walls, floor, ceiling, and even the air around him. When he turned his head away from the light, he was able to make out what appeared to be a bank of windows high above and to his right. Beneath that hung another giant screen like the one in the original room in which Ash had questioned him. Dark movement at the windows appeared to be several men, but from their hazy forms, they might have been extraterrestrials.

A metallic voice rang through unseen speakers, clanging in Mark's ears, and he wondered if it sounded as loud to his minder as it did to him. Apparently not. The guy seemed unfazed.

"Place the collar on him."

The goon's hand was removed from beneath Mark's armpit, and Mark felt himself slipping toward the floor. But two arms caught him, and he realized that they couldn't belong to his goon, because now Mark's back was to the light, and he could see the first goon fiddling with something on the top of a shiny steel table. When the guy turned to face Mark, he held something that looked like a dog collar made out of shiny metal that blinded Mark again. He realized the guy was planning to slip the collar around his throat, and his first thought was that this was the moment that he died.

The hands supporting him locked around his elbows, but Mark had no strength to struggle. The collar was cold as ice as it slipped around his throat, and as he waited for it to be drawn so tight that he could not breathe, he heard a sharp clicking noise, and then the goon stepped away.

The hands went back to supporting him under the arms, and he could still breathe.

"W... what is this thing?" he stammered.

The clanging metallic voice assaulted his ears again.

"Place him on the platform!"

He was lifted off his feet and spun to face the light once again, but this time he had the presence of mind to snap his eyes shut. When he opened them to the barest of slits, he realized that the light flowed out of a giant ring of tall tubes the size and shape of metal garbage cans. From there it blasted upward, radiating off every surface in the cavernous room. It seemed to Mark that the light source was so bright that even had everything in the cavern been painted black it would *appear* as white as it did because of the powerful illumination. He was forced slowly up a long, narrow staircase until he and his *helper* stood on a circular platform staring directly into the column of pure light.

Finally, he realized that the metal voice was Ash, speaking through some kind of address system.

"You're going to do a little job for us, Mr. Townsend. All you have to do is step into the light. We'll do the rest. And you can find comfort in the knowledge that you have become an integral part of the greatest experiment in history."

"What are you doing?" shouted Mark, as Martha Argerich and Rachmaninov started pounding through his head.

He was so exhausted, so filled with frustration and rage that he wished Martha would just get on with it, rip through to the finale, lift her beautiful fingers off the keys, bow to her invisible audience, and... get ... off ... the ...fucking ...stage. "What are you trying to prove?"

"That you may survive for one thing."

Inside a laser? That's what this thing had to be, right, the world's biggest laser generator? The only survival Mark could picture in there was in the netherworld.

"I don't have time to explain the science," said Ash gruffly. "You wouldn't understand it anyway. Pity Derek Maynor isn't here."

"What is this experiment?" shouted Mark, playing for time.

The sound over the address system might have been static. Or it might have been Ash, sighing heavily into the mike.

"We have been having a little trouble with our calibration, if you must know. We *are* on the cutting edge here, after all."

Calibration? What the hell was that supposed to mean?

"We have it under control now. If you're interested, we have discovered that we can *aim* better by adding one last bit of data to our matrix, the density of the target. In this case stone. This should be a fascinating trip for you. Step back!"

Evidently the order was directed at Mark's attendant, since suddenly he realized he was unsupported once again. He started to wobble, his knees buckling, and in that instant all the frustration and rage exploded.

"I'll see you in Hell for what you did to Katie!" he screamed.

"What?" Ash shouted over the speakers.

Mark smiled.

Then the floor rumbled and as he stumbled forward into the light, Martha Argerich's fieriest rendition ever of Rachmaninov's *Third Piano Concerto* pounded full blast in his head.

Mark's legs gave way beneath him, and he lurched forward, the music suddenly becoming atonal and jangling. Instead of the sense of lightheadedness that accompanied a fall, instead of the instant searing burn he expected from the light, he found himself suspended in some sort of field, the vibrations roaring right through his body, and then suddenly the drugged stupor disappeared, and an intense clarity overtook him, just as the field gave way and he surged *downward.*

He experienced flashes of strange and impossible-to-decipher images as though they were being burnt onto the front of his brain. He tried to touch his face to see if his eyes were even open, but his hands–which he could feel but not see–seemed to pass right through his head, and everything vibrated, not only around him, but within him as well.

Suddenly the vibration grew so powerful that his thoughts were shattered. The only input was the rolling tympanic rhythm of the rumbling that came from everywhere at once, and he was completely consumed by a terrible fiery pain. He imagined his internal organs blackening, then broiling to dust, and he tried to scream, but if he did the sound was impossible to hear over the maddening roar. Even Agerich's discordant symphony for once was stilled, but as the agony slowly began to fade, he felt his limbs taking shape again, and this time when he reached toward his face it was there, apparently unharmed.

He could still see the light, but he could not recognize any part of himself within it. As the pain finally disappeared altogether, he felt himself falling faster, and he crumpled into a tight ball, landing hard on what felt like cold concrete, the wind knocked from his lungs. He lay there for long seconds in a light as blinding as total darkness, clutching his belly, praying that his diaphragm would relent and let him breathe again.

EARL'S VAN WAS HIDDEN beneath a camouflage tarp between surrounding birches and undergrowth. And it was already loaded with what he called his essential equipment, leaving barely room for the three of them.

"Shiver always told me that if I got nervous to get out of here," said Earl, nodding to himself.

"So, he knew that maybe just providing a new identity wasn't going to be good enough," mused Marilyn, glancing at Tracy.

Earl grinned nervously.

"He's a pretty smart guy."

He climbed behind the wheel, and Tracy took the front passenger seat, forcing Marilyn to nudge a spot for herself in the mass of wires and boxes and tubes on the floor behind Earl. She frowned at Tracy.

"You're smaller and younger," said Tracy.

"If anything happens it would be better if I was in the front seat," said Marilyn, cryptically.

Tracy noticed just how ominously dark the night had become even as she sensed the planet spinning inexorably beneath them toward the sun. It was hard to tell what was sky and what was looming trees overhead, and the fog lights that Earl used to navigate the twin tire ruts turned the path into a yellow mine shaft. The van slowed a bit, and Earl flipped off the lights.

He nodded through the trees ahead. Two sets of headlights drove slowly past.

"We don't get a lot of traffic out here," he said. "Especially this late at night."

Tracy listened to the low rumble of the engine and her own breathing.

"I'll go check the main road," said Marilyn, as the van rolled gently to a stop.

To Tracy's surprise, the girl reached past Earl–who seemed frozen with fear–and turned off the key. The sudden silence was deafening. Tracy stared at Marilyn in disbelief, once again surprised by her courage and calm. She knew as well as Marilyn that they couldn't just go pulling out onto the road now with Ash's men patrolling it. But she didn't want to get out of the van.

"I should go," she said, anyway, reaching for the handle of her door.

Marilyn placed a hand on her shoulder. "I'm sneakier," she said. "It's one of the things Rank taught me."

Tracy nibbled her lip thoughtfully. The girl was probably right. Still, it felt wrong, to let a teenager place herself in danger in her stead.

"All right," she said, at last. "But stay low and keep out of sight. Just find out what they're doing, and then get your butt back here."

Marilyn nodded, and Tracy watched the girl's svelte figure, loping down the lane in front of them and then disappearing around a sharp bend.

"Shiver told me if they came around, I should get gone. We need to go," said Earl, nodding over and over to himself.

"We can't leave Marilyn. And if you start the motor again you might just draw them right to us. We'll be all right."

"You promise?"

"I promise," she said, feeling as though she'd just lied to the Easter Bunny.

She didn't like being responsible for Earl any more than she did for Marilyn or the unknown people on the list. But she had no choice now. She couldn't leave Earl to Ash's men any more than she could desert Marilyn.

The night grew even darker as clouds shrouded the stars, and Tracy rolled down her window, but even the crickets were silent. She could hear Earl breathing quickly between tight lips, and she wondered if he was about to hyperventilate. That would be great, trying to drag his comatose bulk out of the seat so she could drive. Both of them started when a dark figure came racing back around the bend, but it was only Marilyn returning. She leaped into the van, closing the door quickly again, but not before Tracy noticed that she had a pistol in her hand.

"Where did you get that?" Tracy whispered.

"My dad taught me not to take chances," muttered the girl, digging through Tracy's pack and showing her another pistol that she laid on the console between the seats.

Tracy stared at the second pistol, realizing Marilyn was leaving it there for her.

"You hid those in my pack?" she said, her old distrust of guns returning.

Marilyn nodded.

"I figured if we needed them, we'd need them fast, and you always keep that pack with you."

"How many men are there?" Tracy asked, dragging her eyes from the pistol to Marilyn.

"I spotted three cars still on the road, two men in each. At least two other cars pulled up to the house before we got away."

"What are the men on the road doing?"

"They're parked at either end of the lane."

"They're here for me," said Earl at last, sighing heavily. "You should leave me."

His voice was so shaky Tracy thought he might break into tears, but she was touched by his valiant offer. Shiver. Beatrice. Marilyn. Earl. Every one of them had helped her in their own way and had placed their own lives in danger.

That's what human beings do.

Her father's voice was so clear in her head that she was surprised that neither of the others heard it. And it stirred the old confusion. She knew the voice was true. It was something her father would have said under the circumstances, but how could a man who believed something like that wholeheartedly have done the things he did? More and more Tracy was forced to the conclusion that her own senses had betrayed her on that night as she had betrayed her parents later.

"I can walk back to my house through the woods. Then you two can just drive away."

Marilyn slapped Earl on the shoulder.

"Not on your life, buddy. If these guys want you that bad, then we want you even worse. We're all together in this like the Three Musketeers."

Earl tried out a weak smile.

"All for one and one for all."

"Exactly. And if those goofballs are the same people that took my dad, then some of them are going to answer to me."

Tracy could only stare at the girl in wonder. There had to be eight or ten armed, well-trained men not very far away through the woods, men that were hunting for Earl and almost certainly them as well, and Marilyn was still plotting not just escape but revenge. Tracy found herself not only astounded but feeling much the same way.

Those men owed *her* an explanation as well. More than an explanation. They owed her either her parents, alive and well, or their own lives for their part in their murders. She didn't know *how* she was going to get either, any more than Marilyn did, but she was determined to get one or the other. Maybe not tonight, maybe not here, but soon.

Earl smiled shyly and sniffled.

"So what are we going to do then?" said Tracy, afraid that Marilyn was going to suggest an attack.

Marilyn frowned.

"Earl just gave me an idea, but it's dangerous."

Tracy laughed dryly.

"You're kidding right?"

"Well, I mean it's more dangerous than just sitting here for a moment."

"But not more dangerous than sitting here for two moments."

"Probably not."

"Let's hear it."

TRACY INITIALLY VETOED MARILYN'S plan. It *was* simply too dangerous. But they could not drive out onto the road with the cars blocking escape at either end, and if they remained where they were, they were bound to be discovered sooner or later. So, in the end, Tracy insisted on following Marilyn at least as far as the trees surrounding Earl's house. If anything went wrong, she wanted to be there, instead of sitting in the van not knowing.

"Take the other gun," said Marilyn, nodding toward the second pistol, still resting on the top layer of clothes in the pack.

Tracy stared at the weapon, trying to separate it from the other pistol in her mind's eye, the one lying on the floor of her father's study, beside the dead men. She could see the look of surprise on her father's face when he saw her. She could still feel her mother's hands on her shoulders shoving her into the hidey hole.

"I wouldn't be any good with it. I'd probably just shoot myself in the foot."

Marilyn frowned, but she climbed out of the van and waited for Tracy and Earl to follow.

As they crept through the forest Marilyn kept looking back at them and shaking her head, signaling with a finger across her lips to please be quiet, but there was so much *stuff* to make noise. Tracy tripped on unseen roots and bramble, caught her clothes on burrs and twigs, and generally defeated the purpose of their stealthy approach to Earl's house.

The sun was still a secret hidden beyond an enigmatic horizon, only beginning to weave long red ribbons of light through the trees, but birds chirped and flittered around them. Earl grabbed Marilyn's shoulder, nodding ahead into a wall of alder bushes. They could hear muffled voices through the undergrowth.

Marilyn held out a flat palm to freeze Earl and Tracy, then dropped to all fours, disappearing on her belly into the thick green mass of bracken. When she returned, feet first, she brushed herself off quietly, leaning close to Tracy.

"I can get up to the house without being seen, I think."

"And how are you going to create this diversion?"

The girl frowned at Earl.

"How attached are you to that old house?"

Earl shrugged.

"It's just a house."

"Then I'm gonna set it on fire. While they're busy, you should be able to drive away."

"What do you mean *you*?" said Tracy. "You didn't say leaving you was a part of the plan."

"We'll meet behind the store where we got directions. I can get that far on foot through the woods by say ten this morning."

Tracy shook her head. "No way. I'm not leaving you here."

"You don't have any choice. Pretty soon these guys will get around to searching the surrounding area."

Tracy shook her head again.

"Set the fire. Then we all hike away through the woods."

"I can't leave my stuff *and* lose the house," said Earl, nodding back in the direction of the van.

Tracy could tell that no matter how much fear he felt, that was going to be Earl's sticking point. He'd allow the equipment in the house to be destroyed, or he'd let them take the van full of whatever, and he'd go back to the house. But he wasn't going to part with both.

"I can get up to the house and get the fire started, but I may not be able to make it back this way," argued Marilyn. "I might have to hide in the woods on the other side, and if we wait too long to run for it there's too much chance of giving ourselves away. I don't even want to touch it off until you guys are back to the van."

Tracy had the sinking feeling that Marilyn was doing the only thing she could under the circumstances, and once again she felt as though *she* should have not only suggested the plan but taken the lead. She hadn't exactly had what could be called a full life, but she was older, and there was at least some reason to believe that her own actions might have been the cause of the hell that had befallen these two.

Instead, she was allowing a teenager to not only plan the diversion but risk her life creating it.

"I should be the one," she said.

Marilyn studied her for a moment before shaking her head.

"Don't worry so much. I'm smaller, wirier... I have no problem with guns, and besides, as you've noticed I have a little practice sneaking around."

Tracy nodded slowly.

"You should tell me more about that sometime."

The girl smiled.

"When I get back."

"Here," said Earl, digging in his pocket, handing Marilyn a heavy key ring with a large plastic pendant attached and pointing to one key. "This one is to the bulkhead out back. There's an oil tank in the cellar, and a couple of jerry cans of gas for the emergency generator, and there's a fireplace lighter down there by the furnace somewhere."

Marilyn grinned.

"A man after my own heart," she said, eliciting a wide smile from Earl who didn't seem to care at all that he was aiding in the torching of his own home.

"Ten o'clock," said Tracy, glancing up at the sky that was just beginning to turn blue. But now the light seemed as ominous as a searchlight's beam.

Marilyn shoved Tracy in the opposite direction.

"Get going. Watch for the smoke, and I'll see you at the store. Don't worry. I can do this."

With that she dropped to the ground again and skittered away into the thick brush again.

THE BIG GOON TURNED toward the sound of Ash's voice as it echoed through the giant room again.

"All right. Stand away from the equipment. We're going to bring him back."

The technician beside the goon smirked, muttering,

"I'm not cleaning this one up."

"They got that monkey back through in one piece," said the goon.

The technician shrugged.

"The first body that came back looked like parts of it were stone. They made a lot of adjustments after that." Then he whispered just loud enough for the goon to hear. "Not."

"But why not send him directly here in the past? That's where Ash wants to get to, right?"

"This test is to see if we can place a subject inside a very densely constructed building without melding him right into one of the walls."

"Jesus."

"And of course, we don't want him just running around loose back there."

The humming noise that seemed to be a part of the cavernous room itself grew so loud that both the goon and the tech had to replace their protective earplugs. The column of light pulsed, and the air carried a charge powerful enough to raise the hair on their heads that was already whipped by the indoor wind.

Once again Ash's voice sliced the air, cutting right through the plugs. "Go into the second phase!"

The vibration through the floor now had a harmonic rhythm to it, as though more than one great wheel were turning somewhere beneath their feet. The light danced and jumped and then *bent* like a snake rising out of a basket. It began to spin around like a wobbling top, and the noise level climbed one more notch until it was no longer distinguishable as noise but just another incredibly intense vibration.

Then suddenly the lights went out, and the entire chamber was bathed in absolute darkness. It was a couple of seconds before emergency fixtures flickered on behind the tech and the goon, and they slipped off their dark glasses. Ash's staticky voice sounded in mid-sentence.

"...have lost power again? Get it back online, now! I want him back here!"

The tech looked at the goon and shrugged.

TRACY CROUCHED BEHIND A pile of dead brush, peeking up and down the road. Back toward Earl's place red flames were just beginning to lick the sky above the pines. The men in the cars saw it too, or else they were responding to calls from the other men at the house, because they whirled their big sedans around and disappeared up Earl's drive just as Marilyn had predicted.

Tracy raced back to the van and leaped inside. Earl was already shifting into gear.

"Wait here a few minutes for Marilyn," said Tracy, peering anxiously through the trees.

Earl shook his head, easing toward the road. Two more cars raced by in the direction of his house.

"She told us what to do. We should do it."

"But what if they catch her?"

"I reckon they might."

She stared at him as though seeing him for the first time.

"She's going to meet us."

Earl nodded.

"If she's supposed to meet us she will. If she isn't, she won't."

Tracy still hadn't decided if Earl was semi-retarded or simply some sort of absent-minded professor. But as much as she hated to admit it, she knew he was right. If they stayed where they were, Marilyn had risked her life for nothing.

"All right," she said, nodding down the road away from the house. "Let's get out of here, then."

But to her surprise, once they were off the narrow peninsula Earl turned away from the direction of the little convenience store and quickly pulled up another winding drive.

"Where are we going?" she asked.

"Friend's cabin," said Earl. "We'll hide out there until it's time to meet. We can't just sit at the store. Most likely bump right into some more of those people."

"Can you trust this guy?" said Tracy, glancing ahead through the trees, looking for the cabin.

"He died a couple of years ago," said Earl. "His kids don't want the place, but they pay taxes on it. The power's turned off, but there's a generator, and lots of canned food. I come here sometimes when I need to get away from my machines and think."

The *cabin* turned out to be a three-bedroom cape with side windows overlooking a narrow winding creek. The stream itself was nearly dry, but the cove it fed into was just visible as a thin silver line through the trees where the sun was now a gleaming metal ball. The house had a cozy if vacant feeling, with dusty overstuffed furniture, and heavy old chenille curtains. Cheap brass wall sconces were meant to illuminate framed Currier and Ives prints.

"How come they're after you?" asked Earl, opening the blinds. "You build machines, too?"

Tracy shook her head. "Evidently they think I know more than I do. But I'm not even really sure who *they* are except for Ash."

"They're the bad guys," said Earl.

Tracy tried to smile.

"So, we're the good guys."

"Yep. The Three Musketeers."

She envied his simple outlook on life. But it occurred to her that he had been living alone for a long time, just like her, and yet he didn't have the feel of the hermit that she had developed. It was easy to see that Earl had no walls around his heart.

"Do you have any family?" she asked.

He shook his head.

"I'm an orphan. I was raised in an institution till I was twelve. Then I lived with a couple of foster families. We never bonded. That's what they call it. Bonded. How about you?"

"My story's a little more complicated."

Earl nodded.

"Like my machines. They're complicated, but I can understand 'em."

"You wouldn't understand my relationship with my family. I don't."

"I always wanted a real family, but after a while, I got to making do on my own."

He frowned, and she saw the sadness in his eyes. Clearly not bonding with any of his foster parents had been more painful than he wanted to admit.

"Me, too. I haven't spoken to any of my family in a year now."

"But you love 'em, right?"

The defense attorney in her parents' competency hearing had used almost those exact words. He wanted the judge to see that the girl on the stand was not some wild teenager exacting revenge on overly strict parents. She was an upstanding young woman who had managed to maintain her sanity amid the madness surrounding her.

"Yes," she whispered.

Earl was embarrassed and confused by the emotions he'd stirred up. He excused himself to check the generator, and Tracy peered out the window up the drive, her fingers tracing the butt of the pistol on the top of the pack.

Marilyn was out there, risking her life for them, and for her father, the fact sending another wave of guilt through Tracy. She could almost feel her mother's hand on her shoulder, consoling her, just as she had done so many times in Tracy's youth. She could almost hear her mother's gentle voice.

Tracy, the world isn't just what you can see and touch. There are always going to be people who can't understand. Don't you be one of them.

What was she supposed to understand, murder, treason?

Whenever her ghost mother appeared to her, she found it impossible to reconcile the gentle voice and the woman standing over the bloody corpses. The voice that spoke of reason and the one that believed in astrology and the power of crystals to influence destiny.

She stared at the gun, thinking of Marilyn. Finally, she lifted the weapon and slipped it into her belt where it felt bulky but deadly. She hoped if she ever did have to use it, she could hit what she aimed at, or at least not shoot herself or Earl.

"Earl," said Tracy, when he plodded back into the room. "Just how smart are you? What kind of formal training do you have, physics, what?"

Earl shook his head, laughing.

"I never graduated."

"But you must have taken a lot of science courses."

"From high school. I have what they call a learning disability. I'm dyslexic."

"But the machine," she said, shaking her head. "All that equipment. You transmuted metal and made things levitate. How did you learn to do that?"

"I've just always had what they call an *affinity* for things like that. I can read schematics good. It's English I have trouble with."

"Who the heck is Shiver?" Tracy muttered to herself. "And what do we all have in common?"

"I don't know," said Earl. "But I know he was telling me the truth when he said I'd better keep on my toes."

In the distance, she heard the sirens of fire trucks.

"We'll be safe here until time for the meeting," said Earl, dropping into a recliner and raising a cloud of dust.

Tracy nodded, still staring out the window.

"But what if they catch Marilyn?"

"I can find that out, I think," said Earl, fishing in the back pocket of his pants and lifting out a black box that looked like a hand-held computer.

"What's that?" asked Tracy, sidling closer to inspect the device.

Earl shrugged.

"I'm always losing my house keys. At the post office, at the grocery store. Once I dropped them over the cliff while I was cutting limbs. Luckily by then, I'd put a locator beacon on them. This little gizmo reads a copy of the GPS signal received by my keyring."

"And you can tell where the ring is?"

"As long as I know the coordinates," he said, giving her a funny look. "But I know where most everything is located in this area pretty good."

"Where is she?"

"She's still near the house."

Tracy shook her head. Marilyn should be far from there by now unless something had gone wrong.

Earl read her worried look.

"She might be just hiding in the woods, watching to see what those guys are doing. Maybe it's not safe for her to make a break yet."

Tracy shook her head.

"She wouldn't hang around there after setting the fire. How accurate is that readout?"

Earl frowned.

"It's good to within about fifteen feet."

"Is she in the woods?"

"Sometimes it isn't that accurate."

"Where is she?"

"Somewhere out front. Maybe in the driveway."

She nodded.

"They have her. She's in one of their cars."

"She might have dropped the keys. The bad guys might have them."

The fault in Earl's logic only escaped her for a moment.

"She wouldn't have been out front where they could spot her, and the house must be burning to the ground by now. There's no reason for those guys to keep a set of worthless keys even if they did find them. Marilyn has them on her."

"Probably," Earl admitted grudgingly. "But it doesn't make any difference, does it? If they have her, they'll probably be leaving soon."

She nodded.

"It makes a lot of difference. With *that,*" she pointed toward the black box. "We can follow them."

"We don't want to do that," said Earl, shaking his head violently. "Anyway, we'll know where she is all the time. We have the GPS."

She nodded.

"As long as they keep the keys and Marilyn together. But what if they don't? We'll have no way of knowing what they've done with her."

Earl wasn't sold.

"Those people do bad things," he said. "I don't want to get mixed up with them again. We got away once, but we might not be so lucky again. We could get ourselves killed."

"Marilyn's going to get herself killed, and all she wanted was to help you and me."

She knew that at least half of that was true. If Earl gave it any real thought, he'd realize that his house might still be whole, and he might not have needed help if they had never shown up.

"They're moving now, anyway," said Earl, staring at the GPS.

"I'm going to follow them," she said, rising. "Give me the key to the van."

Earl sat petulantly, crossing his arms.

"It's my van."

"Then I'll just walk out of here," said Tracy, nodding toward the door. "Where will that leave you? No house and probably the bad guys still wondering where the owner is. They'll be back. I promise you that. Do you think you'll be okay on your own? Where will you go?"

Earl stomped his foot.

"We can't go back there. They'll be waiting for us."

"Then find us another way around so we can tail them. They don't know where we are or what we're driving yet."

"How can you be sure?"

"Because your garage was attached to the house. They'll probably assume if there was another car there besides Marilyn's, it burned up in the fire."

Earl seemed to accept that, climbing slowly to his feet, and digging for the car keys. She jerked them out of his hands and raced out of the house. He barely made it into the van before she backed down the drive.

"How do I catch them?" she said.

He shrugged.

"They're heading for Route 1. Take the next left, and we can get behind them."

"Where can we buy a map with coordinates on it that correspond to your GPS."

"We don't need one," said Earl, frowning. "There's mapping software in it."

"You said-"

"I didn't want to do this, remember?"

Instead of following, they ended up paralleling the caravan along back roads, passing by wharves and behind packing sheds rather than along main streets where they might be spotted. When the sedans sped toward the interstate, though, Earl informed Tracy that they were going to have to close up.

"They can cruise at eighty on the turnpike," said Earl. "Even if they hold it to seventy so as not to get pulled over, we still can't keep up on the side roads."

"But we have the locator."

"Yeah. But it's got a limited range. If we're more than maybe fifteen or twenty miles away, we'll lose them."

"It's a GPS."

Earl frowned.

"But the GPS is in the keyring. It relays its location to my readout here."

"Which is it?" said Tracy, not surprised at all that Earl had come up with such a Rube Goldberg electronic system. "Fifteen or twenty miles?"

Earl shrugged.

"I built it to find my keys," he said.

"All right," said Tracy, pulling over in front of a small white house in a shady subdivision of small white houses. Just ahead she could see the intersection with the main road on which Ash's men were traveling. "We'll have to tighten up, then."

"What are you gonna do?"

"I haven't got a plan yet. I just know we can't let Marilyn get hauled off somewhere where they can torture her and probably kill her and get away with it."

At that moment the first car in the convoy rolled slowly past the intersection ahead. Tracy slipped down in her seat, but the two men in the sedan were intent on the road in front of them. It was the same for the second and third cars. In the fourth car, she noticed a passenger in the rear seat, but they were too far away to tell if it was Marilyn. One more car followed, and it too had three people inside.

"Damn," she whispered. "Which one is she in?"

Earl shrugged, staring at the readout on his box.

"They're moving, and too close together to tell."

She waited a couple of minutes, then pulled out onto the highway, glancing at Earl and the device in his lap.

"Don't let me get too far away."

Earl shrugged.

"If you do," she said. "So help me, I'll leave you."

"Okay, okay!" he said, straightening in his seat. "Just keep going. We're doing all right."

Twenty more miles of meandering through small towns that seemed to have no reason for being other than to slow them down, then they reached the on-ramp to Interstate 95 South. As they pulled onto the highway Tracy could just make out the last of the dark sedans vanishing over a hill in the distance. She calculated that the cars were a little over a mile away, and she hung back.

"Don't lose the signal," she cautioned Earl again.

"I won't."

But she hadn't counted on the entire caravan pulling in at the first rest stop. She and Earl cruised past, eying the line of black sedans parked in front of the Burger King.

"Now what?" said Earl.

She surprised him by taking the next exit.

"I don't want to sit and wait on the shoulder," she explained, making a U-turn at the first intersection to pass back through the toll booth and ease partway up the on-ramp. She pulled over and waited, the guy in the booth giving her a glance. She waved and shook her head, watching the line of cars from the north.

"Those guys aren't going to Kennebunk," said Earl. "They're headed for Washington or someplace like that. They're gonna take 95 all the way out of state."

She nodded. Once again Earl had surprised her.

When the caravan reappeared and passed them, Tracy eased back onto the highway. Earl stared at the locator. When he looked her in the eye and nodded, she settled back in her seat. The pistol pressed uncomfortably against her belly, but she was getting used to it.

MARK DECIDED THAT IF he was dead, death was one hell of a ride. But for some reason it was not Martha but Samuel Feinberg's version of The *Appassionata* by Beethoven that now wrapped itself around his disoriented head. The pre-World War II recording he'd heard played so many times on the old stereo in his father's study was devoid of the scratches and distortion that had distracted him as a child.

Although the space around him was an inky haze, the music was clear and crisp, the headlong thrust and energy of Feinberg's keyboard virtuosity sweeter than ever in his mind. The man had a knack for timing, with crucial pauses just long enough to force the listener to really *listen,* and the *Andante con moto* flowed so incredibly smoothly, with a grace that other later pianists could only emulate, and poorly at that.

As his eyes grew slowly accustomed to the gloom and air rushed into his stinging lungs, he was barely able to make out the silhouette of a grid pattern in front of him. He shoved himself into a sitting position, discovering a wall behind him that was as cold and bare as the floor, just as movement revealed a man shape against the grid, and the music finally stilled, leaving a ringing in his ears.

"Who the fuck are you?" said a raspy voice in a harsh whisper.

Mark shook his head, trying to get a look at the guy. If it was one of Ash's goons, he'd certainly managed to surprise the bastard.

Suddenly he was lifted to his feet and deposited onto something that felt roughly like the cot in his cell. Had the experiment been a success, and now he was back in lockup? He ran his fingers along the bunk. This one had a blanket. And why was it so dark? The light in the cell had never gone off.

"Where did you come from, Buster?" said the voice.

He could barely make out the man's face. Dark, sunken eyes in a skull that looked as though it had been beaten lopsided with a sledgehammer. A couple of teeth missing. And the guy was wearing some kind of loose-fitting shirt and pants, not a poorly made suit.

"Where am I?" muttered Mark.

The guy nodded thoughtfully.

"The question is," he said, glancing slowly around in the darkness. "How the fuck did you get here?"

Mark's eyes had almost adjusted to the dim light. There was one small table and a wooden, straight-backed chair, a filthy porcelain sink, and in the corner an equally disgusting toilet with no seat. The air reeked of urine and sweat and the moldy smell of damp concrete.

"I don't know," said Mark.

That wasn't exactly a lie, and he didn't have any idea what this guy's reaction would be if he told him he'd just been *transported* here like Spock.

"Don't know," said the prisoner, in a threatening growl.

"Well, you'd better be finding out before Mr. Cripps comes along, or you're going to be in a shitload of trouble, and me, too. Now if you know a way out of here, you show me."

"I don't," said Mark. "Where am I?"

"You're in B block, as if you didn't know. What's that you got on your neck?"

Mark ran his fingers along the polished surface of the collar, searching for a latch. He found one. Unfortunately, he also found the keyhole, and he had no key. He delved in both pockets, but the handcuff key was gone, and it probably wouldn't have fit anyway.

"It's some kind of tracking collar," he said.

"Shit," whispered the prisoner, slapping a heavily calloused hand over Mark's mouth. In the distance, Mark could hear the sound of something hard striking steel bars.

The big prisoner glanced all around, but it was clear to Mark that there was no escape and no place to hide a second human being in the tiny cell. He sat resignedly, awaiting his fate, while the prisoner dropped onto his hands and knees, searching every inch of the perimeter of his cell for the hole Mark had to have come in through. Mark felt sorry for the guy.

A flashlight beam played along the catwalk outside the cell, and Mark watched in silence as it passed the barred door, and the guard finally appeared. He was a big man, too, with broad shoulders and a hard-billed cap on his head. He stopped suddenly, whirling the flashlight beam into Mark's eyes.

"What the-" he said, taking a step back. "Koenig! What the fuck is going on? Who is this guy?"

"I don't know Mr. Cripps. Honest, I don't know where he come from."

Cripps jerked a whistle into his mouth, and the shrill blast stung Mark's already tortured ears. Far down the iron catwalk, he could hear boot soles pounding ominously.

"Who are you?" asked Cripps, in a voice far more threatening than Koenig's.

Mark shook his head. It wouldn't do any good to tell the man. He had the feeling he wasn't going to be here that long.

Keys clanked, and the cell door slid open. Two more brawny guards appeared behind Cripps, and the prisoner called Koenig automatically turned to face the wall, spread his legs and arms, and leaned against it.

"Stand up," said Cripps, glowering down at Mark.

Mark climbed shakily to his feet, trying to stand at something that looked like attention.

"What's that thing on your neck?" said Cripps, frowning at the collar.

"I think it's some kind of locator, so they can bring me back."

"Who?"

"The people who sent me here."

"How did you get here?"

Mark frowned, but he couldn't seem to think up a plausible story, so he could either refuse to talk or tell the truth. Either one seemed extremely problematic as he stared first into Cripps' hard eyes and then at the heavy truncheon swinging lightly in his hand.

"A man named Ash put me into a machine, and here I am. I know it sounds crazy. That's what happened."

One of the guards on the catwalk laughed, and Cripps glared at him.

"So you just popped up here?" said Cripps, nodding and frowning, but glancing around the cell, not at Mark.

Mark shrugged.

Cripps tapped him lightly on the temple with the end of the baton.

"A story like that should interest the assistant warden. He likes that science fiction shit. Come on, Koenig. We're going for a walk."

Mark noticed that all three guards carried sidearms in large leather holsters. Not automatics, big Colt revolvers. That was odd. Prison guards weren't supposed to carry firearms onto cellblocks.

"I didn't do nothing," said Koenig, shaking his head, refusing to look at the man.

"I said, come on," said Cripps in a low but firm voice. "Don't make me come get you."

Koenig turned around like a small child, frightened of a whipping. He scowled at Mark as they walked side by side between the three guards down the long iron walkway.

Mark's strength seemed to be returning, while the drugged haze he'd been under when he was forced into the light had not, as though the light or the vibrations or the pain had somehow burned it out of him. Although the excruciating agony was entirely gone, the memory of it still clung to his mind.

The assistant warden's office had a scarred panel door with a green glass window. The light inside seemed feeble and distant as Cripps knocked lightly.

"Yes?" The man's voice sounded surprised.

"It's Mr. Cripps, sir. I have someone you need to see."

"Come in, then."

The man behind the polished wooden desk appeared to be about thirty years old, wearing thick horn-rimmed glasses, a dark business jacket, and a very thin black tie over a starched white shirt. He frowned as the five visitors crowded into his small office. A small brass plaque on the desk *read Carl Elgin–Assistant Warden, Leavenworth.* Although there were two chairs Mark didn't expect to be offered a seat.

Elgin looked over the entire group before focusing again on Cripps and politely asking the guard why he was being bothered at this hour. It was three in the morning according to the big round clock high on the wall. Mark half listened as Cripps informed Elgin of everything he knew about what had happened. Finally, Elgin's eyes fell on Mark and Koenig again. He questioned Koenig first, but Koenig stuck to his story that he didn't know a damned thing. Finally, Elgin stood and walked slowly around his desk to face Mark.

The assistant warden looked bigger seated than he did standing. Mark found himself staring down into the man's acne-scarred face. But there was no mistaking the hardness behind his blue eyes. Here was a man who had worked his way up through the system and intended to make warden one day. He wasn't going to have people popping into his cells and screwing up his roll call.

"What's your story?" he said, brusquely.

Mark shrugged, telling it again, watching Elgin's eyes harden even more, wishing he could come up with another, more believable tale. But what? How did someone just appear inside a locked cell?

"And what's this?" asked Elgin, fingering Mark's collar.

"He says it's a tracking collar or something," said Cripps, smirking.

Elgin tapped an impatient foot on the floor. For the first time, Mark noticed that there was no computer monitor on the man's desk, no laptop, no fax machine in the corner. And the big old black phone had no buttons nor dial. Mark peered up at the clock on the wall again and realized that there was a long extension cord running from it to a wall socket. The cord was cloth bound.

"What year is this?" asked Mark, trying to find his voice again.

Elgin let out a long sigh of disgust. "How did you really get into Koenig's cell? And quit with the amnesia crap."

Mark sighed.

"I stepped into a machine designed by a rogue government agency, and the next thing I know here I am."

Cripps stepped forward ominously, but Elgin waved a surprisingly effeminate hand at him, and the big guard stopped. Elgin shook his head in disgust.

"I've got a migraine that would kill a horse. We'll sort this out when the warden gets here in the morning. In the meantime, put both of them in solitary."

Cripps nodded, nudging Mark toward the door.

"And while you're at it," said Elgin, "get that collar off of him, and bring it to me."

WHEN THEY HAD MANAGED to maneuver around the traffic-burdened outskirts of New York City and back onto 95 South, Tracy breathed a sigh of relief. For a while, she'd been certain they were going to lose the convoy in the nightmare of automobiles snarling through the spaghetti-like highway system. Earl sat quietly enough, reading the mapping software on his handheld device, but she could tell by the imprint of his right foot on the carpet that she made him more than a little nervous with her driving.

"It's Washington," she said, nodding to herself.

"Told you," said Earl.

She shook her head.

"If they make it into DC, there's no way we're getting Marilyn back. Washington is security masquerading as a town, and Ash's people control the system there."

Earl shook his head.

"There's no way for us to stop them."

The fact that he was right didn't change things. She couldn't let Marilyn be dragged into some hellhole beneath Washington, and she had no doubt in her mind that Ash had one. She knew in her heart that if the situation were reversed the girl would not let *her* be taken without a fight.

"Come on, Earl," she said, nodding back over her shoulder into the van. "Don't you have any more miracle toys in all that junk?"

Earl shook his head.

"Well, then," she muttered, resting her fingers on the pistol.

"You're crazy," he said.

"I'm beginning to believe that myself," she said, lifting the gun and pulling back the slide to check the chamber the way she'd seen Marilyn do.

"What are you going to do with that?" asked Earl.

"I don't know yet."

She floored the van and sped through traffic until the black convoy was clearly visible in the distance.

"You're sure you have no more neat little toys?" she said, still passing cars.

"I got the machine I built so I could get some sleep."

"Get some sleep? What the hell is that going to do for us?"

Earl shrugged.

"I don't like the lobster boats. Sometimes when the water's calm I can hear their motors in the morning. It wakes me up."

He climbed back through the mass of electronic junk, shoving stuff roughly aside, finally returning with a shoe-box-sized object that appeared to be made of cardboard and Styrofoam. A six-inch piece of white PVC pipe extruded from the top of the gizmo. It looked more like a kid's homemade model of a steamboat than any sort of electronic device.

"I was gonna take it on a trip I was planning," explained Earl, smiling. "Now I guess I won't be going on it."

The smile faded.

"I don't think that's going to help us," she said. "What else have you got?"

"Nothing," said Earl, sadly. "I just use this to stop the lobster boats."

"You *stop* the boats?" she said, staring at the gadget.

He nodded.

"Does it have to be plugged in?" she asked.

He smiled, popping open the glovebox and holding up a black electrical line.

"I have an adaptor."

She grinned at him, and his smile spread.

Tracy watched as Earl leaned out the passenger window and aimed the PVC pipe at a semi alongside. There was a short buzzing noise, the truck's motor went silent without so much as a sputter, and the cursing driver fought the big rig over to the shoulder.

"I'll be damned," said Tracy. "How does it do that?"

"I think it's a unidirectional electromagnetic pulse."

"You think?"

He shrugged.

"It's like my other box. I can get it to work, but I'm not always sure why. I know it fucks up the electrical and electronics systems."

"Will the truck start again now?"

Earl shook his head.

"You did that to lobster fishermen?" she said, frowning.

"They were always waking me up on calm days. They quit coming around at all after a while."

She nodded, smiling. At least it had only been calm days.

"I imagine they would. They probably thought that part of the Atlantic was some kind of mini-Bermuda Triangle."

"So, what do we do now?" he asked.

"Shit," said Tracy, speeding up again as she noticed the last cars in the convoy taking an exit. "Where are they going?"

"She isn't with those guys," said Earl, glancing at his locator, then nodding ahead.

Tracy could just see two of the black sedans, still cruising down the interstate. That was good news, at least. Now there were fewer men to deal with.

"What are you doing?" asked Earl, as Tracy continued to accelerate, bringing them closer to the two cars.

"Can you tell which one she's in yet?" she asked, glancing at Earl.

"Can you?" said Earl, irritably.

"No need to bite my head off."

"Sorry," he said, staring at the bumper of the rear sedan. "I'm a little nervous."

"Okay," she said. "We know we can stop them. Now all I have to do is come up with a plan for when we do. You sure you don't have any other miracle up your sleeve?"

"None that would help us," he said, shaking his head.

"How can you be so sure?"

"Because I am!"

"All right, then," she said, trying to sound more confident than she felt. "We'll just have to make do."

They drove in silence for another hour, Tracy wracking her brain for a plan, Earl complaining that he needed to go pee.

"They're going to have to stop again soon," said Tracy, glancing at their own gas gauge that was pegged just above empty.

"I can't wait that long," said Earl, crossing his legs and holding his crotch.

"There," said Tracy, pointing at a sign for a food and gas stop three miles ahead.

Sure enough, the two sedans pulled off, and Tracy took her time at the bottom of the ramp before rolling slowly across the lot toward the MacDonald's.

"I'm not going in there," said Earl, shaking his head.

"I don't blame you. But you can slip into the trees out back."

"Okay," said Earl, reluctantly.

"Earl," said Tracy, nodding toward one of the two parked sedans six spots away where a blond head was just visible through the rear window. "Marilyn's in that car. Do you see her?"

Earl peered through his window and nodded.

"How do you work that box?" asked Tracy.

He pointed to a single toggle switch beside the PVC pipe.

She reached across and took the box from him. "When the time comes, I'm going to blast their cars with this, then take Marilyn at gunpoint. It might be better if you weren't in the van right then. If anything happens to Marilyn or me, you can just kind of melt away. Otherwise, if it all goes the way it should, you need to get back into the van fast."

"But what if they see me?"

Yes. What?

"Shiver gave you a new identity, right?"

Earl nodded.

"Were you Earl Carter when you did your demo in Terra Diablo?"

Earl shook his head.

"Tommy Setlow."

"Do you look the same now?"

"I used to wear my hair a lot longer and I had a beard."

She nodded.

"They won't be expecting you here. If they spot you just act casual."

Earl swallowed a large lump in his throat before opening the door, walking behind the two sedans, and then slipping behind the rest stop into the trees. Tracy saw Marilyn's head swivel as the van rolled past. Tracy drove slowly up to one of the full-service pumps. A pimply young man with snow-white hair moseyed up to her window.

"Fill her up," she said, ignoring his curious look at the box in her lap.

She wondered what he'd have thought if he'd seen the pistol underneath it. Neither of the sedans had yet pulled around to the pumps. Before the young man could stick the gas nozzle into the tank, she asked him to check the oil.

"Just let me get this, Ma'am," he said, nodding toward the nozzle.

"Check the oil first," she said.

"The gas will pump while I check it."

"I'm afraid it will run over."

"It's got an automatic shutoff."

"Humor me."

The kid shook his head in disgust, left the nozzle in the tank but not turned on, and then went to the front of the van waiting for Tracy to pop the hood. She faked trouble finding the release, still watching her mirror. Just as one of the sedans eased around the corner, she jerked the lever, slinking down in her seat.

When she leaned forward just a bit, she noticed that the pump hid her from the driver and front seat passenger of the sedan. Marilyn was in the back, staring at her. She saw fear in the girl's eyes but determination as well, and Tracy felt her heart sinking as the confrontation approached. She heard but did not see the second sedan pull in behind her.

Now she was shaking.

What the devil was she thinking? There were four armed men in those two cars. But as she glanced at Marilyn again, she knew that if she left her in their clutches the girl was as good as dead. Even so, Marilyn slowly shook her head and mouthed one word.

Go.

Tracy shook her own head. If she drove off now the guilt that had been her constant companion for a year would have a new weight added to it that she would not be able to carry. If she was about to be killed here in this parking lot, she could accept that as long as she did something and realized that her breathing slowed, and her heart's furious pumping eased a little. She discovered that her fingers were no longer shaking on the box.

When the passenger door of the van jerked open, she started, reaching for the pistol. Earl jumped into the seat, still zipping his pants.

"They're right there!" he whispered, pointing past her.

"You don't think I know that?"

The hood slammed, and the kid started toward the first sedan.

"My gas," said Tracy.

"Just gonna start theirs, too."

"Mine first. I was here before them."

The kid gave her a look that said she was a pain in the ass, but Tracy just smiled.

"I'm not going to be able to do this by myself, after all," she said, turning to Earl. "I thought I could, but I can't."

Earl sighed, but he seemed to realize that it was way too late to argue.

"What do you want me to do?"

Tracy nibbled her lip.

"I'm going to try to time it, so I pull out just a little bit ahead of those guys. I'll turn the van so you're on their side. I want you to leave the box on your seat, get out, and fiddle with the hood like you're trying to open it. But keep your back to them. When they start rolling come back like you're climbing into the car, take the box, and shut them down."

She passed the box to him, and he nestled it on the seat beside him.

"And then what?"

"I'm going to slip out on my side with the gun. While they're confused about what's just happened to their cars I'm going to get Marilyn."

"What happens if they start shooting?"

Tracy swallowed a large lump in her own throat, not wanting to tell Earl that they would almost certainly start shooting.

"I'll have to shoot back."

"Jesus," muttered Earl.

The kid returned, topped off the tank, and gave Tracy a funny look.

"Twenty gallons even. That'll be eighty-five fifty with tax."

Tracy handed him a hundred.

"Keep the change," she said.

The kid smiled for the first time.

"Mostly what I do here is argue with drivers over the price or get their license plates when they drive off. Thanks."

"If you hear any loud noises," she said, catching his eye. "Keep your head down."

His eyebrows knitted together, and he walked off shaking his head.

Tracy waited until she heard the ka-ching of another nozzle being shoved back into the pump before starting the van and rolling slowly out across the wide lot toward the entrance to the freeway. Her heart pounded again, but her hands didn't shake on the wheel. She took a deep breath, imagining aiming the pistol, imagining firing it. If she was going to have to shoot someone she wanted to damn well hit them. The men who were going to come barreling out of those cars were probably excellent marksmen, and they weren't likely to hesitate.

Earl sat stiffly beside her, staring straight ahead.

She tapped her brakes as though testing them, then rolled to a stop, watching her rearview as both drivers paid for their gas. Then she started toward the ramp again and suddenly angled across the ramp as though the van had stalled, and she couldn't make it to the shoulder. She nodded to Earl, but now he wouldn't look at her. Instead, he stared straight out the windshield, shaking his head.

"Earl!" she said. "Get out and check the hood! All you have to do is grab the box off the seat and fire it at the cars."

He kept shaking his head, frozen in place.

"Fine," she said, reaching for her door handle. "Stay in your seat."

He coughed, and she noticed tears in his eyes. He was shaking like a leaf.

"I can't do this kind of stuff," he said. "I just can't."

She sighed.

After all, it wasn't Earl's fault. Until a few hours ago he'd been living a nice little life with his machines, then she and Marilyn had shown up.

"All right," she said, sticking the pistol back in her pants and reaching for the box.

"You're still going to do it?"

"I don't have a choice! Right now those men are already wondering why we're sitting here."

Earl took a deep breath, wiping his eyes with both fists. He opened his door and slid out on his side of the van just as Tracy exited on the far side. She jerked the pistol out of her pants, holding the gun in front of her face with both hands. She could hear Earl slapping the hood and muttering to himself, and she suddenly wondered if her feet were visible under the vehicle.

"They're coming down the ramp," said Earl.

"Do it!" she shouted.

She heard the low rumble of the two sedan engines, the humming of tires, then another higher-pitched noise, and suddenly the engines were silent. She whirled around the rear of the van and was nearly run down by the first sedan–carrying Marilyn–as it crashed between the van and the guard rail. The engine had stopped, but the momentum of the car carried it past Tracy. The men in the front seat glared at her, reaching inside their jackets.

She fired the pistol without thinking, watching the passenger's head rock to the side as Marilyn kicked the driver so hard with both feet *his* head dropped onto the steering wheel. Tracy raced around the front of the van. The second car had crashed up onto the embankment, and the driver was already out, reaching for his gun. She shot him twice, but the passenger had already exited on the other side.

"Get Marilyn into the van!" she shouted at Earl.

There was a bang and the sound of ripping metal as a shot struck the side of the van. She ducked, returning fire at the gunman who crouched behind the second car. Glass exploded and the gunman ducked again. Instinctively Tracy dropped to the ground, spotted the man's feet, and fired three quick shots. The man screamed and dropped onto his side. She shot him twice more and leaped to her feet, turning back toward the van.

"Get in!" screamed Earl from the driver's seat.

Tracy jumped in, glancing over her shoulder and wondering if she could possibly be as pale as Marilyn who crouched in the back. As the van roared down the entrance to the freeway Tracy felt bile rising in her throat, and she gasped for breath.

"That was exciting," said Marilyn in a shaky voice.

Tracy was throwing up on the front floorboard.

"THAT WAS A STUPID stunt," said Marilyn, frowning over the paperclip she was flicking around in the keyhole of her handcuffs.

But Tracy could see through the girl's bravado. Her hands were shaking so badly that the clip kept bouncing out of the hole. Tracy slipped into the back and knelt on the floorboard hugging Marilyn and the girl leaned against her, still frowning, but sniffling, too.

"You're welcome," said Tracy.

"I'm sorry," said Earl, glancing over his shoulder at them both. "I kind of freaked out."

"You did fine," said Tracy.

"The Three Musketeers, "he said, his smile like a beacon. Then it died. "Those guys back there, the ones you shot-"

Tracy felt bile rising in her throat again. "It just happ ened... so fast... I didn't know what to do."

"I'm glad they're dead," said Marilyn.

Sometimes there seemed a hardness about the girl that was too dark and brittle even to have been caused by the kidnapping of her father.

"Maybe we should say a prayer for them or something," whispered Tracy.

"Are you serious?" asked Marilyn.

"They were human beings," Tracy whispered, slipping back into her own seat.

She had realized from the beginning, on a subliminal level, that what she was doing was dangerous, but now she had killed with her own hands. She had planned the confrontation knowing it would likely result in someone's death, and when the battle had started, she had killed without thinking. She needed some sort of absolution even if she wasn't religious.

"They weren't human," said Marilyn, her eyes hard. "To be human you have to act like a human being. Forget it."

But Tracy couldn't forget it. She knew that she'd remember the moment until the day she died because she could never forget that other moment, the one where both her parents were unable to explain the scene of horror she'd stumbled upon.

Marilyn finally clicked open her cuffs, tossing them disgustedly onto the floor at her feet.

"How did you know how to do that?" asked Tracy, staring at the manacles.

Marilyn shrugged.

"Rank taught me."

"He seems to have taught you a lot of interesting skills."

"You'd be surprised. My father never liked Rank, and I have to admit he had his bad side. But maybe now my dad would be happy that I learned some of the stuff I did."

"I am," muttered Tracy, grabbing the dash as Earl took an exit on two wheels.

"Slow down," said Marilyn, in a calm voice, resting her hand on Earl's shoulder.

"Which direction?" asked Earl, his voice still shaky.

"It doesn't matter," said Tracy. "Drive until you get to another highway, then take it. Do that until we're lost."

The little beacon on the locator between the seats wasn't moving.

"You left Earl's keys in the car," she said.

Marilyn frowned, glancing at the device.

"I wondered how you knew which car to follow."

Tracy smiled.

"Earl's full of surprises."

She rested the pistol on the console beside the locator, discovering that touching the gun no longer bothered her. In fact, she now felt safer knowing the pistol was within her reach. The speed of the transformation troubled her because she had no idea what this new person was capable of. When she looked up at Marilyn again the girl smiled, but there was steel in her blue eyes.

"You have a plan," said Tracy.

"Go to ground," said Earl, nodding.

Marilyn shook her head.

"We can turn around and use that locator to follow the men who took me."

"I know where they're going."

"Where?" asked Marilyn.

"Ash's office in downtown DC."

"That's not where they took my dad," said Marilyn.

"How do you know?"

"Because I overheard the men talking about the *others*. They were wondering if I was going to end up out west with them."

"So, they're alive," said Tracy, a faint trace of hope rising.

Perhaps, just perhaps, Beatrice wasn't dead. Maybe Ash had taken her as he had Marilyn's parents. But why capture them and try to murder *her?*

"Better to keep on the move," repeated Earl. "Find some place to hide."

Marilyn shook her head.

"I'm not hiding anymore. I'm finding my dad and getting him back."

"I'm tired of running, too," said Tracy, staring at the gun.

The pistol wasn't likely to do them much good against the powers holding Marilyn's dad and the others, but it was a symbol of her decision to stop being a passive foil for others' plans.

"Head west," she said, "toward Terra Diablo."

"Do you know the exact location," asked Tracy, staring at Earl.

He shook his head.

"They took me there in the back of a panel wagon."

"We know it's in New Mexico," said Marilyn. "We can detour along the way to check out any names on the list in between."

Earl appeared to be fighting a terrible inner battle. His head cocked first this way, then that, his lips sucked in between his teeth, his eyes fretful and watery. Finally, he sighed a great sigh and nodded, stuttering.

"All f...for one. And one f...for all."

He stuck out his hand, and Tracy and Marilyn placed their own atop it.

"Through the looking glass it is," said Marilyn, with an evil grin.

"You have no idea," muttered Tracy.

"It isn't exactly stealing," Marilyn assured Earl, who hovered in the shadows beside his van.

Tracy watched the girl's nimble fingers as she used tools from one of Earl's kits to hotwire the Jeep on the back of the dealership lot.

"Another of Rank's talents?" asked Tracy.

The girl was full of surprises both physical and emotional. She had the guts of an Army Ranger and apparently nearly as much special training.

Marilyn nodded, slamming the hood.

They'd chosen the rig because of its remoteness from the highway out front and because it had deeply tinted windows all around. The big V-8 was another selling point. If they needed to move, Tracy wanted to be able to move fast.

"We're leaving your van as a trade-in," Marilyn informed Earl.

"I still like my van better," he whined, helping Tracy transfer machinery into the SUV, anyway.

"I know you do," said Marilyn, placing a set of stolen plates on the new car. "But unfortunately, I'm afraid that the bad guys will figure out who you are and find your registration listed with the county. They'll be looking for the van. Besides, if it rains those bullets holes are gonna be pretty leaky."

Tracy shoved more stuff into the rear seat until there was barely space for anyone to sit. "

They'll find the van back here pretty quick," said Earl.

"There are a lot of other cars," said Marilyn. "With any luck no one will even notice it for a few hours in the morning, maybe even a day or two will go by. Lots like this take in a high inventory of trade-ins."

"Well, one can hope," said Tracy, climbing behind the wheel.

She drove slowly along the highway lined with car dealerships and tall metal streetlights that turned the night into a glaringly bad copy of the day.

"Maybe we're making a big mistake," said Earl, struggling with his seat. "Maybe no one on the list knows anything, and we're just going to draw attention to ourselves."

Marilyn shook her head.

"Tracy's right. Someone on that list must know what's going on."

Earl shrugged, finally getting his seat to recline and closing his eyes as though the argument were over. Almost instantly he started snoring in his seat.

"Maybe we should find a safe hiding place for him and his gear, too," mused Tracy.

"You think he'll slow us down?"

"I just don't want to get him hurt."

Marilyn shook her head.

"Earl's safer with us than he'd be on his own. He's not an easy type to hide in case you haven't noticed."

"I guess he would be pretty conspicuous anywhere we put him," Tracy agreed. "Unless one of the people on the list would take him in."

She tapped the address book.

"That might be an idea... if any of them are home, or alive," agreed Marilyn. "On the other hand, we might be looking at things backward."

"How do you mean?"

"Earl saved our asses with his gizmos."

Tracy frowned. She'd been worried about taking care of Earl when in fact it was Earl's inventiveness that had been taking care of them. Without the locator, Marilyn would be long gone. Without the surprise they created using the device for *stopping lobster boats* there was little chance they could have successfully separated the girl from the trained gunmen.

"But we're the ones who got him into trouble," she argued.

"I don't think so," said Marilyn. "He was already in trouble or your buddy, Shiver, wouldn't have hidden him out like that. Shiver kept a book that he knew was dangerous, you stole it, and somewhere along the way, this guy Ash got wind of where all those people were hiding. Maybe because of something you did. Maybe not. But that's a pretty long and fuzzy line of guilt if you ask me. We're just middlemen."

Marilyn leaned back in the seat, stretching like a cat, and Tracy was amazed by the sense of calm she exuded. In the reflected glow of the headlights, the girl's natural beauty shone softly, like an alabaster vase caught in an errant moonbeam, and suddenly Tracy couldn't get a darker image out of her mind, a picture of Marilyn dead and bleeding, her body twisted, her face bruised and swollen.

Because of her.

She was responsible for the other two lives in this car, and instead of shepherding them into hiding she was leading them into more danger. But she knew instinctively that Marilyn was right, and it was the only thing they could do. If they tried to hide Ash would find them eventually, when they least expected it.

She shook her head, trying to erase the images from her mind, trying to think of some way out of the mess they were in. She knew there was one place she could hide Earl, and Marilyn for that matter, if the girl would submit to it. But Tracy wasn't ready to face going there, not even to save her life or the lives of the others.

"I loved my dad so much," Marilyn blurted.

Tracy nodded, noticing the girl's use of past tense.

"I'm sure he's okay," she lied.

Marilyn shook her head.

"I didn't mean it like that. I meant... the last few years things... I don't know."

"What happened?"

"I got kind of wild my junior year in high school. Rebelling a lot. My dad was the strict disciplinarian sort, and that made things worse. I hung out with a bad crowd. Did things I'm not too proud of, just to do them. You know what I mean?"

Tracy nodded. She could relate to Marilyn's feelings of rejection and rebellion. She'd never gotten into trouble with the law, but she'd tried drugs, and alcohol, and run with the crazy crowd for a while just to be *in* with anyone who would accept a child of nutty parents.

"Rank was attractive *because* my dad disliked him so much," said Marilyn. "But it's funny. He never disliked my dad. In fact, he told me a lot of times that Dad was right to distrust the government, and the law. Rank and my dad were opposite sides of the same coin. Only one hated the government because he knew they couldn't be trusted, and the other feared them because he was a criminal. It took me a while to understand the difference."

"But you do now?"

Marilyn nodded.

"Don't you?"

"I'm not sure anymore," said Tracy, staring out the window. "My situation is a little different."

"Why?"

"Because my parents were criminals," she whispered. "Or at least that's what I thought."

"You're not sure?"

"I'm not sure of anything anymore," she admitted.

She had never wanted to believe that her parents could be the deranged killers the government had made them out to be. But the only evidence she'd had to the contrary was a cryptic note her mother had shoved into Tracy's fist that night before forcing her into hiding.

AventCorp was all the note said.

Give it to Ki, her mother told her. *Make sure that Ki gets it.*

Tracy had disobeyed, later turning herself in to the police, and then deciding to investigate the mysterious company herself. Now she wondered if she'd made another mistake.

Marilyn nodded.

"Things change."

Once again, the girl had made a statement as deep as a haiku, taking Tracy's breath away.

"Yes," she whispered. "They do."

"I hated my dad for a while," said Marilyn, her eyes watering. "But never really. You know what I mean?"

Tracy was unable to speak, staring straight ahead as the night rolled past.

"I'd come in sometimes all fucked up and get so mad at him I couldn't even think straight," said Marilyn. "I'd scream, and rant, and throw things, and I'd really wish that he'd get that mad, too, so that we could just have it out at last. Whatever the hell *it* was. But he'd just catch me and wrap me in his arms and hold me and tell me that everything was going to be all right until all I could do was cry. And then he'd put me to bed, and I'd just want to die for hurting him again. But my pride wouldn't let me say I was sorry."

Tracy felt as though her throat had constricted to the point at which a pin could not slip through much less enough air to breathe.

"I ran away with Rank for a couple of weeks. That really did piss my dad off, but after a while, he gave up arguing with me, trying to lock me in my room, stupid things like that. Then one day I woke up and there was a picture on my bed, an old photograph of him, me, and my mom. I don't know who took it, but we were sitting around the kitchen table laughing. And I could remember what we were talking about, it was something silly I'd done at school that day. I was about twelve, right before my mom died. I held that picture for so long... and I cried and cried, and when my dad came back in the room he just sat on the side of my bed and held me again and didn't say anything. I hugged him so tight, and I felt so bad, and we didn't say anything."

Tracy turned toward the window, wishing that she and her parents had been blessed with a moment like that. Instead, they had parted still strangers.

"Finally, he stood up and looked at me and smiled, and he said *Mare, I can't stand to lose you, not ever. It would break my heart. So you do whatever you want to do whenever you need to do it with whoever you want to do it with, and I'll be there when you need me. Just please be careful, because if anything ever happens to you it's gonna kill me.* That was when I knew that I had to break up with Rank and why."

Tracy nodded.

"So, give me the next address," said Marilyn, reaching for the book. "And I'll find the shortest route there."

Tracy passed her the notebook.

"You understand now why I'm gonna kill all those bastards?" asked Marilyn.

Tracy nodded, fingering the pistol in her belt.

MARK SAT ON THE floor of the tiny punishment cell that was lit only by a paper-thin beam of light from beneath the iron door. There was nowhere else to sit. The room was a concrete box barely large enough for him to lie down in, and it was frigid to boot. The cold radiating from the floor seeped into him, and he couldn't help but recall the freezing water of the tank. It seemed as though fate had willed that he was destined to freeze to death in some dark hole.

His mind floated through its own deep, slow-moving state of iciness that had started upon his arrival in Koenig's cell, dropped a degree or two in Elgin's office, then dipped near zero as he was escorted back into the long hallway.

Carl Elgin
Assistant Warden
Leavenworth.

As the unbelievable reality of his situation dawned on him, Mark felt as though he were inside the beam of light again, as though his body were starting to disassociate from his mind. As hard as it was to accept, Mark knew that he had traveled not only through space, but through time, and he recalled Ash's words.

If you're interested, we aim by the density of the target.

Stone.

That explained why he was here. Leavenworth was constructed of more stone than probably any other building complex in the country and built over solid bedrock. And where better to send a guinea pig than the most secure lockup in the country where he'd be certain to remain for at least as long as it took to retrieve him? Only how long was that?

It occurred to Mark that *his* time and Ash's were two different things. Ash could send him here, then wait a year and still retrieve him a minute after Mark got here, or vice versa. So why hadn't he? The only reason Mark could figure was that Ash had intended he stay here for a certain amount of time, perhaps less than an hour, and then return. Only Elgin's order to remove the collar had either fouled Ash's plans, something had gone wrong back on Ash's end, or Ash had never intended to bring him back to begin with. Yet obviously that was what the collar was for. It wasn't just a locator, it was a way of tracking the traveler so the machine could pull him back into the *present.*

The guards had managed to cut the collar off with a hacksaw when none of them had been able to pick the lock. He'd noticed that all of their watches were the old-fashioned, three-handed numbers. Not one of them wore a digital. There wasn't one calendar watch in the bunch. Now when had calendar watches come out?

Not that it mattered. He was in solitary confinement in the toughest prison in the country, at some unknown date, and the most he could hope for was that someone would decide that he was crazy and move him into a mental facility from which it might be easier to escape. But when he conjured up a picture of an early mental hospital, he wondered if he wasn't better off where he was.

Now–without the collar–he didn't even have any way of getting back to his own time. Of course, reappearing in the present in Ash's lab probably wasn't going to be much better than being left in this hole in Leavenworth sometime in the past. Mark could imagine what would happen to him if Ash got him back.

Questioning again. Ash's particular kind of questioning. Until Ash was certain that he had drained every drop of information out of Mark. Then death and after that an autopsy. The thought that the autopsy might come *before* death didn't bear mulling over.

He began to shiver, and he wondered how many prisoners had died in these punishment cells. He'd heard stories about penal conditions in the early to mid-years of the past century, tales about inmates dying and their bodies disappearing into shallow, unmarked graves. So far, he hadn't been beaten, but neither had he been fed or offered water or warmer clothing. And the look in Cripps' eyes–and the fear in Koenig's–had served to assure Mark that violence was an everyday occurrence here.

He leaned back against the wall farthest from the door, surprised that the concrete didn't seem as cold there as the floor. He rested his head against it, and the shivers that wracked his body seemed to shift inside as though his terrible mental chill were their actual cause.

It was as if he vibrated on some frequency that affected his internal organs but didn't extend to his skin.

He lifted his hands to his face, trying to see their silhouette against the knife edge of dim light beneath the steel door. They were moving so fast that the edges blurred, and he wondered if he was about to pass out. Suddenly he had the sickening feeling of sinking into the concrete wall behind him, and he sat bolt upright, then wobbled to his feet. He reached for the wall only to stumble forward when his hand passed through it as though it were not there.

Was the wall real or not? Was it just a shadow, the cell bigger than he had thought? He withdrew his hand, feeling it pass through something as ephemeral as mist.

He stepped forward and his nose contacted the concrete painfully. So, it wasn't a shadow. He shook his head. What the hell was going on? Still experiencing the powerful quivering throughout his body, he reached for the wall again, steadying himself as his hand once more passed through it, and suddenly he realized that whatever was occurring inside his body was affecting things around him and his senses of touch and sight as well.

He could see inside the wall and sense its structure down to the atomic level. Everywhere his hand passed he could feel the movement of molecules, atoms, and structures far smaller, a system of *being* that created and formed the wall and the gravelly base beyond. Incredibly, he discovered that he could change the structure of both, watching as the concrete steamed away like rapidly melting ice. Wherever he pointed his fingers, cement and steel and then even the soil and bedrock beyond flowed away. It was as though the mass in front of him was no more substantial than a marshmallow, and he directed a powerful blowtorch.

He jerked his hand away, and after a moment the shivering stopped, but the hole–big enough to crawl through and perhaps three feet deep–remained. Testing, he reached out with his hand again and tried to *see* the structure. Slowly he felt his body beginning to quiver and once more he withdrew his hand.

Had the journey through Ash's machine–through time and space–done something to him, somehow *twisted* him to give him this incredible power? Perhaps the drug cocktail had something to do with it as well, although he had no idea of why or how. Somehow, he was able to understand the world around him on a new level, a level that no man had ever understood before, and not only understand it. He could change it as well.

So now he had a way out.

The trouble was that behind the wall lay a huge mass of dirt and stone. He guessed that he was at least twenty feet underground, and the exterior walls of the prison were probably a hundred feet away or more. He had no idea if he could tunnel that far using this newfound talent, but there was nothing else to do. He didn't want to consider what was going to happen to him when the warden arrived in the morning. Mr. Cripps might not be as adept as Ash at torture, but Mark was pretty sure the man had his own techniques for getting answers out of taciturn prisoners.

Before they decided that he was a nutcase and gave up on discovering how he'd appeared inside a locked cell, he might well be a vegetable. Beyond that Ash might not be happy leaving him here. It was quite possible that when he recovered the empty collar, he'd send someone back to get Mark. Or more likely just to ensure that Mark never lived to tell anyone his unbelievable tale. He had to get out tonight.

Only it occurred to him once again that *tonight* meant nothing to Ash. Ash could probably send a whole kill team here at any minute, or Mark might leave some historical trace of his movement, and the team might be eating sandwiches right now, waiting for him to pop his head above ground. Reasoning out the possibilities gave Mark a headache, and none of it was getting him anywhere.

He took a deep breath and reached back into the hole, shifting the atomic structure of the matter, turning some of the dirt to finer dust, some to oxygen and helium, some to water that quickly soaked away into the soil. But much of it seemed to be converted to simple energy. The tunnel glowed with a brilliant light that helped him orient himself, and for a while, the heat grew intense, until he learned to control that as well. He crawled slowly forward, sweeping both hands before him like a seer gesturing in front of a crystal ball.

When he reached the giant foundation stones of the exterior prison wall he stopped, and as he did the light died quickly away, leaving him in total darkness. But when he started tunneling again, edging the hole up sharply toward the surface and broke through, he saw that he was in a wide, brightly lit killing zone overlooked by a walkway along the high wall. The men pacing above were preoccupied with the interior grounds, but he knew he could not chance busting out this close to the prison. He headed downward again, tunneling toward a copse of trees in the distance.

By the time he ran across the deep roots of the woods, he'd begun to realize the limits of his powers. He was shaking both from the internal quivering and exhaustion as he dragged himself weakly up out of the hole and onto the grass. The moon was full, and a million, tiny blue stars clustered overhead as he lay there on his back, knowing that there was no prison on earth that could hold him now, and that there was nowhere in this world that he could hide.

THE SUN HADN'T YET risen, but a dim glow in the east told Mark it was about to.

Before he made it a quarter mile through the woods a fog blew in. Then it started to drizzle, and by the time he reached the first road the light mist had turned to a steady rain. He'd lost all track of time in the tunnel, but it had been late night when they'd thrown him into the solitary cell, and sooner or later they were bound to remember to feed him. He figured he had only a couple of hours at best before his escape was noticed and every police officer in the county was out looking for him. Finally, he stumbled across a farmstead with an old pickup parked in the drive, with the keys in the ignition.

He wondered what kind of situation he was going to put these people in, leaving them with no transportation out here in the sticks. But what option did he have? The best he could do was to leave the truck somewhere unharmed so that it would be returned to them. He worked the wobbly stick shift into neutral, letting the vehicle coast down to the road before revving the engine and taking off as fast at the old truck would go.

He had no idea where he was headed, simply that he had to get as far away from Leavenworth as possible in as short an amount of time as he could manage. He had no money, no ID, and no clothes other than what he had on his back. He needed to get quickly out of what would surely become the first search zone, then find someplace to hole up and think.

By the time the sun was long up he was running low on gas just outside Tulsa, and he rummaged through the glovebox, finding two dollars in change. He stopped in a gas station on the outskirts of the city, surprised when the old man running the place offered to not only gas him up but check the oil and the tires. Mark told him to put in a dollar-and-a-half worth of gas, then bought a Coke for nickel, and twenty cents worth of peanuts. The candy bars seemed just a little too big, and he noticed that the payphone beside the door took a nickel just like the soda machine.

It turned out that he'd gotten almost seven gallons for his money. The tank was half full again. He noticed a calendar hanging in the front window of the station as he pulled out. 1959, and June 6th, was circled.

The nuts settled his stomach as he drove down the road again, but he still had no idea of where to go. He watched in fascination as what looked like the world's largest classic car show rolled around him. He hadn't realized that Studebakers had been so popular. He felt as though he were in the middle of some old documentary, only the colors were too bright. The sky was a rich blue, fading to crimson where another rainstorm had passed in the distance.

The buildings in Tulsa, though blocky looking–with little glass and almost no stainless steel–still shone bright granite gray in the late afternoon sun. And the kids he saw all seemed to be wearing sleeveless sweaters and riding shiny red bikes with giant white-wall balloon tires and baskets. There was a noticeable lack of magnetic signs, no electronic time or temperature displays, and an excess of curly neon lights.

He kept heading west.

A hundred miles down the highway he knew he had to make a decision. The old truck was a gas guzzler, and pretty soon he was going to have to eat something *real*. And he was going to need to sleep. All of which required money. He pulled off the main road onto a small lane bordered by open farmland and a few scattered houses, looking for a home with no car in the drive. When he spotted one, he pulled up beside it, considering his options.

He really didn't want to steal again, certainly not from poor farmers, but he was lost in a world in which he had no place. He had to at least find a refuge where he could figure out how to create an identity for himself. Then he'd look for some kind of work to pay the bills while he tried to figure out if there was any possible way to get home.

He stared at the weathered old house, trying to make up his mind. A light breeze blew white curtains into and out of tall windows alongside the porch, and cattle lowed in the fields out back. But it looked as though everyone was gone. Maybe he could find a can of gas and enough to eat inside, and that would be that. He stepped lightly up onto the porch, easing open the screen. It screeched like a wounded cat, and he instinctively closed it slowly behind him, but that only made the noise lower-pitched, but more pronounced.

Finally, he just let it slap shut.

The kitchen was right off the tiny front parlor, and when he opened the old fridge crowned by its big, round, loudly humming compressor, he was pleased to find a half-eaten apple pie on the top shelf. He carried that and some sliced ham to the table where he discovered that he was hungrier than he'd ever been in his life, devouring the entire pie and most of the ham, and washing it down with cold milk. He carried the dishes to the sink, washed them, and placed them in a drainer.

By the time his hunger was sated, he had decided that there was no way he was stealing anything else from these people. He was headed toward the door when a man's creaky voice stopped him.

"That you, Ted?"

Mark spun and found himself eye-to-eye with a wrinkled geezer in a pair of overalls faded the color of blue ice. The man–lolling back in a rickety old rocker that had been empty when Mark had passed by before–cocked his bald head, squinting, raising one shaky hand to point at Mark.

"Who are you?"

Mark shook his head.

"You don't know me," he said, his shoulders sagging. "I was hungry."

The man nodded, waggling a finger at Mark.

"Come here, boy."

As Mark stepped into the tiny bedroom that smelled of Old Spice and tobacco juice, he noticed a brass spittoon on the floor beside the man's leg.

"Say you're hungry?" said the man, appraising him.

He was thin as a withered sapling, with a thick underbrush of white whiskers sprouting out of his wrinkled face.

"Yes, sir," said Mark. "I'm afraid I stole some food from your refrigerator."

The man nodded.

"Take what you want out of that icebox, son," said the man. "And don't hang your head. I been that hungry myself once or twicet upon a time."

"Thank you," said Mark, weakly.

"You ain't hurt no one, have you?"

"No, sir," said Mark.

Not lately, anyway.

"You broken any laws?"

"I took your food," said Mark.

He neglected to mention the stolen truck or the huge hole in the grounds of a federal penitentiary.

"Well, that's no great crime. What're you running from, then?"

"It's a long story," said Mark. "And I don't think you'd believe it."

"Why don't you tell me anyway," said the old man, revealing a toothless grin. "Ted's gone to Guthrie for tractor parts. Martha and the kids are visiting relatives for a couple of days, and I'm here all by my lonesome."

Mark shook his head. "You really wouldn't believe my story. I don't."

The old man chuckled and waved toward the quilt-covered day bed.

"Sit. I'm up for a good fairy tale. I been living here doing just about nothing for so long I'm starting to think maybe Methuselah and I are in some kind of contest. How much crazier can your story be than that?"

"Crazier," said Mark.

The old man shrugged.

"Let me hear it, then. There's nothing good on the radio anymore. And that television stuff... it's just crap. You can pay for your meal with a tall tale."

So, Mark told him everything, right from the beginning, including the part about him being from the future. It wasn't as though the old man was ever going to understand or believe, and no one was likely to believe the old guy if *he* retold the story. But the telling seemed to help Mark organize his thoughts.

"And you just tunneled your way out of Leavenworth," muttered the old man.

He'd seemed to grow a little more uneasy as the tale progressed, but Mark just couldn't find a good place to stop. Now he was sure the geezer thought he was an escapee from a looney bin, not Leavenworth.

"Unhuh," said Mark, sighing.

"With your hands."

Mark nodded, glancing at his fingertips. With a sudden burst of insight, he began searching for the feeling he'd gotten inside the solitary cell. He felt the internal vibration starting up, and he was afraid for a moment that he might inadvertently hurt the old codger. The man's eyes grew wide and frightened.

"What're you doing, boy?" he said. "Stop clenching your teeth like that. Your face looks hard as an anvil."

"Watch," muttered Mark, aiming his fingertips toward the cracked and worn linoleum on the floor.

Wherever Mark pointed the floor was cut as though sliced by a laser, and the old man shoved the rocker back until it slammed against the wall.

"What the hell you doing, boy?" he shouted.

"I told you," said Mark, discovering that not only could he cut the floor right through to the joists, but he could open it like a trapdoor. He lifted it easily, waving toward the crawlspace below. "This is how I tunneled out of Leavenworth."

The old man leaned forward to peer through the hole in the floor.

"That's the damndest thing I ever seen. You say these fellas that sent you here to the *past* gave you the ability to do this?"

"I don't think they meant to."

"Can you fix that?" said the old man, nodding toward the floor. "Ted'll be fit to be tied if he comes home and sees a mess like that."

"I don't know," said Mark, frowning.

He lowered the section of floor back into place and discovered to his surprise that it was even easier remelding the material than it was cutting it to begin with.

"Well," said the old man, rising to his feet, and giving the floor a stomp to test it out. "I guess you do beat all."

"That's as good a way of putting it as any," said Mark, smiling.

The old man studied Mark's face, frowning.

"You got no place to go do ya?"

Mark shook his head.

"You can't stay here for long. Good folks around for the most part. But they gossip worse'n old hens. Come with me," he said, heading down the hall.

Mark followed him out the back door where he had Mark help him down off the stoop.

"Where are you going?" asked Mark, as the old man started across the dusty backyard toward a ramshackle shed.

The old man stopped, glancing at Mark's pickup.

"You must have stolen that when you escaped, right?"

Mark nodded, embarrassed, but the old man said nothing about catching him in a lie.

"They'll be looking for it," said the geezer.

He tried to shove the garage door aside but didn't have the strength. Mark opened it for him.

"This is a nineteen-thirty-six Packard," said the old man, jerking a dusty tarp off the big black sedan that gleamed in the sun. "I bought it the year before Cloris died. Never got a chance to drive it much, and when Ted got back from the war, he didn't want it, had to have a new coupe for him and Martha. But I've kept it up. It's full of gas, and it runs like a top. The keys are in it. Pull it out, and park your truck in there. No one opens this old shed except me."

Mark shook his head.

"Why would you do this?"

The old man shrugged.

"Why wouldn't I do it? I believe your story right enough now. There's no sense I can see of you spending the rest of your life in a nuthouse or prison because you got mixed up with the wrong sort of people. And I got no use for this old car. I was just keeping it for sentimental reasons, but I guess the good Lord had another plan for it."

Mark started the car and parked it alongside the house. Then he pulled the truck into the garage and closed the doors. The old man was already trying to renegotiate the back stoop, and Mark helped him into the house again.

"Come on," said the old man, leading the way to the kitchen. "You raid the ice box. Take whatever you want. There's wax paper over the sink, and paper bags under it. I'll tell Ted a bum come to the door beggin'. He knows me well enough to know I'd be a sucker for that."

Mark stood there for a moment, watching the old man disappear into his bedroom again, wondering what strange twist of fate had brought him to this farm, what coincidence had mixed up his atoms, or added the right combination of drugs, to give him the power he needed to escape the highest security prison in the US. Shaking his head he turned back to the fridge, found a loaf of bread, and began making a large pile of ham sandwiches. When the bag was full, he placed it on the counter just as the old man called him.

The codger was leaning over the open top drawer of his dresser, and as Mark eased alongside the old man handed him a thick white envelope.

"It's not much to some, I reckon," said the old man. "There's a lot of ones and fives in there, but it's nearly two hundred dollars. It's all I've got."

"I can't take this," said Mark, trying to slip the money back into the drawer, but the old man shoved it shut.

"It's just pin money. Ted and Martha see to everything I want. You're going to need it a hell of a lot more than I do."

Mark sighed.

He really did hate taking the old man's savings, but it was better than stealing.

"If there's any way, I'll pay you back."

The old man shook his head.

"Don't you go coming around here again or go trying to contact me. In a couple of nights, I'll wait till everyone's asleep, and drive that pickup down the road and drop it off. But don't you be coming back this way. Not for a long while, anyways."

Mark nodded.

"I can't ever thank you enough."

The old man harumphed.

"I reckon I'll get my thanks soon. Nobody beats Methuselah at his own game."

Mark shook his head.

"Of all the houses I could have stopped at..."

The old man smiled, patting his shoulder.

"The good Lord deals a funny hand sometimes. You never know how the chips are going to fall, but in the long run things work out. They balance."

"You really believe that?"

"Don't you?"

Mark shrugged.

"My life has been out of balance for a while, I think."

"Sometimes we got to get it back into balance our ownselves."

Mark frowned.

"Have you got a pen?"

"A pencil," said the old man, producing a piece of one from a cup on the dresser.

Mark tore off the flap of the envelope and wrote a brief note, handing it and twenty dollars to the old man.

"Is that enough, you think?"

The old man nodded. "I'll get their address from the truck registration and mail this and the money to them. Don't you worry. Folks understand people falling on hard times."

He shook hands with Mark, then stood on the front porch shielding his eyes from the setting sun and waving as Mark drove away down the road.

EARL SPRAWLED ACROSS THE back seat, quietly playing a harmonica he'd dug out of a small bag buried beneath his gear–some tune that sounded like the Rolling Stones–while Marilyn drove. As the highway rolled endlessly ahead, Tracy pictured the three of them adrift in a small boat, hopefully heading for shore, but just as likely to be swallowed by a whale.

For years–long before that hateful night separated her and her parents forever–she had felt lost and alone. Now she was no longer alone, but she had only succeeded in getting her two companions lost with her, and she lifted her eyes to the stars, voicing a private prayer that nothing bad would happen to them. On the eastern plains of Colorado, the night sky was an immense black bowl, and she imagined them all magically transported into that vast empty *safeness* where no danger could reach them.

Suddenly one of the stars *jerked*, and Tracy frowned, wondering if her vision had just developed a glitch. Sometimes you saw things out of the corner of your eye that weren't really there. Then it happened again. The third time the star traveled far and fast enough that she had to turn her head to keep up.

"I'll be damned," she muttered.

"What?" said Marilyn.

Tracy pointed to a constellation ahead. "Something moved up there."

"Moved?"

Just then the star shot back across the sky close to its original position.

"Wow," said Marilyn, smiling.

"What do you think it is?" asked Tracy.

The girl shrugged. "It's a UFO."

"No. I mean really. Could it be a helicopter or something?"

"Not unless helicopters can fly at like three or four thousand miles an hour. Look!"

The star began a series of impossible maneuvers, jinking up, down, across, back and forth like a fly in a bottle.

"Now, that's cool," said Marilyn.

"There must be an explanation," said Tracy, frowning.

"I just gave you the only explanation I know of."

Tracy glared at her.

"It's a trick of the light. Swamp gas. Venus. Reflections off the upper atmosphere."

Marilyn laughed.

"Done a lot of reading, have you?"

Tracy's expression softened a little.

"It's not a UFO."

"All UFO means is it's unidentified. Even if it is one of the things you listed, we don't know which. That makes it a UFO."

Tracy sighed, nodding.

"There it goes," said Marilyn, lifting her chin skyward as the white dot zipped away over the mountains.

Tracy turned to stare at the empty land and sky outside her passenger window, feeling suddenly as though the disappearing light had stolen both the safety and the magic out of the night.

"My parents believed in UFOs," she said. "They also believed in pyramids, crystal therapy, voodoo spells, cattle mutilations, crop circles, Ouija boards, and poltergeists. Maybe fairies. I'm not sure."

"And that embarrassed you."

Tracy nodded. More than embarrassed. Humiliated. Abashed. Mortified.

"When I was little, I believed in UFOs, among other things, but by the time I was twelve I had discovered how very different my family was. The other houses on the block didn't have charms made out of feathers and leaves hanging from the curtains or geometric designs cut into the grass on the front lawn. Halloween wasn't fun for me. It was the night the other kids hid out front of our house chanting about the weirdos."

Marilyn shook her head.

"Kids can be a lot crueler than adults."

"The adults were cruel enough. My parents hired a staff of civil rights attorneys to keep neighborhood groups from forcing us out, at least until they'd made enough money to buy us a place with no neighbors. One of the cases actually went to the Supreme Court. My parents won, but that was just another blow to me, seeing their pictures in the paper. I assume you know what tie-dye looks like?"

Marilyn nodded.

"How did they support themselves? If they could afford property and attorneys, they must have had jobs."

Tracy shook her head.

"Not the kind of jobs you're thinking of. They published *The New Age Bulletin and Lifechance Gazette Blog and Newsletter.*"

"Lifechance?"

"It's a term my mother came up with. She believed that everyone was born with just so many chances, kind of like a cat. Supposedly the Gazette taught people how to find out what their chances were and how to grab them once they spotted them. By the time I left home for college, there were over half a million subscribers worldwide."

"Wow. That's a lot of readers. They must have been doing something right."

Tracy's frown was so sad Marilyn turned back to the road.

"Because of them, I had no life and no friends. Because of them I... had to do things I can never forget and never forgive myself for. A child shouldn't have to grow up that way."

"I'm sorry," said Marilyn, quietly. "I know people...R ank for instance...who never had any love in their lives. I never had to live that way. It must have been terribly hard."

Tracy's throat constricted so that her whisper sounded like a croak.

"There was love," she muttered. "There was lots of love."

She didn't want to remember that, but she had no choice. To deny it would be a lie, and then what else might be a lie as well? Any warmth remembered threatened her reasons for doing what she'd had to do. She recalled the nights when she was little and crawled into bed with her parents because she was frightened of the shadows in her room or a passing storm, and her father's strong arms around her felt warm and safe. That was not the action of a cold man, a man who could do the things he'd been accused of later.

She recalled the sound of her mother's voice on the day she had fallen from her bike, not only breaking her arm but dislocating a shoulder. The pain was intense, and she dearly wanted her father's arms around her then, but he was gone on some errand, leaving her and her mother alone. She lay there on the hard surface of the driveway, feeling the pain rising like a fire in her small body, wondering if she'd peed in her panties and disgraced herself, trying desperately to push herself up on her one good arm. She felt her mother's hands gently cradling her face, and saw tears in her mother's eyes, but she felt strength in her mother as well, and it gave her courage even through the agony that was almost more than she could bear.

"It's going to be all right, sweetheart," her mother said. "It's going to be all right."

Unbelievably, her mother–who wasn't much larger than a child herself, lifted her off the ground as though she weighed no more than a feather, and carried her to the car, placing her gently in the back seat and quickly returning with a blanket to cover her. All the way to the doctor's house–a friend of the family, not one of those corporate hacks her father was certain were running illegal experiments for the government–her mother kept up a running monologue.

"Don't you worry. You just hold on. Everything's going to be all right. Think of a nice place, a quiet pretty place. Try to put the pain somewhere else. Outside yourself. I love you, sweetie. You're going to be all right. I promise. You're going to be just fine."

Babbling of course. But it didn't sound like babbling to a frightened, pain-filled eight-year-old. It sounded like an angel's voice, reassuring her that the pain was going to go away, that she wasn't going to be deformed, crippled for life, or bleed to death, all the things that were rattling through her mind but that she didn't have the strength to mention because she was clamping her jaw shut so tight her teeth ached.

An angel's voice.

Her father's arms.

What was she missing? How could the man who had held her in her sleep, the woman who had lifted her as though she were the crown jewels of England and cared for her like the most precious of patients in the weeks after, how could these people be the same people she knew them to be, callous, cold-blooded murderers? They couldn't have been, of course. She'd been deceived, by Ash and by AventCorp, but how and why? What could Ash have possibly cared about a couple of New-Age, California kooks?

She felt Marilyn's hand on her shoulder, and it felt warm and comforting.

"I was ashamed of my dad for a while, too," said Marilyn. "Being an appliance repair man didn't seem like much to me. Now... I don't really know what he was, but I haven't felt ashamed since he was taken. Just fear and anger and frustration and rage. And love. No matter what happens. I'll always love my dad."

"I had them committed," said Tracy, sinking back into the seat and closing her eyes.

IN 1959 THE CONDUCTOR, Eduard van Beinum died. So did Mario Lanza. Richard Rogers produced *The Sound of Music* on Broadway. Henry Cowell first performed his *Symphony No. 13, Madras.* Bill Mauldin won his second Pulitzer.

Mark sat on the edge of the bed in the tiny motel cabin, listening to trucks racing by on Highway 56, comparing this world, this roadside hostelry to the world from which he'd recently been evicted. The black-and-white television on the dresser announced a program called *Highway Patrol* in an excited staticky voice, but Mark didn't want to watch a show about men hunting other men. He spun the dial and listened for a moment to a pair of sports announcers arguing about a bowler named Ed Lubanski. On another channel, a news commentator was talking about the new ruler of Cuba, Fidel Castro, and what it meant to have a communist-controlled country so close to American shores. He seemed to be implying that Castro's next stop might be Miami.

Katie was twenty-three years from being born and decades away from dying.

He tried to wrap his mind around that concept. What would life really mean if you could go back and experience it again and again, replaying the same symphony until you were sick of it? In one way it was as though she were alive forever in her own tiny slice of time, and he tried to find comfort in that thought. But the image of her death kept getting in the way. It was all so damned confusing, *remembering* the future that had led him here to the past.

Mark's partner, Rory, would die before Katie, lying beside the lake in southern Maryland where he and Mark had chosen to meet. The two men who had been sent to kill them died also, and only Mark survived the ambush. But not before one of the gunmen told him that Katie was marked as well.

It had been raining heavily–on that bitter day in the future–and as he raced home Mark skidded between the other cars that kept appearing out of the blinding sheets of water, ripping off onto an exit just as he spotted a highway patrol car hiding under the next overpass. It wouldn't have mattered if the cop *had* pursued him. He wasn't stopping short of being killed. It wasn't much more than an hour's drive from the lake to Mark and Katie's house, and that day he made it in a little over half that even with the weather, with the agent's last words–the instant before Mark put a bullet in the treacherous bastard's brain–still chilling him to the core.

"We're all expendable. Your partner... you...your wife."

Katie.

Katie had never even known what he really did for a living, and yet Ash had marked her for death.

Even as he skidded his car to the curb out front of the brownstone that he and Katie shared he knew he was too late. His footsteps splashed a counterpoint to the driving rhythm in his mind as he ran through the open front door, pistol in hand. But the house was grave-silent, and the sense of death hung so heavy in the air that he stopped in the center of the marble entry floor and gasped for breath, tears welling in his eyes as the music in his head dropped into a minor key, funereal and slow like the last beats of a heart.

They were gone.

The killers had already done their work and were reporting to the madman at the helm. Oral reports, nothing written. Soon a cleanup team would arrive, and Mark suspected that their job would be to pin the murder on him. Still, against all odds, he clung to the hope that he was wrong, that Katie was alive.

He stumbled down the hallway, past the dining room with its crystal chandelier and ornate rococo table that Katie loved, past the living room where one of the chairs had been overturned and books lay scattered from the shelves. A thin trail of blood led across the carpet into the study, and he stood there for a moment, steeling himself to face the unfaceable.

Opening the door, he spotted her immediately, curled up on the floor wearing the blue shorts that he'd last seen her in, her white blouse soaked in blood, one tennis shoe on, the other foot bare of even a matching sock. He staggered to her, feeling for the pulse that he knew he would not find.

She had been stabbed in the chest, the upper arms, the legs. Any police officer would recognize the pattern, an emotional, inexperienced killer, attacking over and over in the heat of rage, never realizing that any one of the wounds was probably fatal. Of course, the agency had no intention of anyone ever discovering that Mark would never have killed in that manner, that he was anything other than what he was supposed to be, a financier. That's who the cops would be looking for, but they were never intended to catch him.

AventCorp would see to that. Mark would simply disappear. Just one more wife murderer who was never caught.

He held her body against him, heedless of the blood soaking his own shirt. He had been trained to ignore death around him, to have no feelings but those for the better good, for completion of the mission, but he could not ignore this death. He kissed her lightly on the forehead, feeling the heat of grief chilling to an icy resolve.

He glanced at the clock on the mantel as he lowered her gently back to the floor and rose to his feet, stumbling into the living room where he slid aside one of the heavy bookcases on hidden rollers and retrieved the large satchel there.

The cleanup team would be arriving at any moment.

He slipped back down the hallway and out the front door and into the rain again. A new symphony played in his head then. Placido Domingo, wailing through Wagner's *Gotterdammerung*, the tenor's powerful voice ringing with animal fury. Hurrying to his car he pulled into the neighbor's drive, easing past the house and parking in front of the garage in the rear. Both the husband and wife worked. No one would be home. He climbed back out into the rain just as he heard another car pulling up out front.

Whenever he had killed before the deaths had been ordered well in advance. They were callous, merciless affairs. But now an icy wrath spurred him, and he surrendered to it. He strode around the corner of the hedge, as three men stopped in mid-stride on the front walk, their mouths agape, eyes wide, hands full of metal suitcases that Mark was certain held cleaning gear as well as plenty of nasty things like his own skin, hair, and nail filings that would be torn and shoved into Katie's precious skin, beneath her nails.

As one case clattered to the ground–the man scrabbling to reach beneath his coat–Mark shot him in the face. A second man turned to run. Mark shot him twice in the back. The last man froze in place, shaking, a suitcase dangling from either hand, shaking like a leaf, the stain running down his pant leg clearly not from the rain. Mark placed his pistol directly against the man's forehead.

"You want me to take a message to Ash?" said the man hopefully.

Mark pulled the trigger.

"That'll be message enough," he said, striding back to his car.

He called the police to inform them of the killings, then called his foster father, Senator John Medlock. But he was informed that Medlock could not be reached. Ash must have gone completely mad, and if he had, murdering his own father, and Mark's foster father, could not be ruled out.

Mark drove all night to contact a man in Miami he'd dealt with before, a man who lived on the fringe, working both for the company and sometimes for people the company was working for and *sometimes* for people the company was working against. He was a man who would do anything for money, and money was a commodity that Mark had. The man produced a whole new identity on the spot, even hacking the IRS and Social Security files to insert background data. Within twenty-four hours Mark had a driver's license, and a new passport. Paying cash for a low-mileage used car, he drove to a secluded farm on the outskirts of Gettysburg where, by the light of the full moon, he silently crossed an apple orchard to unearth a vacuum-bagged suitcase filled with more cash and weapons. Then he spent three days in a motel outside of DC planning.

His only concern for his own safety was that he lived long enough to kill Ash and the men who had murdered Katie, and that was going to take some doing. Ash was better protected than the President, but even he had to be aware that no one was safe from a man who didn't care about his own life. If he understood Mark at all then he would certainly know that by killing Rory and Katie–and possibly John Medford–he had pushed the right buttons to turn Mark into a kamikaze.

On the night of the third day, he managed to slip through the first round of security around the AventCorp complex by riding inside the trunk of a low-level staffer whose address he accessed by hacking a government database. Had the gate guards been more diligent that night two of them would have been shot, and Mark might have regretted that a little...maybe. But luckily for them, the car passed through, and when Mark eased the trunk lid open just a crease, he was gratified to see that the driver was a good company man. Even though the lot was nearly empty, he had not had the effrontery to park in any of the reserved spaces nearer the building.

Still, even at that distance, Mark could see the roving security cameras.

He watched the blacked-out windows of the building through the crack in the trunk lid, wondering if anyone was looking out at the parking lot. That was a chance he was going to have to take. The Lincoln Towncar he was looking for sat closest to the doors, in the brightest light. But there was nothing he could do about that. The Towncar would have to pass closely enough for him to hear, and it was only going to take a split second to leap from the trunk and kill the sonofabitch. Of course, the car would be armored. But not strongly enough to save Ash from the satchel charge in Mark's case. He closed the lid quietly and tried to relax, playing Bolero inside his head.

The sound of a car passing slowly by awakened him, and he peered through the crack in the open trunk. The Towncar was rolling past, but Mark noticed immediately that the only one inside was the driver. The new head of the agency was still safely ensconced in one of the highest security buildings in DC.

As the Towncar exited the compound Mark closed the trunk lid again and allowed a soft rendition of Brahms' *Violin Sonata No. 2 in A major, Op. 100* to lull him to sleep.

He awakened as the engine started up. He heard light banter at the gate, and then the car was on the road again. He relaxed, already updating his plan. Although killing Ash in the very parking lot of the organization he had sabotaged was far more pleasing, Mark realized that he would have to take him at his home where security—although still nothing to be sneered at—would be less tight. He pictured Ash in his own living room, kneeling before him, begging for mercy. A vibration against his leg caused him to start. Then he remembered the cell phone. He lifted it to his ear and whispered into it.

"Yeah?"

The laugh on the other end was like glass caught in the man's throat.

"Do you think you can evade me so easily, Mr. *Carleton*?"

The use of Mark's new name drove the air from his lungs. That was fast even for AventCorp. There was only one explanation. His associate with the know-how had talked.

"You're dead," was all Mark said.

"Oh, come on. Are you really that stupid?"

"You murdered my wife."

A very long pause.

"I'm afraid we've had a misfortunate misunderstanding."

"You're dead," Mark repeated, counting the seconds.

It would take them a while longer to triangulate the phone, especially in a moving car.

"You're a traitor, and you're going to pay for it."

"You're out of your mind. Why did you have to kill Katie? Did you murder John, too?"

There was a hesitation on the other end of the line.

"I don't know what you're talking about."

Mark could barely keep himself from crushing the phone.

"Come in," said Ash, reasonably, "and let's talk."

"You really are mad. You know I can get to you."

The laugh again, but less mirthful this time.

"Only if you're suicidal."

"Why wouldn't I be?"

No laughter at all this time, just another long pause.

"We're coming. There's no place you can hide."

"Fuck you," said Mark, hanging up and dialing John Medlock's home number again without much hope.

This time Medlock answered on the second ring and recognized Mark's voice immediately.

"Where are you?" he asked after Mark told him about Rory and Katie.

"I'd rather not say."

"Stay under cover and let me work on this."

"Why did you ever let Ash take the helm?"

Another hesitation.

"I thought he was ready. He's a great organizer."

"Yeah. I've seen it."

"I honestly had no idea he was going over the edge."

"Too late for psychoanalysis now."

Medlock sighed.

"I don't want you hurt."

"I'll take care of myself."

"I'll see that Katie gets a nice funeral."

Mark swallowed a large lump.

"Yeah," he said, hanging up.

Forty-eight hours later he had a new identity again. This time he shot the forger before he left his shop and then destroyed the man's computer. Three days later he went under the knife of a plastic surgeon in Houston who had lost his license because of his penchant for alcohol and prescription drugs, and his proclivity for side work for criminals–mostly members of drug cartels and organized crime–who wanted to disappear.

Again, Mark shot the man before he left and burned his underground operating room.

In a small beachfront cabana on the Gulf coast of Mississippi, he spent six weeks recuperating while a helpful old woman who thought that he was a burn victim brought him soup and sandwiches. He moved to Florida before removing the bandages, then used techniques he'd learned from the ID expert to replace the driver's license and passport photos with new ones he'd taken himself. He purchased a used sailboat and hung out in the Keys.

Mark Townsend was born.

But he wasn't done with Ash or AventCorp. He felt even more like a tightly coiled viper, awaiting the opportunity to strike. One day when he saw John Medlock on television, he watched entranced. John had seemed ancient when he'd taken Mark in. But even now–when he had to be at least approaching eighty–he still had the old charisma and way with words, and he didn't look as though he thought his life was in any danger. Of course, he'd never have acted that way if he did.

Mark called him again.

"Where are you?" Medlock asked when Mark identified himself.

Mark didn't reply.

"Mmhmm," said Medlock, "how's the weather?"

"Same old same old. How are you doing?"

"Me? I'm fine. Couldn't be better. Katie had a nice sendoff."

Mark felt as though he'd been stabbed in the heart. One of the only good things about being on the run was that there was no one to keep offering condolences for Katie's death.

"I'm going to kill all the sonsofbitches that did it."

"Please don't do anything stupid."

"Have you ever known me to?"

"Don't start. I'm working on it. Ash will pay in the end."

"He's your son."

"Not anymore."

Mark glanced at the phone and then his watch. He hung up without saying goodbye. At least he could take some small solace from the knowledge that the company would never sleep until his demise was a fact and that they would continue spending inordinate amounts of money and manpower to track him down.

So, a couple of days later, when he'd pulled into the dilapidated dock in Punta Mara for provisions and been handed the letter from Professor Maynor, he'd been more than nonplused. That *anyone* could find him under his new identity was disturbing, but after reading the letter he'd realized that Maynor had probably tracked him by checking database files for likely research assistants, and Mark's deceased ID expert had simply done his usual excellent work, hacking background information like diplomas and driving records where they would be expected to be found. But MIT professors could have the pick of the litter. They didn't need to go fishing in the Keys. Mark stood on the old pier with his burner phone, wondering why he was making the call, but a deep-seated hunch forced him to punch out the number.

"Got your letters," Mark had said by way of greeting.

"Mr. Townsend?"

"That's right. I called to tell you I don't need the job."

"I didn't think you did."

Mark had expected the man to be curious about the call, perhaps to say that he was sorry, but he had already filled the position.

"How did you get my name?"

"I'd rather not say."

Why not? Obviously, he had done just as Mark thought and accessed a college database. Hadn't he? "What the hell does that mean?"

"I don't care for language like that, Mr. Townsend. We will not get along if you continue to use it."

"Why the fuck should I care?"

"Call me back when you are in a better mood and more in control of yourself," said Maynor, hanging up.

Mark stomped off the pier. The coldness that had taken him after Katie's death had frozen him solid, and for the first time since he felt blood pulsing in his veins.

An hour and three beers later he called Maynor again.

"Sorry," he said, stumbling over the unfamiliar word.

"Are you ready to talk about your employment?"

"Like I said, I don't need a job."

"I mentioned that I was aware of that."

"Then why the... why are we even talking?"

"You called me."

Once again Mark's equilibrium was off. The guy was just enigmatic enough to hold his interest. His eyes ran along the wharf that had once been worn, weathered, and working and was now worn, weathered, and covered with tourist kitsch. He caught the eye of a leggy blond in a few patches of cloth that might have been a bikini. When he frowned, she kept on walking.

"I wanted to be polite," said Mark.

Maynor's laugh reminded Mark of his own inner chill. "I'm sure."

"I only have a bachelor's degree in science."

"I'm also aware of your rather... eclectic tastes in academia."

"What is it exactly you think you know about me?" asked Mark, wondering if he was reading more into Maynor's intonation and words than he should. Years of suspicion were hard to overcome. It was impossible that this academic knew anything about him other than the persona he had so assiduously created. Unless Maynor was more than he seemed. Unless he was working for AventCorp. But that wasn't their style. They didn't play games. If they'd really tracked him down they'd simply have killed him on the boat or lured him off it.

Was *that* what this was about?

"There is no need for me to go into that other than to say that I am not a man who makes a habit of revealing other's secrets."

It wasn't possible, but Maynor certainly acted as though he knew something.

"So, then who are you and... once again... why me?"

Maynor recited a long list of his credits, degrees, doctorates, papers published, and his current seat at MIT.

"I am interested in doing some research that is a bit off the beaten path. I need a man who is well traveled, smart, can fit in with blue bloods or sewer workers, and one who has enough background in science to at least have some glimmering of what he's looking at once he finds it."

"Like I said, just a B.A. I have to be honest with you, Professor, I like my anonymity."

"Another reason I chose you."

"Why should I take the job?"

"Because I have what you need."

"And what's that?"

"Revenge."

Mark stared at the phone as though a poisonous insect had just crawled out of it. Who was this guy and why the fuck did he think he knew so much about him? Or rather who was this guy and why did he know so much about him?

"You're crazy. Why would I want revenge? Against whom?"

Another wet, lapping laugh.

"Play games if you like, Mr. Townsend, but opportunities such as this knock but once."

Maynor gave him an address in Cambridge.

"I have an office there for you. Be there on Thursday."

He hung up.

Mark tried to call back, but there was no answer. He stopped for one more beer in the ratty tavern at the end of the wharf, ignoring yet another leggy blond before climbing down the rickety old wooden ladder to his inflatable tender and heading back to the boat with every intention of sailing to Tortuga.

But on Thursday he found himself on the grounds of MIT having first spent the night casing the grounds. There were way too many places to die on the campus.

The big old brick buildings with parapeted roofs were a sniper's playground. Still, he was certain that he'd have been able to spot any of the new talent AventCorp could field. But when he spent the morning wandering self-consciously through the biggest gathering of nerds, he'd ever seen in one place *trying* to be spotted, no one paid him the slightest bit of attention.

Sunlight glinted on the river behind him while several men and women appeared to be trying to lift one of the buildings from its foundation with a hot-air balloon. The meeting Maynor had mentioned turned out to be Mark sitting alone in a tiny, dimly lit office cluttered with metal shelves and stacks of old textbooks. When the desk phone rang, he reached for it, but the speaker blared first.

"Good day, Mr. Townsend."

Mark got up from the chair long enough to check both ways down the hall.

"Hello."

"I'm so glad you could come."

"How did you know I was here?" asked Mark, sitting again.

Maynor chuckled.

"Because you answered, of course. Did you have a nice trip?"

"Lovely. Can we get to why I'm here?"

"Always to business. All right, then. Have you found the envelope on the desk?"

Mark had it in his lap already.

"I don't understand it."

"Hilgenberg's *About Gravitation, Vortices, and Waves in Rotating Media* was groundbreaking work. You need to study it."

"It's over my head, Professor, and really not anything I'm interested in."

"Not all of it, I'm sure. In any case, you should at least peruse it. I think you will eventually discover it to be of interest. Did you find everything else in the folder?"

"Your cell phone number, the key to this office."

"Yes. So you're all set then?"

"Set to do what?"

"Your job."

"Why would I take it?"

"For the reason I specified earlier."

"Why do you think I want revenge?"

A hesitation.

"Don't you?"

"Against whom?"

"I would think that would be obvious."

"Act as if it's not."

"I'll be in touch. Read the paper."

As Mark sat on the bed in his mid-twentieth century motel room, decades away from anything resembling home, he had the nagging feeling that Maynor had known him better than anyone who had ever entered his life. How the man had known was still a mystery to him, and one not likely to be solved now, but it was almost certain that he would not be here now if not for his association with Maynor.

He leaned back on the bed, peering through the curtain at the neon sign flashing *Rooms for $9.* Trucks continued to roar along Route 56, but Mark couldn't figure out where they were going. The road system was a maze. There were hardly any interstates. Instead there were narrow farm-to-market lanes that were called highways or turnpikes, and every gas station had its own brand of maps—which weren't always that easy to follow because not all of the roads seemed to be marked—but at least they were free with a fill-up.

He flipped absently through the Arnette paper. The Yankees looked like they had a head start toward the Series and Mark tried to remember who'd won that year. It occurred to him that if he could remember things like that he might make a pretty good living here. The want ads listed used cars in excellent condition, low mileage, for nine hundred dollars, and there were three drive-ins in town. He flopped back onto the bed, covering his eyes with his forearm, trying to will away a pounding headache.

Like every other college student who had taken Physics 101, Mark had toyed with what-ifs regarding time travel. The special theory of relativity allowed for travel into the future, and the general theory for travel into the past. Allowed for it but didn't say it was probable or even definitely possible. Under the general theory, all kinds of paradoxes might happen, and no one knew how to keep them from happening. A man might go back in time and murder his grandfather. Did that mean *he* was never born, or that there was a past timeline and a *normal* timeline? Some people believed that paradoxes weren't possible because none seemed to have happened, that there was some unknown force that would stop the man from shooting his ancestor. To Mark, that was like saying your wife wasn't doing anything when she went out to the bar last night because she was by herself when she came home the next morning.

Then, when you threw quantum physics into the mix things got even stranger, because some physicists believed universes were being created every time a change occurred no matter how small. For instance, if Mark had traveled into the past, he had already affected that past so the future–what had been his present–could no longer exist as it was. At least not in the universe he was currently–if the word currently had any relevance any longer–inhabiting. That would mean that he was in a new universe now, one in which he could murder his grandfather and never be born, yet still continue to exist here, in this time, as simply a traveler from another timeline. The only way to know would be to get back to his *own* time. And even then–unless he killed his grandfather in *that* universe–the question might still be up for debate.

His head pounded even harder.

But how the hell had Ash gotten him here in the first place? The memory of falling into the light set off a chain of ideas.

Physicists had proven that an effect on a particle in one light stream could change a matching particle in another light stream, theoretically at any distance and simultaneously. The theory further supposed that it might be possible to change a particle that existed in the past or future in the same manner, as though the distance in time made no more difference than the distance in space. And some scientists had even proposed that *maybe* the particle in the other light stream wasn't changing at all. Maybe the first particle had appeared there and could be made to appear there at *any time.* Had Ash used independent light streams?

The theory just didn't hold water. There was no light stream in the past for Ash to glom onto. Somehow Mark had simply been aimed at a point on this timeline and popped into existence here. Then of course there was the fact that no matter what theory you used to account for time travel, all of them agreed on one thing, the energy required would be unbelievably massive, on the order of the energy in a solar system to move a guy Mark's size any distance in time at all.

And there was an even bigger question.

If Ash had the ability to translate people through time and space–Mark assumed if he could do it through time, he could simply transport someone across town as well–then what the hell was so important in this past that Ash was looking for it here? Or was he simply getting ready to change history to suit himself? That made no sense for the reasons Mark had already enumerated. Ash had no way of knowing whether changes in the past would actually have any effect on his own present. Even if they did, playing with the past was a dangerous hobby. Getting rid of Nikita Kruschev might seem like a good idea during the Cold War, for instance, but it might just as well lead to more instability and even real war. No, Ash was far too intelligent for that, even if he was a homicidal maniac.

Terra Diablo.

For some time before the final debacle at AventCorp, there had been rumors floating that the company had established a secret facility again in the caves in New Mexico. It occurred to Mark that he'd probably been held in Terra Diablo all along. That explained the cavern he'd awakened in. It wasn't a parking lot but part of the underground complex that was no longer in use.

If there's any answers that's where I'll find them.

In any case, Mark was too exhausted to travel any farther that day, and he still had no idea of what he would do if he managed to get to the underground labs and actually find anything out, which seemed unlikely. A part of him really did feel like just giving up at last. He could make a new life for himself here, but a little voice nagging in the back of his head kept telling him that he wasn't safe here, collar or no collar. Sooner or later Ash would send more people back. Some would probably be just coming to do whatever it was that Ash had intended to do in the first place, but others would come looking for Mark. Ash wasn't the kind of person to leave loose pieces lying around, especially if they were lying around in his past where they might just jump up to bite him in the ass.

It occurred to Mark that he'd been looking at time in a very wrong way again.

If Ash really was going to send someone back to get him, then it could happen any time, any place. In fact, if they missed him in one location they might be able to simply return to their present and come back into the past a few minutes or hours earlier. So, did that mean it wasn't going to happen, or that it was going to happen only later–his later? He climbed off the bed, closed the curtains, and double-locked the door, slipping a chair under the knob. He was even more exhausted as he pulled off his clothes and climbed under the sheets, but sleep would not take him until deep into the night.

ASH PACED THE CONTROL room lost in thought.

He wasn't terribly worried about Townsend getting lost. After all the collar had returned. So, what if the guy had figured out a way to cut his way out of it first? Now he was stuck somewhere back in the fifties where Ash could deal with him at his leisure. It was like putting Townsend in the deep freeze, and the idea amused Ash.

According to his unknown informant, though, the project had to be completed within the next forty-eight hours. Ash had never been told exactly what would happen if it wasn't, only that the results of failure would be catastrophic, and Ash believed the man. They were all playing with forces unimaginable by the ordinary man, and Ash was quite aware that he was taking incredible chances with time. But what choice did he have? Fifty years ago, lay the answer to the problem of energy that was about to destroy civilization today.

Fifty years before captured German scientists working at Terra Diablo had discovered the source of limitless energy, and in doing so they had destroyed themselves, and Ash believed come damned close to destroying the planet. If he could get there just prior to that happening he knew that with modern knowledge of physics, he could stop the event, confiscate the equipment, and be the savior of modern man. If only the damned machinery he had now were reliable!

He needed someone back there in the fifties to tell him what the hell had happened. Someone he could trust. The only man he could think of was Trevor. With that realization, he took note of his surroundings again. Everyone in the room was watching him. He found himself staring into a pretty young woman's eyes as she sat at the console in front of him.

"Someone's helping the girl again," she said, screwing up her lips.

"I know that," muttered Ash in a voice that made the two goons beside the door swallow hard.

They were both looking at the technician as though she were something they really didn't want to see.

The woman shook her head.

"She's the problem. She and whoever's helping her. Not the guy you caught," she said.

Ash had no time to listen to people telling him things he already knew. He slashed downward in a sharp arc with the edge of his hand, pleased by the feel of snapping vertebra, enjoying the look of surprise in the woman's eyes before they dulled. She slid to the floor like an alcohol-soaked earthworm, and Ash strode out of the room that was now completely silent except for the low humming of electronics.

He stood for a moment in the long white corridor composing his thoughts again. He was aware on some level that he was becoming unstable. Over the past few days, he had killed one agent and now a perfectly good technician. Of course, he would never be charged in either case. He was way beyond any such mundane law, protected by levels of secrecy already in place when he took overall command and others he had created, and also by his hated father. Still, it was a waste, and he knew it, and waste for no reason other than gratification or momentary rage was illogical.

But there was no denying he had enjoyed it.

Returning to the control room, Ash wasn't too surprised to find the girl's corpse still lying where he'd left it. He would have been astounded if anyone had moved it without his orders. The two goons studiously ignored the body, standing on either side of the door with arms crossed like a pair of harem eunuchs, but the men and women still at their consoles kept shooting fleeting glances in the direction of the corpse. Ash could smell their fear in the artificially chilled air, but his sense of control was still off, speeding his pulse.

"Walsh will be arriving shortly," he said, waving one hand at the wall of glass that overlooked the transporter. "See that he's shown directly inside."

EVEN THOUGH WEARING A new identity was second nature to Mark, it was mind-boggling to have to learn to fit into an entirely different time.

He ate mostly at diners–which seemed to be everywhere–wearing a t-shirt, denim jacket, chinos, and worn black shoes he'd purchased from a second-hand store. He bought a cheap Timex from a pawn shop, and carried a pack of Lucky Strikes in his pocket because it seemed as though everyone, he met smoked. The kids said things like *neat* and *spiffy*, and the adults were all so clean-cut and *the same*. Mark hadn't even been a baby in the sixties, but now he was beginning to understand just how much of a cultural upheaval the next decade was going to be for these poor, complacent people.

It would almost be worth sticking around just to see it.

One thing he had to say for the tail end of the fifties, the food was better. Hamburgers could be had for a quarter, and they were thick and juicy, loaded with fresh tomatoes, onions, and pickles, and the fries were not prefabricated, frozen potato products, but long greasy, and delicious. Even the water tasted better–different in every town like the burgers–but better.

He passed through the panhandle of Texas into New Mexico with only a large plywood sign to inform him of his arrival. There was no tourist information center waiting ahead with air-conditioned restrooms and walls of brochures hawking sights to see like El Capitan or Carlsbad Caverns. When he'd picked up his last map, he'd idly asked the gas station attendant if he'd ever heard of a place called Terra Diablo.

Incredibly the man had shown him how to find the place as though it were nothing special, asking casually why the hell he wanted to go there, but studying him like he might be some kind of extraterrestrial himself. According to the attendant the base had been shut down a few years after the war. There was a small contingent still there since the Army used it for tank training a few months out of the year. Other than that, there was nothing left but rotting buildings and sagebrush.

Mark figured that was what the government wanted everyone to believe. That was how Terra Diablo disappeared. It didn't vanish through some mysterious cloaking technology. It just faded away. In thirty years few people living would remember it or how to find it.

He drove slowly down state road 502 still headed west, glancing out at what had to be either the ass end of the Sangre de Cristos or the Rockies–or maybe both–in the distance. The desert was dusty and inhospitable. Hank Williams blared out a song on the radio about a *Lonesome Highway.* It wasn't Yoyo Ma, but under the circumstances, Mark found the jangling, twangy singer right on topic, and it kept him from hearing the dirge that wanted to play in his head.

He still had no idea of what he hoped to accomplish at Terra Diablo. The whole trip might turn out to be a dead end, or worse. He might just be running right into men that Ash had sent to wait for him, knowing even better than Mark did where and when he was going to arrive. But he had to do something. He wasn't going to start a new life and spend it waiting for them to show up, and his curiosity was in control now anyway. He had to find out what was going on. What was so important back here that Ash had convinced the government to fund billions of dollars for secret research in order to build a time machine to get here?

Of course, Mark knew that another potential flaw in his reasoning was that Ash might never have been trying to reach this era at all. Mark had been a guinea pig, so maybe the machine was only in the prototype stage. Maybe they couldn't control what date it sent a passenger to any better than they could the location. Maybe they never would be able to control it. In that case, he was probably safe from marauding time goons. On the other hand, he'd certainly never get home.

But he knew in his heart that Ash hadn't *accidentally* landed him inside a cell in Leavenworth, and Maynor hadn't had him researching for nothing. Placing Mark in the tightest lockup in the country without popping him into outer space or having him end up somewhere near the earth's core had required pinpoint accuracy. Ash had intended for Mark to stay put, at least long enough to jerk him back to the future.

He was surprised to see military road signs for the complex five miles ahead. Apparently–regardless of what the gas station attendant might believe–the military wasn't acting as though the place were a complete write-off yet. They were probably pretty sure of their ability to keep the press out, and ordinary Joes in the fifties weren't in the habit yet of disregarding official warning signs.

The Pentagon Papers were a decade and a war in the future.

As he drove the Packard slowly along, peering out into the scrub he was passed twice by army deuce-and-a-halfs loaded with sunburnt soldiers with old wooden-stocked carbines between their legs. They peered down at him disinterestedly, and he waved, speeding up just enough to follow the trucks to an area surrounded by chain link and barbed wire. He sped past as the small convoy pulled up to a double gate guarded by two white helmeted MPs. Mark didn't stop until the gate was out of sight, but the fence still paralleled the road, disappearing in the distance between the peaks.

No buildings had been visible through the fence. The complex proper had to be over the horizon which meant the guarded area extended for miles. He'd found what he was looking for.

Now what was he going to do about it?

ASH ENJOYED WALSH'S OBVIOUS claustrophobia as the little man shambled along the narrow corridor, hunching his shoulders and wiping constantly at his dripping forehead with a sopping white handkerchief, glancing at his two bodyguards who were each twice the size of either himself or Ash and quite clearly well-armed. Entering a wide cavern, Ash motioned toward what looked like a tiny bulkhead in the distance.

"I'm afraid the next tunnel goes on a bit farther," said Ash, smiling like a sympathetic tiger.

"Why didn't you put in a direct elevator?" said Walsh irritably.

"There was such an elevator, back in the fifties. Unfortunately, it didn't survive the destruction, and the bedrock above has become too unstable to make drilling another shaft feasible. I believe the ceiling is quite well shored up, though."

Walsh stared nervously at the heavy concrete beams lacing through the stalactites high overhead, wiping more perspiration from his brow. "You could have trolleys or something."

"Again, I apologize. We do have carts, but they seem to be out of service."

"This had better be worth dragging me down here to see," said Walsh, glancing for assurance at one of his guards who continued staring fixedly at Ash.

"I think you'll be suitably impressed."

After another walk down a tunnel long enough to start Walsh hyperventilating, Ash pressed his hand to the security screen beside the last steel door. The bulkhead swung inward with a whoosh, and the pressure in the next chamber raised a small breeze.

Walsh shuffled into the well-lighted cavern, obviously glad to be out of the confines of the maze of corridors again, but still nervous.

"That's it?" he said, waving one hand toward the apparatus in the corner.

Ash nodded.

Walsh slowly circumnavigated the machine, sliding his pudgy fingers over the polished steel and copper, standing on tiptoe to peer over the top of the circular walkway.

"It doesn't look like much," he said.

"No," said Ash, sliding up alongside him. "It doesn't. Most of the guts are buried beneath the floor or hidden inside the control room."

He nodded behind him toward the wall of glass where several white-coated technicians moved efficiently about. He smiled at Walsh's discomfort at the word *guts.*

Walsh stared up at the wall of windows.

"Do you believe you're now capable of attaining the original device before it's stolen from the complex," asked Walsh.

"Yes."

"And there's no chance of a paradox?"

Ash shook his head. "I think not. No more paradoxical than us sending anyone else back in time. After all, we don't know for *certain* that the device was actually stolen to begin with. It may simply have been destroyed when the labs went up."

"Are you still trying to return Townsend?"

"I know where he will have gone."

"How?"

"Because I now know where and when and how he died."

Walsh stopped to stare at Ash, checking the position of his guards yet again.

"If your plans haven't changed, what was so important you had to bring me down here?"

"Come," said Ash, leading the way up the narrow metal steps to the platform around the machine. Walsh huffed his way to the top, signaling his men to remain behind. He stared down into the empty maw of the device, filled with tightly wound coils of copper and what appeared to be row upon row of gun barrels, pointing obliquely up at him.

"I don't know what I'm looking for," said Walsh, shaking his head.

"You will," said Ash, suddenly behind them.

Walsh spun as fast as his fat little body would allow. His men were even quicker, but not quick enough. One of them reached for a pistol. Ash shot him, aiming at the other guard's head before the man could draw. One of Ash's men shot the other guard before Ash could pull the trigger. Ash nodded as he climbed calmly down off the platform.

"What do you think you're doing?" shouted Walsh, starting down after him. "Have you gone mad?"

Ash's pistol waved the little man back onto the platform.

"Simply carrying on with my work."

"You can't just murder me. Do you think no one will know?"

"I think no one will care once I get what I want. Your death would simply be another unfortunate accident, but, in any case, I don't intend to kill you. Not yet at any rate."

He waved toward the men and women in the control room. A high-decibel vibration started somewhere in the floor and then rose to engulf the entire chamber.

"Watch the light," said Ash, pointing the gun past Walsh, toward the center of the device. "All you have to do is step into it."

"You're crazy!" said Walsh, covering his ears as the roar became unbearable. "You didn't give me a collar! How am I supposed to get back?"

"Back?" shouted Ash, slipping on ear protectors.

While the techs in the control room slipped on dark glasses, Ash stared directly into the weaving light until the machine had done its dance and Walsh had disappeared.

"That looked like fun," shouted Trevor, entering through a side door.

"Kind of you to show up," Ash shouted back.

"Wish I could have gotten here a little earlier. Looks like I missed a lot."

"Like you missed the girl?"

"They used some kind of ray device on the cars," said Trevor. "Shot my men before they had a chance-"

"My men," Ash said.

Trevor shrugged.

"That would have been one of Mr. Carter's toys," said Ash.

"You should have maybe hung onto him when you had him."

"Had I realized why he was important I would have," said Ash, suddenly poking his pistol directly into Trevor's face and removing the man's own gun before Trevor could react. "That does definitely seem like something I should have done. Thank you for mentioning my oversight."

"What are you doing?" asked Trevor

"Just making certain I don't make any more mistakes, leave any loose ends. You're going to take a little trip for me."

"What kind of trip?"

Ash nodded toward the machine.

"No way," said Trevor, backing away, shaking his head.

"It's painless, I assure you," said Ash. "And when you get back, I'll give you a double bonus."

"Back from where?" said Trevor, glancing nervously at the machine where the massive tower of light still twisted and whipped like a giant kneading machine gone berserk.

Ash nodded back over his shoulder toward the windows. "They're adjusting the coordinates right now. I'd like you to find Mr. Townsend for me."

"In there?" said Trevor, frowning at the machine.

"Exactly. Don't be a coward, now. I'll give you a triple bonus. How's that?"

Trevor grimaced, glancing from the pistol to the light.

"Quadruple if you want me to walk into that thing."

"Done."

"So how do I find Townsend?"

"Don't worry. We know where he's headed, and we're getting better at targeting with every transition. Here." Ash handed him back his pistol, holding it so that Trevor was forced to take it by the barrel slide.

"You'll need this, too," said Ash, handing Trevor a plastic zip-lock bag from his jacket pocket.

"What's this?"

"The time and location of the spot at which you kill Townsend, also a small locator bracelet so that we can bring you home, and identification proving you're Jack Keating, a general in the Air Force working for the War Department. You should have enough clearances in there to bluff your way wherever you need to go. If you don't... you'll just have to think of something, because I'm not bringing you back until I know Townsend is dead."

A lab tech appeared carrying a neatly pressed uniform.

"Put it on," said Ash. "It's authentic."

"You're crazy."

"Would you rather I shot you?"

Trevor stripped and climbed into the new clothes.

"How the hell will you know Townsend's dead?"

Ash smirked.

"We already know. You kill him and leave the body in one of the huts that survive the blast at El Diablo. Just do your job, and we'll bring you right back."

"Already? What the hell is that supposed to mean?"

"Don't be dense. You've already killed Townsend. You just need to go back and get it done."

Trevor frowned, shaking his head.

"You're sending me back to do something I've already done, and you won't bring me back until I do it?"

"That's about the gist of it," said Ash. "By the way, go ahead and take care of Walsh while you're back there."

Trevor climbed the platform slowly.

"You'd better not screw me," he said.

"What would you do if I did?" muttered Ash as the platform shifted like the lid on an automatic trash can, dumping Trevor into the stream of light.

NOT A TREE DISTURBED the dusty essence of the subdivision, not a shrub marred the grass that shone gray in the streetlamp's glow. The night on the desert near the eastern border of Utah was as dry as an Egyptian tomb and just as welcoming. The little ranch-style homes seemed more like feral creatures huddled up against the predators of darkness than abodes of living, breathing people.

"I don't like this place much," muttered Earl.

"I don't like it much, either," said Tracy, shoring herself up for what they might find here.

She hoped against hope that someone in the book, other than just Bea and Earl, would be left at home, but so far that hadn't happened. And worse, Marilyn was worried that Ash might leave someone waiting for them at one of the houses. A nice little surprise.

"I wouldn't mind getting my hands on a little of that magic you don't believe in right now," muttered Marilyn, smiling when Tracy frowned.

"There," said Tracy, pointing to one of the houses with a Ford pickup out front.

Marilyn nodded, cruising slowly down the street. It was almost eleven. Many of the homes were completely dark. A few televisions could be seen through open windows. A dog barked in the distance.

"He's dead," said Earl, swallowing a large lump.

"You don't know that," said Tracy.

They had visited five more of the addresses on the list now, and all five had turned out to be recently deceased or disappeared, address unknown.

"We have to find out."

"Why? Why can't we just get out of here while we have a chance?" asked Earl.

"Because they might be alive," said Marilyn. "Because they might know something that we need to know so that we can stay alive. Besides, we never saw a body."

"What?" said Tracy, turning to the girl.

Marilyn shrugged.

"We were told that those people were dead. We didn't see any dead people."

Tracy frowned.

"That guy said he attended Austin McCord's funeral."

Marilyn shook her head.

"The ones that died all died violently according to the locals. Car wrecks, fires in the home..."

"So, what are you getting at?"

"None of those bodies might have been recognizable."

"Are you saying that they might be alive, that they might have been switched?"

"It's possible."

"Why bother? Why not just kidnap them the way Ash's people did with your father?"

"I don't know. I'm just theorizing. But kidnappings kind of draw attention where car wrecks and house fires don't."

That made sense.

If Ash had wanted to kidnap the other people on the list. His men sure hadn't been trying to kidnap her, but then she wasn't on the list. She was some kind of afterthought. They *had* kidnapped Marilyn's father. For all Tracy knew they might have kidnapped her own parents a year before. She just had no more idea of what had happened to them than anyone else seemed to.

Earl sank back into the seat, his lips scrunched tight, his eyes focused on the approaching house. The light from one window traced a narrow strip of white across the lawn, but instead of stopping, Marilyn drove on to the end of the street and then around the block, still cruising slowly, glancing up and down the neighborhood.

"What are you doing?" asked Tracy, feeling as though she'd been about to leap off the high dive and had suddenly been jerked away.

"Looking for anything unusual," said Marilyn.

"Like what?" asked Tracy, nerves tingling as she, too, searched the houses and drives for anything out of the ordinary.

Once again, the girl had demonstrated that she was better at this dangerous game than Tracy.

Marilyn shrugged.

"A car with government plates. A house with more lights on than it should have at this time of night. Someone moving outside. I don't know exactly."

"I don't see anything like that."

"Neither do I."

"I guess it's all right, then."

Marilyn frowned.

"Yeah. Hunky dory."

She pulled back around the block and rolled to a stop in front of the house with the lighted living room. The streetlamps dimmed the stars, turning the sky into a black silk shroud. The dog down the street stopped barking, and the night took one long deep breath as they climbed from the car and strolled nervously up the walk.

"This is the one," said Tracy, hopefully.

Marilyn nodded, but her expression was one of trepidation not assurance, and Tracy noticed the large bulge in the small of her back, beneath her blouse.

Earl brought up the rear as usual, glancing nervously up and down the street like a cat in the dog's neighborhood. When they reached the front porch Marilyn held her finger over the doorbell. When Tracy nodded, the girl pushed the button, and they could all hear the bell echoing inside the house.

There was no response, so they peered into the living room through the open drapes. A book lay on the sofa. A can of soda sat on the coffee table.

Marilyn reached in her pocket and pulled out the paper clip she'd used to remove the handcuffs, but before she could insert it in the lock Tracy tapped her on the shoulder. The girl spun, dropping the clip and slipping her hand behind her back as a large, black man came hurrying around the corner of the house next door.

But instead of a gun, the man carried a small rectangular bundle wrapped in cloth.

He had salt-and-pepper hair and deep furrows in his brow, but his eyes were soft like those of a man who has been through the pit and returned to the light knowing that there was no way he had accomplished the journey alone. He stopped at the bottom of the steps, smiling shyly.

"Might one of you be called Shiver?" he asked.

Tracy gasped, and the man held up one hand in apology.

"Sorry!" he whispered, talking to Earl, but then switching his attention to the women. "Woody told me you'd be anxious about your anonymity. You don't have to worry. I won't tell a soul you've been here."

"Thanks," said Marilyn, stepping between Tracy and Earl to face the man.

"Pete Roche," said the man, extending a hand the size of a catcher's mitt.

Marilyn shook with him, introducing Tracy and herself but not giving Earl's name.

"Pleased to meet all of you," said Pete, clutching the cloth-bound package again, and nodding to everyone but especially Earl. "I been keeping this for Woody. He said you might be coming, and if you did that it was important you got it."

"Where is Woody?" asked Marilyn, staring at the package.

Pete shrugged.

"He left the day before yesterday. Said things were heating up too much... Well, that's not the way he said it, but in his broken speech, I got the idea, you know? He hinted that he'd seen someone following him."

Marilyn nodded.

"What do you know about the people Woody was afraid of?"

Pete frowned.

"I know that Woody is a scientist and that the government wanted him to do things he didn't want to. I'm a Christian Scientist myself, and I can tell you we know all about the government. I'm on your side. Are you going to find Woody and help him?"

"We want to," said Marilyn.

"Good. Then take this and get out of here. I've seen cars coming around at all hours since Woody skedaddled. I think they just missed him. There were a couple of guys yesterday kind of creeping around, and I think they went inside, too."

Suddenly the house seemed to emit a warning vibration that tingled all the way up Tracy's spine. She could tell that Marilyn felt it too when the girl glanced nervously over her shoulder at the half-open drapes.

"How did you know we were on Woody's side?" Tracy asked.

"He said you'd look sneaky, too. But you wouldn't have the meanness in your eyes the others do. You don't."

Tracy smiled.

"That's good to know," she said, accepting the package that felt heavy and solid beneath the cotton cloth.

"Go on," said Pete. "They might come back any time. God go with you."

"Thank you," said Tracy, shaking Pete's hand in farewell as did Marilyn, and finally Earl.

Marilyn drove quickly out of the neighborhood and back to the highway as Tracy peeled away small strips of tape and opened the cloth to reveal a large spiral notebook. The first page was covered in jagged Gothic script.

"German, I'm pretty sure," said Tracy. "I don't suppose you-"

"English is my language," said Marilyn. "American English. I can translate some hip-hop into rap."

Earl leaned between the seats to examine the book beneath the dim map light. The first few pages were all the same German script. Then the contents changed. Tracy and Marilyn continued to frown, but Earl grinned from ear to ear.

"*That* I can read," he said, nodding at the esoteric mathematical symbols that filled page after page.

"Equations," said Marilyn, glancing over and then back at the road.

"For what?" asked Tracy.

"Give it to Earl."

Earl accepted the book as though it were made of eggshells, his eyes roving the pages.

"Does it make sense to you?" asked Tracy as he neared the end.

He shook his head.

"Not yet."

"But you think you could figure it out?"

He frowned.

"Maybe. There are a lot of symbols here that don't make sense. Or else I've never seen them used for what he's using them for. I know he's trying to figure out a way to explain gravitic effects, or at least that's what he starts out doing, but this stuff," He pointed toward two pages of extremely small print, and his frown spread all the way to his wrinkled brow. "This stuff is more like...it almost reminds me of-"

"Of what?" said Marilyn in an exasperated voice.

Earl stared out the windows as though he'd forgotten he was in a moving vehicle, barreling through the night.

"Of what I do with the machine. I think this part of the equation is leaving itself open to *adjustments*, maybe human adjustments. I think he's trying to figure out how to tune a machine."

"Like the way you do?" asked Tracy.

"Maybe," said Earl, frowning at the book again. "But I think he's trying to understand it on a mechanical level, and I don't know what this thing is he's tuning."

Tracy studied the drawing that covered the top half of the sheet.

"What?" said Marilyn, noticing Tracy's look of surprise.

"It can't be," muttered Tracy.

Suddenly the old guilt, anger, the sense that she might have been wrong all along, the memories of the kids outside her window, chanting in the night–all came crashing down. Slowly she turned back toward the window, now praying to catch sight of the dancing light again.

"You've seen that drawing before?" asked Marilyn.

For a long moment, Tracy stared silently out into the night.

"Well?" said Marilyn. "Have you seen that drawing or not?"

"No."

"Then what's the matter?"

"Head for Big Sur."

"What?"

Tracy sighed.

"I need to go home. There's something there I need to look at again."

A COUPLE OF MILES from the guard post Mark discovered an old mining trail across the road from the chain-link fence and followed it to a small ravine. He parked there for the rest of the day, catnapping in the sweltering heat, nibbling on stale sandwiches, and sipping from a couple of hot Cokes. As soon as the sun went down, he hiked back to the fence and performed his magic trick, remolding the chain link back into place behind him with his fingers.

The dirt road he'd seen entering the complex lay somewhere off to his right, so he set off into the desert in a path parallel to it and perpendicular to the fence. After an hour he spotted headlights, and he crouched in the scrub brush, waiting until the lights were out of sight before hiking on, the Debussy *Sonata for Flute, Viola, and Harp* playing in the back of his head.

There were just too many unknowns, but it had begun to occur to him that there were just as many for Ash. Ash was experimenting so far out on the edge of known science that there was no way he could have any certainty of what he was doing.

Still, even if there was no straight timeline and Mark couldn't make it back to his own present, he hadn't changed anything in *this* time all that much. Whatever it was that was being done here, whatever it was that Ash wanted so badly from this time and place was still here, still happening or being created, and if it was bad enough, powerful enough, for someone like Ash to want it, then Mark was pretty sure that sooner or later someone exactly like Ash would get around to coming back for it.

Mark couldn't allow that to happen for any number of reasons, but the main reason was that he had never had his revenge. If the only revenge he was going to be allowed was to thwart Ash's plans then he was going to screw them up to the absolute best of his ability. There might be no way he could hope to kill the man responsible for Katie's death, but he could see that Ash died without ever accomplishing his goal, even if that death was so far in the future that Mark would never live to see it.

The thought of Katie was an icicle through his heart. He could still hear her voice, feel the pressure of her hands on his back, her cheek against his. He wondered if the memory itself wasn't some kind of time distortion. Perhaps people traveled in time every day, in their minds. What was so crazy about that? Nothing seemed all that crazy anymore.

He spotted roving spotlights ahead, and when he got closer, he saw fifty low, plywood-sided buildings in a compound, ten to a side, typical cheap military construction for the period, picketed by four tall guard towers. Lights were on in only one of the shacks, but when Mark noticed two soldiers patrolling between the buildings with rifles slung, he dropped to the ground, waiting until the pair disappeared before creeping closer. He slipped beneath the building with the light on, crouching behind one of the wooden pilings when he heard the guards returning. They stopped right alongside his hiding place, discussing a whore in Albuquerque of whom both of them seemed enamored.

One of them stubbed out a cigarette in the dust. Then the two marched off again.

When Mark heard muffled voices through the floor, he realized he'd made a mistake. He should have gone to one of the unlighted buildings. It would be simple to cut his way in from underneath, then search the place for any clues as to what was going on here. He was surprised to hear a woman's voice in an argument with a man. He'd just assumed that in this day and time, there would be few women here, certainly few living on site. The fact that the pair was awake at this hour and arguing intrigued him. He placed his ear directly against the plywood floorboard.

It sounded as though they were speaking German.

One word kept coming up in the altercation, and Mark didn't think it was German. The woman kept saying something about *feedback*, and Mark pressed his ear tighter against the floor, his skin tingling.

Eventually, he gave up on trying to understand what the pair were arguing about, crawling instead to the front of the low-slung building to reconnoiter the dirt street out front. He noticed two more guards at either end of the road, standing beside what looked like small guard houses. The more he studied the area the less it looked like any kind of research facility. The buildings were all too small, identical, and nondescript. They looked more like barracks than labs, and each one of them had one small power line draped from the series of poles running down the far side of the street. He figured at least some of the labs would require more electricity than that.

He heard the crunch of booted feet in the dust again and slunk back farther into the shadows. One pair of boots stopped right in front of him, and for a moment Mark was certain he'd been spotted. Then the other pair marched up the small wooden stoop and pounded on the door.

"Doctor Helsenberg!" said the guard's rough voice. "Can you and your wife please show yourselves at the door?"

When there was no movement from inside, the guard spoke again, this time in German, and Mark heard footsteps overhead and a door clicking open. A wedge of light slashed out into the street.

"Danke," said the soldier.

The door closed, and the guards marched on down the street.

Helsenberg.

That name rang a bell from Mark's research. Helsenberg had been experimenting for the Nazis on some weird notion for producing antigravity with pulses of high-voltage electricity. So, he had survived the war, and this was where they'd hidden him. Only he wasn't being treated like Von Braun. You didn't ask an eminent scientist and his wife to *show themselves* in the middle of the night. These people weren't pampered pets, they were extremely well-guarded prisoners and had been for fourteen years.

What had Helsenberg done to deserve a life in a hell hole like this except to have been forced to work for another regime that probably treated him just as badly? Why would he continue to work for them under such circumstances?

On impulse, Mark reached up and began to open the floor.

A LIGHTNING BOLT OF pain shot through Mark's skull, and he dropped to his knees in the dirt beneath the shack. He raised his hands to ward off another blow from the heavy cast-iron pan held high over Helsenberg's shoulder.

"Wie bis du?"

The nonsense words rattled painfully around in his head, echoing down a long deep mineshaft.

"Who are you?" said a clearer, woman's voice.

A dusty bare bulb buzzed on somewhere far above Mark's head, and he stood slowly, climbing into the hallway of the little house as the pair backed away, the pan still held high over the scientist's head. Glancing at his feet Mark saw that he had cut right through a cheap Persian rug. He wondered if his weird ability would allow him to repair *that*. He looked up apologetically at the middle-aged man and woman, both wearing long cotton housecoats and socks.

"I'm not here to hurt you," Mark assured them.

"Was?" said the man, pronouncing it *vas* and glancing at the woman.

"Speak English, Erhardt," said the woman. "Don't play the dunce."

"What did you to my floor?" said Erhardt, nudging the section that Mark had folded back onto itself.

"Sorry," said Mark, reaching for the *trap door.*

Helsenberg waved the pan ominously, but Mark reassured him with gestures, swinging the section of floor back into place. He was gratified to see that his ability did indeed extend to repairing the nap in a handmade carpet.

Helsenberg and his wife watched goggle-eyed as Mark completed the task. When Helsenberg placed a gentle hand on Mark's shoulder Mark studied him.

"Your body," said Helsenberg. "It vibrates."

Mark nodded.

"I feel it...inside. It happens every time I do what I do."

"Who are you?" asked Mrs. Helsenberg.

"That's a little hard to explain," said Mark. "But as God is my witness, I'm not here to hurt either of you."

"Come, then," said Helsenberg, helping Mark to his feet. "Even very unexpected guests we know how to treat. Although my wife is not German, she makes excellent strudel. I cook the coffee."

The kitchen was tiny, and Helsenberg didn't turn on any more lights, working the percolator by the illumination from the open refrigerator door as his wife sliced thick pastry and dished it out cold onto white saucers. Mark had forgotten how hungry he was, and when the Helsenbergs watched him wolf down the dessert they insisted that he eat more.

"Sorry," he said, wiping his lips with a napkin after a third helping. "I think doing that thing I do eats up a lot of energy."

Both the Helsenbergs watched him like a pair of fish enthusiasts on their first trip to the aquarium. When Mark began to speak again, Helsenberg held up one hand, stepping over to a small side table that held a suitcase phonograph. He placed the needle on a record, and a hauntingly familiar sound filled the room. Clearly Helsenberg was worried that the guards might listen as well as watch.

"Now," said Helsenberg as Mark rested his coffee cup on the table.

"That's the Ernest Bloch solo for violoncello," said Mark, nodding along with the music, "performed by the Canadian, Zara Nelsova. A very rare recording."

"You know this piece?" asked Mrs. Helsenberg, studying him. "It's new."

Mark shrugged, thinking that new was a very relative term. "That's *Suite No. 1,* the *Prelude: Attacca.* My favorite is the *Suite No. 2: Andante,* the *Poco piu lento."*

"You like the cello?"

"My mother performed... performs this piece...she's going to play it for the New York Philharmonic."

That was before he was born, years from now, but he'd heard a recording of the concert. She was better than Nelsova, slicker intonation and fingering, but the Canadian played well.

"Who are you?" asked Helsenberg, irritably. "Why are you here? And how is it you do this... thing...you do?"

Mark nodded.

"I'll tell you all that, but first you tell me why you're here. I know who you are."

"Und how do you know that?"

"Because where I come from, you're famous in a certain quarter."

Helsenberg smirked.

"I can't imagine where you come from, then. It's unlikely that anyone will ever know who I am."

"They hold you prisoner here."

Helsenberg and his wife nodded.

"But what are they making you work on?"

Helsenberg frowned.

"Is this it? You are a spy? Or is it you work for them, and you test us?"

Mark shook his head.

"During the war, you worked on anti-gravity research for the Nazis."

"How do you know this if you do not work for the government?"

"Because where I come from, we know that you did that. We also know that the Nazis perfected something that at least worked like anti-gravity. They used it in flying objects our pilots called foo-fighters. After the war, a great number of German scientists were smuggled out of Germany. Is this where they brought all of you?"

"I think I will not tell you more, until you tell me the answers to questions."

"My name would mean nothing to you."

Helsenberg nodded.

"Very well. I call you Shiver for now."

"Shiver?"

His wife laughed.

"Because you vibrate."

"Okay."

"Where you from?" said Helsenberg. "Why you really here?"

"You don't complete your research. I think maybe that's part of why I'm here."

Helsenberg frowned again, and this time there was the slightest inkling of fear in his face.

"You are here to kill me?"

"No," said Mark, shaking his head. "I told you, I'm not here to hurt anyone."

Helsenberg's sigh was one of relief, but sadness crept over his face.

"Then there is no way I cannot complete my research."

"Why not?"

Helsenberg turned to his wife. "

Because I have no choice."

"You think they'd hurt her?" said Mark.

"I know this."

"Who the hell are these people?" said Mark. "This isn't Nazi Germany."

"Is same in USSR, I think," said Helsenberg.

"Not anymore."

"Ehh?"

"Nothing."

"How you do what you do?" said Helsenberg, nodding back down the hall.

"Something happened to me when they sent me here," said Mark.

"How happened?"

Mark stared at Helsenberg for a moment, waiting until his wife was seated again.

"Is what you're doing here, your work with anti-gravity, have you... have any of you come across any time... like maybe time dilation?"

"I don't understand word, dilation."

"Is your research related to time travel?" said Mark, frowning.

Helsenberg's wife's jaw dropped, and Helsenberg's face went white. It took him a moment to speak.

"When you say you sent here. You sent here from where?.... Or when?"

Mark nodded slowly.

"You come from future," Helsenberg whispered, squeezing Mark's forearm as though it were a particularly interesting loaf of bread.

"Yes."

"When they send you back, the machine do something to you, so now you can do this thing with my floor?"

"I think maybe it had something to do with the drugs."

"Drugs?"

Mark explained more of what had happened to him, and as he worked his way through the laborious process of getting the Helsenbergs to understand and accept his story, their frowns slowly softened until their faces were filled with stunned acceptance.

"What I don't understand," said Mark. "Is, if you had a working anti-gravity machine that could lift remotely controlled flying objects in Germany, why have none surfaced in this country? Is security that good?"

Helsenberg shook his head.

"Der *Flieger* worked, but the research facility that researched the power plant was destroyed by bombs, along with Rieger, Van Kelsig, and the rest of people working there. At the end of war, all we have left at Brennerwelt is some unknown devices and the *Flieger* fuselage which we were modifying to fit bigger power plant. We learn how to build power plant from technical papers left by Van Kelsig."

"And you're trying to reproduce the power plant here?"

Helsenberg shook his head.

"We *have* produced more than one, und they work, but much paperwork was lost. We still trying to understand how torsion field converts into working anti-gravity."

"You have a functioning flying craft that uses antigravity?" said Mark, at least as stunned as they were.

"Yes," said Helsenberg, giving Mark a studious look. "We finally have it working, but lately we have been experimenting with a more powerful machine und we have... what you call... anomalies."

"What kind of anomalies?"

"We argue. Other physicists and me. Where test pods go."

"Pods?"

"Ve use steel balls, called pods. Suspend in field. Change amperage, voltage, size of field, experimenting with propulsion effect."

"Let me guess," said Mark. "You fiddled with some of the input and one of the pods disappeared."

"More than one! Many time we experiment. Different voltages. Different amperes, ohms."

"Did any of the balls return yet?"

Helsenberg nodded. "Two."

"You only sent them a short time into the future, and they remained in basically the same space as the machine, so when your time caught up to them, they simply popped back into being."

"We create time machine," whispered Helsenberg.

Helsenberg and his associates couldn't send the pods into the past because there was no time machine then. If Helsenberg could send a man into the past then he would also be able to send the knowledge of how to create a time machine to that past time. He could in fact send someone back to tell *himself* how to create the very machine that he *had* created and that would be an impossible paradox. Ash could send Mark here, because the machine or one like it already existed.

"Could I see the device?"

Helsenberg shook his head.

"Far underground, in deep cave. Many guards. You never get in."

"You'd be surprised," said Mark.

Helsenberg shrugged. "What for you want to see machine?"

"Well, for one thing, it's the only way for me to get home."

But was there really any point in risking his life trying to get back to an elusive *present* in a relatively untested machine? It had sounded to Mark as though Ash had lost *specimens* in his own tests and that had been using 21st century technology. Skipping out of town in the 1959 version might only end him up dead or much worse.

Ash already had a time machine, and Mark suspected that if he had completed that he wasn't that far from catching up to Helsenberg on anti-gravity. He wanted something else back here, and Mark knew he had to find out what it was and stop him from getting it.

"Are you working on anything else?" he said. "A weapon maybe?"

Helsenberg frowned at Alberta, shaking his head.

"No, but everything made in this place will be made to kill...event...eventually, yes? I am not stupid. I know what for we make research. Sooner or later as you say, army learn how to turn whatever we do into a weapon."

"Ash wants something here," Mark muttered to himself, "but what? Why send people back into the past? Surely, he must realize he can't change it. I have to get into that cavern."

"Is impossible. You never even be able to get away from here, much less into lower complex."

"Will you help me?"

"No," said Helsenberg, glancing protectively at his wife. "Will not give you to guards. But cannot help you. Too dangerous."

"Can you at least tell me where the machine is kept?"

The record had slipped into ***Suite No.2***: The *Prelude - Poco Meno*. It reminded Mark of his mother again, but he had no time for the memory.

Helsenberg nodded slowly.

"Five miles from here. Follow road in desert. There is another group of buildings, how you say... Quonset shacks. Small shed has doors leading to shaft."

"How deep underground?"

"Far."

There was no record of any of the research that Helsenberg was talking about ever surfacing anywhere, and after more than fifty years something would have shown up somewhere. As far as Mark could see that left only three options. Either *he* somehow stopped Ash from acquiring whatever it was he wanted, Ash had acquired it *after* he sent Mark back in time and Mark would never find out, or someone or something else had stopped Ash.

All those options still left the possibility that Ash would send someone back to kill him just to neaten up the loose ends, and Mark was determined that if someone was coming back looking for him then he was going to throw as big a monkey wrench into the works as he could first.

"All you people are going to die or disappear," said Mark, quietly.

"What?" gasped Mrs. Helsenberg, grabbing her husband's hand with both of hers.

Mark sighed.

"Do you believe what I tell you, that I'm from the future?"

Helsenberg shrugged.

"Is hard to believe, but what you do in there," he nodded again toward the hall, "is also hard to believe."

Mark nodded.

"There is no record of any of you, anywhere in the future."

"You trying to frighten us into helping you," said Helsenberg, glowering. "But there is no record of us, now."

Mark shook his head.

"I'm trying to understand. Trying to get you to understand. You create something here that a very powerful man in the future wants very badly, and he will stop at nothing in order to get it. He's killed before. He will kill again. As many people as he needs to. And he won't leave you around to tell the tale."

"You must go now," said Helsenberg, rising, shielding his wife from Mark. "Go away and leave us in peace."

"You have to believe that I'm telling you the truth."

"We are scientists. Not secret agents or warriors. What you expect from us? We should fight armed soldiers with our bare hands? We should be caught helping you and certainly get shot?"

Helsenberg's face was hard and yet frightened, and Mark knew that the man would be no help.

"All right," Mark sighed. "I'll have to go out the way I came in, then."

This time Helsenberg and his wife watched like a pair of fascinated children as Mark performed his magic after first sliding aside the rug. As Mark slipped into the hole Helsenberg caught his eye one last time, and the older man's face was incredibly sad.

"Leave us alone," he whispered so that his wife could not hear. "There is nothing you can do for us."

"THIS IS YOUR HOUSE?" said Marilyn, staring at the array of cement block, stucco, concrete-encased glass bottles, and stone that strangely enough seemed to *fit* atop the craggy outcropping of stone overlooking the Pacific sunset. Fat brass figures that might have been men–although they had no legs and balanced on ball-like bottoms–appeared to chase each other around a stone-lined Koy pond where the colorful fish wove intricate patterns in the glassy liquid.

"My parents' house," Tracy corrected her.

"Nice," said Earl, grinning. "I like the ocean. We were kind of living on opposite points of the country with the same view. Like we were meant to get together."

Tracy exited the car first, stepping out onto the meandering stone walkway between acacias, jacarandas, and eucalyptus which all served to soften the house's few hard edges. She had to admit that there was a curious balance to the idea of her crazy parents living exactly one continent away from Earl.

Marilyn caught her arm as she started toward the big, dark wooden doors, each bearing a hand-carved dove in bas-relief.

"There's no reason for them to come here," said Tracy. "My family wasn't on the list, and there hasn't been anyone here for a year or more."

That wasn't exactly true. There were nightmare memories here. The grounds seemed peaceful beneath the deep azure sky and light ocean breeze, but she knew that this tranquil setting was a facade for something horrible, the calm of the afternoon a lie. Deep currents of evil lay ahead in the confines of the structure, ebbing and flowing beneath her feet.

Marilyn nodded questioningly at the lights glowing inside, reflected through stained glass and a million colored bottles.

"Solar panels on the roof and long-life bulbs," said Tracy. "The Conservancy checks the place every month or so for upkeep, but otherwise no one's allowed inside unless there's a problem."

"The Conservancy?" said Marilyn, following her up onto the stoop.

Tracy shrugged. "It's a foundation my parents established."

Rather than searching for a key over the jam, Tracy lifted the mailbox on a hidden hinge and placed her palm against a glass panel there.

"Authenticate," said a computerized voice.

"Tracy."

A clicking announced that the doors were unlocked, and Marilyn's look turned to one of complete confusion.

"Welcome to the real rabbit hole," said Tracy, waving Earl and Marilyn inside.

A cool zephyr greeted them as they stepped onto the granite floor of the wide, high-ceilinged foyer. Hidden lighting gave the stucco walls a soft, cottony appearance that glowed in different earth-toned shades in each of the adjoining rooms that could be seen through large, arched openings. Shelves high on the walls held dream catchers, handmade dolls, and brightly painted African masks. Shimmering water cascaded down a wide expanse of polished black slate along one wall, disappearing into the floor. To their right flames crackled in a kiva fireplace that looked as though a white plaster bubble had ballooned there.

"Who started that?" asked Marilyn, her hand automatically resting on the butt of her pistol.

"Relax," said Tracy, stepping into the large, comfortable-looking living room. The dark hardwood floor accented the heavy leather furniture, and Navajo rugs adorned the walls and hung from rough-hewn beams overhead. "Fire out!"

The flames died with a low hiss.

"Automatic gas fireplace," muttered Tracy. "Triggered when anyone enters the house."

"Cool," said Earl.

Tracy led them through the living room, past a workout area filled with exercise machines that gleamed white and grey, with leather seats that shone black in the soft light. Every step Tracy took into the house raised ghosts like dust.

Her mother smiling from the sofa in the hallway as she chatted on the phone, motioning for Tracy to sit beside her so she could brush her hair.

Her father–also smiling–nodding down at her in the library as she did her homework at his desk.

Her mother again, kneeling beside her bed, taking her temperature.

There had been a period in Tracy's life when she had defended her parents against all comers, when she took their side against the slings and arrows of the hordes of youths who mocked her and them. She could still hear the kids' catcalls in the halls of her school. She could still see her old Volkswagen, slathered with painted slogans like *Go back to Mars* and *The Aliens are Coming!* But after a while it was just easier to give in, to laugh with the mindless mob and not at them, easier to mock her parents behind their backs. Having once done that it became even easier to believe the mockery.

But she never truly became a part of the mob.

They wouldn't have her, and she wasn't ready yet to really betray the people she loved, but at least she could divorce herself from the targets of the mob's witless assault. Then she had discovered the terrible truth, that there was far more to this house and to her parents' madness than the simple gullibility of New Age conspiracy nuts. Her smiling mother and father were not just a pair of *True Believers* espousing crazy theories and living off the other naive believers around the world. They concealed much deeper and deadlier secrets behind their loving veneers, or so she had been led to believe.

She shivered, wrapping her arms around her own shoulders. When Marilyn eyed her, Tracy shook her head and forced her hands back to her sides.

"Not a speck of dust," said Marilyn, running her fingers along the top of an antique side table in the hall.

"The Conservancy cleans the place whenever it's needed, but the humidity is kept at a constant level, and the air is filtered and ionized. You could open an operating room in here."

The image of a human being, his blood seeping out onto the floor, puddling there so brightly, his life pulsing out of him as she watched, sent another shiver through her.

"That must have been a hell of a lucrative magazine," said Marilyn, inspecting a wire sculpture resting on an ornate antique side table.

"Picasso," said Tracy.

"Original?"

She nodded. "The magazine was only one of my parents' ventures. The tour company they founded arrang ed... I should say arranges tours, cruises, seminars-"

"What kind of seminars?"

"The nutty kind. Speakers talk about crop circles, vanished civilizations, people who have been abducted by aliens."

"A lot of people pay for that?"

"Look around you."

Marilyn did just that, taking in the expensive framing on the abstract paintings, the ornate old cases of leather-bound books.

"Karhonen," she said, smiling to herself. "You're Tracy Karhonen. Not Rogers."

Tracy nodded.

"Ira and Sela Karhonen," said Marilyn. "The trial was all over the networks. Pissed me off when the news shows cut into prime time."

"Sorry about that," said Tracy, sarcastically.

"I'm no shrink, but this place doesn't look like the home of a couple of dangerous nuts."

"Maybe it isn't," said Tracy, realizing that she meant it.

Up to and during the trial she had been sold on her parents' guilt. After all, it was she who had discovered them in the act. But in those final minutes–before the other feds had arrived–when her mother placed the note in her hand and hid her away, she'd wondered...

What was so important about something called AventCorp? What did her mother expect Ki to do with the information? In the end, Tracy had kept the information secret, deciding to find out for herself what was true or false about her parent's guilt. After experiencing AventCorp and Ash firsthand, Tracy was forced to wonder just who was crazy.

"Meaning you're changing your mind."

"Meaning I don't know anymore. A lot has happened since then. AventCorp is certainly up to something, but whether they framed my parents, or my parents were involved with them in some way I don't know yet."

"Did your parents kill those FBI agents?" asked Marilyn.

"I thought at the time that they must have. I... saw them. Saw them with the bodies. There was no one else around."

She struggled to get the images out of her mind, but now that Marilyn had conjured them Tracy knew they were just going to get worse. How could they not when eventually she would have to pass right over the spot where the men had died?

"Your parents are the Kookie Karhonens?" said Earl, catching up with the conversation at last.

"That's what they called them. The California press has always had a way with names," muttered Tracy, steeling herself for the inevitable as she turned down a narrower hallway where the light was dimmer. "Be careful. I have to remember how all the security works."

She ran her hand tentatively along the blank stucco wall. As her fingers brushed a familiar rough spot, she whistled, and a machine whistle answered. She used the tip of her toe to touch three floorboards in succession. The whistle returned a quick arpeggio.

"Okay," she said, starting down the corridor again.

"What is the security in this hallway?" asked Marilyn.

Tracy nodded overhead and then waved back down the hall.

"If you manage to get this far in the house and don't follow procedures, the system assumes you're dangerous. Pass that spot back there without authentication, and a steel door drops down to seal the corridor. If you move an incapacitating gas flows through those vents overhead."

"It wouldn't kill us?" said Marilyn, frowning.

"It continues to release enough gas to keep the victims incapacitated until someone hears the alarm and releases them."

"Where is the alarm?"

"In the living room."

"So, someone would come right over from the Conservancy."

Tracy shook her head.

"There is an alarm that runs to the Conservancy, but since I authenticated when we came in, I don't know if it would still be operational."

"Jesus," muttered Marilyn. "You sure you remember where all the security is?"

"Pretty sure. It was one of the first things I was taught. After all, it was put here to protect my family, not hurt me."

"Protect you from who?"

"At one time I would have said from my parents' overactive imaginations."

Marilyn nodded.

"The government said your parents were involved in passing secret information to third-world countries. The FBI agents they murdered were here with federal warrants."

"Yes."

"Were they selling state secrets?"

"They didn't believe in what they thought of as artificial constructs like borders, but whether or not they'd actually sell out our country... I just don't know. I don't like believing that. I'm not sure anymore that those men *were* FBI agents."

"You think they worked for AventCorp?"

"Probably."

"It didn't help their appeal when both of your parents escaped and disappeared. Do you know where they went or who helped them?"

"No. It wasn't the Conservancy, or if it was, they covered their tracks well enough to get the government off their backs. I'm afraid maybe AventCorp took them."

"Like my father."

"Yes."

"You must have believed your parents were guilty of the murders. You testified."

"I told you. I found them with the bodies."

"Aventcorp must have torn this house apart after the murders. How did the agents who searched the house later not stumble on the security?"

"You can override the entire system. That allows for repairs by outside contractors, visits by people with children, things like that. I left it off as long as the investigation went on. I assume the Conservancy turned it back on later. As you can imagine, there's never been a problem with break-ins, even though the house has sat empty since the trial. The window frames emit an electrical shock, and there are *talking* plants in the gardens that scare the shit out of dogs and I suspect most trespassers as well."

"Talking plants would scare the shit out of me," said Earl.

"Didn't anyone bother to ask why the agents could get in with all that security?" asked Marilyn.

Tracy stopped.

"I just assumed my parents let them in. Otherwise, security would have stopped them without anyone getting hurt. The district attorney had the murder weapon with my father's fingerprints. Another agent testified that the four came in one at a time and didn't come out."

Marilyn shook her head.

"Stinks. What excuse did they give for that?"

"What do you mean?"

"Trained field agents would never go into a place like this alone, and certainly not after one or two didn't come out. Who the hell was on the jury, Ash?"

"How in the world would you know what the protocol was for FBI field agents?"

"I watch TV. All I'm saying is the story sounds pretty thin. How many guns did your family own?"

"None, that I was aware of," said Tracy.

That had been another fly in the ointment all along. Both her parents were rabid anti-gun advocates who had fought long and ultimately fruitless battles trying to convince what they saw as a mad country to give up weapons that they felt were nothing less than child-killing machines. Their hatred of firearms eventually translated itself into a phobia in Tracy that she had barely managed to beat in order to save Marilyn at the rest stop.

In her entire life, Tracy had never seen her father or mother touch a gun, had never seen one in the house. Until that day.

That had been a sticking point for the district attorney as well, when the defense brought out file after file of Tracy's father's writings on the subject. But, in the end, when the prosecution was able to display the circuitry and workings of the *other* security systems around the house, the jury accepted the argument that a man who could devise such traps would have no compunction against pulling a trigger regardless of what he'd said in the past.

And his fingerprints were all over the gun.

Tracy tripped another hidden switch that raised a door in front of them. She stepped through, and Marilyn and Earl followed down a long brick-arched stairway into a well-lighted room the size of a tennis court where the painted concrete floor was warmed with bright Navajo rugs.

"This is where it happened?" said Marilyn, glancing around the wide-open library replete with long oak tables and several more of the ubiquitous overstuffed leather chairs and sofas.

"Yes," said Tracy, staring at the floor beneath Marilyn's boot. She could picture a man there, could see the other three lying close beside him, all face down. Her father standing over them with the machine in his hands, furiously punching buttons, his face filled with rage frustration, and... terror. The pistol lying on the floor at his feet.

At his feet.

She had never actually seen it in his hands, although she had testified that she had.

Why had she done that?

She recalled the questioning, the same things asked over and over in different ways. She hadn't started out by telling them about the pistol at all. She had told the district attorney that her father had *something* in his hands. How had it ever gotten around to being the pistol? Because she knew they'd never believe it wasn't? Because both parents begged her never to mention the device? She honestly couldn't remember. Much of her time in custody had become a total blur.

"There's something I need to look at," she said. "Something I'd like Earl to see."

Earl looked up from the chair where he'd been studying the notebook, as Tracy placed her entire body back-first against the wall.

Suddenly she wasn't there any longer, and Marilyn blinked, running her hand over the flat surface against which Tracy had been leaning only a second before.

"What the hell-"

Just as suddenly Tracy bumped into Marilyn's hand, waving it aside as she strode out into the center of the room, clutching a metal object the size of a brick but shaped more like a dog bone. It was made of a grayish metal, polished to a smooth, but dull surface, and lined with bump-like protrusions at odd intervals.

"Where were you? How did you do that?" asked Marilyn, her jaw hanging.

"Holographic wall projection accompanied by a sensory device that mimics the feel of actual masonry through nerve induction."

"What?"

"There's no wall right there," said Tracy, pointing toward the spot where she'd disappeared. "But don't try walking through it. If it doesn't recognize you–and it won't–the same sensory input device that mimics a masonry wall will simulate the pain of you running into that wall, and you won't know the difference in real and imagined. For all intents and purposes the wall is there, and I'm the only one who can walk through it. Except for my parents of course."

"What else is on the other side of the wall?" asked Marilyn.

"Nothing."

"Nothing?"

She shook her head. "They built that safe room to house this."

Earl pointed excitedly at a page in the spiral notebook.

"It's a picture of that machine."

Tracy nodded.

"What is it?" asked Marilyn.

"I think it's what those four agents were here for. My parents showed it to me only once and warned me to stay away from it. The day the killings took place my mother warned me to never ever mention it. I didn't."

"Did they make it?"

Tracy shook her head, sighing. "They said it was an artifact from an alien spaceship."

"You're kidding."

"Nope. They showed me what it did."

"What does it do?"

"Pretty much the same thing Earl's box does."

"But that means your parents were in tune with that thing the way Earl is with his box. What's so dangerous about that, other than maybe throwing a few boxes of candy around the room or upsetting the world gold market?"

"I don't know. But they put a lot of thought and money into making sure this thing was as secure as it could possibly be. Those agents never got near it, and during the months of the trial when the whole house was open no one else found it, either."

"And you didn't tell anyone. Why? They must have questioned you about it, if it's really what they were after."

"They did ask me about it, but I played dumb, and I think my parents managed to convince them that I really didn't know anything. In the back of my mind, a little piece of me wanted to believe that my parents weren't crazy. The fact that people did question me about the device set off a warning bell in the back of my head."

"And if the agents found that thing, and it wasn't an alien artifact but some manmade device..."

She nodded. "My parents might not only have been crazy but liars as well."

"Genius liars," muttered Marilyn, staring at the device.

"I suppose."

Earl couldn't take his eyes off the device.

"Does it make any sense to you now?" asked Tracy, holding it out to him.

He hesitated before taking it.

"I feel *something*, but not like with the box. It's like that thing is trying to talk to me. Turn it over."

Tracy rolled it gingerly, but it looked basically the same on both sides.

Marilyn traced the sketch in Earl's hand with two fingers.

"How could the man who drew this know about this device if your parents kept it so well hidden?" asked Marilyn.

Tracy frowned.

"There are zillions of people out there who have been in contact with my parents at one time or another, conspiracy nuts, UFO believers, hard scientists researching fringe science. What I'm wondering is did my parents tell the man who drew that picture about the device, or did he give the device to my parents?"

"I don't think that's what matters," said Earl, finally taking the device and turning it end over end.

"What do you mean?" asked Marilyn.

Earl pushed one of the buttons.

A dull throbbing seemed to come from every square inch of empty air and the walls, ceiling, and floor around them. The sensation was like being inside a giant pulsing heart, and the sound was so loud it struck Tracy's eardrums like hammer blows.

"Stop it!" she screamed, reaching for the machine.

But Earl backed away, pressing another button that drove the vibration to a higher, more fevered pitch.

Tracy expected books to start flying from the shelves or the furniture itself to become deadly missiles at any moment. Marilyn tried to take a step toward Earl but stopped, clutching her ears. When Tracy was certain she was about to be crushed by the pulsating pressure of the sound, Earl pressed one last button, and everything stopped so suddenly that Tracy sagged to her knees. Marilyn leaned against a bookshelf as though she'd been driven there by an invisible battering ram.

"Take it away from him," she said, waving weakly for Tracy to get the device.

Earl was so intent on the little machine that nothing of the furor around him seemed to have gotten through. He had the same crazy smile on his face he'd had in his cluttered living room, playing with his own machine.

"I'll be double-damned," he muttered, just as Tracy reached for the device.

He pressed two buttons simultaneously, and then he was gone.

"Oh, my God," she whispered, glancing around the room.

"Where the hell did he go?" asked Marilyn. "Another one of your parents' secret rooms?"

Tracy shook her head.

Although the aching in her skull had disappeared almost instantly with the cessation of the sound, she felt nauseous and so dizzy she wasn't sure she could remain on her knees, much less stand. She slid down onto the cool floor, rolling onto her back to stare at the rough stucco ceiling.

Steph was dead. Beatrice was almost certainly dead. At least five of the others on Shiver's list were dead or gone. Now Earl. Zapped out of existence by some crazy machine her parents believed belonged to aliens. Was that what AventCorp was about? Did *Feedback* have something to do with this? Had her parents or someone her parents had known stolen the device from AventCorp? But no one at the company had ever questioned her about it, and if they knew they pretended not to.

The thought of Aventcorp reminded her of bloody corpses, and although she knew on a conscious level that there was no way a twenty-one-year-old young woman walking in on a gruesome scene like that bore any responsibility for it, she still felt the weight of guilt. Both her parents had been the most non-violent of people. Which made it all the harder to accept what she'd seen. She could easily enough call up a perfect image of her father, aiming that machine at the corpses...

The machine. Not the gun.

Marilyn was still staring at the space in front of her where Earl had disappeared, and Tracy followed the girl's gaze. There stood Earl, grinning wildly. She could have slapped him.

"What happened?" Tracy gasped.

Earl shrugged, tapping the machine.

"Where did you guys go?"

"Us guys?" said Marilyn. "Where did *you* go?"

"I didn't go anywhere. You two just disappeared."

Marilyn jerked the device out of Earl's hands.

"I didn't know it did much of anything but *fly* things, as Earl would say," said Tracy, staring into the past that was now present all around her.

She could imagine her father clearly now standing over the fallen FBI agents, pointing the device at them, frantically punching buttons. Her mother finally noticed Tracy, and her face fell. She shook her head, shouting at Tracy to get out, to get away, but Tracy already heard the pounding of feet behind her.

"Are you all right?" asked Marilyn, wrapping an arm around her shoulders.

"That must be what they were doing with the device," Tracy whispered. "They were trying to hide the bodies."

Marilyn frowned.

"Maybe."

"What do you mean, maybe? You weren't there."

"And you're recalling a very traumatic memory from the viewpoint of a terrified spectator. What did you think they were doing with the device until you saw Earl do his shtick? You didn't think they were trying to *fly* the agents out of here, did you?"

"I didn't understand. To me, it was just more evidence of their madness."

"And yet you never told anyone about the device?"

"I couldn't. I promised."

Marilyn nodded.

"Some promises we just keep."

"Yeah."

"What happened that day, after the other agents came?"

Tracy shook her head, trying to clear the image of her father.

"My mother shoved me into the hidey hole and told me to never ever mention the device. She gave me a scrap of paper that just said AventCorp, and said to give it to Ki."

"Ki?"

"He's in charge of the Conservancy."

"What did he do with the paper?"

"I never gave it to him."

Marilyn frowned. "Why not?"

"I don't know. I hid here until late at night when the last of the agents were gone, and Ki came for me. But I insisted on turning myself in to the authorities. I kept that shred of paper like a talisman, anyway. I guess I was clinging to the faintest shred of hope that I was wrong, that my parents weren't crazy killers. After they disappeared, I knew I had to find out for myself. The Conservancy helped me build a new identity. I think they thought I was going into hiding, and I let them believe that. Instead, I went to DC to investigate AventCorp, but I guess I was pretty naive. They were using me all along."

"I think that thing does a lot more than fly things and disappear people," said Earl, quietly.

"Like what?" asked Marilyn.

Earl frowned, concentrating.

"You were gone, and I was here. To you, I was gone, and *you* were here. There's only one explanation I can think of."

"I can't think of any," said Marilyn.

"I was shifted into another universe."

"That's insane," said Tracy, shaking her head, but staring at the device.

"Not really," said Earl. "There *are* alternate universes. That's how time works. I wonder... I suppose that thing must be able to shift time, too. Space, time, they're just two sides of the same coin. That machine has a lot of potential. I can tell you that just by tuning into it."

"Potential?"

"A lot," said Earl, grinning even wider and nodding.

"Potential for what?" asked Tracy.

"For anything."

Marilyn chuckled.

"Earl," she said. "You should have been a politician. You have a great knack for speaking well and saying nothing."

"Thanks."

"When will the Conservancy be coming back around to check on the house again?" Marilyn asked Tracy.

Tracy nodded toward a table near the rear of the room where a computer monitor sat idle. She booted the machine and typed in a password, clicking the mouse several more times.

"They won't be back for a week or more."

Marilyn nodded.

"What are the chances of finding food here?"

Tracy chuckled. "My parents were also survivalists. If you don't mind canned or freeze-dried, we could probably live here for a decade or more."

"Then I suggest we treat ourselves to long hot showers, a decent meal, and a good night's sleep. How's that sound?"

Tracy nodded.

Even with the ghosts of her past all around her, the idea of sleeping in a warm bed in the safety of the house was more than appealing. Suddenly a week's worth of exhaustion seemed to drop on her shoulders, and she hoped that Marilyn or Earl was up to cooking. She started to turn off the computer when Marilyn caught her hand.

"What's that?" asked Marilyn, nodding toward a blinking red light at the bottom of the screen.

"Oh, no," Tracy whispered.

She flicked through the operating system, turning on the security cameras. Suddenly the screen was a patchwork of view angles. An assortment of vehicles, all very official looking were parked out front. Men in black, carrying automatic weapons were taking up positions at every door and window.

"If you know how to turn on all the security this place has," said Marilyn, "I suggest you do it now."

Tracy started clicking icons. Around them, low humming and buzzing noises sounded. Marilyn raced to the door, peeking out into the corridor.

"The steel doors are going down."

Tracy nodded, still staring at the monitor. Several of the men wore flak jackets and carried what appeared to be grenades. She had no doubt they had other more powerful weapons as well.

"We could all hide inside the room where the device was kept until they give up searching," suggested Marilyn.

"It isn't a room. It's more like a tiny closet. There's barely enough space for the device and one person."

Through the computer speakers, they could all hear the agents at the front door as they crashed it in with a hand-held battering ram. So much for knocking or warrants, but these weren't cops. Three men carrying submachine guns raced into the foyer, one turning left, one right, the other covering the area directly in front of them.

"What's the security out there?" asked Marilyn.

"My parents didn't believe in guns," muttered Tracy, "but they felt strongly that the home was inviolable."

"What's that mean?"

"If the exterior of the house is breached violently like that, the security is stepped up to Code Red. It becom es... deadly," whispered Tracy.

"If they catch us here, things will turn deadly for us," said Marilyn, urgently.

Tracy clicked the mouse again. Suddenly the sound coming through the small speakers became a high-pitched whine, and the men in the foyer dropped in their tracks. Several of the men outside fell writhing to the ground clutching their ears. Tracy turned down the volume on the computer speakers.

"Multi-layered high and mid-frequency sound at extremely high decibels."

Marilyn nodded.

"Fries their brains, right?"

"More like shorting them out," said Tracy, nodding toward the men out back who were stuffing in earplugs in preparation for breaking through the rear doors. "The frying happens there."

This time there was no sound, but the men who collapsed inside the kitchen writhed as well. Tracy noticed

Marilyn leaning for a better look. Smoke had begun to wisp upward through the men's clothing.

"What's happening to them?" asked the girl, grimacing.

"Microwave," said Tracy, barely able to watch the screen.

"Nukin' 'em," said Earl, nodding.

The image of the men's agonizing deaths melded with the picture of the dead agents in Tracy's mind, but she thought of Stephanie, and Bea, of all the people on the list who had disappeared. These men or men like them were responsible for that. Not her parents. Certainly not her, and not Marilyn or Earl.

"They're not here to ask us to a dance," she muttered, steeling herself as she held her fingers suspended over the keys.

"It's not all automatic?" asked Marilyn.

Tracy shook her head.

"Most of it is, but there are some auxiliary procedures available."

"Procedures, for example, that might help us against that?" said Marilyn, pointing at the screen in the corner where a van was dislodging a couple of men carrying flame throwers and another hauling something that looked ominously like a small rocket launcher.

Tracy frowned.

"They certainly came prepared."

Marilyn stared raptly at the screen, the slightest tinge of fear in her voice.

"They're going to blow this place up or burn it to the ground with us in it. Seems stupid if they want the machine that badly."

Tracy shrugged, glancing at the device.

"They searched so many times they probably have no idea it's here."

Twenty-foot flames leaped from the throwers.

Tracy pressed two keys and then clicked another icon. Suddenly lawn sprinklers erupted, and Marilyn stared at her in disbelief. Agents scattered around the yard seemed to find that part of the security system funny as well. They laughed and pointed toward the two men carrying the flamethrowers which sputtered but did not gutter.

"That's it?" said Marilyn. "The sprinkler system?"

The men wielding the weapons released more test bursts of flame which licked hungrily at the outside of the building but could do little but scorch the concrete and glass, as the sprinklers continued to pour forth a deluge, creating mini-rainbows in the California sun.

"When the grass and walks are wet enough the system kicks in," said Tracy, quietly.

Suddenly a sinuous blue spark leaped from man to man. A dozen agents either sprawled on the soaking lawn or danced macabrely across the walks before falling to the ground dead. Tiny lightning bolts continued to race across the sodden grass, sparking upward to the dangling branches of the trees, to the fountains of water from the sprinklers that continued flowing.

"Electrocuted," whispered Marilyn, whistling through her teeth.

"There are fuel cells in the basement powerful enough to light Hollywood," said Tracy. "The energy is released in a series of high voltage blasts of DC. Edison believed that DC would work better for electrical executions... So did my parents."

"That wasn't an execution," said Marilyn, quietly. "That was self-defense."

Tracy nodded.

"I should have known if I came near this place again people would die."

"Would you rather those guys had caught us out on the road, undefended?"

"No."

"They're not all dead," said Earl, pointing at the screen.

A couple of agents sat in their cars, afraid to put their feet down outside.

"They'll call in help pretty soon," said Marilyn.

Tracy nodded.

"Earl, do you think it's possible you could get that device to shut down their radios?"

Earl frowned.

"Maybe."

"Not maybe, Earl. We need to know."

He screwed up his face, reaching for the device. When Marilyn handed it to him, he traced his fingers along every inch of it, eyes closed in concentration. Finally, he nodded.

"I think I can do it."

Tracy flicked a couple more icons.

"Let's go, then," she said, starting down the corridor toward the steel doors that were just opening again.

They passed through the kitchen and out the back doors, stepping gingerly over the well-done agents, the smell of burnt flesh so obnoxious that Tracy was sure she was going to vomit. Somehow she made it out onto the porch where Marilyn grabbed her as she stood poised on the bottom step.

"It's okay," said Tracy, following the girl's gaze to the soaking grass. "The power's off."

"You're sure?"

"I'm more worried about those two out front in their cars. They can still shoot us as we go by."

Marilyn nodded, waving both Earl and Tracy into their Jeep with her pistol.

"Just shut down their radios," Tracy told Earl, as they all climbed in.

"Too late," said Marilyn, cocking her head.

A radio in a sedan parked out front sputtered, and they all stopped to listen. Tracy could make out enough to hear that the men were already calling for backup.

Marilyn cranked the engine and eased out onto the lawn, at the same time nodding toward the pistol in Tracy's belt. Tracy frowned but rolled down her window. It was silly to worry about a stupid phobia now.

"Just keep their heads down," said Marilyn, reading Tracy's face. "And Earl, try to screw up their cars if you can."

Earl nodded, his face tight, his hands shaking on the device that now rattled where he rested it on his own window frame.

Marilyn dropped the shifter into reverse and floored the pedal. The tires spun on the wet grass, and the car clipped one of the sedans in passing. As they blasted out onto the road the agents leaned out of their doors just as Tracy opened fire at their windshield. Behind her, she heard the device buzzing to life.

For an instant, everything stopped as though the earth had suddenly lurched on its axis. The agents were frozen in their seats. Even Tracy's finger on the trigger was paralyzed. One minute the two cars were there, the agents staring at them in disbelief. Then the cars and agents were gone, and just as suddenly as it had happened, the strange petrification was over, and Tracy, Marilyn, and Earl were roaring away down the road.

An owl hooted in the night, and a cold breeze blew down off the mountains making Mark wish he had something much warmer to wear than his light denim jacket. The road through the desert was a well-worn track where thousands of military tires had eroded the dusty sand down to hardpack. He trudged through the darkness, glad that the army had not yet gotten around to developing night vision scopes or motion detectors.

In any case, he was reasonably certain that this far onto the grounds of the massive facility the security would be almost nonexistent at this late hour, at least until he reached the outskirts of the underground complex.

When he'd hiked about five miles and had seen no lights he began to wonder if Helsenberg hadn't been lying to him, either about the facility or the distance to it, and he began to worry about being caught out in the open by a Jeep load of MPs or a truck carrying the next shift of scientists to work. Of course, he could get away again, but that would just stir up a hornet's nest of security around the complex, making his getting near the labs again impossible.

It might also leave some official record of his time and location that Ash could use in the future to target him here in the past.

He hiked another couple of miles before lights did finally glow in the distance. Moving searchlights on more guard towers.

He wondered just how alert the soldiers would be. Guards on duty might have been standing the same watches for months without seeing anything more exciting than a jackrabbit. Odds were the searchlights roved in a set pattern, and the guys weren't even looking. On the other hand, they might just be so surprised to see a human being suddenly appear out of the darkness that they'd shoot first and ask questions later.

It was almost four AM, but it was still hard to tell if the skyline behind him was getting lighter or not. If the scientists kept to a military schedule they'd be moving soon. He trotted on toward the lights.

The closer he got to the towers, the more certain he became that the men inside were not as alert as they might have been. He could make out tiny silhouettes, helmeted figures leaning wearily on their searchlights, passing them across the desert floor in what he began to realize was not a random pattern. Huddling behind a small sandstone outcrop he timed the lights' circuits. He could see the Quonset huts and the small shed set off to one side that Helsenberg had told him to look for. Blocky shadows beyond the searchlights' glow might have been deuce-and-a-half trucks, or they might be stacks of crated material.

Watching as the nearest light completed its slow track, he rose to his feet and raced hunch-shouldered to the base of the first tower, pasting himself against the creosote-coated pillar like a lizard, staring up at the winding wooden stairway and the closed trapdoor high overhead. The other towers all shone their lights across the Quonset huts and then started their dancing light show across the desert again, and he knew that in only a moment the one to his right would shine right where he was standing.

He ran the thirty yards to the nearest hut imagining eyes on his back the entire way, waiting for the shout to halt, for bullets to burn into his back. He slammed against the cold corrugated tin side of the building counting the seconds until the next tower ran its own sweep of the complex. Ten seconds, tops. No time during this sweep to make it a hundred yards to the entrance shack. He raced around the corner to the door of the Quonset hut and tried the handle.

Locked, of course.

Just as the light swooped in his direction again, he trotted back around the side of the hut and leaned against the metal again, staring directly at the third tower where the bored guard had his back to Mark, directing his light toward the mountains.

One second.

Two.

The light from the second tower swung in his direction.

He turned and slid his hand along the corrugated metal, opening the hut like a can of sardines. Slipping inside he closed the magic door, feeling the weird power flowing through him. He could sense every molecule fitting back into place, every atomic bond reuniting.

When the joint was resealed, he stared at the edge of his hand, wondering for the first time if the talent that he had been given bore any dangerous side effects. Was he going to eventually melt himself, become part of whatever molecular bonds he was transforming–like The Fly–or start losing his mind like Dr. Jekyll?

After a moment he decided none of those ideas bore consideration. If he was slowly malfunctioning there was nothing he could do about it, and no doctor would understand much less have a cure.

The Quonset hut was lit only by thin starlight and the occasional beam of a searchlight through the window on the door, but in that gloom, it was plain to see that the shack was empty. What did the military use this building for? There was no equipment stored here, no desks or files, not even a broom.

He slipped closer to the door, glancing out to time the searchlights' pattern again in preparation for a run to the entry shack. Just then the floor began to vibrate beneath his feet. In a moment the vibration became movement as the building slowly tipped, and he gripped the metal stud beside the door, climbing onto the one beside it like a ladder as the entire building rose to lean on end like a giant trap door, a high-pitched rushing sound like wind through a tunnel blasting his ears.

The building was shaken by more rolling vibrations that threatened to dislodge Mark's fingers and feet from his precarious perch, but he clung there, peering out the small window on the hut's door. With a final thunderous quiver, a silver disk as broad as the hut was long blasted skyward on end then quickly leveled out and zoomed away toward the distant mountains.

A saucer, flying at incredible speed, maneuvering as no vehicle he had ever seen could maneuver. As the building slowly lowered itself back into place Mark stepped down again, gazing in wonder at the floor.

A fucking flying saucer. Just like Helsenberg said.

There had to be a wide shaft directly beneath his feet for the craft to have flown out of. A shaft leading directly to the underground research facility of Terra Diablo. And if the cavern was as deep underground as Helsenberg said then the saucer was probably the only reason for that shaft. Surely no one expected an intruder to come right through the bottom of the Quonset hut and *climb* down.

He tested the floor by creating an opening in the bare plywood large enough to stick his head through.

The wide, deep, well-lighted shaft dropped away beneath him. He resealed the opening and created a larger one near the wall. Taking a deep breath, he leaned into the hole and tried an experiment. As he suspected he was able to touch the concrete face with his toe and cut a foot hold. Lowering himself laboriously below the level of the floor, he could see that perspective caused the shaft to look as though it narrowed to nothing near the bottom. It had to be several hundred feet down.

Taking one step at a time—and not looking down again—he began to descend.

ASH GLARED AT THE man in the white frock standing just outside the door of the control room. The man's eyes revealed fear, but his stance told Ash that he was aware of his position as well. Ash couldn't afford to kill him, but that wouldn't stop Ash from making the man's life a living hell if he so chose.

"There must be a way," said Ash.

"You know as well as I do that there's not."

That was the problem. He *did* know. But he dearly needed someone to come along and tell him differently. Of course, that would mean that *he* had made a mistake in his calculations, and that was impossible.

He was caught in a Catch-22 of his own design. Time was running out as Walsh had so perspicaciously noted. Less than two hours ago he'd received a call from the Senator's office demanding his presence that day. Ash had managed to buy himself another twenty-four hours asking for time to pull some reports together.

"There is only one brief time period, and we have to hit it on the nose," said the weasel-faced little toad. "And once we send someone there at that particular time-that particular place–we can never do it again. From the best reading I can get I think you hit the nail almost on the head when you sent Walsh back. Closer than Trevor, anyway."

"Wonderful. I didn't care particularly whether Walsh ended up in darkest Africa during the Boer War. And he's the one who hits the target. Great work."

The weasel shook his head. "Now it's going to be tough to send anybody back between the time he got there and the *event.* That was a real stupid thing to do."

The man realized he'd overstepped, and his lips slapped shut.

Ash was as aware as the weasel that sending three full grown men through the machine in such comparatively rapid succession had disturbed the ether again and that he had been responsible for that decision as well.

"I'm going through as soon as we power up again."

The weasel looked stunned. "You?"

Ash sighed. Why not kill him? It would be so easy. So enjoyable.

"I can't take a chance of sending someone back who won't get the job done," he said, hating explaining himself and at the same time realizing why he couldn't enjoy himself just yet. "And you have to bring me back. How soon will we be ready to fire her up again?"

The man frowned again.

"Five, maybe six hours. The timeline seems to be settling down. But you saw what happened just now. Something disturbed it again, and we didn't do anything."

"None of the men we brought in can tune the machine any better than you?"

The weasel smirked.

"I don't know what you thought you were accomplishing by bringing them here. They don't understand our setup at all."

Then why had his informant bothered to even track the men down for him? He had implied that they might have information Ash could use. But he knew more about the physics than they did. They were cretins compared to him.

"At the earliest possible moment," said Ash, striding down the hall.

The weasel waited until Ash was completely out of sight to wipe his brow and return to the control room.

Unlike the shaft—which was reinforced concrete—the tunnel at the bottom appeared to have been blasted out of solid rock. Strands of metal conduit overhead fed hundreds of incandescent bulbs, and Mark felt naked in their glare. His footsteps on the uneven stone surface echoed like pistol shots, so he took off his shoes, tied the laces together, and slung them over his shoulder.

It was over two miles before he reached the end of the tunnel and stared down a long slope into a vast cavern that looked all too familiar. Then he recognized one weirdly shaped stalactite high overhead. It was the same cave from which Ash had launched him into the past. Only there were no cement block partition walls dividing it, and no shoring beams on the ceiling.

Directly in front of him stood a large concrete platform that—by its shape and size—had to be a cradle for the saucer. Across the wide expanse of floor, he saw white-coated men at work around lab tables, while others huddled about gleaming machinery that he couldn't make out. In one corner several labcoats flittered around a wide stainless steel ring of tubes that looked frighteningly familiar. From the center of the ring a white radiance brighter than the sun flashed, a giant white snake, writhing, reflected off the ceiling of the cavern so brightly that all the men working below wore dark glasses.

The original time machine.

Mark took advantage of the fact that everyone seemed preoccupied with their own work to slide down the long incline and take cover behind the cradle. Apparently, with the saucer gone, there was nothing at this end of the cave to attract anyone's attention. He peered back down the tunnel, wondering again at the incredible maneuverability of the saucer. The tunnel was barely larger than the shaft, and the machine had seemed almost as wide as that. Perhaps it had some kind of protective field that stopped it from bouncing off the rock walls. If the Germans had come up with anti-grav, he supposed that wasn't too much of a stretch.

But the more he stared at the time machine in the corner, bouncing its dancing light off the stalactites high overhead, the more he pictured the saucer in his head. Could the Nazis really have produced that thing? It just seemed too far-fetched. The Nazis hadn't even succeeded in building enough jets and rockets to win the war, and they were on the cutting edge of that technology. How close could they really have been to anti-gravity?

Staring around the vast, brightly lit cavern it was hard to credit what he knew was going to happen. Nevertheless, he was almost certain now that he could walk out of here, and at the allotted time every person in the cavern, every piece of equipment, would be destroyed because none of it made it into the future or Ash wouldn't be trying so hard to steal it from the past. Mark could still try to make a life for himself here in this time knowing in all likelihood that Ash had been foiled.

Only he wouldn't be.

If Ash could send him here, now, then he could send someone else minutes or hours in the future to get whatever it was he wanted. But why cut it so close? Was it because whatever Ash wanted wasn't completed yet? Or was it a foul-up in the future, and Ash was still trying to get back? Of course, there was one other possibility. Ash was already back but not here yet. The ramifications of time travel could drive you crazy.

But one thought stirred Mark to action.

Katie.

She was dead because of Ash, and even the remote possibility that Ash *would* end up with anti-gravity or whatever else he was trying to discover here was more than Mark could bear. There was a delicious irony in the idea that Ash, testing a machine that would allow him to return and recover lost secrets had inadvertently returned the one man to the past who would bury those secrets.

The problem was that while Mark might be able to come up with some kind of device large enough and powerful enough to collapse the cavern, there was no guarantee that he could destroy everything in it. To do so he'd have to make sure he killed every one of the German scientists so that they couldn't pass on what they'd developed to the future. He didn't know if he could do that. He was no longer the man who could kill without question for a cause. The end didn't always justify the means. These people might have served a murderous xenophobic regime in the past, and some of them might really deserve to die, but he suspected from what he'd witnessed so far that most of the people working here were slaves and had been for most of their lives.

He couldn't be their judge, jury, and executioner.

A rumbling noise from the far end of the complex revealed a large set of steel doors–painted to match the surrounding stone–opening inward. Labcoats in the distance stretched their arms in fatigue and waved at the incoming group of scientists. Mark wondered if Helsenberg was among them. Probably. Leaving his wife sitting back in that tiny shack out in the desert, staring at the walls. Who was she, and why had she chosen to marry Helsenberg? She was obviously American. Had they met before the war, or was it possible that she'd married him after, knowing that he was a prisoner, possibly even knowing what her life would be like?

Once again, he thought of Katie. Would *she* have stuck by him had she known what he was, what he really did? He wanted to think so.

He worked his way closer to the lab tables and the light, which increased in intensity the closer he came to the center of the cavern so that he had to squint and shield his eyes. The sound of voices carried across the wide-open expanse, sometimes echoing loudly, sometimes muffled as though whispered through thick wool, and most of them were German. He wasn't going to learn anything by simply eavesdropping.

Finally, as the first shift exited through the heavy doors that rumbled slowly closed behind them, he noticed that they hung their lab coats along the wall there. After studying the new group for a while and assuring himself that they were as dedicated to what they were doing as the first group, he strode purposefully out the thirty-odd yards to the hanging smocks and quickly slipped into one, glancing at the name tag–Reichman, Georg–before fumbling dark glasses out of the pocket and placing them over his teary eyes. He scuttled away from the wall where he was easy to spot standing alone and walked slowly past the long line of lab tables almost unnoticed.

The tables were littered with electronic equipment that to Mark's eye appeared antique; vacuum tubes interspersed with brightly colored transistors, and solid-state boards that looked like something out of the Dark Ages. Of course, here, now, many of them were state of the art. Oscilloscopes sputtered and whined, their bubble screens turning from undulating lines to waves and back, and on one table a static-generating silver sphere fired tiny bolts of blue lightning in all directions, right out of an old Frankenstein movie. Several of the scientists huddled in small groups chattering in German, but Mark passed them by with a nod, receiving only an occasional curious nod in reply.

The work just seemed so disorganized. That was the only way to describe it, and it certainly didn't look like something the government would fund. He couldn't understand what the mass of seemingly unrelated items on the tables had to do with a functional flying saucer or the time machine in the corner.

Nearing the light, he noticed that the contents of the tables changed.

There were items that–although he had no idea of what they were–were clearly not produced in 1959–and certainly not during the war. Most of them appeared to be made of dull gray metal, of varying–but all very odd–shapes and descriptions. The largest of the *devices* was the size of a washing machine but designed as though it had been molded from clay. It was convoluted and eerily organic-looking with several tubes that appeared to be made of glass protruding from one side. A low humming noise came from the tubes, in and out, as though the machine were breathing, and rows of oddly shaped buttons lined one side of the contraption, but there were no designations on any of them to tell an operator what function each one might control.

He stared at the light again and the men gathered around it, wondering for the first time if Helsenberg had been lying. Had these men journeyed through time after all? Were they bringing future technology back to this era? Once again Mark wondered what Ash could possibly want here. He had a time machine. Wouldn't he be just as capable as these scientists of journeying to the future to rob it of anything he required?

"Make it work you frigging Nazi! You did it before."

The scream was so high pitched and so vehement that Mark spun on his heel, staring in disbelief as a man clad in one of the white lab coats but clearly wearing a military uniform underneath brought a Billy club down across the shoulder of another of the white-coated men. The beaten man, holding up both hands to block another blow, jabbered in German, but the officer refused to listen, striking at the man's bared arms, leaving nasty red whelps with each strike. The other scientists stared not at the scene but at the lab tables in front of them. It was then that Mark noticed that two other white-coated attendants stood to one side, also wearing barely concealed uniforms. When they started to turn in his direction, he eased closer to the table beside him and pretended to stare at the odd mixture of flow-formed metal devices there.

The scientist beside him whispered in German, and Mark shook his head and shrugged.

Mark felt the man's eyes probing.

"You are not one of us," said the man in grammatical but heavily accented English.

Mark said nothing, staring at the device that made no sense to him.

"You will be killed," said the man simply.

Mark took a chance.

"What are you doing here?"

The man snorted.

"We are not doing anything. Our warders wish us to do the impossible."

"The device in the corner, the light. What do you use it for?"

The man shrugged.

"It is Helsenberg's machine. He created it from some of what you see here and by studying the propulsion records of the original disk designs. It is basically an enlarged version of the disk engine. He wants to understand better what powers these devices."

"What does power them?"

The man shook his head.

"What does the soldier want you to *make work*?"

The man snorted again.

"Everything you see before you. They do not understand that the men who worked with these wonders during the war are dead. I suspect even they would not be able to make everything you see here work. Perhaps much of it never did."

"But what is this stuff supposed to do?"

"Who knows?"

That wasn't the answer Mark was expecting, but there was no subterfuge in the man's face.

"So, what are you doing here?"

"Exactly as Herr Grunig says," said the man, frowning in the direction of the officer who had finally stopped beating the other scientist. "Making things work. Or not, as the case seems to be. I fear that time is running out for Herr Grunig and the others. They have been charged with making these machines function, and we are here to see that they succeed. I have come to believe that our continued failure to do so will be as unpleasant for Herr Grunig as it is for us. We get the devices running some times... But that can be a dangerous game. Long ago we managed to make one of the machines cause invisibility when it was connected to a large metal object. Then the device was taken away. Probably for testing elsewhere."

Jesus. That's too fucking wild. Is he talking about the Philadelphia Experiment?

"But where did this stuff come from?"

The man's frown spread and was now redirected at Mark.

"Who are you? Where are you from?"

"Let's say I'm not a friend of Herr Grunig."

"Are you a Communist? Is that what you want here? You will find no one to help one of your kind."

"I'm not a Communist. I'm an American citizen who doesn't believe in what the government is doing here."

"You don't even know what the government is doing here."

"I know they're beating people."

"Beatings. This is nothing. There is much worse that can happen to a man."

"Like having his family held hostage?"

The man hesitated before replying, his eyes narrowing.

"And you could do what about this?"

"I don't know yet. But would you be interested if I could help you?"

"Why would you help people you didn't know?"

The officer dusted himself off and turned in Mark's direction, and Mark turned back to the man beside him. The scientist gestured toward a small piece of metal equipment shaped like a dog bone and spoke slowly in German, turning the device over. Mark nodded and pushed the button the man pointed at. A couple of lights came on inside and the metal glowed as though it were melting but radiated no heat.

After a moment the lights went back out, and the officer and his two guards lost interest, wandering off toward the tower of light, but Mark noticed that the device felt warm to his touch now, familiar, as though he had held it before, although quite obviously he had never seen anything like it. He began to shiver, but quickly released the device and took a deep breath, stilling the power before it could start. He stared at the machine, wondering what had just happened. It was as though he and the device had been in harmony, resonating to one another's internal rhythms. How could a machine do that?

How the hell do I do the things I do?

Someone shouted from the area of the time machine, and Mark dragged his attention away from the device on the table.

"What are they doing with Helsenberg's machine?" he asked, nodding toward the light.

"You understand physics?"

Mark shrugged.

The man sighed.

"They experiment with gravity. You understand how I mean?"

"Anti-gravity."

"Correct."

"And it works?"

The man chuckled.

"You've seen the saucer?"

Mark nodded.

"So, if they have it working, then what are they doing over there?"

"Still trying to understand how it works. How did you get in here knowing so little?"

"You wouldn't believe me if I told you."

"I give you the same answer, then."

Mark noticed that one of the guards was eyeing him again, and he pretended to fiddle with another piece of equipment. This time there was no accompanying resonance.

"You must get other stuff doing something or they wouldn't have kept you here this long."

"Yes. We built the saucer from the diagrams that were salvaged after the war. We get the anti-gravity machine and the invisibility machine running. This we do. Sometimes we get one of these other machines working for a short time as you saw. As I said, that is not always a good thing."

"What do you mean?"

The man nodded toward the dog-bone-shaped device.

"You push the wrong button or wrong sequence, you end up dead. Sometimes worse than dead. That is why there is only the captain and two sergeants down here."

Mark pictured the empty Quonset huts far overhead. The military wasn't even willing to keep key personnel up there, shielded by hundreds of feet of solid rock. He eyed the small device more warily this time.

"Where did the devices come from?" he asked. "No one in Germany invented this stuff, did they?"

The scientist shook his head.

"It was discovered. Not invented."

"Discovered where?"

"Near Brennervelt, in 1942."

Mark nodded, the reality finally sinking in, although it was such a strange and unbelievable reality that he had trouble crediting what he knew. The Nazis hadn't invented foo fighters. They had simply reverse-engineered them. This wasn't future technology. It was alien technology. He stared past the saucer cradle, wondering if he should climb back out the way he'd come in or simply slip through the steel doors using his talents and exit that way. A hand on his arm jolted him, and he spun, ready to strike with the other hand.

It was Helsenberg.

"What you do here?" gasped the scientist, glancing nervously around.

"Looking. You knew I was coming."

Helsenberg seemed to shrink into himself.

"Almost fourteen years I work here," he said, sighing, "In this hole in the ground. My wife stays by my side even though I try to talk her into leaving at first. When she still could."

"How in the world did you two meet? They certainly weren't flying mail-order brides out here," said Mark.

"In the beginning, we had American research assistants. I believe at first, she simply felt pity for me. Now it is love. Pity does not last so long. If you cannot help us, then you must get out and survive, so that you can tell others what took place here. But please one thing. If you can, please help my wife."

The plea was so pitiful it struck Mark through the heart. Helsenberg loved his wife as much as Mark had ever loved Katie, and Mark knew in that instant that he would die to honor the man's request.

"I will."

"And remember to tell people what happened here."

"I'm afraid I don't know enough about what happened here to get anyone to believe me."

Helsenberg gripped both of Mark's arms.

"You feel it, just as I do. I can see it in your eyes. We opened Pandora's box, and I don't think it will be us that closes it. If you are so certain what you say is about to happen, then go!"

"I don't know *when* anything happens here," said Mark, shaking his head. "I just know it does, and soon. Maybe I cause it."

Helsenberg shrugged.

"Maybe you. Maybe us. We are playing with God's own fire."

Mark studied the scientist's weary face and saw an image of himself after Katie's death. Helsenberg was already thinking of himself as dead.

"Go back to my house," said Helsenberg, frowning. "Hide. If I live out the day, I will tell you all I know when I see you."

Mark allowed himself to be shoved back toward the tunnel. There was nothing more he could think of to do here, but as he hiked up the long slope toward the vertical shaft Helsenberg's words echoed in his mind.

We opened Pandora's box. If I live out the day...

Once more Gotterdammerung pounded through Mark's head as he raced down the shaft. Whatever was about to happen was going to be powerful. Powerful enough to maybe atomize everyone and everything down in the cavern. He climbed rapidly, trying to figure out how he was going to get as far away as possible when he reached the surface since it was surely daylight by now.

An image of Mrs. Helsenberg–dishing out strudel and pouring coffee for the man she pitied, a man she loved–was stuck in his head, and before he reached the halfway point in his climb Placido Domingo had given way to the finale from Gounod's *Romeo and Juliet.* Katie, who couldn't stand the opera, had always loved that one. He remembered the tears in her eyes the first time he'd taken her to see it.

He had no idea if he could do anything for the men in the caverns, but he wasn't leaving Terra Diablo without Helsenberg's wife.

By the time Mark reached the concrete floor of the Quonset hut his hands were shaking in the stone handholds. As he locked one fist tightly in a hole in order to reach up for the ceiling, the shaft rumbled and shook, and the hut lifted noisily away, revealing blue sky overhead.

He pasted himself against the wall as the saucer blasted by, the wind of its passage threatening to rip him from his perch, the sound of a high-pitched scream stitching needles of pain and then numb silence through his ears. The craft vanished into the tunnel, and slowly the hut dropped into place overhead again. With the last of his strength, he cut an opening and dragged himself into the hut, too spent to close the trap door behind him. He lay there with his eyes closed, a ringing in his ears signaling that his hearing was already returning.

Finally, he struggled to his feet and glanced out the window in the door toward the closest tower. The day guards appeared to be as bored as the night shift, but there was no way short of creating a mile-long tunnel that he could get back to the Helsenbergs' hut now. He'd have to pray that the doom both he and Helsenberg sensed approaching would hold off until dark so that he could slip back across the desert.

He was mopping perspiration from his brow with the back of his sleeve when he noticed a pudgy man sitting on the floor at the far end of the hut, shaking uncontrollably as though it were closer to freezing than boiling inside. The man–who climbed unsteadily to his feet–had definitely not been there only a second before, and he didn't look like anyone who might belong there. He had neither the pale complexion of the sun-deprived, night-shift scientists nor the authoritative look and uniforms of their military guardians. Instead, he was dressed in a suit that looked curiously out of place, far too modern, and more Fifth Avenue than Sears Roebuck.

Mark tiptoed over to him, peering into the little man's beady eyes that were shielded by thick horn-rimmed glasses.

When the man focused on Mark his expression changed from one of intense dismay to fear, then curiosity and something that looked far too much like animal cunning.

"Where am I?" he whispered.

"I'd say the question was more when were you," said Mark, recalling his idea about Ash sending someone back for whatever it was he was looking for. But this guy?

"So, you know... But of course, you would," said the man, giving himself one last good shake that seemed to still his convulsions. Although Mark was certain they'd never met there was something familiar about the pudgy little fellow.

"How would you know what I know?" said Mark, casually frisking through the man's jacket, under his arms, feeling the small of his back.

"You're Mr. Townsend, of course."

"And you are?"

"My name is Walsh."

"And you know me, why?"

The man's eyes became even cagier.

"I know what Ash did to you. As you can see–unless we're not where I think we are–he did the same thing to me."

"What's your connection to Ash?" said Mark, glowering.

The little man held both hands in front of him.

"I had nothing to do with what happened to you. That was all Ash's doing. I wanted to stop him. That's why I'm here."

"What does Ash want here? Why is he doing this?"

Walsh slowly took in the confines of the hut.

"Where are we exactly?"

"We're in a Quonset above the Terra Diablo labs."

Walsh couldn't conceal the excitement in his face.

"Have you been into the labs?"

Mark nodded, and the gleam in Walsh's eyes became almost blinding, but Mark noticed an element of fear remaining.

"I have to get down there!"

"Right," said Mark, snorting, as he appraised the fat little bastard. "I just barely survived the climb back out. You wouldn't even make it down."

"What is the date?" asked Walsh.

"The eighth of June."

"The year?"

"1959."

Walsh nodded, glancing at the sunlight through the far window.

"And the time?"

"Eight-fifteen in the morning."

Walsh closed his eyes, tapping his fingers on the floor. When he reopened his eyes, they had a calculating glint in them again.

"Don't you want revenge against Ash?" he said.

Why were people always asking him that?

"You mean for sending me here?"

Surely this little man knew nothing of why he really craved revenge. Or did he? What was his real connection to Ash and AventCorp?

Walsh nodded.

"I have to admit the idea has some allure," Mark admitted. "But I doubt that you're the one to help me do it."

"You might be surprised what I can help you with."

"Who are you, really?"

"Let's just say that I was an *associate* of Ash, but we disagreed on procedure."

"You mean like kidnapping and murder?"

"Those would be two of the techniques I had qualms with, yes."

"But not enough qualms to turn Ash in."

"To whom? Certainly, you of all people are not so naive."

Mark had to admit that it was a specious question. People like Ash weren't liable under the normal channels of justice. Still, Mark didn't see any reason to trust

Walsh. He was after all an admitted associate of Ash, even if he did claim to have moral scruples. Morals were relative in the world Mark knew Walsh inhabited.

"Revenge isn't that high on my list right now," he lied.

"Pity," said Walsh, shaking his head.

He dusted himself off and strolled over to the door, glancing out the window. "We only have a couple of hours."

Mark felt cold sweat breaking out in his palms. Martha hung her fingertips over the keyboard, but he willed her to freeze.

"You know what happens here?"

"We believe that on June 8th, 1959, in the underground laboratories at Terra Diablo, German scientists who had been secretly held since the war by a special department set up by the Department of Defense finally succeeded in activating a machine capable of exploiting Zero Point energy."

"Zero Point is a myth."

"So are flying saucers," chuckled Walsh. "But you claim to have been inside the labs. Did you see it?"

Mark nodded.

"You know for a fact it's all going to be destroyed?" he said, thinking of the men scurrying around the time machine that they did not understand. The powerful beam of light writhing like the arm of a vengeful god about to strike with fire and brimstone.

Walsh nodded.

"Completely. Although the cavern itself will remain, every person in it, every bit of equipment, the saucer, even all the wiring that connects the lab to the ground above, and the towers and buildings you see here will disappear as though they had never been."

"An explosion couldn't do that."

"I never said it was an explosion."

The idea of tunneling several miles to safety was beginning to seem like a decent prospect. Mark had no desire to be atomized by some surge of energy radiating out of the earth far below. If this little shit wanted to follow him, he had no problem with that, but he wouldn't lift a hand to save him.

Walsh was on his own.

"Then I'll just be going," said Mark, glancing around, trying to figure out the best way to start tunneling. He'd have to drop back down into the shaft and cut horizontally through the rock in order not to be seen by the towers outside.

"But this is absolutely your last chance to get back at Ash," said Walsh, still beating what Mark considered a very dead horse.

"Ash wins nothing," said Mark. "You said yourself, everything is going to be destroyed. All I care about now is getting out of here alive."

"What about your wife?"

Mark's breath slipped slowly away. When he spoke, his voice was raspy and hollow, but the implied violence behind it was easily read.

"What do you know about my wife?"

"I know that Ash ordered her murder."

"You're not telling me anything I don't know," said Mark, motioning for Walsh to continue incriminating himself.

"He never expected you to be at your home when the cleanup team arrived, of course. Or that you would be so resourceful in disappearing after your bungled attempt at revenge. When you reappeared as Mark Townsend, I saw no reason to inform him that we had discovered your new identity."

"Who's we? And how did you do that?"

Walsh shrugged.

"I have my informants, as Ash has his. It pays to be informed around Ash."

Mark grabbed Walsh's lapels and hammered him against the wall beside the door, heedless of the dull thud that must have been audible outside.

"You bastards murdered my wife!"

Walsh's eyes widened, and he wriggled like a greased stoat, shoving ineffectually at Mark's chest.

"I had nothing to do with it! I tried to stop it."

"You were part of it, part of the group that took over the company. You had to know."

"All right!" gasped Walsh, as Mark's finger slipped toward his throat. "I knew, but I didn't think it was the optimum way. I, for one, thought it would have been just as simple to start a new organization, but by the time I was hired, it was all in motion. There was nothing I could do. Do you want revenge or not?"

"What happened to John Medlock after Ash sent me back here?"

"Medlock?" said Walsh, confusion plain as the nose on his face.

"Did Ash kill him?"

Walsh laughed.

"I doubt that. He wouldn't dare touch Medlock. Now I repeat, do you want your revenge, or not?"

In the end it was that final question, burning its way over and over into Mark's brain that saved Walsh's life. Mark let his hands slide down the front of the fat little man's shirt, wiping the filthy feel of Walsh's sweat off his fingertips.

"How?" he said, at last.

"We have to get into the labs."

"Tell me why."

Walsh shook his head.

"Not until you get me down there."

Mark grabbed his throat again, but the look in the little man's eyes told him that he'd die before he'd say anymore.

"There's no way we can make that climb together."

"Climb?"

Mark explained how he'd gotten into the lab. Fear spread across Walsh's face.

"I can't climb down, not through a tunnel. It's bad enough I have to go back into the caverns."

"There's no other way."

"Don't be dense. You just have to think of something else," said Walsh.

TRACY SUCKED IN A deep breath, rolling up the window, staring back over her shoulder at Earl who wore one of his characteristic ear-to-ear smiles, as the wind tussled his hair.

"Those agents' radio *and* car won't work now," he said, patting the machine in his lap.

"I expect not," said Marilyn, shaking her head.

"What happened?" asked Tracy. "I didn't ask you to do that."

Earl shrugged.

"You guys still don't believe in alternate universes?"

"I don't know what I believe, anymore," said Tracy, sinking back into her seat.

Marilyn was driving twenty miles over the speed limit, and her eyes roved every side road, every driveway, but Tracy spotted no pursuit in the mirrors, and no helicopter appeared overhead.

"This car is like a bullseye now," said Marilyn.

"Take a left."

"Where to?"

"The Conservancy."

"That's probably not a good idea. If they know to look for us at your parents' house, they must know about the Conservancy."

Tracy shook her head.

"Trust me."

Marilyn shrugged, whipping the big car into a hard turn. The tires screeched and Tracy looked at her.

"Sorry," said Marilyn.

"Two miles up there's a cemetery. Pull in and drive to the rear."

"A cemetery?"

Tracy smiled.

"Nobody's very interested in dead people."

"I'm pretty interested in not becoming one."

The cemetery turned out to be one of those peculiarly Californian affairs, something between a pastoral last resting place and a Hippie architect's vision of a Greek God's landscaping plan. Eucalyptus trees shaded white sarcophagi, and crushed granite walks meandered between ornate headstones replete with doves and angels and eternal balls of polished marble and glass. Spiritual-sounding elevator music poured from hidden speakers.

"Peaceful," said Earl, nodding to himself.

Marilyn raised her eyebrows but said nothing, following Tracy's instructions and pulling the car under the cover of an open-sided, blue tarp tent near the rear. They climbed out of the Jeep and Marilyn stared at a bright yellow excavator parked alongside. The grounds were bordered by thick woods, but through a wall of Ponderosa pine, the waters of the Pacific could be seen glistening in the sun.

"We can't hang around here long," said Marilyn.

"We won't have to," said Tracy, as a telltale creaking announced the opening of heavy iron doors on a crypt a few yards away.

Marilyn instinctively reached for her pistol, but Tracy placed a hand on the girl's arm, shaking her head. She led them into the darkened mausoleum that smelled of mildewed stone and musty air.

"Miss Tracy," said a small, oriental man with close-cropped gray hair and wearing a bright Hawaiian shirt. His toothy smile was as guileless as Earl's, but his slanted eyes belied a canny intelligence. "It has been far too long. Welcome home."

He crossed his arms and bowed low.

"Hello Ki," she said, hugging the little man whose smile lit up like fireworks. "I missed you, too."

The interior of the sarcophagus held one stone coffin. As the heavy metal doors closed automatically behind them, a light went on overhead and the coffin slid aside revealing narrow stone steps.

Marilyn shook her head.

"Another rabbit hole?"

Tracy smiled.

"You ain't seen nothin' yet."

"Not much could surprise me now."

Tracy chuckled.

They followed Ki down into the innards of a large underground facility. A long corridor was fronted by several hand-carved doors–all bearing carved doves–and soft light flowed from tiny alcoves cut into the walls.

"You've redecorated," said Tracy.

Ki nodded.

"It has been too long since you have visited. I hope you do not think we waste Conservancy funds on frills."

"Of course not."

He frowned, stopping with his hand resting on one of the doors.

"We were very worried when you disappeared from your job."

"You knew?"

"Of course. We were only a few hours behind you at the woman's farm, but then we lost you again."

"You were at the farm? What happened to Beatrice?"

Ki spread his hands sadly.

"There was no one there. When we realized you had escaped again, we were gratified, but the only thing we could do was follow the operative. He has gone to ground in New Mexico and has not reappeared."

"I've been in good hands," said Tracy, nodding towards Marilyn.

Ki studied Earl, then turned to the girl. Then he spread his hands in a curiously oriental manner that seemed to say so much more than a Westerner affecting the same motion.

"Our car," said Tracy.

"Taken care of," said Ki, opening the door in front of them.

The room was large enough to comfortably hold the twenty-odd men and women working at computer consoles along the walls, and the area in the middle was filled with double desks, at each of which a man or woman spoke quietly into headsets. The office had a feeling of barely suppressed excitement. Several people smiled or waved, others stared at Tracy with the awe someone might hold for a rock or movie star.

"We are *all* glad to have you back safely, Miss Tracy," said Ki.

Marilyn leaned toward a monitor, but Ki slid gracefully in front of her.

"Please," he said, quietly. "We do not wish to restrict your presence here, but some of what we do is... you would call it classified."

Marilyn nodded.

"I'm not in the club yet."

"You may never be in the club," said Ki. "I am one of the only ones who knows where *all* the shoes drop, as they say."

"Then we'll just need a car to be going," said Tracy.

Ki frowned.

"Going?"

Tracy nodded.

"Thank you for disposing of the old car. Now we need new transport. A hot meal would be good first, though. You can arrange that, right?"

"Of course! But where will you go? You are safe here."

"I'm not sure I'm safe anywhere, but that isn't the point."

"What is the point?"

"Either my friends and I are *in* the club, or we're not. If we are then we are all the way in. All of us. Do you understand?"

"But Miss Tracy, I am only following protocol that has been established since you were a small child-"

"Which I'm not any longer. Where does the Conservancy get its funds?"

Ki's frown spread as did his hands.

"You are aware of-"

"Where do they come from?"

"All the monies are drawn on accounts that your father established, investments-"

"And are you aware that as of a year ago all property of my parents was legally transferred to me?"

"Yes, but-"

"I *own* the Conservancy," she said, quiet enough that none of the men or women at the desks or consoles could hear, "and everything you see around you. Out of respect for my parents and... for reasons of my own, I have chosen not to take an active part in operations. I have no intention of shutting it down or doing anything to harm it. If you choose not to accept Marilyn, Earl, and I as full-fledged members, we'll accede to your *protocol* and leave. We will require a hot meal and a new car. Some cash would be helpful as well and perhaps new identities if that can be arranged."

Ki bowed even lower this time.

"You are certainly aware Miss Tracy that all of that can be arranged. However, please accept my apologies. I meant no offense to you or your companions. The facilities of the Conservancy and the Conservancy itself are yours to command. Please do not leave."

Tracy gave the moment the importance and hesitation it deserved.

"Thank you," she said, imperiously. "A meal and a hot bath for all of us would be a great blessing."

"This way," said Ki, motioning them back out into the corridor.

"What do you know of the men who attacked Tracy's parents' house?" asked Marilyn, as Ki closed the door quietly behind them.

"They are agents of AventCorp," said Ki, giving Tracy a look that said *he* would have known about AventCorp sooner if not for her. "We are quietly keeping the grounds under observation. Many more agents have arrived and are tearing the house apart inch by inch at this moment."

"They'll really be stirred up now," muttered Marilyn.

"Indeed. The air above us is aswarm with helicopters. The roads are blocked. That the three of you could disappear once again must be maddening to these men."

"Heads will roll."

"No doubt," said Ki, smiling.

"WHAT ELSE DO YOU know about what's about to happen here?" whispered Mark, leaning close to Walsh.

The little man had started to sweat the moment Mark began to construct a narrow tunnel from the hut to the shack concealing the elevator.

"I can't crawl through that," gasped Walsh, peering down through the hole in the floor toward the tiny dirt-lined shaft and shaking his head.

"Stay here, then," said Mark, climbing back out.

"There must be another way."

"Down there," said Mark, pointing toward the handholds in the concrete face.

Walsh's face went completely white. He peered into Mark's unforgiving eyes, and finally Mark saw a decision being made. The little shit might be claustrophobic as hell, but he wanted into the labs bad.

"Follow me if you really want to get down there," said Mark, climbing back into the little tunnel and beginning to burrow.

In a moment he heard Walsh grunting into the space behind him. By the time they broke out of the tunnel, Walsh was a ball of sweat, but he strode doggedly onto the elevator.

Crossing the wide cavern floor, Walsh's white lab coat–the smallest Mark could find on the rack–still hung nearly to the floor, and the sleeves bloused out where he had rolled them under, but the scientists studiously ignored them.

Walsh glanced nervously toward Mark's watch.

"Nine thirty," said Mark.

Walsh nodded. "In one hour and twenty-nine minutes, this cavern will be empty. Nothing, and I mean *nothing* will remain."

"I believe you," said Mark, glancing at the row upon row of tables laden with machinery and alien devices, at the machine at the far end of the cavern still radiating its anaconda light toward the far-away ceiling.

"Tomorrow a two-man team sent to discover why the security at Terra Diablo has not been calling in will report that they found all the complex above *missing*, the cavern empty and partially collapsed."

"So how do they know the exact time it happened?"

"A guard's watch will be discovered later in the sands above. That is the time at which it stopped."

"What happens to all the scientists, all the guards?"

"Gone. All gone," said Walsh as they reached the first row of tables.

Walsh gave the machinery there only a cursory once-over before passing on to the next table where more exotic devices were being experimented with. He nodded perfunctorily at one of the scientists, and the man studied him for only a moment before returning to what he was doing. The scientists knew that neither of them belonged here, but probably figured they were safer knowing nothing and keeping their mouths shut.

Mark shook his head.

"What about the other shift, the men and women left in the encampment?"

"Also gone, although those buildings will survive."

"Where did they all go?"

"I suspect now that *we* took them somewhere."

"What?"

"Think about it. Our records show that every man and woman disappeared from this facility. We know they were here at eight-thirty because we have a report from a man named Grunig who was down here at the time. Later that day they were all gone."

"What's that got to do with us?"

"We are anomalies here. We are not supposed to be here, and yet we are here. I find this curiously ironic and, in a way, fulfilling."

"You're crazier than Ash."

"I doubt that's possible. In any case, time is running out."

He studied Mark's face, and then he began to smile.

"Or perhaps it's not. For you perhaps the very idea is irrelevant."

"No one at all remains?"

"One man, the test pilot. He is found unconscious in his Jeep."

Mark shook his head.

"I can't travel through time at will. After Ash shifted me here, I did pick up that weird talent you just saw, but it isn't time travel."

"It's certainly interesting."

"It doesn't get all of us out of here. What if I just refuse to do anything?"

"That isn't going to happen."

"Because it didn't."

"Exactly. If my theory is wrong and you had nothing to do with removing all the equipment and the scientists, then I'm afraid something very drastic and very unexpected is about to happen here, and I have no idea what it is, but I suspect it won't end with any of us being alive."

"You think maybe one of these machines malfunctions?"

"Or perhaps functions might be the more applicable term."

"This is pointless," said Mark, turning away. "What is going to happen will happen whether we're here or not."

"What about your wife?" asked Walsh, stopping Mark in his tracks.

"Bring her up again, and I may just kill you where you stand."

"Time travel," said Walsh. "Think of it. You might save her-"

"You know better."

Walsh frowned.

"You could *see* her. Alive."

Walsh's whining voice, echoing the same thoughts that had tortured Mark already, was more than he could bear. He closed his eyes and leaned against the table wondering... could it really be possible? Could he see Katie, alive again? See her smile, listen to her laughter, if only from a distance?

Walsh chanced edging closer.

"Think of it. If you can travel in time, she can live forever. You can visit her at any period in her life."

Mark slapped him hard, driving him back against the table and causing an oscilloscope to crash to the floor. Slowly the men around the light edged toward them, until all the labcoats gathered around, but still gave Mark a healthy space. In the back of the group, he caught Helsenberg's eye.

"Translate for me," said Mark.

"IF WE HAVE ONLY this short time," said Helsenberg. "We must get going."

Mark wanted to tell him that for such a great scientist, he only had a very weak grasp of the obvious, but he kept the opinion to himself as he stared at the saucer.

"Where's the pilot?"

Helsenberg shrugged, but he appeared to be fighting off a shudder.

"What's the matter?" asked Mark.

"The pilot... he is worse than the guards. He hates us. The man is brutal."

"How hard is it to fly?"

Helsenberg grimaced.

"The pilot seemed to learn basic maneuvers in only a few days."

A few days. A trained test pilot.

Mark pictured the narrow tunnel making a dizzying ninety degree turn up out of the shaft that was barely wide enough to accommodate the craft. That was some break-in flight for that guy. He wondered how many others had perished during training.

Helsenberg followed his eyes.

"Machine has built in... buffer systems. It will not hit tunnel walls."

Mark nodded.

"So, it can't run into anything?"

Helsenberg frowned.

"It is programmed not to strike tunnel walls. It can *run into* things, as you say. There have been crashes of prototypes in the past. During the development stages, we had one bad crash near town called Roswell. Pilot and copilot were... damaged... beyond recognition."

Mark couldn't help but smile and shake his head.

"If it is true that we have only time you say then there is no other way," said Helsenberg after a moment, and Mark nodded.

He raced to the stand and climbed into the cockpit. Surprisingly the circular fuselage held ten seats besides the ones for the pilot and copilot. He dropped into the pilot's chair, and Helsenberg sat beside him.

"How do I start her up?" Mark asked, glancing at his watch. Thirty minutes.

Helsenberg pushed two buttons the size of his fist, and although there was no sound, a high-pitched vibration rattled up through Mark's seat. He felt the craft lift and lurch, then settle as though floating above its cradle. The clear plastic bubble began sliding into place. Mark noticed Walsh clutching the small machine that *he* had experimented with earlier, and heading up the ramp.

"I need to test-flight her!" Mark shouted before the canopy closed.

There were no pedals, no control sticks, no wheel, just a grey panel in front of him with more of the buttons.

In reply to Mark's questioning look, Helsenberg shrugged.

"I've never flown in craft. None of us have."

"Who taught the pilots?"

"They learn by what you call...trial and error."

Twenty-seven minutes.

"Oh, hell," muttered Mark, placing his hands on the two nearest buttons.

To his surprise, he discovered that he was shaking.

"You shiver again," said Helsenberg, frowning.

"Yeah," said Mark. "I noticed."

He took a deep breath, stilling his thoughts. Schumann's *Introduction and Allegro appassionato* to his *Piano Concerto No.2 in B-flat, Op. 83* performed by Idil Biret on piano, accompanied by the Polish National Radio Symphony Orchestra, began softly in the back of Mark's mind, the beautiful limpid, and yet militaristic fanfare seemed fitting. Instinctively he let his mind respond to the alien controls and the music at the same time. He began to sense the machinery behind the buttons, to understand the workings of the craft on a sub-atomic level, and he realized that the craft was meant to be flown in this manner, designed to respond to the person at the controls as though he were a symphony conductor rather than someone exerting mechanical forces.

Slowly the Schumann evolved into the San Francisco Symphony's version of Wagner's *Flying Dutchman*, and Mark smiled. The music seemed to meld through his fingertips with the internal workings of the machine, and he gently brushed the invisible controls here, and then there, strumming the craft like a guitar.

The saucer rocked again, swinging slowly until they were facing the tunnel.

"Hang on," he said.

As the saucer rocketed forward, he realized that neither he nor Helsenberg had buckled in, and he fumbled for a belt, surprised to discover that there was none.

"Don't worry," said Helsenberg, guessing at his motions. "Craft creates its own inertia field. You will experience no acceleration or G forces."

"Of course," muttered Mark as the saucer zipped up the shaft toward the Quonset hut, and he realized that he had told no one to throw the switch to raise the hut. The gray dot that was the concrete floor high overhead rapidly swelled into a flat hard surface, and just when he was certain he and Helsenberg were about to be smashed into jam, the hut lifted away, and they shot skyward like a cannon shell.

The ground below was a blur, and the mountains approached at meteoric speed, but as his fingers danced across the panel the music and internal workings of the craft continued to meld in Mark's mind. He punched a button, and ghost instruments lit up on the canopy. According to the ground speed indicator, the craft was flying at just over twenty-five hundred miles per hour. He took two swift turns over the far peaks and turned back toward the base again. It was going to be tight, but he could do it.

Only the compound wasn't there.

The guard towers were gone, nothing left of them but the bases of their thick creosote posts, cut off clean as though chainsawed at ground level. The huts, too, were gone, leaving only their bare concrete slabs. He landed the saucer with a thump near the site of one of the missing towers, he and Helsenberg staring out across the empty desert.

Helsenberg shrugged.

"I believe the saucer must sometimes cause time distortion. Now and then pilot reports changes in the surrounding areas. Houses that are not there in our time, strange automobiles and aircraft. Not everyone believe him."

Mark nodded, trying to wrap his mind around the implications. Helsenberg had built his larger device–the time machine–using the propulsion device of the saucer for guidance. It made sense that if the flying machine was pressed hard enough the propulsion system might function in the same manner as the larger machine, but how much time distortion? Was this the nineteen-sixties or some far-flung future? He lifted off and headed west, slower this time, touching the controls with a little more care.

When he spotted traffic along a stretch of desert highway, he slowed the saucer and dropped down for a closer look. Cars immediately began pulling to the side of the road, people hopping out, waving, pointing.

"That's a '63 Chevy," muttered Mark. "There's another one, and they look new. I don't see any other models I know for sure, but I'd say by the looks of those people's clothes and haircuts we're no later than mid-sixties."

Helsenberg nodded, entranced by the people and cars from his future.

"The question is now," said Mark, more to himself than to his passenger. "Can I get us back?"

He placed his hands on the console again and closed his eyes, reading the inner workings of the craft, meshing it with the music in his head until they were one and the same. He turned the saucer back toward the base without looking, as he began to *tickle* the guts of the machine.

There was a vast symphony all around him now, part Wagner, part machine, part something ethereal and indescribable, a strange amalgam of the hidden world of atoms–and a structure much smaller even than that–a world of strings that spun and twisted, knotted and unraveled into infinity. In that instant, he knew that he was looking directly into the mystery of time itself, and he knew that he could travel the *road* in front of them just as surely as he could create handholds in a stone wall with his toes.

He did a flyby of the complex again–low this time–and wasn't too surprised to find the towers back in place, the guards goggling up at the craft.

"We go now to get the others?" asked Helsenberg.

Mark smiled, feeling the machine around him now more like his own skin than an alien flying saucer.

"The soldiers here," said Mark, nodding down toward the men in the towers. "Are they paid in scrip or American greenbacks?"

"I do not understand greenbacks," said Helsenberg.

"Dollars."

Helsenberg nodded.

"Dollars. We, ourselves, receive a pittance, although I do not know why. Sometimes we buy from the soldiers. You call it the black market. Yes?"

"Yes," said Mark. "Where do they keep all that cash?"

"Their pockets," said Helsenberg, frowning. Then he seemed to understand. "Ahh. There is a safe in the Commandant's office."

"Great," said Mark, turning the saucer in the direction of the barracks encampment. "We're going to need to make a little withdrawal."

MARK SHIFTED THE SAUCER in time just far enough to take it back into the deepest darkness before dawn of the same morning he had first entered Terra Diablo. Landing on the desert a mile from the camp he left Helsenberg with the craft. Although the scientist assured Mark that by this time he had already been on his way to the cavern and would not be in the camp, Mark didn't want to take any chance of creating a paradox by the man meeting himself.

Unfortunately as he neared the camp he realized that on this side of the encampment there were no rock outcroppings, no arroyos, and no brush. But most of the guards seemed to be asleep, and he trotted easily to the rear of the nearest shack. Crawling underneath he skittered to the front to reconnoiter. Lights were on in the Helsenberg bungalow. It would probably have been pretty hard for Mrs. Helsenberg to go back to sleep, after having been visited in the middle of the night by a man from the future who cut through her floor with his bare hands.

He slipped out of the protection of the building's front stoop, just as a pair of sentries disappeared around the corner of the furthest house. He ran across the street sliding under the Helsenberg's hut like a baseball player into home plate. After he was certain he hadn't been spotted he crawled to the area where he'd cut his way in before. As he reached up to form a door he was surprised to hear a man's voice inside, speaking English. Mark pressed his ear tightly against the floorboard.

"If you try that again, I'll kill you."

Mark had never heard the man's voice before, but he'd heard enough others like it to know there was no bluff in it, and the sound chilled him.

When Helsenberg's wife answered her voice was high pitched, but there was no quaver to it, and he remembered the strong features of her face, the soft eyes with a hard edge behind them. She was frightened but not cowed. "What are you going to do? Why are you here?"

"We're just gonna wait," said the man. "When he gets here I'll let you go."

No way this guy was waiting for Helsenberg. Anyone who could gain entry into the Helsenberg's house–other than himself–had to be authorized to be there, government, military... and any of those people would have had access to Helsenberg any time they wanted. The only other person the man could be lying in wait for was Mark.

Ash's man.

Somewhere in the future Mark must have left some record of being here, but then, why couldn't he just turn around and get the hell out of here now? What would the guy do then? The empty desert now seemed much more inviting, but Mark knew that way was a trap, too. A time trap.

More than likely the killer would just show up ahead of him again where he least expected it, and besides, he knew that even if he died here, he had to at least try to save Mrs. Helsenberg. The thought of her dying now was simply unacceptable to him. Martha Argerich's rendition of Rachmaninov's *Third Piano Concerto* began softly in his head.

Death was here.

So was Rachmaninov.

Mark crawled silently to the far corner of the small house. He hadn't been through the whole building, but from the little of the interior he had seen earlier, he was pretty sure he must now be underneath the Helsenberg's bedroom. Reaching overhead to the rough-sawn joists he began to cut. For the first time, as he delved into that place in his mind where the atomic changes took place, he understood that he was doing more than just rearranging molecules or atoms. He was *displacing* them. All along the slice where the joists and then the floorboards opened up, the area was clean of material, and he knew that when he closed the door, the molecules would return, but was he moving them in space... or time?

He was beginning to understand how either would amount to the same thing, and he realized he was doing something else as well. He was *directing* time and space, adjusting it the way a conductor adjusts the tempo from adagio to allegretto.

When he had an opening just large enough to slip through he dragged himself quietly into the dark room. There was a sliver of light beneath the closed door. He leaned against it, listening, but silence reigned in the house. He hoped that everyone had simply gone quiet because they had nothing further to say, but whatever the reason, if his opponents–he had to assume there might be more than the one he'd heard–wouldn't give themselves away, then that meant that he was going to have to go find them.

Slowly he twisted the doorknob, putting weight on it to keep the hinges from creaking as he opened the door just enough to peek quickly down the short hall. The lone bulb hanging from its twisted cord cloaked the narrow space in gray light.

There were two closed doors. One was certainly the bathroom, and the other either a small study or perhaps a large closet, then there was the open entry to the kitchen. The closed doors told Mark there was only one killer. Professionals wouldn't like to be separated by doors as well as walls. They'd want to be able to communicate quietly and move swiftly, and Mark didn't believe Ash would be stupid enough to send them back in time with radio headsets. More than likely the killer was here with only the accouterments he needed to access the base, meaning he *fit*. If Mark had been running the show he'd have the woman subdued in the bedroom, probably tied to the bed and gagged–at least he hadn't killed her–and then have agents in all the rooms.

It dawned on him that Mrs. Helsenberg might never have told the killer about *how* Mark had first appeared. If all the man knew about his being here was some old report he'd discovered then it probably just amounted to the fact that Mark had visited the Helsenbergs, not how he'd gotten in. The killer was simply waiting for a knock on a door or window. So he and Mrs. Helsenberg were probably in the kitchen.

They wouldn't have read a report on me just being here.

They'd have read a report on me being killed here.

A chill ran up his back, and Martha's keyboard virtuosity seemed to send the cold right down into his bones. For an instant he thought again of turning around, at least trying to disappear, but Helsenberg's wife was so close, that he could almost hear her breathing. He had been too late for Katie, and a man just like the one holding Mrs. Helsenberg had murdered her. He could never allow that to happen again.

As he took a silent step toward the kitchen a click behind him caused him to whirl, certain that he'd made a mistake, that someone *was* in one of the rooms. His movement caused a screeching sound as his shoe sole twisted on the wood floor, and he tensed, but none of the doors were opening, and he spun toward the kitchen again, too late.

Light blinded him as a silenced pistol fired almost in his face. The shot ripped along his jawbone, knocking his head to one side, and rocking him off balance as another shot brushed the hair above his ear. As he fell back against the wall he kicked upward, catching the pistol a glancing blow, driving it out of the man's hands. He shoved himself off the wall, kicking the gunman in the side, forcing him back into the kitchen, but he had no chance to reach the gun, either, as the man spun, slashing with a long-bladed knife. Mrs. Helsenberg crouched in the corner of the cupboards. Mark glanced back at the pistol, and again the man laughed.

"Go for it," said the attacker who was dressed as Air Force Brass from the fifties, but Mark knew this guy wasn't military.

For the first time, Mark noticed the bracelet around the man's wrist that looked like a miniature copy of the collar Ash had ordered placed around his own throat.

"You can walk out of here and return alive," said Mark, nodding toward the device.

The man never took his eyes off of Mark, but this time his laugh held less mirth.

"The only way I get back is when you're dead."

"Then I hope you enjoy Hopalong Cassidy and Bing Crosby."

"Very funny," said the man, sidestepping as Mark maneuvered into the kitchen.

The knife flashed, and Mark dodged, lashing out with a kick that just missed ripping off his opponent's kneecap. He spun, throwing a reverse roundhouse kick at the man's head, but once again all he got was air.

The man backed away as Helsenberg's wife sidled around the table.

"AventCorp is through," said Mark. "Give it up."

The man smirked.

"You don't know shit about the company."

"I was there before it *was* AventCorp."

The man's face tensed in concentration, and he stared at Mark, searching for the lie. Slowly realization dawned.

"I knew you were good," he said. "If you hadn't been I'd have gotten you the first time."

"What first time?" said Mark, edging away from the door, hoping the guy would try to slip past to the gun.

If the fight went on much longer, they were going to draw the attention of the guards.

The man's eyes were squinty and cold, and Mark knew he'd lunge at any moment. He prepared himself for the attack, balancing on the balls of his feet, ready to sidestep, or slide past and rip toward the nose with an open hand.

"At your house," said the man. "I wanted to wait for you there, but Ash was sure the guys at the Estate would do the job. If I'd stayed, you'd be dead like your wife."

Suddenly the house was as frigid as a winter crypt. Mark's heart stopped pounding, and his breath stilled in his lungs. The only movement in the entire room was the man's eyebrows, rising as he took in the expression slowly burning its way across Mark's face, the rage that kindled behind his eyes.

"You," whispered Mark.

"They call me Trevor." said the man, a wide grin spreading.

"I'll put it on your tombstone."

"I didn't do it fast, either. I bled her like a pig, a little at a time. She crawled around begging me to stop, and she called your name a lot, too. How come you didn't come to save her?"

Mark leaped. There was no finesse to the attack, just pure unadulterated wrath. Trevor's grin turned to a grimace, but he stepped easily aside and twisted the knife, aiming for Mark's gut.

Mark swung downward with the edge of his open hand, severing Trevor's arm as though it were made of cake. It flopped to the floor, and a thick column of bright crimson blood spurted, washing Mark's chest. As the man's jaw dropped and he stood dumfounded–staring at the bleeding stump where his arm had just been–Mark slashed again, this time opening another artery in his opponent's throat. Trevor dropped to his knees, his eyes wider still but the light behind them slowly dimming. Mark knelt to catch him by the shoulders, pulling him face to face. He wanted to dismember the bastard, to feel more of the warm blood soaking his fingers.

"You... you die here," coughed Trevor, barely able to shake his head. "They find your body..."

"They find *a* body," said Mark, still glaring.

The light faded from the man's eyes, and finally, the rage died inside Mark as well, leaving him empty of even the music.

"That was for Katie," he said, shoving the body onto its back so hard Trevor's head cracked loudly on the linoleum.

He had no idea how long he knelt there before he felt soft hands on his shoulders, and he looked up into the eyes of Helsenberg's wife.

"You're hurt," she said, making a face as she gently daubed his cheek with a kitchen cloth.

He saw the blood on her hands and reached up to feel the wound. The bullet seemed to have skittered along his jawbone and then exited near his ear. The skin hung in flaps, and although the blood seeped rather than spurted, it was a messy laceration.

"That needs to be bandaged," she said.

Mark shook his head, gently pushing her hands away. "We don't have time."

Instead, he held the skin together and slowly reconnected it. It wasn't like closing a door made of wood, and it was much more complicated than repairing a Persian rug, even trickier than flying through time. Living tissue was not some machine to be finessed, there was a wonderful *chaos* to it that he sensed held order on a level that not even his newfound miraculous talent could help him understand. It wouldn't be pretty, but he felt certain he could make the scar at least lie flat along his face so that the skin didn't pucker. Perhaps another plastic surgeon could disguise it in the future. It occurred to him that he might go to the same man he'd later killed, and the thought brought a painful smile to his face. He might be able to repair the skin, but the damaged muscle still ached.

"You shiver again," said Mrs. Helsenberg, as she watched slack-jawed.

He nodded.

"I think I'm gonna use that from now on."

"Use what?"

"The name."

"Why did you come back here?"

He rose slowly, staring at the pool of blood on the white floor. The dim light reflected from the hallway made it appear almost black, and that too had a curious irony. Black blood from a black heart. He wished now that he'd had more time to deal with the man. Trevor deserved to die much slower for what he'd done to Katie, and there was probably a lot of information that Mark could have gleaned from him, but there was nothing to be done about it now. For just an instant he considered going back to the saucer, shifting back an hour or so in time, and coming back to catch the killer before he was ready, but of course he couldn't do that, or he'd already have done it. He shook his head to clear it.

"We have to get out of here," he said. "We're taking the saucer."

"We?"

"All the scientists and their families."

"You can do that?"

"I have to do that. I know what time it's all going to happen now."

"When?"

"Very soon."

When he knelt and began stripping the body she gasped, so he stopped.

"I'm going to take his clothes," he said. "You may not want to stay in here."

She smirked.

"Seeing him naked and dead will not hurt my feelings."

Mark knew exactly how she felt, and he shrugged, undoing the man's trousers. Regardless of what she'd said, though, as he jerked them down the corpse's thighs, Mrs. Helsenberg scurried out of the room. The pants and what was left of the blouse and jacket were a tight fit, missing one sleeve, and everything was splotched with blood, but with the greatcoat, he'd just spotted hanging on the wall, and in the darkness, the stains probably wouldn't be visible. He snagged a garrison cap off the same hook as the coat and pulled it low on his forehead. A gleam caught his eye, and he followed it to the severed arm. On the wrist the wide solid metallic bracelet gleamed, and he knelt to inspect it, shaking his head.

"Give me a piece of paper and a pen," he called down the hallway.

When Helsenberg's wife returned he took the pen and small spiral notebook she offered.

She stared at him as he dashed off a quick note, tore off the sheet, and slipped it between the bracelet and Trevor's severed arm. When Mark was done, he picked up the pistol from the hallway floor and stuffed it into the back of his pants. The uniform wasn't a perfect fit, but it was good enough for the darkness outside, and the greatcoat would disguise the fact that one arm of the uniform jacket was missing from the elbow down.

Helsenberg's wife stared at him as they stood at the front door. He smiled at her, feeling the new scar twist his expression, and he wondered if it was nearly as reassuring as he had intended it to be. He opened the door and peered warily up and down the street. Stepping quickly out onto the stoop without taking time to wonder how stupid the stunt was, he strode out across the street, leading her by the hand toward the Commandant's office.

The two guards walking the beat stopped at the end of the street and stared. He stared back until both saluted, and he returned their salutes peremptorily. Stepping up onto the landing of the office, he pulled aside the screen and sliced a hole in the door, unlocking it from inside. He let them in, closed the door, and repaired the hole.

He quickly bypassed the desk in the front room and found the Commandant's office. There in the corner stood a stout black safe. He was tempted to just slice through the hinges and the interior bolts and let the heavy door drop to the floor. But it dawned on him that the soldiers here had to think everything was normal for at least the next few hours or God only knew who would be waiting when he came back. It might be the army, called out by the Commandant, but it might just as well be a horde of Ash's men who knew about the disturbance, the day, and the time. So he gently removed a section of the safe door large enough to pass his hand through, then rummaged around inside.

There were several files and one large canvas bag with a rope closure. He had to make the hole bigger to get both of them through. Then he closed the hole and opened the bag, discovering bundles of ones, fives, tens, and twenties. He took off the greatcoat and slipped the rope onto his shoulder before replacing the coat. Through the window, he could see the guards just making their turn at the end of the street again. He hastily cut yet another hole in the floor. Sticking his head through, he stared out at the empty desert darkness before helping Mrs. Helsenberg down with him, the two of them scrabbling to the rear of the building and climbing slowly to their feet in the shelter of its lee. Instead of staying low and timing the lights, instinct kicked in. He snatched his companion's hand again and ran.

They were several hundred yards away from the camp when he was blinded by spotlights and heard the first whine of a bullet past his ears. Mrs. Helsenberg shrieked. Another bullet struck the hard desert floor and ricocheted away into the darkness. Mark knew those had been warning shots, but if they stopped now and raised their hands, within minutes they'd be surrounded by armed guards who'd no longer be sleepy or bored. He dragged Mrs. Helsenberg along, zigzagging like a jackrabbit, farther away from the base and closer to the saucer out there somewhere ahead in the darkness.

With the light catching him, then losing him, then catching him again, it was impossible for his eyes to adjust. He was certain that the low rise ahead was where the craft lay hidden, but when they reached it and dropped behind its welcome shelter, the saucer was gone. Already he could hear the thumping of a Jeep bouncing over the uneven ground in his direction. He rested his fingers on the grip of the pistol in his pants, but knew he couldn't use it. These guards were not icy-eyed murderers like the man who'd been sent to kill him. As much as he wanted to hate them, they were simply soldiers doing their jobs. He signaled for Helsenberg's wife to stay where she was and crawled back to the top of the rise. The Jeep was barreling across the uneven desert sands. Headlights pointed directly at him, but silhouetted above them he could see a fifty-caliber machine gun mounted and a man gripping it.

The pistol was going to be of no use in any case.

Just as the gunner spotted him and wheeled the weapon in his direction a flash of metal blocked Mark's view. The saucer crashed to a grinding landing, plowing the desert floor. Mark grabbed the woman, leaped over the top of the rise, and raced to it. They staggered up into the machine, shouting for Helsenberg to close the canopy even as the confused soldiers came to the conclusion that this was no authorized use of government property and began to fire.

Mark saw the bright yellow bursts from the machine gun as he leaned hard onto the panel and piloted the saucer upward and away. Behind the craft, a volcano of sand slowly fell on the men who were now scrabbling under the Jeep for cover. The base had come to life like a stirred hornet's nest, and Mark had no doubt that the soldier he saw halfway across the main street pulling on a jacket was the Commandant. Now he knew they couldn't leave the other scientists in the camp for later. As soon as these guys got to a radio or a phone more soldiers would be on the way.

"How many men are on duty in the encampment?" he asked Helsenberg.

When the man gave him a quizzical look Mark tried again.

"How many soldiers?" asked Mark, nodding down toward the camp.

Helsenberg closed his eyes.

"Fifteen."

Shit. That was a lot of armed men.

"How many scientists and their wives will be there right now?"

Helsenberg opened, then closed his eyes again, concentrating. Mark saw him tapping finger to finger.

"Sixteen."

"Do the trucks have radios? Are there phones in any of the huts other than the Commandant's?"

"No radios in trucks. Commandant's shack is only communications center. He may have phone in his own house, but I believe is only connected to the guard houses and his office."

"All right."

He dove the saucer in a breathtaking swoop toward the center street as Helsenberg and his wife leaned way back in their seats. Bits of sand and debris that had still managed to cling to the fuselage now blasted away in the wind as the ground leaped up at them. They flashed by the watchtowers so fast that the guards clutched at the wooden railings, their caps flung away into the night. Mark saw the Commandant leaping for cover under the front stoop of his office just as the saucer leveled off and Mark managed a perfect landing down the middle of the street. He shoved at the canopy as it began its torturous rise, slipping out from under it just as the officer was climbing shakily to his feet. So far none of the guards had gotten over their shock enough to train guns in his direction. Mark jerked the pistol out of his belt and aimed it at the pudgy Major with a pencil-thin black mustache and a jerky lower lip.

"Get in," he said, waving the pistol back toward the saucer.

The man stared at the gun, then into Mark's eyes, and raised his hands, climbing into the craft just ahead of Mark. Mark pointed toward one of the rear seats, and handed the pistol to Helsenberg.

"If he moves, shoot him," he said.

Helsenberg smiled and nodded, turning to face the Major.

Mark raised the craft until it hovered in the center of the street. When Helsenberg nodded toward the button to close the canopy Mark shook his head.

"We mean you no harm!" he shouted, watching the men in the towers and on the ground chattering nervously to each other. "Get in the trucks. Load everyone here and take them with you to the labs. We'll be watching."

When no one moved Mark turned to the Major.

"Tell them to do it."

The man found some courage, at last, shaking his head.

Mark turned to Helsenberg.

“Shoot him in the right knee, and then I’ll ask again”

Helsenberg’s eyebrows peaked.

“Do it,” said Mark.

Helsenberg shrugged, pushing the gun barrel against the major’s kneecap. The man grimaced as Helsenberg slipped his finger off the trigger guard and onto the trigger.

“All right!” screamed the major, slapping at the pistol.

Helsenberg smiled evilly.

“Tell them!” Mark ordered, lowering the craft so that all the guards in the towers could see their commanding officer.

The major commanded his men to do as Mark had said. Mark closed the canopy and raised the craft to a point where he could watch the movement below. In less than fifteen minutes everyone was loaded in two trucks and the little convoy had started to roll.

“We follow them?” asked Helsenberg.

Mark watched the line of headlights rolling toward the labs and shook his head. “I’m going to drop you and the Major off at the labs. If the others get there before I get back, just hold the major in one of the huts. I have a couple of errands to run.”

“Errands?” said Helsenberg.

Mark nodded.

"I need to pick up a copy of the Wall Street Journal."

Helsenberg looked at him as though he’d gone mad.

"AND THIS CAME IN when?" said Ash, frowning at the paper in his hand.

The messenger, a young man of barely college age but enough good sense to know that he was in the presence of death, stared past Ash at the blank wall beyond, standing at stiff attention. "Less than two minutes ago, sir. I was ordered to bring it directly to you and disturb you no matter what you were doing."

Clearly, that order bothered the boy immensely, and Ash was gratified, but the messenger's supervisor–a man smart enough not to deliver the message himself–was correct in his assessment. Ash stared at the handwritten fax.

Hope all is well. But I have decided that since you have finally managed to screw everything up, it is time that I must intercede.

It was the closing lines that bothered Ash the most.

Don't stare into the light so much. I've told you before you'll hurt your eyes.

All the best.

Walsh.

It wasn't possible. Still, Ash was certain that the handwriting was the same he'd seen on numerous yellow notepads. Through the glass of the operations room, he could see the dancing light that had only become operational again moments before. *That* was the only functional time machine in the world. There was no way for Walsh to have returned to write that note, and yet Ash knew that he had. His fingers traced the other item on his desk.

One of the new bracelets.

The ringlet and a man's severed arm were all that had returned when the technicians tried to recall Trevor. He stared at the blood-stained piece of paper that had been stuffed between the wrist and the bracelet.

Be seeing you.

Mark.

Was it remotely possible that Townsend and Walsh had both somehow escaped the time prison he had created for them? If so, either one of them could ruin him now, knowing what they knew. And if they really did have the ability to time travel then God only knew what else they'd wrought back in the past.

Ash noticed that the messenger was still there, staring at the wall, one tiny bead of sweat waiting to slip from the crease between his eyebrows down the bony bridge of his nose.

"I want all our agents called in," said Ash, waving the fax in the kid's face. "I want this facility crawling with them inside the hour. Put us in lock-down mode."

The kid nodded, spinning on his heel, relief at escaping evident as he raced out of the room. Ash shoved the bracelet away across the desk leaving a trail of blood, but the message still glared at him.

Be seeing you.

Mark.

TRACY AWAKENED IN TOTAL darkness, certain that she was buried alive. Her heart raced, and she clawed wildly at the linen cloth that bound her. Her movement caused recessed fixtures to flood the small bedroom with soft golden light, and as she finally managed to unwind from the tangled sheets she relaxed.

The room, entombed deep beneath the ground and encased in protective steel, concrete, and sound-deadening insulation, was as silent as any of the graves far above. She wondered if she had slept another day away. She'd been exhausted enough, and the hot bath and giant meal that Ki had supplied had only added to her weariness.

She had taken no interest in the Conservancy as a teenager. The covert and secretive organization was just one more proof that her parents were weird, but at least it was one of the manifestations of their insanity of which the public at large was unaware. Tracy had acted as though this band of oddballs didn't even exist, and only her association with another couple of outcasts and several run-ins with death had convinced her that coming here might be a good idea.

Now she was beginning to wonder if her parents–and these same misfits–weren't the only really sane people left.

She stretched lazily, staring at the pajamas she'd found in the built-in drawers along the wall and she wondered if Ki or her mother had placed them there. It would have been just like her mother to plan for some apocalyptic future by stocking this underground fortress with clothes for a grown-up daughter. Tracy took the night clothes off gently, as though they were the finest silk, laying them reverently atop the bed before dressing quickly and pressing the intercom beside the door.

Ki's voice answered almost immediately.

"Yes, Miss Tracy? You slept well?"

"Very well. How long was I asleep?"

"Twelve hours and eleven minutes."

Tracy smiled. Ki could be trusted to be unfailingly accurate although whether he was timing from the moment she entered the room or the instant her head hit the pillow she wasn't sure. There were no cameras that she could see, and she didn't believe he'd spy on her.

"My companions?"

"Mr. Carter still sleeps. Miss Marilyn just stepped into the computer room."

Although Ki's voice was flat as glass Tracy could still detect just the slightest irritation. He might acknowledge her hegemony here, but he didn't have to like allowing outsiders into the inner sanctum.

"Thank you. I'll meet you there."

"Shall I wake Mr. Carter?"

"That's not necessary. He can use the rest."

She paced down the long corridor, nodding to men and women who acknowledged her with nods of their own that seemed to Tracy more like respectful bows. She didn't like the feeling that they saw her as more than she was, almost like a returning princess. It gave her a sense of responsibility that she knew could easily turn to even more guilt if anything should happen to any of them. Once again, the computer room grew silent as Tracy entered.

"You all know who Miss Tracy is," said Ki, and everyone smiled.

"Welcome back," said several people at once.

Tracy nodded.

"What are you people doing here, exactly?" she asked, leaning over one of the monitors where Marilyn was inspecting what looked like an underwater shot. But the image was blurry with floating debris and muck.

"An excavation off the coast of Malta," explained Ki. "A team has unearthed pottery shards that are over thirty thousand years old."

Tracy frowned, moving on to the next monitor where illegible streams of data flowed downward. Marilyn followed

"And this?" asked Tracy.

"Incoming transmissions from a star system beyond the Andromeda Galaxy."

"Transmissions?"

"We have not been able to decipher them as yet," said Ki, smiling at the young blond woman at the monitor. "But Lara is one of the best code breakers in the business."

"You mean you believe it's from an intelligent species? Extraterrestrials?"

Ki nodded, studying Marilyn closely.

"Miss Tracy does not hold with all our beliefs. Is that not true, Miss Tracy?"

"It is."

"So I must assume that much of what you see here will seem... outlandish to you."

"What else *is* there here?" asked Marilyn, glancing at the desks, and the other monitors.

"We track reports of UFOs as they come into numerous sources both governmental and private in many countries worldwide. We also have ongoing investigations at locations of poltergeist and afterlife remnant phenomenon."

"Afterlife remnants?"

"Ghosts," said Tracy.

"In addition, there are our cryptozoological teams-"

"Sasquatch, the Loch Ness monster, things like that," said Tracy.

Ki nodded.

The girl gave Tracy a *look*, but she just shrugged.

"This is not what you were expecting," said Ki, smiling at Marilyn.

"No," said Marilyn. "But then since I met Tracy, I haven't been able to predict much in advance of my next breath."

"Caitlin!" said Ki, waving at a small brunette with feathered earrings who was tapping furiously at a keyboard on the centermost desk.

The girl hurried over to them, snapping to a very relaxed version of attention, her dark eyes shining with fervor.

"Could you please give Miss Marilyn and Miss Tracy a rundown on what you have learned since the latest attack on the Karhonen Estate?"

The dark eyes blinked and went blank for a moment. To Tracy, the girl looked like a computer booting up.

"Nine AventCorp field agents died due to injuries inflicted by the security system. Two remaining agents who seemed to have...reappeared out of nowhere... are in a special government medical facility outside of Yorba Linda. They are stable but the limited reports we have received indicate that they are ambulatory but mentally unresponsive."

"Unresponsive?" said Tracy.

Caitlin nodded.

"We assume that either the...event itself sent them into shock, or the device caused some type of brain damage. Whether it is permanent or temporary we have no way of knowing."

Caitlin gave Tracy a questioning look, but Tracy merely nodded for her to continue.

"Aventcorp is now conducting a manhunt in the area, and the perimeter is expanding. We predict that within the next two hours, it will reach its maximum potential, and they will have to admit defeat."

"They'll give up," said Tracy.

Caitlin nodded.

"They will assume you have eluded them and will begin watching for you to appear on their radar again.

The likelihood is they will begin looking for more of the people on the list."

Tracy gawked.

"You *know* about them?"

"Of course," said Ki. "When we realized that the agency had compromised some of their identities and had already kidnapped several of them, we immediately initiated emergency protocol-" he stopped when Tracy frowned at the word. "Procedures. We *killed* some of them...You understand?"

Tracy nodded.

"You faked their deaths."

Ki bowed his head.

"Others simply disappeared because we didn't have time or resources for a more elaborate escape. Now most of them are ensconced in safe houses, but our people are doing so at great danger to themselves. Mr. Reich, we had to actually take from the agents holding him."

"My father!" gasped Marilyn.

Ki nodded.

"He is safe."

"Where is he?"

"In hiding with some of our people, right now. As soon as we are in direct communication again you will be able to speak to him."

"How could you possibly know about the people on the list?" asked Tracy.

Ki smiled.

"Miss Tracy, your parents helped create the identities on that list."

The rabbit hole kept getting deeper and more twisted, but a thin rope of hope seemed to dangle just out of reach.

"Ki, do you know where my parents are?"

Ki's smile melted into a sad frown.

"No, Miss Tracy. I do not. We have searched for them endlessly, but there is no trail. There never was."

She stared around the room filled with highly trained technicians and state-of-the-art equipment.

"How could that be? People don't just vanish into thin air. You should have found *something* after all this time."

"Yes, and so should the authorities."

"Which leads you to suspect?"

"Nothing. It leads me to suspect nothing. We have no evidence."

"So, you believe they are no longer alive?"

Ki shook his head, but his eyes said yes.

"Do you know a man called Shiver?" she asked.

"Of course."

Deeper and much more twisted. Now Marilyn's allusion to a rabbit hole seemed inadequate. This was no hole, it was a vast maw opening up beneath their feet.

"How do you know him?"

"He is the man who brought the people on the list out of bondage. He helped your parents to found the Conservancy."

Tracy shook her head.

"That can't be the same man. The Conservancy is... what...thirty years old?"

"Yes."

"But Shiver can't be much more than thirty himself."

"I have no idea of his age. I would suspect it would depend on when you met him."

Tracy blinked, trying to turn on her internal computer the way Caitlin had.

"I met him about a week ago."

"Then I am glad he was alive and well. He's a most interesting man."

"But he can't be the same man who founded the Conservancy. He wouldn't even have been born."

Ki's smile was so oriental Tracy wanted to scream.

"He was also the same age in 1959," said Ki.

"That's impossible," said Tracy, the date slapping her in the face. "And why 1959? What do you know about that year?"

"It is the year from which the survivors fled."

"Time travel?" said Marilyn, shaking her head and grinning. "Are you serious?"

"It is another *fringe* area that is covered here," said Ki, nodding toward Caitlin.

"You're saying the government has time travel?" said Marilyn.

"I wouldn't say the government," said Ki. "But we know that AventCorp has been experimenting with it. Shiver told us as much. The machine is located at-"

"Terra Diablo," said Marilyn.

Ki nodded.

"Who are the people on the list?"

"German scientists who were held against their will at Terra Diablo. It was they who created the original time machine adapting technology from an alien vessel that crashed in Germany during the war. They also worked on the other devices that had been discovered in the crash."

"Devices like the one we have."

"You have the device?"

Tracy told him about the hiding place in the house and the note her mother had given her.

"You should have told me, Miss Tracy."

"I know," said Tracy, wondering if Steph would be alive today if she had. "Why is Ash after all the people on the list if AventCorp has their own time machine?"

"Time travel is a mere offshoot of the power he seeks. He cannot truly control the machine he has now or wreak the benefits from it he suspects the machine holds. He seeks the original device which is a source of almost limitless power."

"Earl can control it," said Tracy, quietly.

Ki nodded.

"And Shiver."

"So, what happens now?" asked Tracy.

"We must wait," said Ki. "Ash is not the only one in power about whom we worry. The anthill is buzzing now. We must see who comes out on top before we make any moves at all. After all, you have the device."

"I don't like waiting," said Marilyn.

Ki bowed his head, his eyes inscrutable.

"There is a difference between the waiting of the prophet and the standing still of the fool."

"Very inscrutable," said Marilyn, glancing at Tracy who just frowned and shook her head.

MARK QUICKLY DISCOVERED THAT he could travel back in time as far as the creation of the machine in the labs at Terra Diablo, but only forward until a few days after Ash sent him back to the past. At both ends he hit a wall. The block in the past made sense, since he could not travel to a time when there had been no time machine. He didn't know exactly *how* that theory might get around the fact that alien ships had existed before the saucer, and that they more than likely distorted time just like the saucer he flew. That was a problem for better heads than his.

But why the wall in the future? That frightened him.

What if Ash *had* somehow gotten his hands on whatever the hell it was he wanted at Terra Diablo? What if he had perfected it to the point at which it could do a lot more than simply destroy a cavern complex and maybe a few scientists and soldiers? What if there *was* nothing beyond that point in the future?

There was no sense dwelling on that when his priority was saving all those people in the past. That and doing his damndest to assure that if Ash *did* get his hands on whatever he was looking for it wouldn't be because it got left at the labs.

Oh...and of course killing Ash with his bare hands. Mark had been forced to put that one on the back burner for too long. Now he sensed that time was truly on his side.

On his first trip, he stopped outside of New York around 1980 to pick up the Wall Street Journal he was looking for, but not just the one copy. He stole a decade's worth of archives from a small local library. Then slipping back ten years he spent a few days creating new identities for the Helsenbergs–which was a lot easier in the nineteen-seventies than the computerized, databased twenty-first century.

Then–returning to 1959–he and Helsenberg took several trips flying all the soldiers–including those guarding the underground complex–high into the mountains, leaving them with water and food. Mark calculated that they could hike to safety within a few days. Then he flew Helsenberg and his wife to the time and location he'd prepared, leaving them with most of the cash and instructions on how to invest it. Then and only then, he went back for the others.

On his return to Terra Diablo, he discovered that he had been gone a total of twenty minutes–although to Mark it was days. The scientists clustered around the saucer and Walsh pushed to the front, his pudgy hands wrapped tightly around the small device. When he started to climb inside Mark shook his head.

"The others first. You'll go on the last load."

Walsh still tried to clamber over the lip of the machine, but Mark shoved him easily aside, letting others pour in to fill the seats. He'd already decided Walsh's fate, although he wasn't ready yet to inform the little bastard. Let him sweat.

"Mein Frau," said a short, gray-haired man, as he dropped into a seat.

Mark nodded, pointing overhead.

"Don't worry."

"He doesn't understand much English," said another of the younger scientists.

"Tell him all your families are being brought to places of safety. You will be joining them soon."

"Danke."

"You're welcome," said Mark, placing his hands on the panel.

They rocketed away up the shaft so fast the scientists all let out a collective gasp, and Mark realized by the smell that regardless of the lack of sense of momentum one or more of the men had succumbed to motion sickness.

"Welcome to the future," he said, as they blasted along high above clouds that looked like puffs of cannon fire, appearing, spreading across the sky, and then disappearing in less than the blinking of an eye.

Glancing back at the goggle-eyed men, he realized that none but perhaps Helsenberg had really understood all the implications of what they were doing. They oohed and aahed, peering toward the ground as Mark swooped lower, but the craft was traveling so fast that it was impossible to see much of anything. He did notice that new roads raced ahead of them like snakes crawling out into a barren landscape, and he pointed these out to the men who nodded and smiled.

Landing the craft in a dell behind a large farmhouse, he ordered the man who spoke English to keep the others quiet while he was gone. He trotted across the fallow field with the full moon shining behind him like a giant guard towner. The lights of the house were on, and two people stood silhouetted on the broad back porch, but Mark wasn't certain they were Beatrice and Helsenberg. Something seemed different, and he slowed, listening, sniffing for danger.

The house seemed different as well, but he wasn't sure what it was about it that caught his attention. Then he noticed that there was a small wing attached to one side that hadn't been there before.

Of course. He'd traveled to the spot in time where he was supposed to meet them, but he hadn't taken into account all the ramifications of leaving them to travel through time the old-fashioned way, by simply living it.

They'd made renovations to the house. They'd aged. As he drew closer, he noticed ridges on Beatrice's forehead and worry lines around her eyes that had not been there when he'd left her. Helsenberg seemed to stoop a little as he stepped down off the porch.

"At last, you've come," said Beatrice, hugging him, but glancing past him into the darkness.

Mark turned to Helsenberg.

"You're looking well."

Helsenberg shrugged.

"A little older, a little wiser. But all thanks to you."

"Your English has certainly improved. How about our investments?"

Helsenberg's face split into a wide smile.

"I am quite happy with them. I also have bookies all over the country who follow my bets like clockwork."

"You lose-"

Helsenberg nodded.

"Enough to convince them I am not psychic, but almost always I win, and our legal investments are good. I suspect that some of them will become good *later?"*

Mark smiled.

"You're gonna love that Microsoft stock."

"I suspect I will like *all* the stocks. Xerox certainly did well."

"The identities are all in place?"

Helsenberg nodded, reaching into his pocket for a small spiral notebook and passing it to Mark.

Mark read the names addresses, and bank account numbers.

"Their background files are under the mattresses in each of their homes, like you ordered," said Helsenberg.

"Good job," said Mark, glancing around the farmhouse. "Might as well turn out the lights now. It's time to be going."

But Helsenberg shook his head.

"No," he said. "This is our home now."

"But we agreed to place everyone in the same year-"

"Why? We will have no contact with the others. What does it matter that some of us age faster or *sooner*? And everything will be as new to me now as it would be to me then. Besides I still have bets to place for you!"

"You're sure?"

Beatrice suddenly hugged him again, and Mark realized that while to him their last parting had only been moments before, to her it had been years since she'd seen the man who'd saved her and her husband. His throat constricted as he hugged her back while Helsenberg patted his shoulder.

Mark slowly eased out of Beatrice's grip, nodding.

"Have a good life, Shiver, my friend," said Helsenberg.

"Live long and prosper, Werner Smith," he said.

"That is a good saying," said Helsenberg. "I shall remember it."

"You should watch more television," said Mark, smiling as he ran back to the saucer.

IT TOOK TWO MORE trips to get all but the last few out of the Terra Diablo labs, and each time Walsh had tried to worm his way into the craft until Mark was forced to give the pistol to a blocky man named Kroner and pantomime shooting Walsh if he moved. Kroner, like Helsenberg before, seemed to have no problem with that, and Walsh was smart enough to sit down in a chair beside one of the worktables and shut up.

10:51. Eight minutes to zero.

Mark climbed out of the craft and began to help the last of the crew of white coats up into it, listening to the soundtrack of *Exodus* in his head. Kroner led Walsh up the ramp ahead of him, but before they reached the saucer Mark stopped them, taking the pistol back and motioning Kroner into the saucer. Walsh stared at the gun and then Mark with a resigned look on his face.

"You can't leave me here," he said, shaking his head.

"Why not? What do I owe you?"

"I can help you get to Ash."

"I don't need you for that. I've got all the time in the world."

The little man's eyes got sneaky again, and Mark wondered if it wouldn't be better just to shoot him and be done with it. The thought reminded him of the soldiers, and the idea of even one more killing suddenly became unpalatable.

"But what if you can't get to him in time?"

"In time for what? He isn't going to get what he wanted from Terra Diablo."

"Terra Diablo isn't everything. Ash has a backup plan."

Mark frowned.

"What kind of backup plan? If he can't steal the technology from here, what's he got?"

"He's already got the machine."

Mark tried to understand what Walsh was getting at. What was Ash going to accomplish now with his time machine? He couldn't get the alien technology from Terra Diablo because the cavern was going to go up any minute, and he couldn't steal any from the future because of the wall that Mark had run into.

"There's nothing he can do with it," said Mark, climbing aboard the saucer.

Walsh seemed to finally accept that he was being left behind, but instead of standing docilely on the ramp of the saucer cradle he raced away down the ramp. Mark shook his head, as he dropped into the pilot's seat preparing to close the canopy.

To his surprise two of the scientists became very agitated, slapping his shoulder, speaking in rapid-fire German, pointing toward Walsh. The little bastard had the odd-shaped device in his hands, fingering the buttons madly, and for just an instant Mark was certain he knew what happened to the labs.

Walsh blew the caverns up in one last fit of rage, trying to get one of the alien machines to work.

Mark reached for the canopy button again as the saucer began to whine, but the two scientists were still gesticulating wildly. Even though his watch told him it was now 10:55 he stayed his hand, staring once again at Walsh.

The little creep was pointing the machine directly at them. And he was still punching buttons, but the sound playing in Mark's head was no longer cinematic background but something stranger than anything he had ever heard. If it was music at all it was proof that music was the ultimate form of communication, because he felt at that moment as though he were in communion with the entire universe, that he could read it and understand it on every one of its myriad levels.

The saucer, the time machine, and the other numerous alien machines on the table, were all just instruments in an orchestra that spanned all time and space. Each of them was a powerful and dangerous device in its own right, but the machine in Walsh's hands was something else altogether. Walsh was like a nine-year-old beating wildly on the keys of a concert grand and one of the keys was attached to dynamite, but Mark also knew instinctively that Walsh wasn't about to destroy more than just the cavern with that thing. Whatever did that was still four minutes away. The device Walsh was toying with had the power to destroy everything, as though the universe had never been. It was a machine for *tuning* Zero Point, the energy on which the entire cosmos was built, and Walsh was playing it very badly.

Mark climbed hurriedly out of the saucer and raced down the ramp toward Walsh, but the little guy was ignoring him now, staring at the device with a rage much larger than his body could hold. Mark could sense the device resonating with Walsh's emotions like a drum-head to the stick.

"Give it to me!" shouted Mark.

The beady eyes took him in, confused, dazed, then turned back to the machine.

When Mark reached him, he grasped the device, preparing to jerk it away. Instead, he felt himself locked into the internal rhythm, the *music* changing subtly to a duet, but it was like trying to play alongside a chimpanzee. There was no finesse to Walsh's movements and the device seemed to sense the little man's lack of confidence. Mark could feel the rhythms working their way through the device, resonating with the floor.

"Let go!" he shouted, kicking Walsh in the thigh, jerking at the machine.

The little man bent double, but his fingers would not release their death grip. The internal rhythm worked its way up to a fever pitch and the external vibrations became a shudder through the floor. In desperation, Mark struggled to understand the *music* to control at least his end of the cosmic keyboard. The device transmuted mass and energy, just as his talent did, but it had infinite other functions as well. It was a universal wand, and it was now in the hands of an idiot.

Although Walsh fought wildly to maintain his grip on the machine, he still wasn't in nearly the shape that Mark was. Mark could sense the little man's stamina flagging, but he also knew that he didn't have time left to fight with him. He squeezed the machine tighter, riding the internal wave, controlling the device with two imaginary arms waving imaginary batons.

And then there was no Walsh.

Mark stood there for only a moment staring at the space on the other side of the device where the little man had stood. Empty. The machine sagged in his hands. A great rumble shook the cavern and Mark stared at the dancing light that now writhed madly in the corner. Stalactites crashed to the floor and a huge crack raced across the ceiling. Either the device in Mark's hands had set up some kind of internal sympathetic vibration within the light, or the machine, left on its own for too long was reaching some sort of overload, but this was how Terra Diablo ended. As though from a great distance he heard the Germans shouting. He turned and ran to the saucer.

As they blasted up out of the tunnel into bright sunlight again, Mark glanced at his watch.

10:57 and counting. Two minutes to zero.

He was tempted to hang around and watch the show, but there was no telling what was about to happen here. A force that could not only destroy all evidence in the labs below without actually collapsing the cave *and* removing the camp above...who knew how far that energy might extend?

He leaned back in the pilot's seat, still listening to the music of the spheres resonating inside his head and guided the saucer forward through time again. It took several *days* to place the last scientists and their families, to indoctrinate them into their new identities, to convince them that they were free and safe at last. Then, and only then, he traveled to the one time and place he thought someone might believe his story, where the device might be safely stored until he needed it.

Haight Ashbury. 1969.

Mark smiled as he walked the hilly streets, weaving between long-haired, young men and women wearing tie-dyed shirts and cutoffs, hawking underground comics and Acid. The air in the neighborhood was so laced with pot and patchouli he could taste incense on his tongue.

He found Ira Karhonen and his girlfriend, Sela, running a New Age bookstore beside a free clinic. When he asked to speak to them on a private matter, they both giggled as though he were from Mars, and when he demonstrated his talent by slicing cleanly through a plaster wall, they were sure of it. They closed the store for the day and took a little trip with Mark into the mountains. The three of them buried the device there, and Ira and Sela promised to return to it when they had a more secure site in which to store it. Mark knew they'd be true to their word. After all, Katie had subscribed to the *The New Age Bulletin and Lifechance Gazette* which would not even go into print for another twelve months.

"This is so wild," said Ira, grinning and tugging his ponytail that drooped over his shoulder like a handle.

"It's gonna get wilder," said Mark. "Don't trust anyone and take care of that machine."

"Don't worry," said Sela, wrapping her arm around Ira. "We will."

"I know you will," said Mark, turning to go.

"Peace," said Ira, giving Mark the two-finger signal.

"Peace," said Mark, returning it.

And so, it was done. The scientists were safely ensconced in their new lives, the machine was taken care of for the time being...Still, Mark worried about the soldiers. Their reports were sitting in some dusty file, somewhere, just waiting for Ash to find them in the future, in Mark's old present. They were like a ticking bomb hanging over his head.

But finally, he decided that come what may, he could not harm those men. He wasn't going to travel back into the past again to eliminate them, because he knew that he never had. He couldn't have. He didn't have it in him any longer. There was only one man that Mark still wanted to see dead, and that was a rendezvous he had in the future.

At the wall.

Before that, there was one more thing he had to do.

MARK LONGED TO HEAR the soft, heartrending tones of Johannes Brahms' *Violin Sonata No. 1 in G major, Op. 78.* That was what the moment called for, music so sweet and sad it hurt the ear.

Instead, Jean Sibelius' *Seventh Symphony* slowly built to its ominous conclusion in his head. He left the car on the street to race through the rain along the sidewalk he knew so well, staring at the familiar manicured lawns now sodden, listening to a neighbor's Corgi barking as it perched on the back of the sofa in the front window of the big brick Georgian home next door. Even through the downpour the smell of lilacs still hung in the air from numerous well-trimmed bushes along the street, one of the reasons that Katie so loved the neighborhood.

He slipped up onto the wide concrete stoop, punching the numbers into the lock, entering silently, and quickly coding more numbers into the security system before the alarm could sound.

This was as close as he'd come in four attempts.

Every time he tried to reach the house to intercept the killers he had been stopped at different points down the block. It was as though he walked into an invisible wall that would not let him pass any farther than the corner of the street where he watched in horror as Trevor exited his big black Ford sedan out front and–just as expertly as Mark–entered Mark's home unannounced. Mark had stood frozen in mute witness as the man came out again, slipping an evil-looking dagger back into his jacket. Mark pressed against the invisible wall with every ounce of his will, but he was forced to watch as the evil sonofabitch drove away, and only moments later his own car roared to a stop in almost the same spot. He had never known until then how close he had come to saving her.

If only he hadn't taken so long at the lake. If only he'd never gone to meet Rory. If only. If only.

Now, as he passed into the house minutes before the murder, he knew in his heart that there was nothing he could do. Some things could not be changed because they had not been changed. His only hope was that he would be allowed to at least see Katie again, perhaps hear her voice, but he had to be silent and stealthy as a ghost because he suspected time itself would not allow him to disturb her.

He was shocked when she stepped out of the bedroom in those familiar blue shorts and gasped, then smiled the smile he had been praying to see if only one last time.

"You're back?" she said, giving him a funny look. "Did you forget something?"

He was speechless. Stepping forward he drew her into his arms and squeezed her so tightly she gasped again, chuckling. The feel of her was intoxicating. He breathed in deeply, memorizing the moment.

"You're hurting me," she said, pushing against his chest.

She stared into his eyes, questioning him.

What to say to her? Run? Get out now? It was still a few minutes until the assassin got here.

He started to tell her to tell her to hide but discovered that he couldn't. It was as though he were suffering some kind of stroke, no words–not even the images that he sought would form–and slowly the realization dawned on him. He could be here now because his being here changed nothing. He could hold her, love her, see her alive, smell her sweet, morning breath fresh with toothpaste, but he could not warn her away from her fate.

"You changed," she said, pinching his white shirt between two fingers and frowning. "Where did you get this?"

"Spilled coffee," was all he could manage.

"Did you burn yourself?"

He shook his head, realizing that he couldn't allow her to see the scar, cocking his head to one side.

"Did Rory loan you this outfit?" she said, leaning back in his arms. "It looks like something he'd wear."

Mark nodded, trying out a smile that wouldn't quite make it past his heart.

"I love you more than you'll ever know," he said, choking back a sob.

She frowned, squeezing him back just a little.

"I love you, too. You know that."

He nodded.

"You came back to tell me that?" she said, kissing him lightly on the unscarred cheek. "I thought you had a big meeting this morning."

"I did," he said, struggling to keep the sadness out of his voice.

A big meeting with Rory and a couple of other killers, but that was happening at this moment... No. It had already happened. About now he was driving like a maniac through the rain, almost here. Only to get here too late. He was too early *and* too late, and there was no way he could change either. It was maddening.

She slipped out of his arms but took his hand. "I was just going to make a pot of coffee," she said, leading him down the hall. "Try not to spill any this time."

He could see the door to the study, farther ahead, open wide. The assassin must pull it behind him, a few minutes from now, leaving it barely ajar.

They turned into the kitchen, and she released his hand. He stood frozen beside the counter, drinking in the sight of her, her hips swaying as she swished from the cupboards to the Mr. Coffee, her tiny hands expertly practicing an act she had performed a thousand times as she continued to regard him with a careful eye.

"Are you sure you're all right?" she asked again.

He nodded.

"I just missed you all of a sudden."

"You're acting funny," she said, kissing him yet again and staring deeply into his eyes. "Did you have a bad dream last night or something?"

"Yes," he said.

A bad dream. A very bad dream. And it was about to happen over, and over, and over.

"And you came home to hold me?" she asked, snuggling closer.

"Yes," he whispered, his fingers tracing the fine hairs at the base of her neck.

"That's sweet," she said, squeezing him, then pushing out to arm's length again, her smile bright as sunshine. "But you have work to do, and so do I. I'm going to organize the den today. I have papers all over the place."

He nodded. The den. Where the assassin would find her... when? Minutes from now, he realized, glancing at the bright red clock over the stove.

He refused to let go of her arms, and her smile lowered almost into a frown.

"Honey," she said, kissing him one last time. "It's all right. It was only a dream. Now we both need to get to work."

"I know," he said, quietly, his fingers slipping lovingly along her arms as she backed away.

He could feel the same force, the same *wall* that had compelled him to keep his distance, now pressing him away from her, causing him to back slowly out of the room as she smiled ruefully, waving.

"Go to your meeting and forget it," she said. "Tomorrow you won't even remember."

Yes, I will. Tomorrow and all the tomorrows.

Then he was out in the hall, on the porch, closing the door behind him, the force shoving him down the walk and into the rain, back the way he had come. Time would not be denied.

He reached the corner as tires squealed to a stop down the block behind him, and he hurried away toward his car, unable to look at the man whose shoes he heard slapping up the walk of the house where Katie was now sipping coffee, heading for the study...

Across the street—through the veil of rain—he saw a man running in the direction of the house.

It was himself on his first-time trip back. Too late and about to hit the wall. He turned away toward his car.

Suddenly he stopped, staring unseeing into the placid morning light, as the symphony roared to a thunderous finale, realizing the terrible mistake he'd just made.

He'd come back so close to the event, to the murder. He should have gone back farther. Maybe a lot farther.

Katie hadn't said anything like *You're back again* or *You always come back...*

He could never do this again. Never visit her at some other point in time.

Because he hadn't.

He stumbled on down the street, ignoring the mail-man who stared at his tear-stained face, nodded, and then turned politely away.

TRACY MEANDERED THROUGH THE tunnels of the Conservancy until she stood in front of the door of her father's office. She opened it slowly, stepped inside, and closed it behind her. The automatic lighting was even more subdued than everywhere else in the subterranean complex, and as she crossed the floor to the highly polished wooden desk with its glass top, she noticed how quiet it was, as though the room soaked up sound.

But perhaps it was because she was holding her breath.

When she did breathe, she caught the unmistakable aroma of her father's pipe, heavy with cherry. Even after all this time, it clung to the space, and she was shocked to realize that Ki must have sealed this room hermetically. She might have been the first person other than him to enter it since her father had been taken away by federal agents.

The smell brought so many memories with it. Warm afternoons sitting on the back porch watching the breakers as the sun lowered behind them like one giant drip from a golden candle, talking until the twilight brought a chill to the yard. Her father had always been a wonderful conversationalist, a better listener than he was a talker. It had seemed so natural for him to want to hear everything his only child had to say. She could see his smile now as though his face were a part of that long-ago sunset, see him nodding to himself, puffs of blue smoke rising and then disappearing in the breeze.

She crossed to the desk, flicked on the green lamp, and dropped into the red leather armchair that she had sat in so many times as a child. Originally the chair had resided in her father's study at home. Apparently, Ki had brought it here, after... The chair, too, brought so many memories.

Doing homework while her father toyed with some electronic machinery on the other side of the desk or wrote longhand with one of his numerous fountain pens on a yellow legal pad. Leaning way back, kicking her short legs up on the desk, and pretending to dictate to him while he pretended to write on the same pad.

She stared at the one picture in the one frame.

The three of them, walking on the beach. Tracy was thirteen, and her high cheekbones peeked through baby fat, her breasts beginning to protrude beneath the flat expanse of her bathing suit, legs stretching to take on definition. It was the first time she had studied the photo from an adult's perspective, and she was shaken by how much she looked like her mother now. As a child, she had always considered her father handsome and her mother beautiful. Peering at her mother's image she understood for the first time why her father had always stared at her the way he had.

The desk was littered with the same handwritten pages she remembered. Ki must have left it as it was, as part of the memorial that the office had become.

Most of the papers had to do with some theory her father was working on regarding the possibility of the planet shifting magnetic poles in the next twenty years. He believed that the pyramids contained astrophysical clues to the date of the last shift, and geological evidence dated from that time predicted another shift soon. If that had been her father's one great theory, and he had stuck to it, he might have convinced someone. Maybe. But the papers beneath those were about another wild idea, the location of Atlantis. Apparently, it was buried beneath the Antarctic ice cap. How convenient. Right where no one could prove it or disprove it in this lifetime.

Without even thinking she began to neaten the desk, organizing the fountain pens according to size and color, stacking the papers to one side, and straightening the computer monitor. She started to close one drawer that had been left ajar, then opened it instead. Inside was a stack of the same legal pads, and she began to read. Finally, with a trembling hand, she removed the top tablet, reading slowly, taking in every word.

"Ki," she said, pressing the button on the intercom.

"Yes, Miss Tracy," came the answer after only a second.

"Could you please bring Earl and Marilyn to my father's office?"

"THAT'S IT," SAID EARL, nodding at the yellow pad as he flipped through the little spiral notebook to the picture of the dog bone device.

"Do you understand these equations?" asked Tracy, pointing to her father's writings beneath his own sketch.

Earl ran his thick fingers across the text of both pads, slowly flipping pages. Marilyn stood to one side, making a face, while Ki crossed his arms and gave all of them an inscrutable frown. Finally, Earl shook his head.

"I think he was trying to understand it, too," he said, tapping the spiral notebook. "Just like the guy in here."

"Shiver must understand it," said Tracy. "The device did something with Earl, in my father's study at the house. He just disappeared."

Ki shrugged.

Tracy stared at Earl, wondering how close he'd come to exiling himself so far away that even God couldn't have found him. Earl seemed as unconcerned as usual.

"But that doesn't explain how Shiver does what he does with his hands," she said.

"I do not understand that myself, "said Ki. "Apparently, something happened to him when he was first removed into the past."

"He's like my machine," said Earl, nodding toward the pad.

They all stared at him.

"What do you mean?" asked Tracy.

Earl smiled.

"He's tuned himself."

"Tuned himself?" said Marilyn, frowning.

"To Zero Point," said Earl, as though that should have been obvious. "He doesn't need a box. He can tap into the energy any time he likes. Man, that must be awesome. I never saw him do any of that stuff. He just picked me up and moved me."

Tracy closed her eyes and nodded.

"In your house that night. You said you got sick after... I thought you meant after you did the demonstration at Terra Diablo."

Earl shook his head.

"No. After I rode in the flying saucer. After I traveled through time."

Tracy didn't bother asking why he'd never told her. It probably hadn't seemed important to Earl, and she'd never asked.

"Ash wants the device really badly," said Marilyn. "What does he want to use it for?"

"It is the key to controlling Zero Point energy," said Ki. "At exactly 10:59 AM on the 8th of June 1959, the labs at Terra Diablo were destroyed. Or rather they were emptied, and the surrounding ground was devastated by what might have been either a high-level explosion or an earthquake of approximately 6.8 on the Richter Scale. All the equipment inside the labs, including the original time machine, and all the alien devices salvaged by the Nazis and later brought to this country disappeared completely."

Tracy frowned.

"Disappeared? So, Ash's plan was to return to the labs *before* the event occurred and to remove the alien artifacts. One in particular."

Earl nodded.

"The device is just for *tuning* Zero Point, which is everywhere, all the time, in infinite supply. When I play with my machine, I get it to transpose metals and fly things. My other machine turns Zero Point into a focusable electromagnetic pulse, but it's still just *tuning* the available Zero Point. Between me and the machines, we can use some of the energy, but if a person wanted to and had the right device, they could learn to tune it and then amp it up until God knows what would happen on the other end. It would be like aiming a nuke like a pistol."

"Oh, my God," whispered Tracy, suddenly understanding. "Earl, where is that device? Where are your boxes?"

Earl shrugged.

"In my room."

"Go get them, and for God's sake don't turn them on. Marilyn, maybe you'd better go with him.""

"You knew?" she asked Ki, as Marilyn and Earl hurried out of the room.

He shook his head.

"We assumed it was something of the sort. Shiver warned your father about the device. That was why he constructed the hiding room in your home. Why he insisted on such extreme security, and why Shiver later returned to ensure that the Conservancy built this complex as our headquarters, but your father insisted that the device remain at the house forever. Apparently, he wanted it close to him."

"Dad was pointing that machine at the dead agents," she whispered.

Ki waited.

There was more to the moment than just guilt. There was a sense of relief as well, because she knew in her heart that the man who had held her in strong arms when the storm raged outside her window, the woman who had carried her in her own strong arms, were not the killers she had believed they might be. *She* was guilty, not them.

"He didn't kill those agents," she said. "Ash had them murdered just as he did so many others in the company. They were there simply to frame my parents. What was Dad doing with that machine?"

"Trying to save them I suspect," said Ki, opening his hands palms up. "He probably thought that he could somehow use the device to tune the Zero Point energy and give them back their life force, or perhaps even shift them back in time to a moment before they were murdered. But alas, he never learned to use the machine. No one has. Ash thought he could blackmail your parents into giving him the device that he believed they had, but they went through the entire trial without telling him the location, and then they disappeared. Apparently, it was at that point that Ash decided that he might be able to return to Terra Diablo and steal the device before it could make its way into your parents' hands. Of course that would never have worked."

"Why not?"

"Because your parents already had it later."

"Ash's insane."

"Any man who hopes to harness the heart of the universe for his own purposes is insane."

"But he can't do it without the device, right?"

"Maybe," said Earl, stepping back through the door with the alien machine in his hands.

Marilyn followed with Earl's boxes stacked in hers. They gingerly deposited all three devices on the desk. "My machines are just *tuners*. Ash rebuilt a bigger machine. He thinks it's just a time machine, but if he keeps fiddling with it there's no telling what's gonna happen."

"He's supposed to be a brilliant scientist," said Tracy.

"One of the best," agreed Ki.

"You talk as though he impresses you."

"He always has impressed me with his abilities. It's how he chooses to use them that I find appalling."

"Did Ash have something to do with my parent's disappearance?"

That would be the last straw. If she had inadvertently delivered them into his hands, she wouldn't be able to bear it.

"We don't believe so," said Ki.

"But you're not sure?"

"Not certain. But since their disappearance, we have been able to speak to several of the asylum guards under neutral circumstances, and we believe that Ash was not involved. The nature of their escape was too unique. In fact, we at first thought that Shiver had helped them. Certainly, he would have had he been able, but time is not always so easily unraveled. Apparently, there are walls within it that keep a man from being where he is not supposed to be."

"So, you have no idea what happened to them."

She nodded. She'd never be able to tell them how sorry she was.

"Why do you torture yourself so, Miss Tracy?"

She stared into his eyes and realized for the first time that he loved her as a father himself. She rose to her feet and embraced him, sensing his disquiet–as she had in their initial meeting in the crypt–at the unusual display of affection. When he trembled slightly, she pulled him into a tighter hug until he finally surrendered, and she felt the very tentative touch of his hands on her back. When she turned her face to his. his eyes glistened.

"Thank you, Ki," she whispered. "Thank you for always being there for me. Thank you for maintaining all...this. Thank you for being you."

She kissed him lightly on the cheek, and he nudged very gently out of her embrace, staring at the floor.

"You are most welcome."

Earl and Marilyn also seemed to find the carpet very interesting. The unexpected release of emotions left Tracy feeling drained and confused.

"Perhaps you should sit down again," suggested Ki, guiding her back to her seat.

Marilyn nodded, meeting Tracy's eyes again.

"You look white all of a sudden."

She dropped back into a chair, taking a deep breath.

"I feel as though I just awakened from a long, terrible nightmare. I sent my parents first to prison and then to a nuthouse, and they were innocent."

"It was what they wanted you to do, Miss Tracy."

"What?" she gasped.

Ki nodded, lightly resting his hand on her shoulder.

"In the trial, you only told the truth of what you had seen or at least what they wanted you to tell. Your parents knew they were going to be convicted even though they were innocent. Do you believe they would have wanted you to lie?"

She shook her head. Her father had one cardinal rule for her from the time she was able to understand the words. Never lie. Never.

"No. They'd never have wanted me to do that."

"They knew you couldn't save them from imprisonment. But you did save them."

"From the death sentence on the murder charges."

"Of course. No other witness was as persuasive as you."

"I convinced the judge they were insane, that they didn't know right from wrong."

"Others testified to the same thing," said Ki.

Her parents' friends had sounded crazy themselves when they took the stand. So, it was easy for the judge to believe that the Karhonens were nuts. Still, it mitigated her guilt only a little to recall that others shared it.

"But the judge listened to you, because you were the child. You were the last person he expected to say that a parent was insane. Yet you did. You saved their lives."

Could it be as simple as that to slip out from under the terrible weight of her guilt? No, of course, it wasn't. She may have saved their lives as Ki insisted, but she had testified in front of them that she believed them to be mad, and she would go to her grave remembering the sad look in their eyes.

"If Ash has a machine that works even a little like this," Earl interjected, shaking his head and nodding at the second legal pad he'd pulled out of Tracy's father's desk. "that's not a good thing."

Tracy stared at the sketch of a circular device with what looked like rays of light rising out of it. Stick figures surrounding it showed that it was much larger than the handheld device on the desk. "What can he do with it, I mean other than send people through time?"

Earl shrugged.

"It isn't so much what he can do with it as what can happen."

"What do you mean?"

"Well, like I said, the thing about Zero Point is *tuning* it. I can kind of tune my box, but it can only handle so much power. So, I guess I can only do so much damage. But maybe a machine big enough to send people back and forth through time... it might just finally reach an overload point or hit the jackpot or get tuned the wrong way, however, you want to look at it. I'll bet that's what happened in Terra Diablo in 1959."

"So, Ash could blow himself up."

"Yeah- "

"That's not a bad thing in my book," said Tracy.

"It's not just him," said Earl.

"What do you mean?"

He pointed at the figures on the next sheet of paper, but once again they were meaningless squiggles to Tracy.

"Ash's machine must be a hundred times bigger than my box or this thing here on the table," said Earl.

"A hundred times more powerful."

"It doesn't work like that. It's exponential, and his new machine probably doesn't run on the same tubes and stuff they had back in 1959 either. It could be bad... real bad."

"Shit," muttered Tracy. "Why was I certain you were going to say something like that?"

Earl nodded.

"It might just be another boomer like in 1959... if that's what happened. Or it might be a pop like a firecracker. Then again it might be a blast big enough to split this planet or even atomize it. Maybe do a lot more damage than that."

"How could it possibly do more damage than that?" asked Marilyn.

Earl shrugged.

"I told you. Zero Point isn't like normal energy. It doesn't require a chemical or nuclear reaction. It just is. It's everywhere, like water in the ocean, and if you stir it up enough who knows what's gonna happen?"

"You're saying there could be a chain reaction?"

"Maybe."

"I'd like a little better information than that."

"That's all I've got."

She stared at Ki. The little man shrugged.

"So, while we sit here, Ash is playing with a machine that could destroy this entire planet and probably has no idea of the danger," said Tracy.

"Why would you assume he doesn't know?" asked Marilyn.

"Because if he did, he wouldn't be doing it," said Tracy.

"That assumes that he's sane. I don't think that's true. Your parents are the sane ones. Ash is crazy as shit."

Tracy nodded, trying to imagine what her father would do in this situation. What Shiver might do.

"There's no way we can get into Terra Diablo, is there?" she asked Ki.

He shook his head.

"It is one of the most highly secured areas in the country. You would never get in, and I could not allow you to try."

His eyes said that regardless of who was in control of the Conservancy, *that*, at least, was not open to negotiation.

Tracy nodded.

"Then we'll have to figure out some way to get Ash out of there. To get him to come to us."

"Or I could just land a flying saucer there and go in like the Marines."

Everyone spun to face the door.

"Shiver," said Tracy, Earl, and Ki all at once.

Mark smiled, shaking his head.

"You guys can call me Mark. After all, we're old friends."

Ki shook his hand. Earl hugged him like a long-lost brother, and Tracy stood shyly to one side, trying to decide if he'd aged or not since she'd seen him. There definitely seemed to be more worry lines around his eyes and some deeper sadness within them as well.

"You traveled through time to save me," she said, wonderingly.

He nodded.

"Why?"

He frowned.

"I had been watching Ash for a long time. Trying to find a way to get to him. When I saw you run out of the offices that day I followed you. When I figured out what was going on, I knew I couldn't leave you to Ash or his men."

"You saw me killed."

He shook his head.

"No. But I saw you *about to be* killed. That was when I went back and set up to meet you on the roof. I wish I'd known who you were before, but you did a pretty good job of coming up with a new identity, and I'd never seen you in person."

"So, what do we do now?"

"Now everything will play out," he said, frowning.

"How do you mean?" said Marilyn. "That doesn't sound so good."

Mark shrugged, glancing at his watch.

"In a couple of hours' time hits a wall."

"What?" gasped Tracy. "You mean that's it? Ash really does it, destroys everything?"

"I hope not," said Mark.

"But then what does that mean, *time hits a wall?"*

"I'm not sure."

He explained about the time barrier that would not allow a paradox.

"I've tried to get in to stop Ash at different points, but he lives right up to the end, so I can't kill him. I do know a few things that he doesn't."

"So, what are we supposed to do?" said Marilyn.

"Play our parts in the finale," said Mark.

THE DAMNED MACHINE WAS on the fritz again.

Ash glared at it as though the gleaming apparatus with its multibillion-dollar coils and its state-of-the-art innards were a pile of rusting junk. Ten minutes before it had started to act up just as Ash was preparing to enter it.

Then, mysteriously, it had turned itself back on for a few seconds, and the men in the control room had become almost hysterical, punching buttons futilely until it turned off yet again, and now would not start.

The odds were that the machine would come back online eventually. It had a way of doing that, as though it had invisible batteries that had to be recharged, but Ash had the nasty suspicion that between Townsend and Walsh he didn't have any more time. The assholes were out there now, somewhere, just waiting to spoil everything.

He slammed a thick folder down onto the metal desk in the corner of the lab and two black-suited agents jolted, then snapped back to attention.

"How is it that no one figured out that Mark Townsend was originally Agent Clark? Did we not have him right here, in this facility?"

Neither of the agents so much as admitted they'd heard the question, and both were far too intelligent to ask why *he* hadn't caught that slip himself.

"This man is loose. No one can catch him, and he's trying to ruin my entire operation," said Ash for the benefit of the overhead mike. Heads barely nodded in the control room. "I want him caught. I want to know what he learned back there and whether he's now here or not. I need information, people!"

This time he glared at the two agents who both gave him *who me* looks before gladly disappearing. His ears pricked up as the machine began to slowly hum to life again.

"Crank her up," he said, staring through the windows at the machine where the tower of light was just appearing. "And this time let's try raising the amps and tightening the iris."

Something had happened back in 1959 other than just destruction at the labs. Somehow Townsend–and it seemed Walsh as well–had learned how to travel forward in time without Ash *bringing* them back. At least that was the threat implied in the messages, and Ash didn't believe Townsend at least was the type to make idle threats. Of course, there was always the remote possibility that they had simply traveled back through time the old-fashioned way, but Ash didn't believe the men threatening him were eighty-year-olds.

It occurred to him that the destruction of the labs might not have destroyed the device Ash was looking for, that either Townsend, Walsh, or both, had it and had learned to use it to time travel. If that was true, there was no telling what else they'd learned to do with it.

But his suspicions extended beyond the past. He stared at the light roving upward out of the machine, nodding to himself.

Time. It was all about time. Controlling time. That was the ultimate control, but it was a chimera. If he could move back only a day, for more testing... But he had not done so, so he could not. The frustration was enough to drive a man insane.

He could feel those same threads of time winding tightly about him, constricting like a python, choking off his breathing, contracting around his heart. He was losing control, but he was reasonably certain that his enemies could no more look into the future than he. There was still a chance of wresting victory from the grip of defeat. He peered at the frozen figures in the control room, waving his fist and shouting hoarsely.

"That device down there is more than just a time machine. I want to see what else it can do."

"HAD I REALIZED YOU were Tracy Karhonen," said Mark, shaking his head, "I probably would have brought you here instead of wasting time setting up an identity you were never going to use."

"How could you not have known who I was?" asked Tracy, staring at the man who had set her on this insane journey what... a week before? The sadness in his eyes was more pronounced now.

Mark shrugged.

"I was so focused on Ash, on learning what it was he was trying to accomplish and stop him. But I had to be careful, take it a step at a time, because if I went too far into the future and didn't find any way there to get to him, I might have precluded doing so in the past."

Tracy shook her head, trying to make sense of what he was telling her.

"You're sure that's the way time works?"

Suddenly his face was a mask of pain, as though she had touched on a terrible secret.

He nodded slowly.

"That's the way it works. When I saw him in the open, the day he was after you, I wanted to kill him to stop him, but I couldn't because that day was *before* he sent me into the past. He had to live at least that long. So instead, I went back in time and created a new identity for you and then came back for you. The only way to get to Ash now is in this here and now. The same way anyone would get to him."

Tracy noticed that the scar on his cheek had shrunk to a barely visible hairline.

"Why didn't Ki tell you about me? You were in contact, right? Apparently, he was keeping an eye on me."

Mark shook his head.

"I haven't been back here for quite a while. I wasn't worried about your parents because I knew that in the future Ash was still searching for the device. Since he didn't have it, I assumed until too late that your parents were all right. I'm sorry."

"But you could have gone back in time and helped them- "

"It doesn't work that way. Time isn't fluid. I can't just swim around in it like a fish. It's more like a million different corridors all running the same direction. I can travel up and down them and open doors, but when I leave the doors close behind me, and I can never reopen them. Sometimes a lot of other doors close at the same time. I can never change anything in my past that will change my future or even my present, whatever my present may be at the time."

"I'm sorry I took your book," said Tracy, frowning.

Mark nodded.

"You didn't know me. You were alone and afraid. I should have been more careful. It was another stupid mistake on my part."

"So, what do we do now?" asked Marilyn. "How do we *play our part in the finale?"*

"Have you managed to learn any more about Professor Derek Maynor since I was last here?" Mark asked Ki.

Ki shook his head. "We never discovered any information regarding your Professor Maynor. He is a will-o-the-wisp, a ghost."

"Maynor's more than just resourceful," said Mark. "But I think I might know how to flush both him and Ash out."

ASH STARED AT THE television screen in his office as he tried to crush three steel balls in the palm of his right hand. Every channel displayed the same image. A silvery, saucer-shaped craft flying leisurely over Washington DC, trailing a long banner that read '*DM 1-555-107-6468 MT*'.

F-18s scrambled around the craft, and commentators chattered about the missiles that had been fired at it—as it looped slowly over the White House—to no effect. The saucer seemed able to simply disappear and reappear at will, leaving the hapless pilots to auto-destruct the weapons in the air as they passed outside the city. In any case, the UFO seemed intent on advertising its cryptic message, not attacking the seat of government.

As Ash watched, several news helicopters ignored warnings from the Air Force and hovered close enough to the craft to see the human being at the controls.

Mark Townsend smiled and waved.

Ash threw the marbles, shattering a four-hundred-year-old vase.

He lifted his phone and tapped out the number on the banner.

"Hello?" The voice was the same one he remembered, only cocky this time, not addled by fear or drugs.

"You are a thoroughly remarkable man, Mr. Townsend. I believe I have said so before."

"Ash! So good to hear from you. How's the experiment going? Have you heard from your man back at Terra Diablo? What was his name again?"

"Trevor."

"Ah, Trevor. I didn't get time to chat. Did you get his bracelet back?"

"That's quite a flying machine you have there," said Ash, struggling to keep his voice under control. The saucer should be his. All the machines should be his.

"Yessiree, Bob. She's the '59' model, you know. Still very state of the art, though. Did you see me dodging those missiles?"

"Impressive. We need to talk."

"We are talking. Chat away. But make it fast. I'm expecting a call."

"From Professor Maynor."

"Yep."

"He's dead."

Ash enjoyed the sound of silence on the other end of the line.

"No, he's not," said Mark.

But this time the voice wasn't quite so cocky.

"Did you think he could hide from me forever?"

"I considered the possibility that you'd caught him, but I don't believe you. I think Maynor knows as much about Zero Point as you do, maybe more. If you had him, you'd use him. You're crazy, but I never thought you were stupid."

"Thank you, I suppose."

"So, now that we've concluded that you are a liar as well as a psychopath, where do we go from here?"

Ash's knuckles whitened around the phone as Mark waved at the TV camera again, and he realized that he was seeing the scene in real time. Mark was talking to him and staring back at him. The sense of being watched through the passive screen was eerie and disconcerting. He wanted to put a foot through it.

"Why don't you visit my lab, and we can discuss the future."

"Unhuh," said Mark, shaking his head a moment later on the screen. In spite of the sense of real-time, there seemed to be about a two-second delay. It was as though he were speaking to someone just a step away in space and a bit in time as well. "I've visited your labs, remember? Only we were discussing the past at the time."

"Yes," said Ash.

"If you don't shut down that machine, you're going to kill yourself and everyone there, and maybe a lot of other people as well. A lot of people."

"You think I will repeat the mistakes made in 1959?"

"I don't think there were any mistakes in 1959, but I know you're making a big one if you keep messing with that machine."

"Why would you think that?"

"Because very shortly everything stops."

Ash was silent for a moment.

"You've tried to access the future?"

"I have accessed the future. But in a little over an hour, I hit a blank wall. You've hit it, too, haven't you? That's what all the rush was about. You damned well know what's about to happen. You've known all along, and yet you're going to keep on. You're crazy as shit, Ash."

"And you believe you can change the future?"

"Don't you?"

"Why don't you come in? You can tell me about your trip."

"Some other time. As I said, I'm waiting for a call."

Suddenly the phone went dead, and Ash threw it across the room to land atop the shards of porcelain. When one of his agents entered without knocking he was tempted to kill the man. The agent saved himself by speaking quickly.

"We've located the girl."

Ash smiled, his eyes gleaming like the sun.

MARK'S PHONE RANG AGAIN almost immediately, and he raised it to his ear prepared to cross mental swords with Ash once more. Instead, he heard a familiar voice and smiled.

"How are you, Maynor?" he said.

"Fine. Fine. I'm glad to hear that you are well, also. You cut quite a figure on the screen."

Mark laughed.

"You like it? It's what you sent me after."

"Not exactly, but I am impressed."

"That seems to be the standard reaction."

"You've spoken to Ash."

"He called first. He wanted to meet."

"In good time."

"I suspected you'd say something like that."

"You have always been very perceptive."

"That's why you hired me, right? That and the fact that I'm too stupid or hardheaded to know what's good for me."

"I would not have described your qualities in that manner. You are like a badger. Once you set your teeth into something, you do not let go. You alone have succeeded in bringing us to this fateful point in time."

"You want the same things Ash wants."

"Ash is a madman."

"Anyone who tries to control Zero Point is a madman."

"Then we must stop him."

"You know what's going to happen, don't you?"

"I suspect."

"You suspect that Ash is going to keep pressing that machine until there's a Zero Point event. Something will happen like what happened in 1959."

"Probably much worse."

"We have less than an hour."

Maynor didn't ask how he knew. If Maynor didn't know everything already–and Mark suspected that he did–he was smart enough to figure it out.

"I also know that you created Ash," said Mark.

When Maynor finally spoke, there was hesitation and something else in his voice. Something like... admiration, but it might have been fear.

"Very astute."

"You created a lot more than Ash. You created the man who created Ash. The man who created me. You set this all in motion."

"Where is the small device?"

"In good hands."

"The girl."

Mark didn't answer. Everything was rolling toward an unseen, unstoppable conclusion.

"Can you pick us up?" asked Maynor.

"Why in the world would I do that?"

"To stop Ash from killing us all."

"Do you have an a-bomb?"

Maynor chuckled.

No. Something better."

"A squad from Delta Force?"

"Nothing quite so brutal."

"Brutal is good when you're dealing with Ash."

"But not necessary, I assure you."

"Where do you want to meet?"

"Do you recall where you were when we first spoke?" asked Maynor.

"I'll be there."

TRACY STARED AT THE car in front of the crypt and smiled. Marilyn wore a smirk of her own, but Earl simply admired the sleek new sedan.

"Very safe," said Tracy, nodding at Ki who held the front passenger door for her.

Ki seemed to accept the compliment without reservation.

"Your parents always insisted on Volvos. We have found no reason to change our mind about the company or their product. In fact, the Conservancy is rather heavily invested in the company."

Ensconced in the passenger seat, surrounded by front and side airbags and tightly belted both lap and shoulder, Tracy considered the irony. She was certain the automobile had been rebuilt at the factory to include bullet and bomb proofing, with two-inch-thick windows and heavy doors. The car would probably protect all of them from a head-on collision with a military fighting vehicle and then an attack by a fifty-caliber machine gun, but it wasn't likely to save anyone from the wrath of God Ash was about to bring down on the entire world.

As they rolled slowly out of the cemetery, she glanced at the Pacific wondering if they could really trust Shiver's judgement.

Mark, she reminded herself.

The man had a real name now. He wasn't just some crazy magician who had appeared out of nowhere. He was a man who had been through some kind of hell of his own so strange she couldn't even begin to imagine what it might have been like. It was easy to see that Ash had done something to him, something terrible enough to send him on a crusade through time itself. Yet he had taken time out of that quest to save her, at the risk of unraveling a mind-bogglingly intricate plan. How could she not trust him?

"A few minutes before I hit the wall in the future," Mark had told them. "I've seen you entering the caverns. You'll live at least that long."

"But that sounds more like the end than the beginning," said Tracy. "Why don't we just change it, stay here, or run away?"

Mark bit his lip, shaking his head slowly.

"I don't think so. I think you have to be at that time and place. It's one of those doors that's closed. No matter what you do, you and the others are going to Terra Diablo."

"And you think that's a good thing?"

"I'm going to be there, too, and I don't want to die any more than you do, but this is almost the end of the line for my plan. You just have to trust me."

Tracy had shaken her head, fighting to believe in something that to her still sounded too much like prophecy, and a *bad* prophecy to boot. But she could not deny her helpless feeling of being carried along by events. Still, his final words had not engendered much faith.

"When the time comes, just do what he says."

The *he* was obviously Ash.

Pulling onto the freeway, heading east, it was only moments before they were bracketed, front and rear by dark sedans, with another car edging alongside, blocking the traffic in the passing lane behind it. Ki held a handwritten sheet of yellow notepad against his window, and Tracy saw the look of surprise on the agent's face in the car beside them. The man chattered with his driver before nodding and pulling into line ahead. Ki handed Tracy the sheet of paper. It read, simply *We'll follow you.*

"That went easy enough," said Tracy, her heart pumping madly in her chest.

Ki smiled.

"Killers they may be, but they do not crave battle. It is much simpler and safer for them if their quarry submits to being caught."

"They're going to kill us, anyway," she whispered.

Ki shook his head.

"I do not believe Shiver would send us to our deaths without at least a chance of success, and we still have the device."

"Why in the world didn't he have us leave it at the Conservancy?" asked Tracy. "Ash will take it as soon as we get to Terra Diablo."

"Yes," said Ki. "We are merely buying time."

"I don't think time is something that can be bought and sold," said Marilyn.

"It was a figure of speech," said Ki, turning back to the road.

Through the tinted rear window of the sedan ahead two agents could be seen staring at them. When they waved toward an upcoming exit Ki slowed the car and followed. The sedan behind them took a moment to be sure they weren't trying an escape, then pulled off as well. Three miles up they pulled into a local airstrip and parked beside a corporate jet with engines already running.

ASH FONDLED THE ALIEN device on the metal table in the corner of the cavern, studying its convoluted form. Even hefting it gave an otherworldly feel. The balance was off, as though it had been created to be held by something other than human hands. This was the prize he had been searching for. He held in his hands the holy grail that would grant him the keys to the kingdom of power, of control. With this machine, he could manipulate Zero Point.

The idiot, Earl, had been right all along. Zero Point was nothing like normal energy. It could not be managed with dials and levers, turbines, or transformers. It was more art than craft, more lifelike than simple inanimate power. It almost had what amounted to a will of its own, but this device was the handle to the lever that could move the world. With it, Ash had control of everything. Nothing and no one could stop him now. All he had to do was learn to play the machine.

He stared at the four people seated in straight-backed chairs–their hands and feet bound tightly with plastic ties–and smiled.

The girl, Marilyn, glared with a hatred that was beyond fear, and the Asiatic simply stared at him with those dark eyes that said nothing and much at the same time. Ash found the man peculiarly distracting, reminding him in some indefinable way of Walsh, but this man was small but well built, quite probably trained in the martial arts, self-contained and dangerous. Walsh was pudgy, trained in nothing but corporate brown-nosing, and capable of chatter that could be disconcerting in its own way but significant of nothing in particular.

Ki was a man to watch closely. Walsh–regardless now of whether or not he had successfully managed to travel through time–was history.

"What do you plan to do now," asked Tracy.

Although he hated to admit it, she also made him uneasy. She would not hold any false notions of her circumstances, and yet she was too self-assured for a woman staring death in the face. He admired her courage, understanding that–like the younger girl's–it was a product of rage. She hated him for what he had done to her parents, to her, to her world, and he enjoyed the knowledge that she would die still filled with the terrible frustration of unfulfilled revenge.

"Not to sound cliche, I plan to take over the world," he said, smiling, still fondling the device.

"With that?"

He nodded.

"And that," he said, glancing at the time machine that still sat dormant in the corner. He looked up at the techs in the room above, and one of them nodded nervously. They would get it working shortly. The monitors were revealing the readouts typical just before the apparatus came online again.

"You spoke to Mark," said Tracy, quietly. "You know that when you turn on that machine and fiddle with that... thing, you're going to kill us all."

Ash laughed.

"You believe that by telling me this you will stop me from completing my mission? That you will keep me from my destiny?"

"There's a wall in time," said Tracy, "and we're all about to hit it."

Ash nodded.

"You believe that that's the end. Is that it?"

"What else could it be?"

"Very simply it is the point at which mankind–at which *I*–gain control of Zero Point. At that instant time travel by others becomes impossible."

Tracy frowned. Was that possible? She had no idea. Mark had never mentioned the possibility. Had it occurred to him?

"That makes no sense," said Ki.

"It makes no sense to someone who doesn't understand Zero Point," said Ash.

"And you do."

"Better than anyone."

Earl laughed, and Ash's face reddened.

"You don't know diddly," said Earl.

Ash backhanded him.

"My destiny will not be denied by cretins and fools."

"You are mad," said Ki, quietly.

"A man who believes in holistic medicine, a man who thinks that aliens seeded our planet with life four billion years ago, who accepts the reality of pyramid and crystal power, calls *me* mad?" said Ash, his laughter tinged with a thinly veiled threat. "Choose your words carefully."

"My beliefs endanger no one," said Ki. "Yours threaten us all with extinction."

"Your extinction is coming, but I wish all of you to live long enough to see what I accomplish. I have studied all the surviving notes from the debacle at Terra Diablo," said Ash, once again fondling the small machine as though it could feel his attention. "This device is the key to controlling Zero Point. The fools that worked in this lab had no way of knowing that, of course. All that is required is the right combination of keystrokes. Your friend, Mr. Townsend is convinced that in a few moments time ends. That is not what occurs."

"What does occur?" asked Tracy.

"Time *changes."*

Tracy shook her head.

"Changes? How could time change?"

"You cannot possibly understand. Mr. Townsend certainly doesn't. The only way I could explain it is that because of my possession of both machines, *he* is no longer able to travel forward in time past a few moments in the future. He assumes from this that time ends. As I said, it simply changes, and only for him."

"But you know what the time is that that happens, too. You must have tried to travel beyond that point."

"I was not in possession of both machines. With this device I can control that one," said Ash, nodding toward the time machine.

"You're mad."

Earl frowned.

"You have to tune it," he said, shaking his head.

"Exactly," said Ash.

"You don't know the music," said Earl.

Ash smirked, turning back toward the control room. Once again, the tech nodded. Ash could hear the machinery beginning to hum.

It wouldn't be long now.

MARK DID ONE LAST flyby of the dock, noticing the long black limousine parked beside the bar from which he'd called Maynor...when...was it only a few months before? His time sense was irredeemably distorted. Regardless of the explanation he'd given Tracy, past, present, and future had become fluid for him, a river flowing in both directions at once, in which he knew he could easily get swept away and drown.

Another limousine was parked farther up the small bayside street, and dark-suited men had created a cordon there, holding back a small crowd. People waved and pointed in the direction of the saucer, but he had only popped into this time and place moments before, too early for even the highly alert, Florida-based Air Force or Navy jets to reach the scene. More than likely the local press would beat them this time, but by then he intended to be long gone.

He landed gently, balancing the saucer on the end of the ratty wharf like a plate on the edge of a knife. He fingered the grip of the pistol in his belt as the canopy rose slowly, and he climbed out to meet Derek Maynor.

Another limousine parked in front of the first, and two men in black got out to open the rear doors. Two old men climbed out to stride resolutely down the dock. One of them Mark recognized instantly. John Medlock, Senator from New Mexico. The most powerful man in the United States Senate and Mark's mentor. Medlock was tall and broad-shouldered with a thick head of gray hair brushed back from a high forehead. He had penetrating blue eyes, and a look that said he had never simply *asked* anyone to do anything in his entire life.

That meant the other, much shorter, fat, balding man in the rumpled gray suit had to be Maynor.

"How good of you to come," said Maynor as Mark climbed down to the dock.

Maynor extended his hand, but Mark ignored him, staring at Medlock. His antennae were buzzing, but he was in control here, not these two old men.

"How have you been?" asked Mark, coldly.

Medlock's eyes were equally cold, and he offered no reply. He'd always been an arrogant sonofabitch, but once Mark had trusted him. Now things started to click. Of course, Ash hadn't killed him.

Maynor slipped past Mark to run his fingertips along the fuselage of the saucer, his eyes wide.

"Amazing. In perfect condition. You have done well."

"I'm glad you appreciate my work," said Mark, turning to study the little man.

Maynor had always made him nervous even when they'd only been in contact over the phone. It was more than just the man's insatiable love of intrigue. There had always been something overtly threatening about him, something that Mark knew was very important, but something he could never quite put his finger on.

"How much time do we have?" asked Medlock in a tone that said he expected to cut through this superfluous chatter.

"A few minutes," said Mark, barely holding himself under control, nodding back toward the saucer. "Get in."

Medlock clambered up the slight incline into the cockpit surprisingly easily for such an old man, and Maynor followed. But at the top, before dropping inside, he turned and faced Mark. They stood there for just a moment studying at each other–Mark's antennae at full buzz–and suddenly he realized that he had placed himself between the saucer and the men-in-black. But none of them appeared to be facing in his direction. Not that it mattered. Medlock and Maynor weren't going anywhere without him.

"You two set this entire thing in motion," said Mark, staring at Maynor.

"Of course," said Maynor, as though a small child should have been capable of discerning the intrigue.

"You set up my parents, too," said Mark, turning once again on Maynor. "You had them killed so that *he* could take me in. I was your creation all along."

Maynor laughed.

"What a tangled web we weave... I had to *create* the man who would eventually leave me in a hole in the ground in New Mexico so that we could *finally* get to this point. Amazing, no?"

"Unfortunately," said Medlock, "we have no more time for you to figure out the entire Machiavellian protocol, and your services are no longer required."

"You can't fly this thing."

"I assure you that Senator Medlock can," said Maynor.

"No way," said Mark. "No one has even seen one of these things for over fifty years."

Maynor laughed.

"John may be a little rusty, but he's kept up his pilot's training, and old test pilots are the best."

As Mark stared into Maynor's face the final piece of the puzzle fell into place. Leaving Walsh had been a mistake after all. Mark had thought to bury the man in the past. Instead, Walsh had joined forces with the lone test pilot–one of the few men alive who would believe him–to travel the hard way through time, back to the present. And while living it Walsh had managed to become Professor Derek Maynor, probably with the young Senator Medlock's help.

Walsh knew that Mark had been sent back in time so Maynor/Walsh spent a great deal of time and probably government funds and acumen to assure that Mark would be the right person at the right time to do so. He was responsible for tracking down the scientists Mark had hidden, for feeding Ash just enough information to keep the ball rolling.

So they could all meet here. Now.

Mark slipped his fingers around the pistol butt.

"I wouldn't do that if I were you," said Maynor.

Mark froze.

"Unlike Ash, I don't kill people for no reason," said Maynor, nodding back toward the closest limousine.

Glancing over his shoulder Mark spotted the sniper who'd been hiding in the car. The lens of the scope glinted in the sun where the man rested his rifle on the open door of the car.

"I'm assured that man is a crack shot," said Maynor, accepting Medlock's help down into the cockpit of the saucer. "It's taken me decades to get here, and it was a circuitous journey, but will be well worth it in the end. You have no idea what you've wrought."

"You have no idea how this all ends," muttered Mark.

Maynor shook his head.

"But I do. You have no concept of what Zero Point is or what it can do. It is the answer to everything. Once we control it nothing, and I mean nothing, is beyond our reach."

"Two old men seeking to run the world. How pitiful."

"But we won't *be* old men forever," said Maynor, grinning like a happy child. "With Zero Point we will be able to not only control time, but to turn back its influence. We will travel to unknown worlds and explore the very meaning of the universe."

"You think you can regain your youth?"

"Why not? You stole it from me."

"You both knew Ash was going to murder my wife. You set it up," said Mark, wondering if he could kill either of them before the sniper's bullet struck.

Maynor waved a dismissive hand.

"It was bound to happen. Don't get your time mixed up."

"Why do you think the two of you will be able to stop Ash?"

"Because he will listen to John."

"His father," said Mark. "Did you plan that, too? Did you have Medlock sire him, then turn him into a madman on purpose?"

Maynor simply smiled.

In his entire life, Mark had never encountered men so ruled by lust for power, so completely evil. What must life have been like for Ash, to have been nothing more ever than a tool to be bent and twisted until it no longer even resembled anything human? It occurred to Mark that if he could get back to 1959 and kill both Walsh and Medlock none of this would happen. But of course that was impossible. That door would never open.

"Get off the saucer," said Medlock, as the canopy slowly clicked shut.

Mark stumbled onto the uneven boards of the wharf as the craft jolted backward. Medlock might know how to fly it, but he was rusty. Mark turned back toward the sniper, wondering if the man truly had orders just to watch him or whether now that he was no longer between Medlock and Walsh the guy had the okay for the kill.

Ten minutes to zero.

He found the thought almost amusing. Zero second. Zero Point.

Everything was coming down to zero.

The man with the rifle waved him forward, but instead of answering the sniper's summons, Mark stood with his arms hanging limply, staring up into the glare of the sun, denying its power to blind him, listening to the last stanzas as Martha Argerich finally began to complete the music she had begun for him so often.

Only the glare wasn't the sun, just a reflection of it.

He noticed that the sniper had seen the strange glinting orb, too. As it swooped toward them like a hawk in a stoop, the gunman dove for cover, but Mark stood perfectly still, smiling to himself, the music pounding in his head.

"PLEASE DON'T DO THIS," said Tracy, as Ash began stroking the device in his hands, touching the buttons lightly.

Ash frowned, motioning for one of the agents to move closer to Tracy.

"If she speaks again, kill her."

The agent nodded, his hand under his jacket.

Suddenly the doors at the far end of the cavern opened and two men strode through, one short and stooped, one tall and very erect. They were silhouetted by the undulating light from the time machine as they passed it, and Ash studied both of them very closely as they approached.

"Stop!" he shouted, and another agent intercepted the men, gun drawn.

The taller of the two men spoke quietly to the agent. The agent holstered his gun and stepped away. Ash's hands flittered nervously across the device, and the tall snakelike light of the time machine seemed disturbed, whipping around the giant chamber like a cobra on amphetamines.

"Stay where you are!" he screamed, as the two men slowly crossed the wide floor to meet him.

The smaller man kept glancing nervously at the light, as though it might strike down at him like a mammoth white sledgehammer, and Tracy wondered if it could do just that. When the pair reached Ash, she recognized the taller of the two old men as Senator Medlock. Everyone had seen him at one time or another on television. He had been touted as a front-runner for president in the next election, but there had been too many worries about his age. What was he doing here? Did he really think he could stop Ash?

The smaller man was familiar, but she couldn't place him. Still, something in his mannerisms–the way he toyed unconsciously with the tip of his tie, the way he leaned to place all his weight on one foot–told her they'd met before.

"Give me the device, Ash," said Medlock, holding out both hands like a man telling a small child to give up the matches he'd stolen from the kitchen counter.

"No," said Ash, backing away a step, shaking his head, clutching the apparatus tightly to his chest.

The blinding white rays of the time machine in the corner bounced off the walls and ceiling, spraying the immense cavern with shards of living light.

Suddenly Medlock's voice echoed through the chamber like the sound of thunderous doom.

"Give it to me, boy!"

"No," pleaded Ash. "It's mine. I built the machine. It's all mine."

"You did nothing more than I allowed you to do!" shouted Medlock. "Now give it to me!"

To Tracy's surprise, Ash dropped to the concrete floor so hard her own knees ached.

Sheer terror oozed from every pore on Ash's face, and he quivered like a man struck by a lash. What power did this man hold over Ash that he could do this? Medlock hovered over him like a vengeful god, glowering down, refusing to reach for the device that was just beneath his hands, insisting that Ash accept the final indignity of handing it up to him. It was not in her nature to enjoy someone else's humiliation, but Ash was the man who'd had Stephanie killed, who had sent murderers into her home to frame her parents, ensuring that *she* would testify against them in court.

"Give it to me!"

As slowly as a man taking his final step onto the gallows, Ash's hands rose to meet those of Medlock's. The senator relieved Ash of the device, but Ash would not look him in the eye.

"You are a fool!" shouted Medlock. "Worse than a fool. I don't know how I could ever have sired a piece of dung like you."

Medlock was Ash's father?

It seemed incredible but staring at the two of them in the strobe-like light of the device, she saw the resemblance. Medlock was tall to Ash's shorter build, but both had the broad shoulders, the high forehead and cheekbones, the deep-set, driven eyes.

Only now Ash's eyes were darting and downcast while Medlock's were cold and filled with something that looked like rage, but which Tracy sensed was far more calculating and cold. She couldn't understand what kind of upbringing could have created such a father/son relationship, but it had to have been so brutal it was beyond imagining. A man like Ash feared few men. Instead, men feared Ash. Yet here he was, on his knees, neck bent in supplication, as though ready to accept the headsman's axe, and Tracy actually wondered if Medlock was about to murder his own son in front of all of them.

Instead, Medlock toyed with the device, and Tracy's mind left Ash long enough to consider that Ash's father might complete the job he had not.

If Medlock pressed the right buttons there was probably no reason he couldn't set off the machine just as successfully as Ash would have. After all, Mark had assured them that very shortly time was coming to an end. He never said who pulled the trigger. He had simply told her to trust him, but she was beginning to wonder if her trust hadn't been misplaced.

As she watched Medlock playing with the machine his expression turned from anger at Ash, to pleasure at his own success, to concentration, to frustration, and finally to fear. It seemed as though the device in Medlock's hands was somehow interacting with the time machine.

The light from the machine in the corner whirled and twisted and danced, then whipped and contorted, dropping so close to their heads that even the shorter of the two men ducked away from it.

"Shut it down!" the little man shouted, waving at Medlock.

"I'm trying!" said Medlock, his fingers tickling the device frantically as though it were some kind of dangerous musical instrument. But Tracy knew that he didn't know how to play it. He only thought he did.

"You said you could control it!"

"It's got an off switch. I saw them use it in the labs!"

"Then do it!"

"It isn't here. The keys are...different!"

"How can that be?" asked the fat little man, rushing to Medlock's side, clutching at the machine as Medlock jerked it away.

Tracy noticed that the two agents were disappearing through the doors at the far end of the cavern. Good luck. No one was going to outrun this. That the men-in-black would die with them was little consolation, though.

She struggled against her bindings, but they were tight and thin, cutting into her skin, and so she stopped. Why bother? Bound or free there was nothing she could do any more than Medlock or Ash could. She could sense the machine winding up to a crescendo.

"Cool," said Earl.

Instead of fear, she saw wonder in his face. Of course, Earl would be loving this. He wasn't thinking about dying. He was just awestruck by the power of the machine, by the tuning of it. She was happy that he wasn't suffering from the fear that overwhelmed her. Marilyn, too, kept up a brave front, staring at the light instead of the two terrified men. She was going to glare at that light right up until the minute it killed her. Ki sat stoically, accepting his bondage and his fate.

Suddenly she realized that there was a new sound in the cavern, a deep, rolling vibration, and she felt something strike her face, and then again. The roof of the cave seemed to be swaying. Large fractures appeared, and she wondered if the machine were not about to cause a cave-in that would kill them all and shut down the devices before they reached the point of no return. Perhaps mankind would survive.

Medlock and the smaller man were on their knees beside Ash—the device between them on the floor—arguing, gesticulating wildly, but their voices were carried away before the louder sound of the devastation that was beginning all around them. A chunk of rock the size of a taxicab dropped from the ceiling toward the time machine, and then disappeared inside the twisting column of light. The machines would not allow themselves to be shut down by something so insignificant as a mere cave collapse. The sound of rending stone echoed in counterpoint to the pulsating pounding of the time machine's heavy vibration, and she knew that nothing would stop their final symphony of destruction.

Suddenly she noticed another silhouette against the dimmer light of the open doorways. Had one of the agents returned? For what? Certainly, duty wasn't strong enough to bring men like that back into this bedlam. The man stepped resolutely into the uproar, but instead of crossing the wide expanse toward them, he strode directly to the time machine, turning his back to all of them, and in that instant—as he peered at the rampaging device—she recognized his stance, the same way he had stood waiting for Ash's men to burst through the door onto the rooftop.

Shiver.

He rested one hand on the side of the machine, then the other.

Suddenly he seemed fuzzy, as though he were vibrating so fast, she couldn't focus on him. After a moment he became even harder to make out, until there was just a blur where he stood, a gray ghost.

He raised his hands above his head, and he looked for all the world like a phantom symphony conductor, the twisting, swirling stream of light echoing the movements of his hands as though it were a deadly concerto that he was playing, and the light was a writhing soloist. The raucous sounds around her began to lessen, the cracking, rending noises deadened, and then stopped, the flashing, whipping light slowed its dance and then finally the tower of white stood tall and straight and then dulled and disappeared, until the cavern was bathed in the dim redness of the emergency bulbs and the sound of her own breathing and her heart pumping wildly in her chest.

Slowly the ghost became a quivering human form again, then a shivering man, and finally a dim shadow, shaking violently. After a moment he straightened, turning toward them, crossing the floor to stand before Medlock and the smaller man who rose shakily to their feet.

"You!" said the smaller man. "How did you get here?"

"Give me the device," said Mark, holding out both hands.

This time it was Medlock who acted like a frightened child in possession of forbidden matches. He backed away, shaking his head, but something in the doorway stopped him in his tracks.

Tracy followed his eyes, wondering if the light was messing up her vision again, or whether the man there was using some power like Mark's to distort his form. He looked way too tall for one thing, having to stoop to pass through the door, and he walked with a peculiar rolling gate that seemed far too graceful for a mere human, seeming to float across the floor. But the two people who followed were human enough.

As the power came back on, the lights returned, and Tracy gasped.

The *man* was not a man at all.

He was some kind of alien, with gray, metal-colored skin and a head too large for his needle-thin and overly long neck. His body was gaunt to the point of emaciation, but his huge, black, comma-shaped eyes were reassuring when they rested for a moment on her. She felt as though he had touched her physically, had told her to be at peace, that everything was going to be alright. His glance passed from her to Ash, to Medlock, and then the little man, and although he had no lips the alien seemed to frown, and the mere expression appeared to strike the three men like a lash.

The little man and Medlock dropped to their knees again beside Ash, bowing their heads.

When the alien spoke, Tracy realized that he was not *speaking* at all. Yet she could hear his soft voice inside her head as though he were standing right beside her.

"You have toyed with powers you cannot even begin to understand."

The remonstrance was painful in its intensity.

Although she had not been responsible for the time machine or the device, she sensed that a little of what he said was aimed at her. She had played with the device. She and Earl had used his machines to fight Ash's men. Just being involved on the periphery of this alien's contempt was mentally agonizing. She could only imagine what the three men on the floor were experiencing.

Her attention was drawn back to the two humans who hurried around the alien toward her. Her mother reached her first, clutching her tightly, holding her face in loving hands, as her father cut away her bonds so that she could rise to her feet and fold herself into their combined embrace. Tears flowed freely, until all their cheeks were slick, and she tasted them in each kiss. Her father's arms were warm and strong, and she drew in breath after breath of his sweet pipe smell. She peered into his eyes, and the love she saw there warmed her, but guilt still chilled her heart.

"I had you locked up," she whispered.

They smiled.

"You had no choice, and you were lied to by everyone around you. The whole world told you we were crazy, that we were murderers and traitors. Tracy, it's all right. We forgive you. We're okay."

"Where have you been? I was afraid after you disappeared that you'd died."

Her mother pointed toward the alien who was ambling back in their direction.

"He came for us. We've been with him, and others like him."

"All this time?"

Her mother nodded.

"We've been away," she said. "Trying to convince the *Andomariy* not to destroy our civilization. We had to assure them that we would help them get back all the machines they had lost in their crash, and that we would destroy all records of them. That's why we're here."

"When Shiver came to us in the late sixties he started us on a lifelong quest for truth," said her father. "But that also put us at odds with both the government–which wanted to find all the missing devices–and the Andomariy who wanted them back. They had just about reached the decision to simply give up looking for all the machines–since they were afraid that by the time they found them we might be able to hide away the knowledge somewhere–when they found us and took us from the mental hospital. We have been arguing with them ever since."

"For a year?"

Her mother laughed.

"No, dear. We came directly here."

Tracy shook her head.

"From the past."

"Not exactly."

"All this time...I felt like I betrayed you, but I couldn't find any way to believe in you-"

"We couldn't come back any earlier," said her father, sadly. "I'm sorry. We had a long way to travel, and we had to arrive when all the machines were together."

"The aliens brought you here with a time machine?"

Her father frowned.

"No. The Andomariy know how dangerous it is to toy with time. We are here now because of the time distortion of travel to and from their world. It's difficult to explain but suffice it to say that time distortion caused by faster than light travel is very different from what these machines do. The Andomariy knew better than to ever create a time machine like that-" he pointed toward the large device where the light was just dying away. "Now we must give them all the machines, both the Andomariy's and Earl's. It's over now. We're going to start a new life."

The alien continued to glower over the three men on the floor, and Tracy could tell by the way they groveled that he was still *talking* to them, although she could no longer hear his voice, and she was glad.

"They framed you. But why didn't you tell the court? Why didn't you tell me?"

"We couldn't," said her father. "Ash told us if we ever talked or tried to defend ourselves, he'd hurt you."

Her mother drew her back into their arms.

"It's over now."

"Thank you for saving my parents," said Tracy, turning to the Andomariy, as he stepped away from the three kneeling men.

"It was a simple thing," said the giant alien, his soft voice echoing in her mind. "To us, life and death are one, but we are aware that your kind cherish this side of it the more. Still, we believe there is a balance to be maintained."

The words echoed with something Shiver had told her... when, a hundred years ago?

The alien stared across the cavern as Mark/Shiver trod wearily toward them.

"He is a very special being. The only one to our knowledge who has ever been so in tune with the Great Balance that he is able to control it using no machines whatsoever. Yet his own life is out of balance due to this man called Ash, this man called Medlock, this man called Walsh."

Finally, the last piece of the puzzle fell into place. Walsh. She'd seen him, entering and leaving Ash's office, his beady eyes roving like those of a rat slipping through a maze.

"I owe Shiver my life," she said, quietly.

The alien nodded.

"Sometimes it is not the owing, but the knowing that is important."

He reached out and placed his hand gently first on Tracy's mother's forehead, then her father's, then Tracy's, and Tracy felt a wonderful sense of release as he did so, glancing up into the impossibly wide, dark eyes.

"You were watching over me," she whispered. "Weren't you?"

He shook his head slowly.

"That was not my mission, although I am pleased that you were not harmed. Your life is part of the Great Balance. You have seen much that is bad. Now it is time for good again."

"Like karma."

"That is a useful word. It does not take in all that is the Great Balance, but it is useful. All things happen for a reason, but only gods know what those reasons may be."

"So, you believe in gods?"

Tracy wasn't sure if the sound that she heard was laughter or something more akin to a verbal shrug.

"We believe in the Great Balance. Whether there are hands upon that Balance, mortals may never know. The Balance does not require us to know. It just is."

"Thank you, anyway, for being part of the Great Balance."

"Live well, Tracy Karhonen," he said, turning to step between the approaching Mark and the three men.

"It is time for me to be going," said the alien to Mark, "but you have done a great service, and you have suffered much. Is there anything that I may do for you in return?"

Once again Tracy noticed the deep sadness in Mark's face as he shook his head, but then his eyes began to burn as he glanced past the alien at the three on the floor.

"I have to do it myself."

He tried to sidestep the *Andomariy*, but the creature moved surprisingly fast to place himself in front of Mark once more.

"Harming them will not bring you what you seek."

Mark glared up at him.

"What is it you think I seek?"

"Peace."

Mark shook his head.

"Revenge will bring me as close to peace as I'm ever going to get."

"Revenge will not bring your life back into balance. Only love can do that."

Mark shuddered, as though he'd been struck.

"Don't speak to me of love in their presence. They defile the word."

"Only your hate holds you here. If you would only open yourself to the possibilities, your love would draw you from this place."

Mark shook his head.

"I don't know what you mean. Love is dead to me."

"I ask you again. Is there nothing I can do for you?"

"Not unless you can *really* turn back time and change it."

The alien shook his head sadly.

"This, unfortunately, no one can do. It is not in the interest of the Great Balance to even contemplate such a possibility. But on occasion, it is fortunate that there are other alternatives."

He waved a long, slender gray arm, and suddenly the giant screen below the windows of the control room burst into life, filled with the image of a book-lined study.

Mark turned toward the alien. The creature twisted its hand, as though gesturing to an orchestra. The camera moved, panning around to focus on a beautiful, dark-haired woman wearing bright blue shorts. Mark was riveted to the screen. His shoulders sagged, and he looked as though he were doing all that he could to simply stand. The giant alien sidled close to him.

"This being is important to you?" asked the Andomariy.

Mark could barely nod, but the alien answered with a slow, graceful nod of his own. As he turned to face the screen once more, the woman glanced toward them, and Tracy noticed how lovely her brown eyes were.

"Katie?" Marked shouted hoarsely.

"The being you call Katie exists on many planes, on many worlds. On the world in which you see her now, the man you call Trevor does not reach her. The man you think of as yourself intercepts him, but in doing so, they both meet their fates. Later, on the day in which you see her now, she will be informed of *your* death."

"Why are you showing me this?" asked Mark, unable to pull his eyes from the screen.

"You have done much in service to the Great Balance, and it would be a great disservice to it to see the two of you suffer. Take this," said the alien, holding out the small device. "And go to her. You will know how to find her. Your love will serve as a beacon, but then you must return here with her, to this world. The future there is too bleak for the two of you."

Mark stared at the device for only a moment before locking his hands around it. He frowned, in concentration, but his fingers began to play instinctively–faster and faster–across the buttons as though they were the keys of an instrument.

And then he was gone.

"How can you be so sure he'll succeed?" whispered Tracy.

The alien turned to her.

"Because the Great Balance wills it."

He reached out a sinuous hand and rested it lightly on her shoulder. She felt a strange tingling power surging through her, the soft embrace of something ephemeral, like some secret gift.

"You have carried their love always with you," he said.

She nodded, admitting to herself that it was true, that there was a hidden power to love, to the memories that she had denied for too long.

"As they have carried yours always. Be with the Great Balance, Tracy Karhonen. Forgive yourself, for they have never condemned you."

She could not stop the tears as she felt her parents' hands, replacing the alien's once again on her shoulders.

"And what will you do now?" she asked the *Andomariy*.

"We will remove all the devices or destroy them utterly, along with all files that pertain to them. Those-" He pointed toward the men who clustered at the windows of the control room and then at Ash, Walsh, and Medlock. "Must come with us. The one you call Earl must also come with us."

"Earl?" said Tracy, glancing sadly at him.

But Earl was smiling broadly.

"I'm going with you?" he asked, excitedly.

The alien nodded.

"Wow," said Earl, and Tracy realized that there was no better place in the universe for him.

"I'll miss you," she said, hugging him.

He hugged her back.

"We'll stay in touch."

"Is that possible?" she asked, staring at the alien.

Another mental shrug.

"It is possible."

"I'd like that," she said, hugging Earl a little tighter.

The alien waved, and the men in the control room began to fade as though they had been mere specters. Walsh and Ash started to protest as Medlock started toward the alien, but they were already turning to mist as was Earl who was still grinning wildly and waving. In an instant, they were all gone. Then the alien faded as well.

"They have a way of doing that," said her mother, laughing at Tracy's goggle-eyed expression.

"But the machine," said Tracy, easing out of their arms to stare at the time machine that now sat idle in the corner.

Suddenly light burst forth from it again, and the cavern began to vibrate beneath Tracy's feet.

"We have to be going," said her father, taking her arm and leading her toward the doors.

THE EERILY MOVING SOUND of voices singing to the accompaniment of some indefinable yet strangely fitting instrument reverberated through the many chambers of the Conservancy and echoed out into the warm air beneath the tent outside the crypt. The poetry of the words integrated perfectly with the formal simplicity and beauty of the tune.

Mark had insisted on choosing the background music for the meeting. *A Feather on the Breath of God* by Hildegard of Bingen, the ninth-century Abbess, philosopher, teacher, and poet. The accompaniment was his mother's cello, a recording she'd made only days before her death.

The guests mingled like the last of the crowd at a wedding–Tracy refused to invoke the funeral symbology the site demanded–smiling, and hugging, waiting for Mark to appear. When he finally exited the mausoleum, he stopped for a moment, staring up into the blue sky, breathing deeply of the salt air, his arm around Katie's shoulders, and Tracy drank in the sight of them. The pair seemed to be the essence of everything that had happened to her. They had been used, and betrayed. The worst that the world could possibly have to offer had been thrown against them, and yet there they were. A pair of miracles, just as she and her parents were miracles, just as Marilyn and her father were.

Suddenly Tracy felt so filled with life that it was difficult to believe she could hold it all in. Marilyn left her father's side, and she and Tracy embraced briefly, as Mark and Katie spoke quietly with Ki and other Conservancy members, including the new members... Beatrice and a couple of middle-aged German men who had been so wrapped up in wonder for the past two days at all the Conservancy could offer that Tracy had barely had a chance to meet them.

"What will you do now?" Tracy asked Marilyn.

The girl shrugged, glancing at Ki.

"He offered me a job."

Tracy laughed.

"Actually, I did. I own the Conservancy, remember?"

"So, you're coming back into the fold... with all of us nuts?"

"Someone has to keep you and my parents out of trouble."

A dark sedan pulled into the gates of the cemetery, and Tracy felt a stab of fear, but the car slowed beside a shaded walk, an old woman exited the rear, hobbling up the hill toward a grave, and Tracy turned away.

"Deja vu?" asked Marilyn.

"I'm getting over it."

"Me, too, but it really is over. I'm glad you and your parents have worked things out."

At the mere mention of the old hurt, Tracy felt her throat constrict. Most of her guilt had melted away, but even reason and the alien's soothing touch had not quite rid her of the residue of it. As she watched her parents laughing with Mark and Katie, she knew that it was a soft hurt, one that she could live with. That was the way life worked. Hard days and soft hurts interspersed with sweetness and love.

The Great Balance.

As Mark spoke animatedly to her father, Katie laughing on his arm, Tracy noticed that Mark's hands were conducting along with the music, and she smiled.

I HOPE YOU ENJOYED **Shiver.** Please take a moment to leave an honest opinion on Amazon. And become a member of my newsletter, Chandler McGrew's Supernatural Suspense News!

Also by Chandler McGrew

Supernatural Suspense

Whispers in the Dark (1st in the Dag Connors Supernatural Suspense Series) Exiled to Maine after personal tragedy, FBI Profiler Dag Connors battles demons both internal and external. When three girls are kidnapped, he's thrust into a web of darkness, joined by a young detective and a seasoned hunter. Guided by unseen forces, he uncovers sinister truths blurring reality and nightmare. With redemption at stake, Dag must confront the ultimate evil before it devours all he holds dear.

Crossroads Sheila Bright talks to the dead, while Kira Graves wields supernatural powers in a world teeming with mystical beings. When tragedy strikes and Kira's family falls to unearthly creatures, she embarks on a perilous journey to Graves Island with her steadfast companion, Jen. But when Kira is unexpectedly transported to another world, she must confront the sinister Empty-Eyed Man to prevent universal chaos, even if it means sacrificing everything.

The Remnant Trace Wentworth, haunted by a childhood encounter with rats, finds unexpected salvation beneath New York City's streets. Fleeing Mormon Fundamentalists he suspects of murdering his fiancée, he discovers she's alive. Joining her Brethren, Trace is thrust into a perilous world of secrets and danger, with one revelation threatening to shatter the Mormon faith forever.

'Truders Fane Smith, a brilliant twelve-year-old, and his mother are besieged in their home after his father's murder by the Watchers. Mysterious visits from Joshua warn Fane of impending danger as time runs short. Meanwhile, autistic prodigy Shep Ward is tasked with confronting Joshua but ends up on the run armed only with his knowledge. Both Fane and Shep are drawn back to their birthplace, Rastley, under the sinister control of Morgan Rastley. As a sociopathic hitman closes in on Shep and Fane faces a grim fate, the fate of the world hangs in the balance.

Shiver Enter a gripping saga where a musician's past collides with a present of time travel, revenge, and advanced tech. Mark Townsend confronts Ash and the secretive Conservancy, unraveling a quest for Zero Point energy. As he battles personal loss and betrayal, every decision resonates through past and future, adding layers of suspense to this riveting tale.

Epic Fantasy Series

Sons of Empire (1st in the Empire Chronicles Series)

Empires Collide (2nd in the Empire Chronicles Series)

Rune of the Sword (1st in the Saga of the Altmages)

Children's Books

Allie and the Nothingwhere Machine In the enchanting realm of Widmark Castle, Allie and her witty cat, Ples, confront a dire threat – the encroaching void of Nothingwhere. When Allie discovers her parents may be trapped within, she embarks on a courageous quest armed with magical inventions. With loyal companions, they journey through enchanted paintings, facing external challenges and internal doubts. Battling Night Walkers, they strive to restore balance, blending courage, magic, and friendship.